THE VANISHING OF RUTH

Janet MacLeod Trotter

Published by MacLeod Trotter Books
New edition: 2011

  ISBN 978-0-9566426-1-5

www.janetmacleodtrotter.com

To all the Swaggies I travelled with to Kathmandu on the Asian Greyhound bus in 1976 - and our driver Geoff for getting us there – thanks for the great memories.

To my big brother Don who came through the snow to greet me at the airport after I got stuck in Delhi – much love. Hold Fast.

◇◇◇

I am indebted to the Lit & Phil Library in Newcastle upon Tyne for the quotes from travel books used in the novel. Thank you to Kay Easson and her very helpful staff; and to Pauline, Berit and Audrey for keeping me going with countless cups of good coffee and flapjack.

Janet MacLeod Trotter was brought up in the North East of England with her four brothers, by Scottish parents. She is a best-selling author of 15 novels, including the hugely popular Jarrow Trilogy, and a childhood memoir, BEATLES & CHIEFS, which was featured on BBC Radio Four. Her novel, THE HUNGRY HILLS, gained her a place on the shortlist of The Sunday Times' Young Writers' Award, and the TEA PLANTER'S LASS was longlisted for the RNA Romantic Novel Award. A graduate of Edinburgh University, she has been editor of the Clan MacLeod Magazine, a columnist on the Newcastle Journal and has had numerous short stories published in women's magazines. She lives in the North of England with her husband, daughter and son. Find out more about Janet and her other popular novels at: www.janetmacleodtrotter.com

Also by Janet MacLeod Trotter

Historical:

The Beltane Fires
The Hungry Hills
The Darkening Skies
The Suffragette
Never Stand Alone
Chasing the Dream
For Love & Glory
The Jarrow Lass
Child of Jarrow
Return to Jarrow
A Crimson Dawn
A Handful of Stars
The Tea Planter's Lass

Teenage:

Love Games

Non Fiction:

Beatles & Chiefs

CHAPTER 1

November 1976, Bamiyan, Afghanistan
Cassidy

He woke to the smell of wood smoke and the sound of someone stoking up the stove. Packed around him on the teahouse floor, cocooned in sleeping bags, were his passengers. They snored and scratched at bites in their sleep. The young Hazara boy tending the stove grinned and pointed at the teapot on top. Cassidy nodded, his temples thumping from last night's cheap brandy.

'Thanks bonny lad.'

Yesterday's drive up from Kabul had been tortuous, the dirt tracks already icy in the shade; he had only just held it on that hairpin bend. Marcus had made a big fuss, ordering everyone off the bus and making them push. Typical bloody Posh Boy trying to undermine him with the group. Marcus: there was something about his co-driver that nagged his aching head, but he couldn't think what. Cassidy took his tea outside, trying to shake off a feeling of foreboding.

The freezing air stung his cheeks and made his eyes stream. Someone was already at work, hammering. The sound bounced off the cliffs behind where the massive Buddha statues sat faceless in their rock niches. As Cassidy slurped off his tea, the hammering took on a jarring under-beat: the sound of boots running down the road. Juliet, arms waving, came tearing out of the half dark.

'Gone,' she panted. 'They've gone – no sign – have you seen them?'

'Gone? Who?'

'Marcus and Ruth.' She skidded to a halt, dust rising between them. 'They're not at the other *chaikhana*, I've checked.'

Cassidy felt his teeth clench. 'Well, they can't have gone far at this time in the morning.'

'They've left their foam mattresses.'

'There you are then – gone for a stroll.'

'But taken their sleeping bags.' Juliet grabbed his arm. 'We need to start looking – I'm worried about Ruth – you know what a state she's been in. What if
she's-?'

'What?' Cassidy felt alarm; it wasn't like Juliet to get panicky.

'Something's happened.'

'No it hasn't.'

'How do you know?' She fixed him with troubled brown eyes. 'We shouldn't have argued with them like that.'

'Like what?'

'Last night, remember? You telling him what a waste of space he was and me accusing them of stealing.'

1

Cassidy rubbed a hand over his face. He had only a vague recollection of the Londoners teaching the Germans the words to *American Pie* while he drank the last of his Turkish brandy. And Devon and Kurt had been discussing recipes for hash brownies like a couple of old housewives, but he didn't even remember Marcus being there.

'Where did we have this argument?'

'Over in their *chaikhana*.'

Now it was coming back to him: Marcus and Ruth splitting off from the group and kipping in a different tea shop. He had a hazy memory of lamplight on a wooden table and two hands; Marcus' thick and calloused fingers entwined with Ruth's pink slim ones.

'Then I stormed out,' Juliet reminded. 'Me and my big mouth, I shouldn't have said those things. Was Ruth okay?'

Cassidy had an image of Ruth: blonde hair falling into her eyes, her face pale and anxious. 'She was all right,' he said.

'So they never said anything about taking off? Cos you must've been the last person to see them.'

Despite the cold, Cassidy felt his back prickle with sweat. He remembered now: the money on the table.

'They never said. But you know Marcus – he takes off when it suits him.'

Juliet gave a helpless shrug. He swung an arm about her shoulders. 'They don't deserve your worry – not after the way they've treated you. Would it be the end of the world if they didn't come back?'

'You don't mean that.'

He sighed, 'No, course not.'

'Help me look for them, Cass.'

He liked it when she called him that. 'Aye, come on, we'll check out the bus first.'

***

The morning was spent in fruitless searching. They asked around the *cay* shops and open-fronted stalls. Owners beckoned them to sit on carpeted verandas and take tea. German Kurt, who could speak Dari, talked to the boys left in charge of the merchants' ponies and carts. The horses stood patiently in their shafts, heads dipping into sacks of feed. No, there had been no blond-haired foreigners asking for lifts. Some of the Australians climbed around the honeycomb of caves that had once been cells for the Buddhist monks, but found nobody.

Cassidy, despite liver salts and gallons of tea, was feeling increasingly unwell, his stomach cramping with anxiety. He drove the bus further up the valley but there was no sign of them.

'Perhaps they've gone on to the lakes at Band-e Amir,' he suggested to Juliet.

'But how?'

'Marcus would find a way.'

'Can we go up there?'

Cassidy sighed. 'Not in this bus, it's too risky this time of year – we'd probably get stuck. I've got all the others to think about. We really should be down the Shibar Pass before its dark.'

She didn't argue. He knew she was feeling guilty about last night's row, but what else could he do? He had a trip to run and over twenty other passengers to look after. Back at Bamiyan they found Devon and the Australians playing a hybrid game of football with some local boys, their shrieks and calls ringing around in the clear air. It took him a further hour to gather up all his passengers, dragging them out of teashops and from sunny spots under the golden poplars.

'Listen guys,' Cassidy said as they grouped around the dusty bus. 'My guess is they've headed on to the Lakes. The point is: do we hang around here a bit longer or go back to Kabul and wait? I've only got a week's visa for the bus, so time's limited.'

Arguments broke out.

'Not here, it's too cold.'

'But we can't just leave them.'

'They should've said where they were going.'

'Bet we'll find them back in Kabul.'

'We're already two weeks behind schedule, let's go!'

'But Ruth's only twenty, we shouldn't go without her.'

'They're both adults.'

Juliet suddenly piped up. 'Let Cassidy decide, he's in charge.' She turned to him. 'Tell us what we should do.'

Before he could answer, Kurt came running up the street with a youth dressed in *shalwar kameez* and a faded pinstriped jacket.

'Listen, listen!' said the German.

The boy had seen a foreign couple boarding a truck just before dawn, at the call to prayer. He pointed back through the village and the mountains beyond.

'Up, up!' said the youth.

'To Band-e Amir?' Juliet asked. He nodded.

'What sort of truck?'

The boy swivelled and pointed at the sheep grazing under the trees.

'Struth!' an Australian snorted. 'They'll stink. Have to hose 'em down before we let 'em back on the bus.'

'Do you think it's them?' Juliet said.

'Who else is mad enough to take off that early in a sheep truck?' asked Cassidy.

'Yea, the guy's a loony,' said one of the Londoners.

Kurt asked the boy to describe the couple, and then translated. 'The woman was dressed in jeans and coat and a pink woollen hat.'

'Yes, pink,' the boy nodded in understanding. 'Lady pink.'

A group of children were gathering quickly around the bus, laughing at the older boy's attempt at English.

'The boy says the man had a red beard and was dressed like a Pashtun,' said Kurt, 'except he wore a veil like a woman.'

3

Cassidy grunted, 'His *keffiyeh*; that's our Lawrence of Arabia all right.' He turned to the local boy and fished out a ten Afghani note from his jeans. 'If they come back this way, tell them we've gone to Kabul. We'll wait till Wednesday then we'll have to push on to Pakistan. They can catch us up in Lahore.'

Kurt translated for Cassidy; the youth nodded and smiled. The other children giggled and pushed against him.

Cassidy herded his group back on board. There was a hasty shoving of rolled up mattresses between the seats, ducking under strings of overhead washing and a noisy settling down. Maggie, the Irish nurse, pushed past to rummage through the box of cassette tapes. Juliet and Kurt were the last to mount the steps.

'They'll be all right,' Cassidy said. 'Some people just aren't suited to group tours – that's their choice.'

Juliet gave him a tired smile and offered him a squashed toffee from her pocket. He took the sweet hoping she'd sit down at the front, but the card players at the back shouted that it was her turn to deal. Kurt followed like her shadow.

Cassidy revved up the engine. Maggie slammed in a cassette and plonked into the front seat beside Devon. 'Well at least we won't have to put up with Marcus and his feckin' poetry,' she said. 'Rustum this, and Rumi that.'

Devon gave a soft chuckle. 'Hey man, I liked his poetry.'

Cassidy swung the bus into a three-point turn, juddering over the rutted road.

'And Ruth,' Maggie said, 'well, she gave me the creeps - all that screaming in the desert.'

'I think Ruth's kinda cute.'

'Mad as a fish, you mean.'

Electric piano burst from the cassette deck as the bus jolted forward. Picking up speed, they bumped across the plateau towards the swirling green waters of the gorge, raising clouds of dust to the thump of Steely Dan. Shadows were already creeping across the valley and the tension returned to Cassidy's shoulders at the thought of the hairpin descent.

A fragment of memory from the night before surfaced like a shard of glass. *'Dare to die, Cassidy!'*

Marcus, his bearded face mocking in the lamplight, had leaned towards him and whispered, 'Dare to die, Cassidy! That's the meaning of life.'

And Cassidy had thrust the money at him and shouted, 'Fuck off and die then!'

Cassidy's hands were clammy as he gripped the wheel. The pair of them were gone. He'd got what he wanted, hadn't he? He tried to rid his head of Marcus's taunting voice and Ruth's frightened pinched face. But they haunted him all the way back to Kabul.

CHAPTER 2

County Durham, England. The present.
Amber English
The chapel door banged open and shut, bringing a blast of cold, damp air. Amber glanced round to see who had arrived late to her grandmother Sarah's funeral. A man in a battered old Barbour jacket and wild grey hair squeezed in behind the throng of elderly farmers and neighbours. Amber's father caught sight of him and cursed under his breath.

'Who is he?' Amber whispered.

'Souter - bloody reporter,' Daniel hissed. 'Don't stare.' He dug her in the ribs as if she were still a child, not twenty-three. 'And don't you dare speak to him.'

Amber eyes smarted as she turned to the front. She was feeling emotional enough without her dad being so touchy. She knew her father would rather be anywhere but paying respects to his dead mother; it was Amber and her mum who, coming all the way from London, had shamed him into attending. After the divorce, it was Helen who had continued to bring Amber up on holiday to stay with her gran and help out on the smallholding. The three of them sitting together: how rare was that? Gran - such a family person - would have loved to see it. Amber swallowed tears. She should have made more effort to come north and visit when old Sarah had moved into the care home; now she would never see her beloved gran again.

As they stood for a hymn, Amber blew her nose and took another glance round. The journalist was staring right at her. What was he doing here? There was no story in an old woman's death, except that Sarah had once had a daughter who had gone missing and never returned. Her stomach clenched. Could his coming here be in any way connected to her tragic Auntie Ruth: the blonde girl in the picture on Gran's mantelpiece who had vanished in Afghanistan ten years before Amber was born? *'They think she took her own life,'* her mum had been the one to try and explain. *'No one can be sure, but that's what the police thought.'*

As a girl, Amber had been fascinated and appalled at the idea of the teenager in jeans smiling from behind a curtain of fair hair, going off to a faraway land to kill herself. She had envied Ruth's pretty looks and in early teens had tried to straighten her wavy black hair and dye it blonde. No one had ever properly explained to her what had happened though she had longed to know.

Twenty minutes later they were filing out after the coffin and heading up the steep hillside to the small burial ground. The rain had eased but the wind blew them sideways and the old women who followed clung onto their hats. Amber watched her father take one of the cords and help lower the coffin into the ground, wondering if he felt any regret at the long years he had cut his mother out of his life. She couldn't imagine being that angry with anyone for so long, let alone her lovely gran. She knew it was about him being adopted but not finding out till he was almost grown up. '*Never forgave his parents*,' Helen had told her.

But Amber thought it also had to do with the Ruth tragedy and her dad blaming his parents for something. Beyond the tract of brown heather and dead bracken, the valley below disappeared into mist.

Amber's father raised his voice, 'you're all welcome back at the *Bull's Head* for a drink and a sandwich.'

The nearest pub was half an hour away in St John's Chapel. Most of Sarah's elderly friends paid their respects at the cemetery and left. Back at the pub, a dozen mourners stood in self-conscious huddles, among them Sarah's care workers, neighbour Neil Timpson and the Cleggs who were renting Sarah's smallholding. Daniel knocked back two whiskies and went to speak to the Cleggs.

While her mother turned to Neil, Amber chatted to Dorothy and Sharon from the care home, topping up their wine to get them talking. They reminisced about Sarah's love of game shows on television and her habit of wandering out of the building to chat to people passing the gate.

'She used to call me little Miss Chatterbox,' Amber smiled, 'but she was Olympic standard.'

'We've got her things in the boot of the car,' said Dorothy, 'there wasn't very much.'

'Was there a photo album?' Amber asked, remembering how she used to encourage Sarah to get out family photos so she could gaze at fuzzy instamatic snapshots of the leggy Ruth with her quizzical smile.

'Yes,' Sharon said. 'She often used to look at that.'

'Yeah she did with me too; used to like talking about my Auntie Ruth as a girl. Did she mention her at all?'

The women exchanged glances. 'She got very confused towards the end,' said Sharon. 'Poor old soul thought your aunt was coming back – used to go out and look for her.'

Dorothy said they had to be getting back to the home. Amber went out to help them unload her grandmother's boxes. They seemed apologetic; it was mostly old clothes and a portable television.

'Keep the TV,' Amber told them, 'One of the residents can use it, yeah?'

Sharon gave Amber a hug. Dorothy said, 'I've some paperwork to tie up. Perhaps you or your parents could pop in before you leave?'

Amber nodded. 'I'm gonna stay around for a couple of days anyway.'

'Excuse me!' A man moved out of the shelter of the pub wall, grinding a cigarette under his walking boot. The man in the Barbour. 'Can I have a word?'

'Leave the lass alone,' Dorothy scolded, 'it's her grandmother's funeral.'

'Souter,' the man said, ignoring Dorothy's remark and stretching out his hand. 'I'm just here to offer my condolences.'

'Sniffing for a story, you mean,' Dorothy said. 'The old girl's dead, for goodness sake. Let her rest in peace.' She turned to Amber. 'You don't have to speak to this man; he only wants to rake up the past.'

'Charming as ever Dorothy. Let me help with those,' Souter said, piling up and lifting the boxes.

Amber nodded. 'It's okay,' she assured Dorothy. 'I'll see you tomorrow.'

Souter followed as Amber unlocked the hire car she and her mother had driven up from Durham station.

'Sorry about your grandmother,' the journalist said. 'Makes you think doesn't it? That a life can be packed into four boxes after all those years. How old was she? 88, 89?'

As Amber stacked them in the boot she tried to place the man's accent: not local.

'Thanks, but why are you interested in my gran?' she asked, locking the car.

'Just paying my respects.'

'You're a reporter, right? Bet you're itching to have a look through those boxes.'

Souter's putty smoker's face broke into a grin. 'Very sharp.'

'What you expecting to find?'

'Not much after all this time.'

Amber eyed him. 'Is this to do with my auntie disappearing? Cos if you want info on all that, you've come to the wrong person. I've been kept in the dark for years.'

Souter considered her, and then nodded towards the public bar. 'Let me buy you a drink. I promise not to grill you about your family. I really was fond of your grandmother. And maybe I can tell you a thing or two – if you'd like to know?'

Amber's insides twisted; the absent Ruth had hung like a spectre over her growing up. 'Yeah, I really would.'

***

The low-ceilinged bar, with its horse brasses and copper warming pans glinting on dark-panelled walls, was almost deserted. Two youths in paint-splattered overalls, who were playing pool at the other end, stopped to eye the newcomer with her tall athletic figure and large blue eyes.

'I'll have a pint of cider, thanks,' Amber told Souter. Choosing a table by the window, she kicked off the high heels she had borrowed from her mum and sank back.

'Spill the beans then,' she said with a tired smile, pulling back her long wavy hair.

'I covered Ruth's story from the beginning – came up from London and never got away again – this place can do that to you. Got friendly with your grandparents. I think they hoped I might be able to uncover something that others had missed.'

'And did you?' Amber could not keep the eagerness out of her voice.

7

The reporter shrugged. 'Not much.' He gave Amber a shrewd look. 'I noticed you talked of your aunt "disappearing". Does that mean you don't believe your aunt killed herself?'

She shrugged. 'Don't have an opinion. My dad only spoke about it when he was drunk – said he thought some guy had murdered her – the one she went off with. Used to give me nightmares thinking about that.'

Souter nodded. 'Sarah didn't believe it was suicide either. She didn't believe Ruth died at all.'

Amber felt her stomach flutter. 'What would make her think that?'

'Call it a mother's intuition, but she never gave up thinking she would walk back through her kitchen door, never.'

Amber felt her hopes deflate. A hunch was hardly grounds for a case against the suicide verdict or her father's wilder accusations of murder.

She took a sip of the sweet cider and asked, 'and what d' you think?'

'I probably lost a bit of perspective too,' he admitted. 'I went out to try and find her.'

Amber spluttered over her drink. '*You* did? Wow, to Afghanistan?'

'Yes, after your grandmother and father returned none the wiser. Did your father not tell you that? No, I suppose he wouldn't. He resented me for it – muscling in on private family grief as he saw it. Not that he had much contact with his parents by then – he was away at sea a lot – and his relationship with his old man was worse than putrid.'

'Did you find anything about Auntie Ruth?'

Souter shook his head. 'Not a trace. That's what made it worse – there was no body to bury, no way of saying goodbye and drawing a line under things.'

'Were the Afghans the problem - maybe hiding something – like my aunt being murdered?'

Souter gave a snort of indignation. 'Your father's idea? He thought everyone was to blame. It suited him to dismiss them as bumbling or untrustworthy foreigners. But the fact is the Afghans couldn't have been more helpful and kind. They treated your grandmother with respect and went to great trouble to take her to the area in the mountains where Ruth and the missing man were last thought to have been.' He took a swig of beer and wiped his lips on the back of his hand. 'But we drew a blank. All the police could go on were suicide notes left in their backpacks in Kabul. They were only discovered weeks later, when the alarm was raised. Ruth was supposed to be going to help at a mission orphanage in India, but never turned up.'

Amber had a sudden thought. 'What else was found in the backpack? What about her clothes and stuff? Did she keep a diary?'

Souter flashed a look. 'Ever thought of becoming an investigative journalist?' he grunted. 'There was a diary; didn't tell a great deal. She wasn't much of a writer. And there were two rolls of film. The police had them developed. Nearly broke your grandmother's heart – seeing her daughter in drunken poses with all these bearded hippy types, smoking goodness knows what. Up till then Sarah thought *Rainbow Tours* was some sort of church group doing the religious sites through the Middle East. Old John told her to destroy the photos.'

'And did she?' Amber's blue eyes were wide with curiosity.

'No.'

'I've never seen them. Are they in Gran's boxes? Is that what you're after?'

Souter gave an impatient sigh. 'I'm not after anything. I know as much as we're ever likely to know. I admit it did cross my mind to do a small piece about the funeral, just to acknowledge your grandmother's love for her daughter and how she never gave up hope. But to be honest, no one's interested any more in what happened to a couple of hippies over three decades ago. It's ancient history. Dorothy's right; your grandmother should rest in peace.'

Amber felt a fresh wave of grief that her gran was gone and that she would never again get a hug of welcome at her cottage door. She gulped at her drink; Souter had nearly finished his.

'Can I buy you one now?' she asked, wanting to keep him there talking. He shook his head. 'Did Grandma ever say anything about me? I used to love coming up here and helping out with the hens and stuff.'

'Yes. She was very fond of you – and your mother. Your visits were the highlight of the year after your grandfather died. I think it made her feel a bit closer to your father too. At least she could hear news of him from you.' Souter drained his glass.

'Yeah, I tried to get him to visit – he only lives in Berwick – but you can't tell Dad what to do.'

Souter grunted and reached for his coat.

'So,' Amber asked quickly, 'how do y' know those photos of Ruth's weren't destroyed?'

Souter glanced at the door and lowered his voice. 'Because I've got them.'

Amber stared at him. 'Oh my God, how - ?'

'Sarah gave them to me for safekeeping – ages ago when there was first talk of her going into the home. I think she worried that Daniel would throw them out. Your father's way of dealing with the whole thing was to pretend it had never happened – wipe out all the painful traces – least that's the way I see it.'

From his musty-smelling Barbour, Souter pulled out a battered brown envelope. 'Sarah would have wanted you to have these.'

Amber gawped at the package that lay between them on the table. 'That's them?'

The reporter nodded. 'Not just the photos, the diary too.'

Amber felt her insides somersault. Here were the last links to her mysterious aunt and the fatal bus trip she took so long ago. What would it tell her?

'Sarah was right,' Souter said, zipping up his coat, 'you're a lovely girl. I'm glad to have met you at last. But better get going before your dad finds you consorting with the enemy.'

9

'Why are you the enemy?' Amber asked, reluctant to see the man go when she had so many questions.

Souter shrugged. 'For befriending Sarah and taking your father's place? I dunno.'

Amber stood too, clutching the envelope and grabbing her shoes. 'But I want to know more. Did anyone go back to Afghanistan again? Did Gran?'

'She wanted to, but after the Russians invaded in 1980 it was impossible. And your grandfather got cancer, so she had to look after him. Old John hadn't been well for a long time – but I think the shock of it all finally ruined his health.'

Amber walked outside with him in her stocking feet. 'What about the articles you wrote at the time – do you have copies I can read?'

Souter pulled out his cigarettes and offered one. Amber shook her head and Souter put his back to the wind and lit up. 'Yes, I've copies. I'll send them to you. Give me your address.' He tore off part of the cigarette packet and got Amber to write it down with a pencil stub from his pocket. He must have sensed her eagerness and frustration – perhaps it mirrored his own from years before – because he put a hand on her arm.

'If you really want to find out more about the trip Ruth went on, I could probably put you in touch with Cassidy.'

'Cassidy? Who's he?'

'Your dad really hasn't told you anything has he?' Souter's look was pitying. 'Cassidy was the bus driver. I reckon he might talk to you if we can find him.'

Just then, someone rapped hard on the pub window. Amber saw her father's flushed face mouthing angrily.

'Time I went,' Souter said, hunching into his weathered jacket. He thrust a grubby creased business card at Amber. 'You can get me on this number. Ring in a couple of days and I'll see if I can run Cassidy to ground.'

'Cool,' Amber smiled, 'and thanks so much.'

Souter nodded and turned into the gale. Amber watched him being buffeted towards the car park. Something made her shout after the journalist.

'Hey, what's Cassidy's take on it all?'

Souter turned and shouted against the wind. 'It's a long story – but he thought that one of the other women on the trip knew more than she ever let on.'

'What woman?' Amber called.

Daniel banged again at the window and beckoned her inside. Amber just caught Souter's reply.

'Juliet – Juliet Forbes!'

CHAPTER 3

'Requisites for Travelling: An umbrella is required, not only as protection from the rain, but from the sun; it should be of double silk. A straw hat with a wide brim is the best in hot countries. A green veil or blue spectacles are useful as a protection from the glare of the sun. A small tent, a hammock, and a small carpet ...A basin of block tin, a looking glass, table cloths, sheets and towels, a thermometer, a case of mathematical instruments, a telescope, drawing paper, pencils, Indian rubber, a camp stool, measuring tape, and pedometer should be taken.'
Handbook for Travels in the East, 1840

London, September 1976
Juliet Forbes

She put all her weight against the large suitcase, straining to get the metal catches to click into place. Outside, in the dark, a car went past playing The Beach Boys. It was five in the morning but she couldn't sleep. The hotel room was too stuffy and she was too excited. In two hours she would be on her way to India! She felt she had been in preparation for this moment all of her thirty-one years – even before - when the shock of her father's RAF plane crashing into the mountains of Baluchistan had caused her mother to go into labour.

Opening the case again she wondered what she could bear to leave behind: the yellow maxi cheesecloth skirt or one of her travel books.

'You're never taking all of those?' her friend Joan had asked incredulously.

'Why not? They're old friends.'

Her father had collected travelogues – outdated and out of print - and they had been her escape from the kindly boredom of her paternal grandparents' house where she had grown up. Smoking illicit cigarettes in the garden shed she would roam Persia and the Levant with Gertrude Bell and Freya Stark. At school she had learned about reincarnation from her German teacher, and became obsessed with the idea that in a previous life she had been an Edwardian explorer. Why else did she so strongly identify with these women and their thirst for travel? She called her reincarnated self Grace – after her favourite traveller Grace Ellison – and knew one day it was her destiny to go east.

Her Pop and Nan discouraged such ambitions, and saw no need for Juliet to venture any further than her job at the motor tax department at county hall. To alleviate the monotony of processing tax discs, Juliet taught herself graphology, delighting her fellow clerks by analysing their handwriting and those of their boyfriends to see if they were compatible. Her strange hobbies and fanciful conversations had baffled Pop and Nan, but now they were gone and Juliet felt no obligation to stay in Durham. From their modest legacy (the house had been rented since 1920 and so yielded up no capital) she managed to scrape together enough to go travelling.

She had never been further than a school trip to Paris, so yearned to strike east and see for herself the treasures promised in her books. More than this, she wanted to explore the lonely deserts of Baluchistan described in the last letter her father had ever sent home. He had flown over serrated mountaintops, camel trains a mile long and seen a coastal island that rose and fell in the sea like magic.

Then, with the war nearly over, his plane had gone down in a storm, Juliet had been born and her mother had died of 'complications' as her stoical grandmother had put it. A year later, a parcel had turned up via various air bases with a present of a child's waistcoat - embroidered velvet and studded with tiny mirrors - and a letter from a merchant called Aziz Baloch. Juliet's father had commissioned the garment for his unborn baby but never returned for it. Mr Baloch had heard with great sorrow of the death of Sahib Forbes. As a friend and a brother, Aziz Baloch was sending the waistcoat and sought no payment for it. He hoped the family Forbes were well and comforted by God. *Inshallah*!

Juliet's grandfather had sent back a polite note to the address in Quetta with a photograph of baby Forbes. Occasional postcards, smelling faintly spicy, would arrive from Pakistan sending greetings and blessings to the family Forbes. When Juliet began to plot her route east, she hoped to visit Quetta and possibly make contact with Aziz Baloch, though his postcards had stopped several years ago and he had not replied to any letters since her grandparents' deaths.

***

The man in the specialist travel agency seemed amused by her enthusiasm for Asia Minor.

'When do you wanna go?'

'I'm told the autumn's a good time to go east.'

'Yea, avoid the monsoon and the shits,' he grinned. 'Camping or hotels?'

'Got to be camping,' she smiled, thinking of the romance of tents in the desert.

'Buses are more comfy than trucks. How about *Rainbow Tours*? They're reliable and not too pricey. Three months to Kathmandu: accommodation, meals and entry to historic sites, all in for £250.'

Fifteen minutes later Juliet had left the shop having signed up for the overland bus leaving in late September. The world lay beyond, mapped and beckoning. She would shed her possessions and stride out towards a new life with just a sleeping bag and a handful of clothes.

***

And a suitcaseful of books. Juliet sighed as she stared into the case that would not shut. She opened the case, took out the cheesecloth skirt and a large box of sanitary towels. Travel could make periods stop, so she had read somewhere, or maybe her friend Joan had told her. Joan had been full of dire warnings and grisly tales of rapes and deaths and mutilations along the hippy trail. But then Joan lived in daily expectation of being mugged on the Number 24 bus and always wore her handbag slung across her chest like a bandolier to prevent someone snatching it.

Juliet grabbed her suede coat and hauled her luggage onto the landing. The suitcase was impractically heavy. She piled her overnight bag and sleeping bag on top and shoved them along to the lift. Grinning inanely at the desk clerk, she went outside to wait for the taxi. The dawn air was chilly and London strangely quiet. Sunday morning.

***

On Earl's Court Road a huddle of figures, wrapped in jackets and hats, squatted on the pavement beside heaps of rucksacks and cases. A small van was parked in the empty road. Juliet could just make out the fat curly lettering of *Rainbow Tours*. The taxi driver heaved out her luggage.

'You sure this is it?'

'Well I hope we're not going in that,' she nodded at the van and laughed, 'or some of us will be running along behind.'

She paid him off, and then took a better look at the group. They looked half-asleep, blank-faced and subdued. How could they not be feeling as excited as she was? Someone tapped her on the shoulder and she glanced round startled. A young girl in a pink woollen beret, hunched under a huge pack, gave her an anxious smile.

'Excuse me; are you waiting for the bus to Kathmandu?' She had a soft voice and a Durham accent that Juliet recognised immediately.

'Yes,' Juliet laughed, wanting to hug her. She looked far too young to be travelling to India.

The girl blushed. 'I know it sounds daft but I'm worried about getting on the wrong one.'

'Yeah, me too. It would be a bit humiliating to end up in Bermondsey instead of Istanbul.'

'Nuffin' wrong with Bermondsey,' a London voice piped up from the pavement.

'Even better now you've left it,' said another. They looked like brothers.

The human luggage pile began to stir and yawn and chat. As the sky lightened, an old-fashioned blue Bristol bus chugged into view with a bang and a cloud of black exhaust smoke. It came to a juddering sigh beside them, the same garish rainbow pattern and yellow lettering as on the van. Juliet thought how Joan would panic; it made the Number 24 look like a royal carriage. The door hissed open and out jumped a stocky man with long brown hair and a droopy moustache. Despite the cold morning he wore only a pair of threadbare beige cords and a washed-out black t-shirt. He grinned at them with all the relish of a sergeant for a group of raw recruits.

13

'Morning travellers! All right? I'm Cassidy your driver. We'll do introductions later. Let's get busy, eh?'

He banged on the window of the van. 'Wakey wakey, you lazy Kiwi bastard. I've got a ferry to catch.'

A lean balding man with long sideburns tumbled out, loudly cleared his throat and spat on the pavement. Cassidy whistled tunefully as they unloaded the van of cooking equipment, boxes of food, tents, jerry cans and foam mattresses. He swung up onto the roof of his vehicle and began loading the roof rack with supplies.

'All the main cases and rucksacks go on top,' Cassidy called down. 'Anything you need for the next week you put in your hand luggage. You won't be seeing your suitcases till Venice, okay?'

There were murmurs of discontent and a sudden scrambling into rucksacks.

'Told you in the bloody brochure,' the New Zealander grunted.

'Aye and they told us we'd be travelling in a feckin' bus,' retorted a dark-haired Irish woman in a long multi-coloured scarf, 'not something out the steam age.'

Cassidy snorted with laughter, leaping down in two agile moves and began chivvying his troops for their luggage. 'Haway, we want to get to Kathmandu before Christmas.'

Juliet's stomach twisted in excitement at the exotic name; this was really happening! The New Zealander reached for her case and balked at the weight.

'Struth! What you got in here – gold ingots?'

'Sort of, yes. They're my travel books.'

He rolled his eyes. 'Well, sort of they're too heavy. You'll have to throw some out.'

Juliet stood her ground; trying to win him with her broad smile. 'My case isn't as big as some of the others here. Can't you just squeeze it in?'

Cassidy intervened, reaching for the offending case. 'It's nothing a man can't handle.' He winked at Juliet. 'Get yourself on board, pet.'

He's a Geordie; she was comforted by the familiar accent.

Juliet picked up her tartan overnight bag and sleeping bag and followed the Irishwoman – 'I'm Maggie, you can stick with me' - who was already pushing her way past the others to reach one of the tables at the back of the bus. The seats were worn and musty smelling and the floor sticky. She squeezed past three tanned and freckled young women with Australian accents and a plump middle-aged American couple in matching waterproof jackets.

'Chuck honey, can you get down my bag again, I'll need my bifocals.'

'Sure thing.'

A row of seats on either side of the aisle had been removed to accommodate two tables, and the rows in front reversed. Maggie had already commandeered two table seats facing forward and stored away her luggage in the overhead rack. Juliet quickly shoved her bag down behind the reversed seats and plonked herself next to Maggie.

It was a scene of chaos, people struggling with bags, coats, blankets and sleeping bags, trying to find places for them in racks or under seats. The young girl with the pink hat looked lost, so Juliet waved her over.

'There's a seat here if you don't mind travelling backwards.'

'That's fine,' she smiled, pulling off her hat and letting blonde hair tumble. Her eyes were an intense blue. 'I'm Ruth, by the way.'

'Struth this floor's filthy!' complained one of the tanned Australians.

The New Zealander came elbowing his way up the aisle and started removing bags from behind the table seats, including Juliet's.

'Can't leave 'em here. Foamies go here.'

'What are foamies?'

'Mattresses.' He dumped her bag on the table. 'Feels like you've got another bookcase worth in here.'

Before she could ask him where it was to go, he was rowing his way back down the bus with his elbows. Shortly afterwards Cassidy came round making sure everyone had stored away their luggage and had a seat. He read out a list of names, checking them off like a school register. There were twenty-two. Two more were to be picked up in Paris. One hadn't turned up.

'Devon MacPherson?' he called out again.

'Is that a place or a person?' quipped one of the Londoners.

The New Zealander muttered, 'Well if he's not here in ten minutes you'll just have to go without him.'

'He's beginning to piss me off,' Irish Maggie complained.

'Don't worry,' Cassidy grinned, 'Mr Sunshine isn't coming with us. He's taking out the trip in two weeks time.'

'That's a relief,' said Juliet, 'I thought he was the second driver.'

Cassidy pulled a rueful smile. 'At the moment there isn't one. Lad went down with hepatitis. But we should have another by Italy. Don't worry.'

Cassidy smoked outside as he waited for his last passenger, but no one came. Climbing aboard, he switched on the engine.

'Got any tunes, mate?' someone called out.

'Sorry, tape deck's not working.'

Several people swore at once.

'How can we get to Nirvana without Led Zep?' shouted a young man with lank fair hair.

'You hum it and I'll whistle,' Cassidy said, revving the engine and closing the door. As he eased the bus away from the curb he began to sing. Just then, Juliet caught sight of a gangling figure with an Afro and a goatee, loping along the pavement with a guitar strapped to his back. He grinned up at them and gave a peace sign.

'I think someone wants us to stop,' she called out.

'Must be Devon,' Maggie said, 'he looks a dish. Stop the bus, Cassidy.'

But the driver was singing so loudly as the bus trundled forward that he didn't hear. The lanky man picked up speed alongside, waving more vigorously.

A chorus of 'stop!' rippled down the bus. When Cassidy realised they weren't protesting at his singing, he banged on the brakes and they lurched to a sudden halt. He jumped up and opened the door. Devon reached it and climbed aboard. Apart from the guitar he only carried a small haversack and a colourful blanket slung over his shoulder.

'Greetings earthlings,' he smiled.

'You're late,' Cassidy said, 'and you interrupted my singing.'

Devon chuckled and gave him a mock salute. 'Carry on, my leader.'

Cassidy returned the gesture. 'Grab a seat, eh?'

'Room at the back!' called Maggie. 'You can budge up, Ruth, can't you?'

The girl was gazing out of the window and didn't seem to hear. She brushed a tear from the corner of her eye.

'I'll move round,' Juliet offered. She touched Ruth on the shoulder, manoeuvring her into the window seat and sat beside her. 'Homesick already?' Juliet murmured, pressing a handkerchief at her.

Ruth blinked away tears and smiled. 'No, I'm happy, really happy.'

Devon joined them. 'Wow ladies, this is gonna be a blast!'

Then the bus was accelerating up the road and heading out of London.

CHAPTER 4

Ruth's Diary
Sunday 26th September – Day 1!
We're started for India! No going back now. Felt sick with nerves getting on the bus. Nice woman called Juliet found me a seat at back table – she's from Durham way too. Crossing dead rough, hated it but had nice chat with Peach – she's American and quite old and she's got a daughter a bit older than me called Sherrie and says I remind her of her girl. Poor Juliet was standing in the queue at the duty-free and this drunk guy with red hair spewed all over her denim skirt! Me and Peach tried to clean her up but she still stank!

Oh boy, did she get teased on the bus! Paul (he's got long greasy hair and is dead funny) told her she shouldn't have had that second pint! (She doesn't even drink beer). Maggie made a big fuss (God, she's a pain) and made her take off her skirt and tights and hang them out the window. Juliet was going to sit there in her knickers (she doesn't give a monkeys that there are lads around) but Devon leant her his Indian blanket and Peach gave her a snakeskin belt to keep it tied so she looked like she was wearing a huge kilt! Cassidy (he's our nice driver) said he'd get her case down in Paris.

Folk at my table – me, Juliet (really nice, quite pretty for someone over 30, chatty) Maggie (Irish, dead pretty but thinks she's God's gift to men, flirts a lot)

Devon (black American guy, friendly, been busking round Britain, has stickers all over guitar case).

At the other table – Gino from Australia (curly dark hair) and likes to play cards – asked Juliet if she wanted to play strip poker while she only had a couple of things on. I think he fancies Maggie.

Catriona (plump, friendly, Scots and knows one of the boys in Bay City Rollers!)

Ron and Denis – two brothers from London (not sure which is which yet), very strong accents, laugh a lot at each other, love to play cards too.

This afternoon was a real laugh – driving through France (flat, boring, like south of England) singing You are my Sunshine and Waltzing Matilda with the Australians, and Juliet's skirt flapping at the window. Didn't think about home at all.

Later – writing this by torchlight – am sharing tent with Juliet, Catriona and Maggie. Went into Paris with Peach and Chuck. They spent time trying to put call through to Sherrie in Tucson – wish I'd gone drinking with the others. Juliet's just come in wearing men's pyjamas – feel safe with her around. Maggie not back yet – saw her snogging with Gino at the back of the bus.

CHAPTER 5

Berwick
Amber

Two days after the funeral, Amber drove with her father back to Berwick, wondering why she had agreed to do so. Her mum had told her it would be a good opportunity to talk. Growing up, Amber had only seen her dad for sudden weekends when Daniel was home from working on the rigs or the statutory two weeks in the summer holidays when her mum insisted that he take her. She had longed for those times when he took her sailing in his dinghy, cooked fresh fish on the beach and scrambled the Berwickshire cliffs. But as she got older, awkwardness had grown between them and the holidays dwindled.

Since leaving school Amber had hardly seen him, except during one summer vacation when she'd been on a dig along the Northumberland coast excavating a Mesolithic site. They'd met a couple of times for a drink with her student friends and he'd been shocked to find her drinking pints and wearing a nose ring.

Her dad's house was an '80s semi on the fringe of the town: boxlike with small square windows and an unkempt pocket of garden. Amber's mother had said being left for weeks on end with a toddler on an estate where everyone else went out to work and Daniel was on the rigs, had driven her demented. An hour after arriving, the daylight went.

'I'll do your garden tomorrow,' Amber offered, 'if you like.'

They were the first words spoken between them for an hour. But the previous two days had been full of stormy accusations about Amber sneaking off to talk to the reporter, of arguing over what to do with her grandmother's boxes, and of Sarah's will that had left the cottage and smallholding to Amber. She'd been tearful at her gran's generosity, yet awkward at the unexpected gift.

'We could share it Dad, couldn't we?'

'I couldn't care less,' Daniel had snapped. 'I'd never live in it. Sell it and make some money.'

'I think I might hang onto it,' Amber had said.

'Why would you do that?'

Amber shrugged. 'Keep renting it out.' She didn't want to say that she felt more at home in the place than she ever had in London or Berwick.

'A nest egg,' her mother had nodded in encouragement.

Daniel had given Helen an angry look as if it had been her suggestion. 'Well, if the lass isn't going to get a proper job or marry someone who has, she'll need something to live on.'

'Dad, you're a Neanderthal.'

Helen had given her that warning look that said it wasn't worth making an issue over. What was so wrong with working in a garden centre? At least she had a job. It kept her fit and she loved working outdoors; dirt under the fingernails was a small price to pay.

'We'll get a carry-out,' Daniel said, 'and a fish supper.' There was no food in the house.

'How about going into town and having a pub meal?' Amber suggested, balking at the thought of a long strained Friday evening ahead.

'Suit yourself.'

Cheery lights beckoned across the bridge in the walled coastal town, promising warmth and escape. Amber chose a lively tapas bar and ordered chorizo stew, pork, salads and beers. Daniel looked in amazement across the rough wooden tables at the animated guitarist and singer.

'Didn't know Berwick had such a place.'

After her father had downed three beers, Amber pushed back her unruly dark hair and asked, 'what were you doing at my age - like before you met Mum?'

Daniel shot her a suspicious look and then shrugged. 'By your age I'd been at sea for four years. South America and back three times.'

'Cool. Did you enjoy travelling?'

'Ports are much the same the world over.' He paused. 'The sea; it was the sea I loved.'

'So you never wanted to be a stonemason like granddad?' Amber asked.

'Maybe as a boy.' Daniel's face tightened. 'Until I found out my so-called parents had been lying to me all my life. Then I couldn't wait to get away.'

'You mean when they told you about being adopted?'

'They were never going to tell me,' he said bitterly. 'I only got to know when I applied for a passport and needed my birth certificate.'

'What did it say?'

Daniel's mouth twisted. 'Can't remember.'

Amber didn't believe him, but knew not to press further.

'Tell me about South America. I'd love to go there some day.'

'I'm no expert.'

They walked out into the cold dark. On the way home, Daniel led the way into a neon-lit bar near the station. He ordered her a cider; a pint and whisky chaser for himself.

Deciding to risk a rebuff, Amber asked, 'Do you think that's why Auntie Ruth wanted to travel too - cos you went to far away places?'

'It wasn't me put the daft idea in her head,' Daniel growled. 'It was some busy-body missionary. I'm surprised her parents let her go.'

'She was twenty,' Amber pointed out, 'they could hardly stop her.'

'Oh, they could get her to do whatever they wanted,' Daniel contradicted, 'specially the old girl.'

'Maybe that's why she decided to go so far away, then, to get away from them?'

Daniel knocked back his whisky. 'I encouraged her to go to catering college in Edinburgh – cut the apron strings. They smothered her. She was the child they'd prayed for and thought they couldn't have. That's why they adopted me. Then bingo, a miracle girl is born. I was only four but I can remember the day; it's the only time I ever saw the old man cry.' He quaffed his beer. 'But Ruth was happy in Edinburgh. I would see her when I got leave and she was a different girl – liked a drink and a party – really living at last. Then suddenly she got this idea in her head about orphans and she was off to India to save the world.' He shook his head in incomprehension.

'Did you see her before she went?'

Daniel gripped his glass. 'Briefly. My ship was in Glasgow. She came to say goodbye.'

Amber said, 'It must've been bad going out to Afghanistan to look for her – for Gran too.'

Daniel gave her a fierce look. 'It was a waste of time. I knew something terrible had happened when I heard she'd gone off with that man. She was that naïve with boys – too trusting. Sarah kept kidding herself – she couldn't admit it was her and the old man that had driven her away. She just thought she could fetch her back like she'd missed the school bus or something. That Souter kept egging her on, keeping her hopes alive just so he could get a juicy story out of it. The sick bastard.'

Amber saw his agitation, but knew this might be the only time they talked about such things.

'What did Granddad think?'

Daniel stared at his pint. 'Blamed Sarah for filling Ruth's head with religion and letting her leave England. His religion was patriotism – England for the English, he used to say.'

'God, I remember Gran telling me that,' Amber said, 'but I always used to think it was a joke about our family name – cos of us being called English.'

'No, he never joked about that. He was a POW in the Second World War and never got over it – hated the Germans.' Daniel drained off his beer. 'He could be a poisonous bastard. Made everyone's life a misery.'

Amber was shocked by the savagery of his words and let the matter drop. There must have been so many painful accusations flying around about whom was to blame; no one could have predicted such a tragedy. Why couldn't it have brought them closer together, rather than stirring up this bitter brew of hatred? As a little girl, the only thing she'd really wanted was for them all to live happily together at Gran's house.

On the way home, she slipped her arm through her dad's and was pleased when he didn't pull away. When they got back to the house, Daniel brought out a whisky bottle. Amber hoped they would talk more, but her father turned on the TV.

She must have fallen asleep on the sofa, because the next she knew, Daniel was shaking her shoulder.

'You want to know what she was like?' he slurred and sat down heavily. 'Here. Look.'

Daniel thrust a narrow box at her, the kind that might once have held a necklace. Amber squinted and sat up. Inside was a wodge of tissue paper. Amber unwrapped it.

'Careful,' he said.

A thin swatch of hair, so pale it was hard to see against the yellowing paper, lay tied at one end by a baby blue ribbon.

'Oh my God,' Amber gasped, electrified. 'Ruth's?'

Daniel nodded solemnly. Amber ran her finger along its length. The hairs were very fine, blonde and soft to the touch; the kind she'd always dreamed of having as a teenager.

'When did she … ?'

Daniel's eyes glittered. 'She cut it off as a keepsake,' he mumbled, 'before she went to India. So I'd never forget her.'

Carefully her father re-wrapped the pelt of hair. He stood unsteadily and left the room without another word. Amber sat staring after him. Just touching the hair brought Ruth alive for her more than any amount of photos or diary. It had been part of her aunt when she had lived and breathed.

She went to bed and called Souter on her mobile. 'It's Amber English. Sorry it's late but - '

'I thought I'd hear from you,' the reporter said cheerfully. 'Everything okay?'

Amber told him about the lock of hair, then immediately regretted it. This man might still be after a story. But Souter was eager to tell her about tracking down Cassidy.

'He's still in Newcastle. I rang his old home number and he's only moved five doors up the street. He's not on the phone, but you can leave messages at Ali's Bazaar - it's a grocer's apparently.'

Amber added the address to her mobile. 'Thanks a million.'

'Will you go and see him?' Souter asked.

'Yeah,' Amber made up her mind on the spot. 'On my way back to London.'

CHAPTER 6

'Nowhere can you more easily dispense with man's society than in your tent, after a long day's fatigue. It is a pleasure, which words cannot tell, to watch that portable home, everywhere the same, spreading around its magic circle ... as cord by cord is picketed down, it assumes its wonted forms, and then spreads wide its festooned porch, displaying within mosaic carpets and piled cushions. There the traveller reclines, after the labour of the day and the toil of the road ...'

The Spirit of the East: Journal of Travels through Roumeli during an Eventful Period, by David Urquhart, 1838

Juliet

In the Bois de Boulogne that evening, they pitched the orange tents for the first time. Cassidy ordered them to find camping companions, except for the married ones: Americans Chuck and Peach, and a young New Zealand couple called Shane and Lucy, who got tents to themselves. Juliet found herself being commandeered by Maggie – 'you look like the girl guide type who can put up a tent in two minutes' – and joined by the amiable Glaswegian, Catriona.

'Can I come in with you three?' asked Ruth.

'No room,' said Maggie.

'I'm sure there's space for a fellow Durham girl,' said Juliet. She glanced around. The other women had teamed up easily – three Australians who were travelling together and four middle-class Brits with plummy accents who had gravitated towards each other like magnets. Cassidy had already nicknamed them the Poshettes.

'Are you any good with a mallet?' Juliet asked.

'Yeah,' the girl grinned. 'Me and my brother were always camping out on the moors as kids.'

Juliet smiled and threw her the hammer. 'Get pegging then.'

Maggie gave a loud huff. 'Fine. You get it sorted. I'll take a shower.' Grabbing her wash-bag and towel, she sauntered off towards the shower block, stopping by the London brothers' sagging tent to make a bawdy quip about slow erections.

'Don't mind madam,' Catriona winked at Ruth. 'I'll bet you five francs she'll be out of our tent in a week, shagging her way round the boys.'

Ruth went pink and busied herself with pegging into the hard ground. By the time Maggie had returned, wet-haired and gleaming, they had the tent up, the mattresses and sleeping bags unfurled – three in a line and Ruth's across the top – and their bags piled in the entrance.

Cassidy issued them each with a pink toilet roll and cooked up hot dogs and beans from a portable gas stove.

'From tomorrow, you get into shopping and cooking groups – three in each means you do it less than once a week. I keep charge of the kitty.'

He offered to get Juliet's case down from the bus roof.

'Mind you, that blanket suits you,' he winked, can of beer in hand. 'Sort of Dorothy Lamour meets Stanley Baxter.'

'Not quite the image I'm after,' Juliet laughed.

While most of the group went into Paris for the evening, she stayed and washed her smelly clothes, changing into her pyjamas – comfortable cotton men's striped ones – and a baggy woollen jumper that she had packed instead of a dressing gown. She returned Devon's Navaho blanket along with a bar of Swiss chocolate, placing it inside the tent he was sharing with two Germans.

A cultured voice from the back of the tent said, 'My mother always told me that washing with vinegar was good for taking out bad smells.'

Juliet stared into the gloom; she had thought the tent empty. The older of the two Germans with a tanned chiselled face, spectacles and untidy greying hair was propped against a faded canvas bag reading by torchlight.

'Now you tell me,' Juliet said with a cautious smile.

He gave a soft laugh and put down his book. 'Cigarette?' He pulled out a battered packet of Galois.

'Great idea,' she answered with only a moment's hesitation, squatting down on Devon's blanket in the entrance. They lit up and he introduced himself as Kurt. Juliet felt contentment settle inside at the first aromatic whiff of smoke. 'Umm, the smell of France.'

'A Francophile,' said Kurt.

'Isn't everyone?' she murmured, and then gave him an embarrassed look. Maybe this man had fought on French soil? The war had ended barely thirty years ago and he looked in his fifties. Or what if he had been in the Luftwaffe and had flown against her father? She felt the burden of history lying between them like a dead weight.

'France is beautiful,' he nodded, 'but I prefer to go east – Turkey, Persia – it is all so interesting, so full of the past. So many cradles of civilization, yes?'

'Oh, I agree. I'm very excited about the whole trip. I've been reading about these places half my life in old travel books and biographies. I tell you, those Victorians knew how to have adventures – quite fearless - even the women.'

'Especially the women,' Kurt chuckled.

'How is your English so good?'

'I worked at the British Museum for three years in the '60s. I'm an archaeologist. I like London and go back often to see friends.'

'Is that your son you're travelling with?'

Kurt shook his head and blew out smoke. 'Tomas is a friend – a doctor. He works too hard. He wanted to take time off and asked me to show him some of the wonders of the world. When his spirit is refreshed, then he can go back to treating bronchitis and piles. And you?'

Juliet hesitated. Motor tax department sounded deadly dull; graphologist would be lying. 'I'm a reincarnation of an Edwardian traveller, Grace Ellison. I've returned as Juliet Forbes because there's so much more of the world to explore – places to see, people to meet.'

His cigarette glowed in the dark. 'How interesting. We are similar I think.'

Juliet snorted with laughter at his unexpected reply. 'In what way? Are you reincarnated too?'

'I don't think so. But we are both nosey about people and what makes them – how you say? – tick? You are interested in the living and I look for clues about people who have been dead for centuries.'

Juliet liked him. 'Tell me more about what you do.'

Kurt spoke of his work on early Buddhist iconography. She listened enthralled as he described the ebb and flow of cultures and empires that had shaped central Asia from Alexander the Great to Babur of the Mughals.

'Buddhism spread north and east from India along the old trade routes. Then monks and pilgrims came in the opposite direction from China and Korea and settled in remote mountain caves. They left rock carvings – petroglyphs – to show the way. Many sites lie unexcavated in remote parts of Afghanistan and Pakistan. I dream of discovering whole ancient worlds out east.' He laughed at himself. 'Tomas says I am too interested in dead things – he only cares for the living.'

'It's possible to care for both, I'm quite sure.' Juliet finished a second cigarette and got up. 'It's been really nice chatting to you.'

'I hope we can do so again.'

'Yes.' She glanced out of the tent to see who might spot her coming out in her pyjamas.

He added, 'Why don't we get the German question out of the way now, then we can relax and be friends?'

She looked at him startled. 'What do you mean?'

'I see the way you look at me, Juliet. You are thinking; this man is old enough to have fought in the war. Did he fight against my father, or my uncle? Did he drop a bomb on Coventry? Was he a concentration camp guard?'

Juliet went red.

'I was a student for most of the war,' Kurt said levelly. 'In 1943 I was conscripted into the army but my eyesight was too bad for fighting, so I ended up as a clerk in Eastern France and was taken prisoner by the British. That is when I learnt my first words of English - and how to make a cup of tea.'

Juliet held onto the tent pole, overwhelmed by a desire to confide. 'My father was in the RAF. I was born a month after he died. His plane crashed in a storm somewhere over the mountains in Baluchistan. That's another reason why I want to go east. I may never find where it happened, but I might feel nearer to him somehow.' She swallowed. 'There's an emptiness – not knowing him – but liking what I heard about him.'

Kurt nodded.

Outside, noise erupted as a Contiki Tours bus returned and disgorged some of the Rainbow passengers too. Juliet did not want to be caught lurking in her pyjamas and turned to go.

'Baluchistan,' Kurt said. 'Some time I must tell you about the Buddhist petroglyphs found near Seistan.'

Juliet smiled. 'Anyone would think you were trying to chat me up.'

His quiet laughter followed her retreating footsteps.

***

Ruth babbled incoherently in her sleep. Catriona snored in a rising crescendo, stopped abruptly as if she had ceased breathing, then let out a long low sigh. Just after Juliet had dozed off, Maggie came back in the early hours, stumbling in the dark.

'Am I in the right tent? Who's that in my bed?'

'Yours is over here,' Juliet whispered.

'Thanks,' Maggie slurred and fell over Juliet. She collapsed on top of her sleeping bag and went straight to sleep.

It seemed only minutes later that Cassidy was banging a pan lid and telling them it was breakfast. Juliet crawled out of the tent into a chilly overcast morning.

Over bread, jam, fruit and tea, Cassidy introduced them to two guys from Liverpool who were joining the trip. One made a beeline for Ruth. She seemed bemused by the attention. It struck Juliet that Ruth had no idea how attractive she was. There was nothing artful in the way she shook back her hair and smiled, revealing pearly slightly crooked teeth. Juliet had a stab of disquiet: an innocent abroad. She would have to keep a protective eye on the girl from the Durham Dales.

CHAPTER 7

Newcastle
Amber

She walked out of Newcastle's cavernous Central Station under massive sandstone arches and into bright spring sunshine. Amber wanted to clear her head before tracking down Ruth's overland driver; she was still reeling from what her dad had said at Berwick station.

Sitting on a bench, Amber released her wild hair from a scrunchie and closed her eyes. She pictured her father studying the electronic notice board while they waited for her train and she gabbled on about how he should get an ipod for all those weeks on the rigs. Daniel had said nothing until the train pulled in. He had picked up her bag, turned to her with a face as impassive as granite, and wrung out the words, 'I am illegitimate. My mother's name was Mary MacRae; my father's was Karl Schmitt. He was a German POW who stayed on after the war mending farm machinery. She was a Scotch maid at the mental hospital. She left me on the minister's doorstep along with my birth certificate.'

Amber had gaped at him, speechless. Her father had given a bitter little smile.

'Aye, imagine what that did to young Danny English – brought up by a bigot who made me fight anyone at school with a foreign name. The only time he allowed us a party was when England beat Germany in 1966. And all the time he knew I was a little foreign bastard. Once Ruth came, he couldn't stand the sight of me.'

'Oh, Dad - !' She had started to hug him, but her bag had got in the way and he had swung it through the carriage door.

'Best get on,' he had said, standing back. Amber had stumbled aboard, still trying to find something to say. 'It doesn't matter' was on the tip of her tongue, but dried there. Of course it mattered – to her dad. Amber wondered if her mum had ever known the full story or was she the first person in a generation to be told? But Daniel had given her no time to ask any questions.

'Bye lass.'

'See you Dad,' Amber had said feeling helpless, 'I'll ring you, okay?' Once in her seat she had waved through the window. Daniel had raised his hand then walked away. She had seen the coastal view through a blur of tears. Why had he waited till the last minute to drop such a bombshell? She'd been trying to get him to open up and talk for days. *Jeez Dad*!

Sitting in Newcastle, letting her coffee go cold, Amber felt a hot wave of shame at her failure to comfort her father. She was really churned up about it and could only imagine what it must be like for him. How had Daniel felt at discovering his true origin – angry, betrayed? Amber tried to imagine the anti-German feeling in the late 60s among the war generation. Amber wondered if her grandfather had taken a perverse

26

pleasure in creating a xenophobe out of his half-German, half-Scots adopted son.

So where did that leave her, Amber? Whenever she'd thought about who she was, she had seen herself as more Londoner than Northerner, growing up in the capital with her mum since she was five. But she had been proud of her Weardale heritage, loved its high desolate moors and its kindly, hardy people. She felt at home there. But her father had sprung from quite different roots. So did Amber have no spiritual claim to her grandmother's little piece of the Durham Dales? Or could upbringing bind tighter than ties of blood? Daniel had obviously not thought so, or he wouldn't have hated his adoptive parents so much. And yet he had stayed close to Ruth; he had never rejected her as his sister.

Screwing up courage she dialled her father's home number. She would tell him that she really didn't care where he came from, he was still her dad and that she loved him to bits. Daniel would probably tell her not to be so soppy, but she would say it anyway.

No one answered, and no answer-phone kicked in.

Amber's eyes stung with tears. God, she was an emotional wreck since her gran had died. Wiping her eyes with her scrunchie she tied back her hair again and took a deep breath.

Get a grip. Better to concentrate on the mystery of Auntie Ruth; that's why she was here, remember? From what she had read of the diary so far she liked her aunt – she seemed normal and uncomplicated - a little bit new-agey perhaps, but likeable and probably a laugh. At least Ruth had been grounded in her own sense of self; she knew who her parents were and where she came from, and that suddenly seemed a very solid basis from which to face the world.

Amber pocketed her mobile and got to her feet.

CHAPTER 8

Ruth's diary
Monday 27th Sept – Day 2
Rained all day. Cassidy just kept on driving. Played lots of cards at back of bus. Mick (stocky guy from Liverpool) got the tape deck working again. No one will let Catriona play Bay City Rollers yet!

Camping at place called Orange. Went to toilet and when came back nearly screamed place down – thought I saw snakes in front of tent! But Juliet calmed me down and said they were just fat worms. Maggie (Irish) and the ones still drinking on the bus thought it was funny, but Devon said he would have been really freaked out by it too.

Thurs 30th – Day 5
Got to Pisa in Italy today. Still raining. Had a laugh on the bus – Juliet can read people's handwriting. She read Mick's and told him he was practical and loyal, but he thought too much about sex – he went as red as his hair! There's a sweet couple, Lucy and Shane from New Zealand – like a couple of lovebirds always holding hands. She told them they were very suited, cos Shane is extravert and loving, and Lucy is stable and easy going with her feet on the ground.

She told Devon that he was kind and introverted (which means quiet though he doesn't seem the shy type to me) but that he'd had something traumatic in his past that he needs to sort out. Devon said having to share a tent with Tomas (he's tall German doctor with a black beard) and his smelly feet was the trauma. (I feel a bit sorry for Tomas cos his English isn't very good and he can't join in much, not like his friend Kurt who is fluent. Tomas bites his nails right down to the stumps and I can see this cloud of sadness hanging round him – it's purple-grey like thunderstorms). I didn't want my handwriting done. We drew funny faces on the steamed up windows.

Didn't go up the leaning tower – hate heights. Instead went to the Cathedral with Juliet and Peach and Chuck. Never been in a Catholic church before – Dad would go ape – it was big and echoed and smelled spicy. It felt full of good vibes, like all the prayers and good feelings over the years were still hanging in the air. I wish Daniel could have felt it too, see that religion doesn't have to be plain and boring like chapel. Juliet lit candles to her dead parents and grandparents even though she's not religious. Peach got all teary and Chuck took her out. They went off to find a phone and ring their daughter Sherrie in Tucson. Sherrie has twin boys. P's really missing them all.

Friday 1st October – Day 6
Michael Angelo campsite, Florence

Arrived yesterday in a thunderstorm – all went to the bar and drank red wine and sang songs till Cassidy dragged us out to put up tents. Met a really nice crowd from a Swagman bus – some of us went off to a disco called the Red Garter. Had a dance with Mick, drinks were dead expensive. Mick tried to kiss me, but I wasn't keen.

Went sightseeing this afternoon but most places just closing for siesta. Saw some old paintings in Uffizi gallery, bit gloomy. Highlight was seeing statue of David (handsome and naked!) and going for ice-cream with the Londoners. ♥

Sat 2nd – Day 7
Writing this on bus with hangover. Had a really good night in the bar with the guys off the Swagman bus again – they've got Tamla Motown cassettes (my favourite) and we had a great dance – me and Juliet and the Australians and the ones that Cassidy calls the Poshettes (four English girls, all in their twenties with long hair and posh voices that go around together) I get them mixed up except the one called Mixie who has beads and tiny plaits in her hair – but they're good fun and don't mind Cassidy teasing them.   ☺ ☺

Then somehow we ended up on the bus and Mick had this bottle of brandy and we were playing Paul's Steppenwolf really loud. Then Chuck came in his pyjamas to tell us to shut up and Maggie called him Wee Willie Winkie cos he had this bobble hat on his head, but that just made him madder. And Chuck said, some folk are trying to getta sleep and Mick said, and some folk are trying to get another drink and thumped the ceiling. Chuck said, don't you think you've all had enough? And everyone shouted no! Then Chuck says, Goddammit, you guys, you're nothing but a bunch of degenerates. Maggie said that sounded like a heavy metal band and Mick shouted, yea, we're the degenerates and started playing air guitar.

Juliet went off the bus to speak to Chuck – I heard them when I went to the toilet. He was complaining about Cassidy not keeping control of things and not being a proper tour leader like it said in the brochure. Juliet said it wasn't his fault cos he didn't have time for all the touristy stuff when his relief driver still hadn't turned up and that anyway, people on the trip didn't want someone nannying them all the time. But Chuck said that somebody should take command. Juliet suggested that he might be happier on a more upmarket kind of trip where they had a courier and stayed in hotels and that it might not be too late to switch, but Chuck said that this was what Peach wanted and that was that. Poor Chuck, I feel sorry for him. I think he and Peach are too old for this kind of thing. I could never imagine my folks doing this ever.

Juliet saw me going back on the bus and said I should get some sleep, but I wanted another drink. I don't remember getting back to the tent last night. I think Paul must have helped me – or maybe it was Mick. The way he keeps winking at me this morning makes me think we must have snogged or something. I'm not going to drink like that again!!!

CHAPTER 9

'As the gondola slipped away from the blaze and bustle of the station down the gloom and silence of the broad canal, I forgot that I had been freezing two days and nights; that I was at that moment very cold and a little homesick. I could at first feel nothing but that beautiful silence, broken only by the star-silvered dip of the oars. Then on either hand I saw stately palaces rise gray and lofty from the dark waters, holding here and there a lamp against their faces, which brought balconies, and columns, and carven arches into momentary relief, and threw long streams of crimson into the canal. I could see by the uncertain glimmer how fair was all, but not how sad and old; and so, unhaunted by any pang for the decay that afterward saddened me amid the forlorn beauty of Venice, I glided on.'

Venetian Life, by W.D. Howells (New and Enlarged Edition) 1875

Venice, Italy
Juliet

Two days later, they drove through banks of fog to Venice and the waterlogged campsite at Fusina. The cases were unloaded from the roof for a weekend stay; on both days they got caught in downpours in the city. Juliet wandered around the rain-splashed streets and over dripping bridges in a bright orange cagoule bought for the trip. It rustled noisily as she walked and the hood restricted her view. With her stripy tights and yellow clogs she could be seen a street away.

'Wow, put your shades on,' cried Devon, 'here comes psychedelic Juliet.'

Juliet loved the camaraderie of the group; everyone was determined to have a good time no matter what the weather. Only Cassidy seemed stressed; his second relief driver had gone down with sickness and diarrhoea two days before they arrived and dysentery was suspected.

With Catriona and Ruth, she tagged onto one of the Australians who had a Michelin guide and was reading out long descriptions of St Mark's Square and the Doge's Palace to anyone who cared to listen, and several who didn't. The New Zealand couple walked behind hand in hand, stopping to take pictures of each other. Kurt and Tomas lingered behind, often in deep discussion. After two hours Fran, another Australian, mutinied.

'Enough, Gwennie, time for pizza.'

The small group fragmented. Juliet was about to follow Kurt and Tomas into a nearby café when Maggie pulled her back.

'Not with them,' she nodded at the Germans, 'they give me the creeps.'

Juliet stood awkwardly at the door. 'But Kurt's really nice; we were chatting the other night.'

'Well I couldn't get that big Tomas to talk. Doesn't want to mix. Just gabbles on in German to his friend – probably his boyfriend,' Maggie sniggered, wheeling Juliet round and pulling her towards the Liverpudlians. 'And remember what he said when you were doing people's handwriting on the bus? "Zis is not science, zis is telling fortune like gypsy".'

Juliet flushed. Maggie had overheard Tomas's remark to Devon.

'I'm sure he was making a joke,' Juliet said.

Ruth followed, splashing through puddles in scuffed walking boots. 'I think Tomas is ill.'

'He doesn't look it,' retorted Maggie. 'And he eats twice as much as the other guys.'

Ruth put a hand over her heart. 'I mean he's suffering in here. There's something sad about him.'

'Mystic Ruth speaks,' Maggie rolled her eyes. 'Come on, I need food.'

***

Late that evening, Juliet left a dozen of her bus mates partying in the camp bar. A handsome blond guy of about her age – one of the barmen perhaps? – was leading them in a drinking game. Passing Kurt's tent she felt a pang of guilt at the way she had allowed Maggie to frogmarch her off to lunch with the rowdy crowd. She caught a pungent whiff of cannabis. Tomas's legs and big boots were sticking out beyond the canvas; the gangling doctor was too long for the standard tent. Voices murmured, punctuated by Devon's slow chuckle.

Juliet found Catriona and Ruth still chatting in the dark and munching through a bag of Italian cakes. There was a smell of cheap wine, which they were drinking out of plastic cups.

'Did you know wee Ruth here is off to work with orphans in Delhi?' Catriona enthused. 'How brave is that?'

Ruth shook her head. 'I'm not brave.'

'Well, I think travelling all the way to India on your own is very brave,' said Juliet, 'let alone staying there to work with orphans. I wouldn't have dreamed of doing that at twenty.'

Ruth said, 'bravery is things like saving people from burning buildings or stopping someone drowning. Daniel's the brave one in our family. He's in the merchant navy and he's seen waves as big as houses. Nothing frightens him.'

'Daniel's her big brother,' Catriona explained.

'He's four years older,' Ruth added. 'He's adopted.'

Juliet wondered why she should mention that. This was the first time she'd heard the girl talk about her family. When she'd asked her before about her life in Weardale, Ruth had laughed it off, 'that's boring; nothing happens up there.'

Juliet settled down beside them. 'So what made you decide to go to India?'

Ruth shook back her curtain of hair. 'I heard this missionary speak when I was at college - showed us a cine film of the place. The children

31

looked so happy even though they hardly had anything. Dad was dead against it but Mum said if God was calling me then I should go.'

'Are you religious then?' Catriona asked.

'Not really. Not like Mum.'

Juliet got into her pyjamas and went off to wash. When she returned they were still talking about Ruth's upbringing and how she was glad to get away from her parents' strictness. It seemed once she had started to talk about home she couldn't stop. 'Once I got to Edinburgh and college I realised how boring my life was. They'd kept me so sheltered from the world – I didn't know anything. Being in a city was brilliant!'

'You should try Glasgow,' Catriona laughed. With a loud belch she crumpled up the empty packet. 'Best bakeries in the world.'

They settled down.

'Sometimes at the chapel I used to see things,' Ruth said into the dark, 'before they happened. Sort of like visions. That's another reason I wanted to leave home.'

'Away you go!' Catriona giggled. 'Like second-sight?'

'Yeah, kind of.'

'Give us an example,' Juliet asked, disbelieving.

'Once I saw our neighbour old Mrs Timpson standing in the doorway of the chapel with bright light shining behind her. A week later she died in a car crash.'

Juliet felt a flutter of anxiety; she hated hearing about violent deaths.

'That's terrible,' Catriona gasped. 'Did you tell anyone?'

'No. I would have told Daniel but he'd just gone to sea. Things were difficult at home – between him and my parents – so I didn't want to give them something else to be upset about.'

'But surely it was just coincidence?' Juliet said. 'And, if you were going through a bad time at home, maybe your imagination got the better of you? The mind can play tricks.'

'No it was a premonition she was going to die,' Ruth was adamant.

'Hey,' Catriona said, 'can you tell us anything that's going to happen on this trip?'

Ruth gave a small sigh.

'Sorry, didn't mean to take the mickey.'

'Let's drop the subject,' Juliet said. She'd begun to shiver.

'I'll tell you what I see,' Ruth said. 'Catriona's going to fall in love.'

'I am? Great. Who with? Cos I quite fancy that Alexei from Liverpool.'

'No, this man's tall, dark and handsome.'

'Not on our bus then,' Catriona snorted.

'He's a Turkish pudding chef. You'll run off with him and he'll make you sticky cakes for ever.'

'You!' Catriona cried and hit her with an inflatable pillow.

'And what about me?' Juliet smiled, relieved that the conversation had turned light-hearted.

Ruth hesitated. 'You're going to get left behind in the desert.'

Juliet froze.

'As long as she's got a pile of books to read she won't even notice,' Catriona teased.

'Sorry,' Ruth said, 'I didn't mean to upset you.'

'You haven't. It was just a joke like the pudding chef, right?'

'Yeah, course it was.'

Despite being really tired, Juliet found it hard to fall asleep. She refused to believe in Ruth's flights of fancy, but found the words disturbing. In fact there was something about the girl herself that bothered her, something she couldn't put her finger on.

Yet on the surface Ruth was attractive and likeable, and she shouldn't take any notice of a wine-induced prediction. Ruth couldn't have possibly known that Juliet had always been frightened by the very idea of deserts. They were empty, hostile places. One had swallowed up her father and broken her mother's heart.

CHAPTER 10

Cassidy

He had trouble prising his passengers from their tents the next morning and wished he hadn't drunk quite so much Johnnie Walker himself. He should be keeping his store of duty free to use as bribes at border posts further east, but a telex waiting for him at the camp had left him pissed off and anxious. There was no one available to replace his sick relief driver for at least two weeks. He could try recruiting one from a westbound trip as a stop gap. Fat chance, he thought. He needed someone now.

There was that friendly lad in the bar last night who had offered; he claimed to have driven long distance but he sounded too posh. There again, Cassidy had been impressed with the way the man had organised the group into bar games and handled one of the Aussies firmly when he'd made a drunken pass at Ruth. He wasn't too young – probably early 30s – and he seemed amiable and willing to help. Perhaps he should seek him out before they left and see whether he was serious?

'Haway, lasses,' Cassidy shouted into the Poshettes tent, 'you should be up making breakfast. We leave in an hour.' He went off to shave.

Emerging from the wash block, he heard the throaty noise of a bus engine and for a moment panicked that someone was driving off with his. But it was another Rainbow bus arriving. Bloody great! Help had come just in time. Yet something about it was not quite right. It pulled in beside Cassidy's. Then he realised that under the coat of filth and dust, the windows had been whitewashed over like a hospital ambulance to keep out the glare of the sun – or to stop others looking in. The engine gave a sickly cough and died.

'Hey, mate,' the driver gave a tired smile as he jumped down. He was gaunt and wild haired, dressed in grubby eastern pantaloons and army jacket.

'Bob?' Cassidy cried in sudden recognition. Bob was a die-hard overlander who had been doing the trail since the 60s; he had last seen him wintering in Delhi in '74. Cassidy clasped him by the hand and slapped him on the back. 'You bugger, I've seen better corpses!'

Bob grunted. 'You should see the others – what's left of them. Got a brew going?'

Bob's passengers dripped out one at a time, yawning and squinting into the early light and huddled around the camp stove. Cassidy was shocked by the state of them: yellow, skinny, travel-weary, ill. Only five or six looked capable of wiping their own backsides. But with a mug of tea in hand, three or four sparked into life, eager to tell their travellers' tales, their tanned faces and hands engrained with the dust of the road.

'Half the group got dysentery and five had hepatitis,' explained Bob. 'Stopped in Tehran for two weeks – six of them in hospital. Had to arrange for flights home, including my co-driver. Another three got sick

34

of waiting and took off. Haven't seen them since. Been a bloody nightmare, mate.'

They perked up over the hot strong tea, and got a bit of colour back. A bleary-eyed Poshette reheated congealed rice from the previous night's meal. The newcomers ate it without complaint, whereas few of Cassidy's lot could face the food. They gathered around, curious and a little wary of the motley crew who had suddenly appeared with the dawn.

'We got shot at in the Khyber Pass,' grinned a bearded South African proudly. 'Still got a bullet hole in the back window.'

'This Afghan guy pulled my earring right out!' said a woman in a red kaftan. 'Ripped my ear and it got infected. Bad scene for girls in Afghanistan, I tell you.'

'That's where the dysentery started …'

'Reckon we got food poisoning at that place in Kandahar …'

'Worse in Mashhad, I was okay till Iran …'

'And Pam got jumped on by a guy in Eastern Turkey. I wouldn't bother stopping there if I was you …'

'Best bit was the beaches on the Med, but we were nearly a month late by then and Bob said we had to keep going - '

'And there were packs of dogs everywhere – the last thing we needed was rabies.'

Cassidy saw the effect their tales were having on his passengers. Their eyes were out on stalks, swallowing the lot. The last thing he needed was panic spreading. He put a stop to it.

'So which of you hardened travellers is going to volunteer as my relief driver?' He tried to sound as matey as his thumping head would allow. 'It'll be a breeze now it's autumn – no Delhi belly, no mad dogs in the heat.'

'No way,' said the kaftan woman, 'we can't wait to get home.'

Bob shook his head. 'Sorry mate, can't help you on this one.'

'I'm your man.' A deep voice spoke from behind.

Turning round, Cassidy saw the muscular guy from last night's party padding forward in flip-flops and faded cut-off jeans, freshly shaven and grinning. He looked the picture of health, thought Cassidy, in stark contrast to the bunch of ghouls who were spreading their germs and gloom among his troop.

'Like I said last night, I'd be happy to help out.'

'Can you really drive a bus, er -?' Cassidy asked, struggling to remember the man's name.

'Marcus,' he prompted. 'Marcus Barclay. Driven all over the Indian subcontinent. I'm an old pro.'

'Go on Cassidy,' Maggie piped up, 'he's a good laugh. I vote we take Marcus with us.'

Several of the Aussies chorused in agreement.

Cassidy hardly hesitated. The guy looked like a godsend. It took Marcus just a few minutes to fetch his belongings: a navy duffle bag, a small tent and a saddlebag made from Afghan carpet. It appeared he was already packed.

Soon they were clearing up and moving out. Cassidy was keen to be gone. There was something about the ill-fated westbound bus and its sad-looking, decimated group that made him shudder. It was as if the blanked out windows hid something more malignant than dysentery, like a fever ship cast adrift with its plague-ridden crew.

Probably just the jumpy thoughts from a bad hangover, but he couldn't help it. He was not a superstitious man, but he found it hard to shake off the feeling that their bad luck might be contagious. He felt sorry leaving Bob, but his friend was on the home stretch now. He gave him the remnants of the whisky bottle and a packet of Woodbines.

'Anything to tell about the road ahead?' Cassidy asked.

Bob shrugged. 'I'd steer clear of southern Iran – rain's washed away part of the route so I was told – and it's still dodgy through Baluchistan – not safe to camp. Stick to the north – Mashhad, Herat, Kabul – that's the way we came.'

Cassidy nodded. Bob seemed on the point of saying something else, but Marcus appeared, asking if he could do anything.

'Good luck, Cassidy mate,' was all Bob said.

Soon they were on the road and heading for the Yugoslav border.

CHAPTER 11

Newcastle
Amber

'Keep ganin' to the top of the hill,' the young woman pushing a fretful toddler told her. 'Then it's off to the right.' She nodded and brushed off Amber's thanks. 'Nee bother.'

After a string of motorcycle shops and newsagents, the West Road morphed into a bustle of Asian shops: curry houses, a halal butcher, and small supermarkets with sacks of Basmati rice piled in the windows. Young women in hijabs and old men in embroidered caps mingled with young couples in tracksuits, baseball caps and high ponytails. She found Ali's Bazaar down a side street of terraced flats.

The door chimed as she entered. It smelt of spices and citrus and earthy vegetables. An Asian radio station was playing in the background.

'No pet, I haven't seen him today,' said a woman behind the counter. She had grey hair swept into a bun and a diaphanous lime green scarf over her *shalwar kameez*. 'Are you family?'

'Niece of a friend,' Amber replied.

'Why don't you try his flat? Number Seventeen. Bell doesn't work. Knock very loud. Sometimes he's playing music very high.'

'Thanks.'

'Okay, pet.'

Rapping hard on the peeling yellow door brought a young guy to the window above. He was bare-chested and rubbing black hair with a towel.

'He's not in. Saw him go off on his bike this morning.' He leaned further out, his hair spiky and eyes very dark. 'Want to leave a message?'

Amber stared; he was Bollywood film star handsome. He waited while she grappled for words. 'Any idea where he might be?'

He grinned. 'God knows.'

'Or when he'll be back?'

He rested on muscled arms. 'Could be half an hour, could be tomorrow. Are you in a hurry?'

Amber bit her lip in frustration. 'I wanted to see him today. I have to be back in London tomorrow.'

'Well, if Cass is expecting you, I bet he won't be long.'

Amber felt foolish. 'Thing is, he doesn't know I'm coming. Actually, he doesn't know me full-stop.'

His brown eyes widened, and then he laughed. 'You are a mystery woman!'

She gave an embarrassed grin. 'Name's Amber.'

'Jez,' he replied, waving a brown arm out of the window in a mock handshake. 'So what do you want with the mighty Cass?'

'Info about a bus trip he took out East years ago. My auntie was on it. Sort of want to find out more. I've got photos but haven't a clue who they all are.'

'Wow, sounds cool. Cass loves talking about India and that. He's still an old hippie. Your aunt not with you then?'

Amber shook her head. 'She died ages ago. I never knew her.'

'Too bad,' Jez said. They gazed at each other in silence. Amber felt she could quite happily chat to him for the rest of the day whether Cassidy turned up or not.

'Listen Amber, sun's shining so he's probably gone to the allotment to chill. If you want to go and look you can leave your gear with me for a couple of hours.' He gave a quirky smile. 'Long as you're not a religious nut or a dodgy drug dealer or something?'

'Nothing more dodgy than a landscape gardener.'

'Cool,' he smiled and disappeared inside.

Two minutes later he was opening the door to her left which lead to the upstairs flat. Jez wore baggy jeans and had pulled on a white hoody that accentuated bulky shoulders and the creamy brown of his skin. He was smaller than she'd imagined; they were about the same height. His brown eyes were flecked with gold light and framed by long dark lashes. His easy smile set off small kicks in her stomach.

Steering her by the arm, he pointed out directions to the allotments. 'You can leave your bag in the hallway, it'll be fine.' He smelt clean and spicy. Amber was reluctant to leave.

'It's really kind ... you sure?'

'No problem. And if you don't find him, come back here and have a brew.'

She smiled. 'I'd like that.'

***

Most of the allotments were deserted. Amber spotted a battered red bicycle propped up against a thicket of dead raspberry canes and blackberry bushes. Two trenches were newly planted. An apple tree, hung with wind chimes, was in bud. But it was the hut beyond that gave the clue: hammered together with old planks and corrugated sheeting, it was painted in myriad colours and swirling designs like an Asian truck. On its roof was a depiction of turquoise lakes and kingfishers, on the sides were golden stupas, scarlet parrots and snow-capped mountains. Every other inch was covered in motifs, flowers, peace signs and unblinking eyes. Above the open door a battered metal sign said, 'Please leave guns outside.'

A radio station was playing rock music; someone was whistling along in tune. Amber called hello and peered inside. An old camping table was covered in newspapers and tin mugs, next to a man reading in a dilapidated armchair. The place reeked from a paraffin heater.

'Mr Cassidy?'

'Who wants him?' the man asked gruffly, lowering his newspaper. In the dull light Amber could see a wiry set of shoulders under a brown woollen jumper, a gaunt face with a walrus moustache, and grey hair pulled back into a ponytail.

'Hi, I'm Amber English. Jez said I'd find you here.'

'And, bonny lass?'

Amber took a deep breath. 'I've just been to my gran's funeral in County Durham. I'm trying to find out more about her daughter – my Auntie Ruth. She was on your trip in '76 – the one who went missing, yeah? You see, no one's ever really explained it to me – why she disappeared and that. I thought you might talk to me. I know it's a bit of a cheek and it's a million years ago, but a guy called Souter - '

'You're Ruth's niece?' As he interrupted, he pushed himself to his feet and came forward, staring hard. 'Daniel's lass?'

'Yes.'

'Holy shite!'

CHAPTER 12

Ruth's diary
Tues 5ᵗʰ Oct – Day 10

We're all getting a bit sick of this rain. Catriona said it reminded her of the west coast of Scotland and fancy coming all this way just to find herself back home. To keep our spirits up we kept singing Raindrops keep falling on my head and Singing in the rain and anything with rain or water in the title!

Stopped at place called Zadar for shopping. Nice square, buildings the colour of biscuits. Juliet bought carrots and bread from a cheerful plump woman in black. Why are so many women in black? Are they all widows? Others went off to buy brandy and beer from a supermarket. Marcus (the new helper driver!) came and carried the shopping - snapped the end off a carrot and ate it. Juliet said that was his ration. Think she likes him.

Writing this on bus. Cassidy has pulled over until the thunder and lightening eases off. He's snoozing. Marcus is telling stories at the back of the bus about going overland. He's so funny. A man in Istanbul once offered him five camels for his girlfriend! He agreed but his girlfriend wasn't pleased. She went off with a Canadian dentist instead!

Marcus is full of energy and words and laughter. He can't keep still. His aura is red. He's like fire. I'm so happy! ♥

CHAPTER 13

'Come! Let us go to Dalmatia. It is summer time, the sky is serene, the breeze soft, and the water blue. Let us revel together in the romantic stories written upon the ancient walls and frowning bastions; the hoary cathedrals and stately palaces; by that greatest of all historians, "Old Father Time."

...from first to last, in all our weeks of voyaging, the skies above us were the bluest of the blue, and the water as unruffled and tranquil as an inland lake. Not a drop of rain, nor a dark cloud, marred the beauty of our trip down the whole length of the Adriatic.'
Delightful Dalmatia, by Alice Lee Moqué, 1914

Split, Yugoslavia
Juliet

That night they camped in the rain at Split where Juliet and her tent-mates attempted to make carrot soup, holding Chuck's golf umbrella over the camping stoves.

'Hey, Mr Cassidy,' Chuck called out, 'it says in the brochure we should be barbecuing and sunbathing by the Adriatic.'

'Feel free,' Cassidy laughed, hunching into his worn leather jacket and lighting up a cigarette.

'Needs more salt,' Maggie ordered, standing over the cooks, drinking beer. Just before they were due to serve up, she poured in a liberal dose of *Slivovic*. 'That should make it cordon bleu, eh girls?'

They stood around or squatted on the groundsheet, slurping soup out of plastic orange mugs.

'Where did Marcus go?' Maggie asked moodily.

'Said something about eating in town,' said one of the Liverpudlians. 'Saw him go off with Fay and Suzy.'

'The Poshettes? Cheek of it!'

'Can't blame him - this is the worst meal so far,' Australian Gino declared cheerfully. 'Tastes like cat's piss.'

'Only you would know,' Maggie retorted. 'Thought you'd been on a catering course, Ruth?'

Ruth didn't answer.

'It's not that bad,' Cassidy defended.

Afterwards, a dozen of them commandeered the bus and drank their way through half the newly bought beer. Juliet sat at the front reading Agnes Conway's travelogue of the Balkans and wondering if they would ever see the spectacular views and the sun-baked fields. Ruth stomped down to put on Steely Dan and blasted it up to full volume. She was in a strange mood. As the light went, a camp guard circled the bus and watched them until the last revellers went to bed. There was no sign of Marcus or the girls.

41

Early the next morning as Juliet stirred the porridge, Cassidy kept her company while he shaved, his mirror and bowl of water balanced on the camping table. The rain had stopped and the mist was lifting to reveal a wooded bay and a calm sea shimmering in the dawn light.

'This is the life, eh?' said Cassidy. 'Best part of the day.'

'I usually hate getting up early,' she admitted, 'but this is good.' She eyed him. 'Why does everyone call you Cassidy? Don't you have a first name?'

'It's who I am,' he grunted.

'Bet you were in the Forces. My Dad was always known by his surname. When my Nan or Pop were in a teasing mood they'd do the same. "Forbes Junior, it's time for tea".'

Cassidy chuckled. 'Forbsy eh? Then that's what I'll call you.'

Looking up, she caught sight of movement behind him. One of the Poshettes crept out on all fours from Marcus's small green tent and stood up, barefoot and holding chunky boots. Cassidy saw Juliet's surprised look and turned. The young woman gave a bashful smile and hurried off to the wash block.

Cassidy snorted, 'That didn't take him long.'

'God, don't tell Maggie, she's earmarked the new bloke for herself.'

They both laughed. As Juliet stirred the pot, Lucy, the married New Zealander, came out of her tent yawning and grimaced.

'Not sure I can eat that.'

'You look a worse colour than the porridge,' Juliet teased. 'What were you doing last night?'

Lucy and Cassidy exchanged a look, but before Juliet could work out what it meant, Chuck passed clean-shaven from the washroom. He gave them a nod but didn't stop.

Juliet whispered, 'he doesn't approve of us - thinks we're a rowdy rabble.'

'You are.' Cassidy rinsed off in cold water.

'And that you can't control us.'

'Right again.'

'Actually, I was trying to persuade him to jump ship and join another bus.'

'Thanks,' Cassidy grunted, 'are you trying to get me sacked?'

'No, I just thought he might be happier.'

'He hasn't come on this trip to be happy,' Cassidy said. 'He and Peach are on a pilgrimage.'

'Meaning?'

'They're following in the footsteps of their son who went to Kathmandu with the Peace Corps. He went part the way on a Rainbow bus, so they want to do the same.'

'Really? How cute!' Lucy exclaimed, nibbling on a biscuit.

The porridge began to bubble. 'So where is he now, the son?' Juliet asked.

'Still in Nepal apparently.'

'That's amazing,' Lucy said. 'I mean how many parents would take the trouble to rough it like this just so they could know what it was like for their child?'

Juliet felt a sudden lump in her throat and the familiar ache of emptiness whenever she tried to imagine what her own parents would have been like.

'You okay?' Cassidy asked.

'Yea, it's just the steam – makes my eyes water.'

***

Later that day they arrived at the walled city of Dubrovnik and walked its ramparts, looking down on its winding streets and red-tiled roofs. Cats padded across cramped squares and washing flapped from high balconies. Juliet slipped away from the others, found a café serving Turkish coffee and sweet sugary cakes, and read her book.

A shadow fell over the page. 'Agnes Conway? She was a friend of my great-aunt.' Marcus was standing looking over her shoulder, his handsome face grinning. He pulled out a chair and asked, 'May I?'

Juliet looked around for the Poshette, but he was alone. 'Sure, please do.'

'My great aunt Isabel was married to a diplomat,' he said, tapping the book. 'He was posted to Athens before the First World War. Agnes wrote up her travels after staying with them. They went to Corfu and Albania, so I'm told. Perhaps it mentions Aunt Isabel in the book?'

Juliet laughed, 'I don't think so, but how amazing! I love this book. It's so descriptive of a lost age. Not that I've ever been this far before.'

'I think you'll find the area hasn't changed much,' Marcus said, 'especially in Montenegro and northern Greece – still oxen ploughing and women harvesting in peasant costumes. So you've never been further east?'

'Not yet, but I can't wait. I've been hooked by travel books since I was a kid. One in particular by Grace Ellison all about Turkey – she saw the Whirling Dervishes and lived with a family in old Stamboul.'

'"*An Englishwoman in a Turkish Harem*",' said Marcus.

'Yes! Don't tell me you've read it too?'

He nodded. 'Wonderful book.'

Juliet was impressed. 'I've never met anyone else who's even heard of it.'

He ordered a coffee and they talked animatedly about books and Turkish antiquities. She warmed to him quickly. 'Konya is the best place to see the Sufi dervishes doing their thing,' he told her, 'but not until December I'm afraid.'

'Even just to be there would be fantastic. It's such a pity our route doesn't go that way,' Juliet said.

He considered her over the rim of his cup. His eyes were an intense aquatic blue that made her insides flutter. 'Maybe we will.'

'Doubt it,' she sighed. 'Cassidy seems quite determined to stick to the schedule.'

'But this is a trip of a lifetime! It's up to all of you to take control and make the route your own.'

Juliet laughed, loving his enthusiasm. 'Yes, you've got a point.'

'Don't worry about Cassidy,' Marcus grinned, 'leave him to me.'

CHAPTER 14

'Good common wine will be found in most of the Greek islands, and at Smyrna; at Athens and Nauplia the common French wine is to be had, but the wine of the country in Greece is resinous and scarcely drinkable to a foreigner, savouring of sealing-wax and vinegar.'
Handbook for Travels in the East, 1840

Thassos Island, Greece
Juliet
'Where the hell are we?' Maggie yawned.

'Isn't that the sea?' asked Catriona.

'Keramoti!' Marcus called out from behind the wheel. 'And that over there is Thassos Island.'

Juliet peered sleepily at the wooded finger of land jutting out of calm blue water, bathed in early sunlight. They had left an overcast and stuffy Athens two days ago, done Delphi, then taken shelter in a wayside taverna when the rain caught up with them yet again. There had been much drinking of Ouzo and resinous Retsina with some local students, and a general mutiny when it came to pitching the tents. Marcus had volunteered to drive overnight instead.

'Hey,' Chuck stood up and called out, 'this can't be Thassos Island! We're supposed to see Mount Olympus first.'

'Tell him,' Peach said in agitation, 'we have to see it. Gerald told us it was a highlight.'

Her husband swayed down the aisle waving the tour brochure. 'Thassos Island comes *after* Mount Olympus.'

The bus veered towards the harbour. 'Everyone was asleep,' Marcus answered, 'so I just kept going until the rain stopped.'

People began to stir and argue. Marcus brought the bus to a halt. Chuck prodded and shook Cassidy out of a deep ouzo-induced sleep.

'Hey, Mr Cassidy, what you gonna do about this?'

'Bout what?' Cassidy squinted out of bloodshot eyes.

Marcus jumped up and faced the passengers. '"The Isles of Greece, the Isles of Greece, where burning Sappho loved and sung!" Byron,' he grinned. 'Listen chaps, you're close to burn out already. You've done enough sightseeing for now. What everyone needs is to chill-out on the beach for a couple of days. You're going to love it here.'

'But what about Mount Olympus?' wailed Peach. 'Gerald said - '

'It's impressive,' Marcus interrupted, 'but you're going to see far better. The amphitheatre at Ephesus – the ruins at Persepolis – they'll blow your mind. The further east you go the better it gets. But you need to prepare for Asia. You have to get into gear, physically and mentally, otherwise you won't last the pace.'

Chuck looked unconvinced. 'Mr Cassidy, are you gonna let this man take over? Tell him he'll have to take us back.'

Cassidy rubbed bleary eyes with his knuckles and sighed.

'I think Marcus is right,' one of the Poshettes, called out, 'I can't wait to lie on a beach and do nothing.'

'Me too,' her friend agreed lifting her beaded head from an Australian shoulder.

'I vote we stay,' shouted Catriona.

There were murmurs of approval. The sight of blue sea and an almost cloudless sky was more tempting than the thought of hours in the bus backtracking.

'Okay,' Cassidy said, 'we'll stay.'

'This is too bad!' Chuck cried. 'I'll be making a call to head office.'

Cassidy closed his eyes again. Marcus put an arm around the middle-aged American's shoulder.

'I'm sorry – it's my fault – don't be hard on him. Listen, Chuck, I know just the place to revive the spirits. Friend of mine runs this taverna on the island and he serves the best calamari in Greece. We'll go there for lunch – my treat – and you can tell me all about Gerald's trip, yeah?'

Juliet watched in admiration as Chuck was charmed into acquiescence. Piling out of the bus, she caught Kurt's look.

'Don't you mind missing the home of the gods?' he asked.

Juliet shrugged. 'I'm quite happy to lie on a beach and read.'

They made camp and caught the ferry across to the island. Some headed straight for the bars and cake shops of the small town, while others wandered along the shore to watch fishermen sorting their nets in the warm breeze. Juliet noticed the New Zealand couple being invited along by Marcus to lunch with Chuck and Peach. Maggie and a Poshette tagged along too. The more adventurous, including Juliet, went in search of a deserted beach. The hill road took them through quiet leafy woods, past chalets closed for the winter and down to a sandy cove of frothy breakers.

At once, Juliet and Catriona stripped down to their underwear and ran shrieking with delight into the sea.

'Come on you lot,' Juliet challenged, 'its wonderful!'

'Mad Pommy bastards,' Australian Fran laughed, throwing off all her clothes and wading in with bulky freckled arms flailing. 'Struth it's cold!'

'No it's not,' Juliet laughed, 'it's like a warm bath.'

Kurt and Tomas changed into swimming trunks and joined them. Ruth dithered. Taking off her shoes and rolling up her jeans she went for a paddle. Within seconds the others had splashed her so much she retreated. 'Stop it, I can't swim!'

Afterwards, drying in the October sun and eating a picnic of bread and honey, goat's cheese and yoghurt, Juliet eyed Ruth. She seemed out of sorts – had been for days. 'Sorry about before, I didn't know you couldn't swim.'

Ruth pulled a face. 'My dad tried to teach me. He would take me up the beck and chuck me into this deep pool. I hated it. Daniel used to jump in and fish me out, even though Dad would be shouting at him that I had to learn for myself.'

'Silly man,' Juliet exclaimed, 'you were never going to learn that way.'

'Daniel did,' Ruth replied, 'he would do anything to please the old man in those days. Anyway, Mum put a stop to it in the end. Whenever it was swimming time, she said I was needed in the kitchen.'

Juliet lay back on the warm sand, enjoying the caress of salty air, and dozed off. When she awoke, Kurt and Tomas had gone.

'Said something about Roman remains,' Catriona said drowsily.

'And Ruth too?'

Catriona looked up. 'Must have. Didn't notice she'd gone.'

***

That evening the group barbecued on the beach round a campfire, close to a taverna. The Liverpudlians and Australians started drinking games with bottles of cheap Domestica, and the Poshettes led a starlit swim while Devon and Marcus took it in turns to play Bob Dylan songs on the guitar.

Tomas had taken himself off to bed, so Juliet sat with Kurt and shared a mug of wine, shaking off her earlier unease about Ruth. The girl had been jumpy and vague about where she had gone that afternoon. She had started drinking early in the taverna and had attached herself to the Poshettes. Juliet had tried to keep an eye on her, but that group had gravitated down the beach and into the dark.

Devon appeared to have paired off with Maggie since the trip across to Thassos Island and was now lying with his head in her lap, legs stretched out into the dark. Juliet wondered if Maggie would switch tents tonight. Two of the Poshettes already appeared to be sharing a tent with two Aussie miners.

'Wouldn't it be lovely to sleep out under the stars tonight?' Juliet mused, offering Kurt a cigarette. In the firelight, his handsome face was thoughtful and composed. She liked his calmness and the way he didn't join in any of the petty jibes or squabbling.

'Yes, sure,' he agreed, his tone amused, 'as long as you are wrapped up in three blankets and a woolly hat.'

'I bet you'd look sweet in a bobble hat.' She lit her cigarette from his.

Kurt laughed. 'Would you like a walk along the beach?'

'Sure.'

They stood up, shaking off sand. The sea lapped benignly behind the merry beach party. As they reached the darkness beyond the spill of lights from the taverna, she linked her arm through his.

'Tell me about your time at the British Museum. What were you working on?'

'Mainly the Bactrian civilization of Central Asia.' She felt him relax.

'I'm afraid I've never heard of it.'

47

'It's rich in art and architecture – a mix of Buddhist, Greek, and Chinese - but there's still so much we don't know,' Kurt enthused. 'The heart of Bactria lies in modern day northern Afghanistan. One of the foremost academics in the study of their language is at Cambridge – Professor Bailey - his grasp of ancient languages is phenomenal. He's unlocking many of the mysteries of Bactrian culture from his analysis of archaeological finds – coins and such like.'

'Is there much to go on?'

'Quite a bit in the Kabul museum I believe. But we've probably only scratched the surface. Much of the area is so remote that little has been excavated. It's very exciting to think that the key to unlocking an ancient civilization can be lying dormant in the ground waiting to be discovered, don't you think?'

Juliet was about to reply when a high-pitched screech pierced the dark. They stopped in their tracks.

'What was that?'

'An animal?' Kurt guessed. 'Somewhere in the woods.'

They stood and listened, but nothing else came. Juliet glanced behind but no one round the fire seemed to have heard. They started to walk forward. Just then, a shadow detached itself from the mass of dark trees that fringed the shore. A figure came tearing towards them, barefoot and wailing. She threw herself at Juliet, hysterical.

'Ruth! Whatever's the - ? It's okay, I've got you,' Juliet said, hugging her. 'Okay, okay, calm down.'

Ruth sobbed, unable to speak. Juliet stroked her dishevelled hair. Her breath was sour, smelling of wine. When Kurt touched her in concern, she tensed and burrowed further into Juliet's hold. Juliet and Kurt exchanged anxious looks.

'Let's get you back to the camp,' Juliet soothed, 'then you can tell us what's wrong.'

Ruth shook and wept as Juliet led her back along the beach, Kurt following.

'Ruth's had some sort of accident,' Juliet interrupted the singsong and coaxed the distressed girl near the fire.

Marcus leapt up to make room for them and at once everyone was asking questions, offering drinks.

'Are you hurt?' Marcus demanded, cradling her with an arm.

Ruth shook her head, gulping down tears.

'Where have you been?' Catriona cried. 'I was looking for you. Thought you were in the taverna with that Greek guy.'

'Try to tell us what happened,' encouraged Juliet.

'I w-went – to – the toilet,' she sobbed. 'He – he gr-grabbed – me – '

'Who did?'

'The Greek guy?'

Juliet silenced the questioners. 'Let her speak.'

'I didn't s-see,' Ruth gulped. 'He was behind - had his h-hand over my mouth.'

'Has he hurt you?' demanded Marcus.

'N-no. I screamed and he let go.' Then she dissolved into tears again.

Juliet stroked her hair. 'A lucky escape.'

'But he might still be out there,' Catriona worried, 'waiting to pounce.'

'I'll go and look,' Cassidy said at once.

'Me too,' Marcus volunteered, climbing to his feet. Some of the Australians followed.

Devon weaved after them, shouting dire threats into the dark.

'Who exactly are they looking for?' Maggie asked, muscling in beside Juliet. Nobody could answer. 'Let me take a look at you girl.' She checked Ruth over. 'You've got a swollen lip but that seems to be all. Must have bitten it when he grabbed you, eh?'

Ruth nodded and her crying subsiding.

'Did he speak to you?' Maggie questioned.

'He said something,' Ruth answered in a small voice. 'I think it was in English, but he was Greek – I think.'

'So even if they find him, you won't be able to tell if it was him?'

Ruth bowed her head. 'I was so scared.'

'It's okay,' Juliet said with a warning look at Maggie, 'enough questions. The main thing is that you're safe.'

Shortly afterwards the search party returned. 'No sign of anyone up the beach,' said Cassidy.

'Dude's long gone,' added Devon.

'That may be so,' said Marcus, 'but we'll have a rota for guarding the girls going to the lavatory tonight.'

'Ooh, lavatory!' Maggie mimicked.

'Shut up,' said Catriona.

Marcus crouched down by Ruth, putting a protective arm around her shoulder. She leaned into him. 'One man to each tent,' Marcus continued, 'sleeping outside. That'll send out the right signal.'

'Seems over the top to me,' said Maggie.

'I think it's a grand idea,' Catriona said. 'I vote Alexei sleeps outside our tent.'

The party broke up amid arguments about who was to sleep where and with whom. Juliet settled Ruth in their tent and told her to wake her if she wanted the loo in the night. She went back out for a late cigarette and found Cassidy and two Poshettes sitting with Devon and Maggie by the dying fire sharing a joint.

'Maybe Marcus has a point,' a Poshette was saying.

'It's not his decision,' Maggie argued.

'Decision about what?' Juliet asked, flopping down.

'Marcus thinks we should hit the road tomorrow and go to Istanbul,' Cassidy explained.

'It's a bad scene here,' Devon said, 'bad karma.'

'Just cos some randy Greek makes a pass at Ruth,' Maggie was scathing. 'It's a total over-reaction.'

'Poor girl's had a bad shock,' said Juliet.

'What's your vibe Cassidy?' Devon asked, holding out the joint.

Cassidy passed it straight to Maggie without smoking. 'Maybe we should go. Don't want any jip with the locals – I can just see one of the Scousers smashing up the bar in revenge.'

'God you men are pathetic,' Maggie muttered, 'she's got you all running round her like scaredy-cats.'

'Hey babe,' Devon drawled, 'cool it.'

'Why're you been so hard on Ruth?' Juliet asked.

'Cos I don't believe her sob story,' Maggie snapped. 'She was last seen in the taverna with a local bloke by Catriona. Then she disappears. Next thing she's running up the beach screaming like a banshee saying she's been jumped on outside the bogs. Except the bogs are in the other direction, or were you all too drunk to notice?'

'So what are you saying?' Juliet demanded. 'That she went too far with some local man and it's her fault?'

'Maybe,' Maggie said, flicking the toke into the fire and standing up. 'She's a little flirt when she's had a drink. Or perhaps she just made it up to get attention. How the feck should I know? Whatever it is, her little story doesn't add up, does it?'

She walked off, leaving the others not knowing what to say.

CHAPTER 15

Newcastle
Amber

'Sit yourself down, lass,' Cassidy nodded at an old armchair with its seat cushion missing.

Cassidy's hand shook as he passed Amber a mug, slopping hot milky tea onto the mildewed carpet. He shook his head and sucked in his breath as Amber explained about her grandmother dying and Ruth's diary and photos. He darted looks at Amber, but said little as she chattered on about her family and fired off questions about Ruth and the long-ago trip. Cassidy reached for a half bottle of whisky on a makeshift shelf and poured some into his tea.

'Want some?'

'No thanks.'

Amber found it hard to keep still. Here she was in the presence of the trip's driver: a man whom Ruth had described with affection in her diary and one of the last people to ever see his aunt alive. A living link to her past. A handshake away.

She gulped at the tea which burnt her mouth. *Calm down.* She put the mug on the floor and tucked a long leg underneath her. 'I just want to know more about her, you know? Anything really. With Gran dying it just brings it home how little I know – and now I can't ever ask her.'

'What about your da? What does he think to you digging up the past?'

Amber said, 'we're not very close – I don't know what he thinks most of the time. But I'm sure he cared for his sister. He seemed to think it was Gran and Gramps fault for driving her away in the first place.'

'Aye, well, he had a go at me an' all – for not waiting with the bus in Afghanistan until she turned up. But I can't blame him – I've had to live with that guilt for half me life.'

Amber saw pain etched on the man's craggy face. 'You weren't to know.'

Cassidy fumbled in his top pocket for a squashed packet of *beedies* and offered one to Amber.

'No thanks.' She fiddled with the beads at her neck as she watched him light up the Indian cigarette. Aromatic smoke filled the shed. 'Go on then, I'll try one.' The sharpness burnt her tongue like hot chilli.

'I never got to see the diary or anything,' Cassidy said, leaning forward, elbows on knees. 'Did it tell you much?'

'Not really. It starts quite full and chatty, but tails off pretty quickly like she couldn't be bothered – travel weary - I dunno. Or maybe there was stuff happening that she didn't want to write down.'

Cassidy eyed her. 'What makes you say that?'

Amber shrugged. 'Well, later on it gets a bit weird, and some of the pages between Yugoslavia and Turkey have been torn out. Did something happen?'

51

Cassidy inhaled deeply and snorted out smoke. 'Aye, she got grabbed outside the toilets one night, at a campsite near Thassos Island in Northern Greece. I don't think anything heavy happened, but it did give her a scare, and it led to a lot of argument about whether we should press on early to Istanbul. Ruth felt bad about that.'

'Oh, right.' Amber nodded. She stubbed out the exotic cigarette and picked up her tea, waiting for Cassidy to say more but he didn't. They sat in silence while the older man smoked, lost in his thoughts. She was itching to question him but didn't want to stress him out.

Finally, Cassidy extinguished the tiny cheroot between calloused finger and thumb. 'Given me a bit of a shock you turning up like this. I haven't thought about these things in a long time – not in any detail, like. How did you find me?'

'Souter, a journalist Gran was friendly with. He gave me the diary and stuff. I'm sorry, I should have got in touch first, but I was in the area after the funeral.'

Cassidy nodded. 'She was a decent woman your grandmother, and brave. Never seemed bitter about the tragedy – just wanted her lass back.'

'So what was she like, Auntie Ruth? I'd really like to know.' Amber held her breath, tense with waiting.

'She was very bonny – and a nice lass with it – nothing stuck up about her. She was always one of the first to help out or volunteer for things – filling up jerry cans from village taps, that kind of thing.' Cassidy hesitated.

'Go on,' Amber encouraged. 'Even if it's bad, I really wanna know.'

'Well, she had a crazy streak – when she'd had a drink – she'd babble on about seeing things and try to jump off high walls – a daredevil. Or maybe it was just that kind of trip – I never really felt in control of it.' He pulled on his thick moustache, reflecting. 'But even though she had her mad moments, Ruth was harmless – like everyone's kid sister. Mind, she could be naïve about people, in my opinion. Too trusting by half.'

'That's what dad said about her,' Amber said. 'He's always thought she was killed by the man she disappeared with - what's his name?'

'Marcus.'

'Yeah, that Marcus guy. What do you think?'

Cassidy let out a long sigh. 'No I don't think so – not murder.'

'Why not?'

Cassidy shrugged but did not elaborate. Amber felt he was holding something back. She tried a different tack. Fishing out the battered pack of photos, she began spreading them out on the Formica-covered table.

CHAPTER 16

Ruth's diary
Sat 16th Oct – Day 21
Esso Campsite, Istanbul.
Felt terrible all day. Splitting headache. Still feel travel sick, even two hours after bus has stopped. Can't stop thinking about last night. Want to tell Juliet but can't – she's been so nice – said I was to treat her like a big sister and talk to her anytime. Said it must be awful not having my mum around at a time like this. Made me cry.

Letters from home waiting at the campsite. Can't bear to read them yet.

Later – in tent
Avoiding Maggie and the Poshettes. They hate me for having to leave Greece early. I've heard them slagging me off in the washroom. But they don't have a clue. Cassidy found me crying outside the bar. Said not to listen to them and I'm not to blame. If anyone gives me a hard time I'm to let him know. Catriona and Juliet, Peach and Chuck have been really great. Devon too – he offered me his Indian blanket. But I feel bad cos Maggie's not speaking to Devon now. She's making a big thing of being friends with Aussie Gino instead. Thank God she's moved out of our tent.

Marcus is trying to be everyone's friend.

CHAPTER 17

'I have come back to Stamboul to laugh, for I have never laughed anywhere as I have in this land of extremes and contradictions and surprises ... At nights I rise and peep through the lattice windows and see the beautiful moon bathing with its silver magnificence the silent, sleeping city and the calm quiet Marmara beyond ... Letters belong to the West – energy belongs to the West – but the sunset and the dreams and the beautiful calm felicity which I now enjoy is the inheritance of the Women of the East.'
An Englishwoman in a Turkish Harem, by Grace Ellison, 1915

Istanbul, Turkey
Juliet

She was distracted by raised voices in the inner courtyard of the Blue Mosque.

'Please,' said the attendant, pursuing a portly middle-aged couple and pointing at their shoes, 'you must take off.'

'I don't think so,' the English woman in a polyester dress replied. The man continued past the racks of shoes as if he had not heard.

'Yes, yes,' insisted the Turkish man, 'it is our custom.'

'Well it's not ours,' the woman snapped. 'To take off your shoes in public is quite vulgar in my opinion. We're tourists – not here to pray.'

The Turk's agitation grew as they brushed past him and headed towards the leather curtain leading to the mosque's interior, talking loudly. Juliet stood with clogs in hand waiting for Catriona to unlace her shoes.

'Right little memsahib,' Catriona muttered.

Juliet waited for the attendant to order the couple out of the mosque or summon help, but he didn't. His face sagged with weary resignation. *This has happened before.* The anxiety of the previous two days ignited her anger.

'Excuse me!' she launched after them, brandishing scuffed yellow clogs in the air.

The pair turned in surprise. The man gave a quizzical half-smile. 'Yes?'

'You can't go in there with your shoes on.'

He gaped at her, but the woman was dismissive. 'I don't see why not. We're here to sight-see and there's nothing in the guide book to say - '

'Please take them off,' Juliet smiled. 'It's a matter of courtesy.'

'Well really!' the woman huffed.

Newcomers to the courtyard were glancing over. The Englishman avoided Juliet's look and coughed nervously. 'Perhaps we should, dear?'

'Oh for heaven's sake! I'm not that interested in the place.' She threw Juliet a furious look and turned on her heels. 'Come on, we'll go to St Sophia's instead.'

The Turkish attendant smiled as Juliet and her friend handed in their shoes and ducked under the curtain.

'Jings!' Catriona gasped as they gazed upwards. Aqueous light filtered through the intricately painted domes and half domes, and rippled over the blue and turquoise tiles. They padded across the carpets, their movements slowed and voices hushed by the graceful tranquillity of the mosque.

Juliet was reminded of the grandeur of French cathedrals in the carved pillars and soaring arches, yet the myriad colours and curling designs were hypnotic and the warm carpeting more intimate. The whole experience was somehow sensual, the space for prayer more open and casual than rigid rows of pews. She closed her eyes and let go a long breath, welcoming the calm after the last fraught couple of days.

Sober, Ruth had been subdued and baffled by the storm she had created. 'I feel terrible,' she told Juliet. 'I hate all this arguing. I don't want to spoil things.'

'It's not your fault.'

'But it is,' she had said, looking miserable.

Juliet had found the whole episode disturbing, not least the callousness of Maggie and some of the others towards the girl, as if being grabbed outside the toilets was no big deal for a woman. But there was something else that nagged at the back of her mind, something that had seemed odd at the time that she couldn't now remember. Too much cheap red wine or too wrapped up in Kurt's conversation about Bactria. She was attracted to Kurt – he was probably the most interesting man on the bus – and would like to know him better. But she couldn't tell if he found her attractive. Catriona said she was wasting her time as it was obvious Kurt wasn't interested in lassies.

Cassidy had dropped them off early that morning at the Hippodrome and the group had dispersed as eagerly as prisoners on release. Ruth had been taken firmly under the wing of the middle-aged Americans and bustled off to Topkapi Palace.

Juliet had looked around for Kurt but he had already vanished; he and Tomas had been deep in conversation on the bus and seemed so preoccupied that she did not like to intrude. In the Blue Mosque, a guide attached himself to Juliet and Catriona and pointed out the black stones from Mecca and the steep white marble *minbar*, the staircase from which the imam prayed at Friday prayers. Afterwards they wandered out into the mild October sunshine, and bumped into the Australian women.

'We're going to the Pudding Shop for lunch,' Fran said. 'Want to come?'

They fell in together. In the restaurant garden, they drank instant coffee and shared a plate of macaroni cheese and chips. It was busy with other overlanders meeting up and swapping news. They saw Maggie and the Poshettes drinking Amstel beer at another table and playing a raucous game of *Scissors, Paper, Stone*.

'Devon's next door in Sitki's smoking a hubble-bubble pipe and getting some peace,' Fran said in amusement.

'As long as Maggie's got someone to play with,' said Catriona with a roll of her eyes, 'the last thing we want is that wee cow back in our tent.'

On the way out, Juliet caught sight of Kurt and Tomas in the pastry shop scanning the notice board. It was overflowing with handwritten notes and advertisements. Detaching herself from the others, she went over.

'Looking for something in particular?'

Kurt swung around startled. 'Not really,' he said with an evasive shrug.

'Not some ancient map for Bactrian treasure?' she teased.

He smiled, recovering his poise. 'Tomas has a friend Rudi who is travelling east. He left Germany a few months ago. We were just checking to see if he's left a message to say where he's gone.'

Tomas looked tense; he shook his head. 'Nothing,' he said in German.

Juliet was surprised Kurt had never mentioned the friend before, but at that moment Fran appeared.

'You guys want to tag along with us?'

Kurt nodded. Together they wandered towards the Galata Bridge. The streets were noisy and narrow as they side-stepped cars and street vendors: a toothless grinning chestnut seller, street porters bent double under huge bales of cloth, water sellers clacking to attract attention and boys balancing brass tea trays as they scurried between dark workshops with glasses of *cay*.

Kurt, who had been to the city before, navigated the covered bazaar and its warren of open stalls muffled in sepia light. Juliet and Catriona rushed about excitedly, picking up belts and fingering jewellery, trying on coats and haggling for brass jugs. As the stallholder wrapped her purchases, Juliet tried to engage the bashful Tomas in conversation.

'This friend you are looking for - is he a doctor too?'

He hesitated, scratching his dark beard in that thoughtful reflexive way that Juliet had noticed. 'No, not doctor – school friend. He – how you say? – works on plants.'

'A horticulturist,' Kurt explained.

'*Ja*. But big interest is water – water for plants.' He wiggled his fingers like falling rain.

Juliet smiled. 'Irrigation.'

Tomas looked at Kurt who nodded and elaborated. 'Rudi is an expert on irrigation – especially in desert conditions. He is hoping to find - '

'Kurt,' Tomas interrupted and said something quickly in German that she didn't catch.

Kurt gave an apologetic shrug. 'Ah, the ladies are done,' he said, making a big show of admiring the jewellery Catriona had just bought. 'Shall we move on?'

He led them off to the Egyptian spice bazaar with its multi-coloured mounds and piles of nuts and fruits. They emerged by the Yeni Mosque to the clatter of flocking pigeons and the salty smell of the Bosphorus. The Galata Bridge was crowded with anglers and fishermen selling cooked fish from charcoal fires balanced precariously on their bobbing boats. They bought fish in hunks of bread, dipped them in bowls of garlic and salt, and ate looking across the busy waterway to the modern city beyond.

'There lies Asia,' Kurt exclaimed.

'It's so exciting,' Juliet enthused between mouthfuls of hot fish. 'All of it.' She waved her hands expansively.

At that moment, Marcus bowled up with a slim-faced young Turkish man in jeans and a suit jacket.

'Hi guys! This is my friend Ekrem. He says he recognises you, Juliet.'

'Really?'

'The lady with the yellow shoes,' the young man explained. 'I see you at the Sultanahmet Mosque this morning.'

'The Blue Mosque?'

'I was the guide behind you.' He smiled and touched his heart with his hand. 'You shout at bad lady to take off shoes.'

'Yes,' Catriona said, 'she's frightening when she's angry, isn't she?'

'Not frightening, beautiful,' he answered with a broad smile.

'What a charmer,' Catriona smirked. 'Got yourself a rival there, Marcus.'

Marcus laughed and made introductions. Ekrem was a medical student, making money guiding. The genial man insisted on taking them all for refreshments. He led them uphill, delighting in Marcus's excitable, gesticulating stabs at speaking Turkish. Tomas said shyly that many of his patients were Turkish guest workers in Germany, but Ekrem was dismissive. 'Ah, they are peasants from the countryside.'

'Ekrem is like a Londoner,' Marcus chuckled, 'he cannot imagine why anyone should want to live anywhere but in his wonderful city.'

'Of course,' grinned the student, 'it is the best.'

At a *cay* shop with a view over cascading rooftops and minarets to the choppy sea below, they were greeted warmly by the patron who brought out glasses of black tea with lumps of sugar, plates of cigarettes, pistachio-studded halva and sticky cakes drenched in honey. They wiled away the afternoon drinking tea and chatting to Ekrem. Older men came and went with a click of prayer beads and a nod of greeting, to smoke their waterpipes in the dim interior. Marcus was expansive about the wonders of Turkey and quoted verses of the Sufi mystic, Rumi, to the gentle ridicule of Ekrem.

'Marcus, you are hippy without the long dress! All from West are looking for mumbo-jumbo mystic men. But in Turkey we leave religion to our old men. Atatürk, he give us modern country – goodbye Sufis, hello science,' he grinned.

'For heaven's sake, don't throw the baby out with the bathwater,' Marcus exclaimed.

'What baby?' Ekrem asked, baffled.

'The Sufi baby – your heritage and culture. Rumi and the others have given you poetry and music and love of good things – wine and ecstasy and spiritual fulfilment.'

Ekrem shrugged. 'You can have their religious music, I prefer Pink Floyd.'

Unexpectedly, Tomas guffawed and thumped the table. 'Pink Floyd – good man!'

Marcus gave a mock expression of pain. 'You Philistines, you don't know what you're missing. A Sufi lives for the moment; he gambles everything for love. Isn't that so, Catriona?' He seized her hand and kissed it.

Catriona pushed him off playfully. 'Away you go, you flirt!'

Juliet let the banter wash over her. She felt deeply content, glad that she had eschewed frantic sightseeing for this aimless afternoon. Even Tomas appeared relaxed.

'It wouldn't surprise me, Tomas,' she said in a lull in the conversation, 'if your friend Rudi never got further than Istanbul. I think I could happily stay here for weeks.'

Tomas flicked a look at Kurt.

Kurt said, 'Rudi will have moved on by now. He wants to see Iran – study the water wells underground.'

'Kanats?' Juliet said. 'I've read about them.'

'Can-whats?' asked Catriona.

Kurt explained. 'A very old system of irrigation. In China too. That is how peoples can live in deserts.'

'That's right,' Marcus agreed, 'in parts of Afghanistan I've heard they once had these amazing underground waterwheels that pumped water for miles, driven by windmills above ground.'

Kurt gave a rapid translation to Tomas, who tensed with excitement.

'Have you seen such things?' Kurt asked.

'Well no, not first hand,' Marcus admitted, 'but I've read about them. An ancestor of mine was part of the Afghan Boundary Commission along the Northern border of British India - when the British were trying to keep the Russians from muscling in on Afghanistan and places. Algernon Barclay surveyed the whole area - he was my great-uncle or third cousin or something.'

Kurt leaned forward. 'And this Algernon wrote about it?'

'Kept a detailed diary and drew up the Commission report. Stirred my interest I can tell you. As a boy I used to act out riding through barren mountains and staking claim to watering holes.' Marcus laughed. 'Proper little Lawrence of Arabia I thought myself.'

Kurt had a rapid-fire conversation with Tomas.

Intrigued, Marcus said, 'I'm tickled that you chaps should be so interested. Why is that?'

'I've been interested in the history of that part of the world for many years,' Kurt smiled, 'the flow of civilizations. The British were just the latest in a long line of empires that rose and fell.'

'Fell maybe,' Marcus replied, 'but left their mark, nevertheless. The borders Algernon helped draw up still stand to this day. Though I'm not sure the Baluch who live there bother with such niceties.'

'Baluchistan!' Juliet exclaimed. 'Have you been there, Marcus?'

'Parts of it, yes. But it's vast. And there's a civil war going on there at the moment – Baluch flexing their muscles against a remote Pakistan government – not that anyone outside the area talks about it.'

'So it's not easy to travel there?' Kurt asked.

'Downright dangerous, I'd say. Why do you ask?'

'Tomas's friend Rudi picked up rumours there was some kind of hippy commune out there. Have you ever heard of such a place?'

'In Baluchistan? Seems highly unlikely.'

'Ja,' Kurt agreed. 'Rudi has some crazy ideas.'

'Do you have your ancestor's diary with you by any chance?' Juliet asked.

'Hardly,' said Marcus. 'If only I'd known Great-uncle Algernon would cause such a stir.'

'I'm not interested in boundaries,' Juliet said, 'just the area. My father -' Suddenly, her throat watered.

Kurt gave her an anxious look. 'Forgive me, please. I was forgetting.'

'Forgetting what?' Catriona asked in bemusement.

His chiselled face full of compassion, Kurt said, 'Her father died there in a plane crash.'

'Poor girl!' Marcus cried. 'How dreadful for you.'

Juliet swallowed and steadied her voice. 'I have his old reconnaissance map. I was hoping to find someone who'd been there who could make sense of it.'

Marcus stretched out and clasped her hand. 'Of course, I'd be happy to.'

CHAPTER 18

Ruth's diary
Sun 17ᵗʰ Oct – Day 22
Mum's letter is full of the usual stuff – visit from the minister, village bring and buy, two bible verses etc. Wants to know about sightseeing and others on the trip. Likes sound of Julia and Catriona, but that's cos I told her they were missionaries! Dad bad with his nerves - not been out since Harvest Festival. Says Daniel on South American route. They don't know he's been in Glasgow or that I've seen him. At least I'm away from all that and don't have to pretend we're Happy Families.

Topkapi palace interesting. Peach missing her son Gerald as much as Mum misses Daniel. Do all mothers love their sons better than their daughters?

Wish I'd gone with Juliet and Catriona. They've just come back with Marcus and this Turkish guy called Ekron (?) - nice looking – and full of what a great day they've had. I'm sitting in the camp café writing this while they all eat meatballs and spaghetti (cold) but I'm not hungry. Ekron says it's not proper Turkish food and that tomorrow he'll take them to a fish restaurant.

Splitting head. Marcus flirting with Catriona.

Mon 18ᵗʰ Oct – Day 23
Today I'm tagging onto Juliet and Cat. Just had a fantastic time at this Turkish baths. Juliet got us lost looking for old part of city where a writer called Grace lived in a harem. Says she's her reincarnation. Catriona said if she was, she should know where she used to live! Ended up at baths near Topkapi – had massage and sat in really steamy room and gossiped about blokes on trip. Catriona gone off Alexei from Liverpool cos shown no interest. Now likes greasy-haired Paul or Cassidy. Juliet says Cassidy nice. Lot of talk about Germans. Catriona thinks are spies.

Cat says Marcus good fun but terrible flirt. What did we think? Juliet says he's definitely got charm and must have interesting family (cos of some chat they had yesterday about a relation in Afghanistan or somewhere). J says he went to Oxford, but prefers to travel than get boring job making money. Cat says must fancy him if knows so much about him. Both tell me I'm being very quiet. I'm bursting to say something but mustn't. Cat says she's still waiting for the Turkish pudding chef I predicted to turn up and sweep her off her feet. That reminds Juliet that we're supposed to be meeting Ekron for a meal.

CHAPTER 19

Istanbul, Turkey
Cassidy

He felt really relaxed for the first time since leaving England: a long steam at the *hamam*, a good nosh of kebab and chips, a couple of beers with the drivers from Encounter and Swagman – a good grouse about the weather, a recommendation about where to stay in Capadocia – and then a smoke with Devon. They were mellow-yellow, as Devon put it.

He liked the Yank a lot; his sense of humour and the way he didn't get hassled. He'd been in the army too: survived 'Nam. He knew that when Cassidy said he'd been with the tanks in Aden that he'd seen some action. He didn't have to spell it out. Devon knew about war – the smell of it, what it did to your guts, what you saw when you closed your eyes at night.

'Heavy shit, man.' That was Devon's verdict and he wasn't wrong.

Coming out the café with the domes and minarets glowing in the setting sun, Cassidy was assailed by the thought that he was glad to be back east. Up till then he'd been in two minds, wanting to get away yet not wanting to leave. You had to be in the right frame of mind. Posh Boy Marcus had said something the other day about needing to gear yourself up for Asia, and he'd been right. It was like getting in training for the start of the football season – physically and mentally – else you couldn't cope. And that had been his problem; half of him had still been back in Newcastle worrying about Paula and whether he could have done anything differently.

But what was done was done, and anyway they had needed a driver at short notice and promised a bonus. He would send it to Paula when he got paid at the other end, even though she had said she wanted nothing more to do with him, ever. Not if he took the trip. *Bloody running away as usual, just as well we don't have a bairn!* Her words had chased him across Europe.

Travel and tinkering with engines: that's what he lived for. And cricket. People were often surprised to find he was keen on a game like cricket, but Cassidy had learnt to play in the army and he carried a cricket bat on board because you never knew when it might come in handy.

'Hey, Cassidy, my dear chap! Where are you going?'

It was Mr Hail and Hearty Marcus wearing a fez and baggy pantaloons with a smart button-downed Ben Sherman shirt with a packet of Camel cigarettes squashed into the breast pocket.

'Back to the bus.'

'Come and have dinner with me and my good friend Ekrem. We're meeting up with some of the gang.' He swung an arm about Cassidy's shoulder and squeezed him in a joss stick-scented grip.

'What?' Cassidy laughed. 'So I can give you a lift back to the campsite when you're all pissed?'

'Not a bit of it,' Marcus protested, 'I'm happy to drive the bus back so you can indulge in a bit of raki.'

'Hey, raki indulgence,' cried Devon, weaving out of the shadows, 'count me in, oh bountiful one.'

'With pleasure, my dear troubadour! Come and sing for our Turkish host. Anything in the Pink Floyd variety will get you free *souvalaki*.' He swung back to Cassidy. 'And the fair Juliet will be there.'

'Meaning?'

But Marcus just laughed and clapped him on the back again. Cassidy wondered if it was that obvious that he liked Juliet? He loved her wackiness, the way she got excited over little things and he kept seeing the image of her on day one strutting up the bus in her panties when someone had been sick on her skirt. Or was Posh Boy just trying to wind him up? It had hacked him off the way his co-driver had taken control of things in Greece, missing out Mount Olympus, then pretending to be all concerned over Ruth, but keeping in with the Poshettes too. He couldn't work him out. But he was prepared to give Marcus the benefit of the doubt – and a night-out in Istanbul was not to be sniffed at – especially if Juliet was going to be there.

***

They ate in a small restaurant that felt like someone's front room, the group who had met Ekrem the day before, plus himself, Devon, Ruth, Peach and Chuck who had been swept up by Marcus too. All thirteen squeezed around one long table.

In twos and threes they were taken into the steaming kitchen to choose their meal from boiling pots of bean soup, rice and chickpeas, and trays of aubergines baked with tomatoes, shish-kebabs and fish, stuffed vine leaves and okra. Cassidy couldn't believe he was hungry again, but he was. Ekrem brought in bottles of white wine and Efes beer, and the volume of the conversation and laughter went up to max. Even Peach and Chuck relaxed and grew giggly; Cassidy bet their limit was usually one glass of wine at Thanksgiving.

Kurt and Marcus had a deep conversation about archaeology and Buddhist petrochemicals – at least that's what Cassidy thought Kurt said - and drew designs on a paper napkin: crude circles and dots that got Kurt excited. 'This is the wheel of life!'

Juliet was lapping it up too, as if she'd never seen such art before. She was looking soft and flushed because she's been to the *hamam* too and Cassidy thought if he touched her skin it would feel downy and warm like a peach.

Posh Boy was full of bullshit. He clapped Kurt on the back and waved the napkin at Ekrem. 'See that, my young unbeliever! The Buddhists spread their message far beyond their place of origin. That's what religion does – fires people up with the zeal to take on the world. That's how civilizations have spread and grown, Ekrem my friend.'

'Marcus, the wine has gone to your head,' Ekrem joked back. The Turkish lad was the only one speaking any sense.

'I'm serious, dear chap. You wouldn't get your leap in science and learning without the patronage of strong rulers fired by religion.' Marcus took off on one of his poncy rants. 'Look at Alexander the Great, Darius of Persia, Akbar of the Mughals, the Arabs, the British – the list is endless.'

'The list of tyrants, yes,' Ekrem snorted.

'Ruthless maybe,' Marcus said, 'but in time things settle down and civilizations flourish.'

'For the ruling classes, not the poor buggers they conquer!' Cassidy chipped in.

'Ah! Cassidy speaks for the common man. There you are Ekrem, a fellow Marxist to keep you company.'

'You don't have to be a Marxist to be against all that colonial bollocks,' Catriona said. Marcus looked surprised, as if he didn't expect the Scots lass to have an opinion on anything other than food.

Yeah,' Devon agreed. 'Religious dudes should stay at home, man, stay cool.'

'It's the tyrants with *no* religion we need to worry about,' Chuck waded in, 'like Hitler and Stalin.'

'And Richard Nixon?' Devon asked with a sarcastic smile.

Chuck scowled. 'At least he was standing up to Communism.'

'Meddling in South East Asia, more like,' said Juliet.

The conversation really started to cook. Marcus seemed pleased as punch at the argument he'd just ignited, but the more wound up Chuck got, the more tearful Peach was looking. Ekrem became anxious at the sudden ding-dong.

Suddenly Tomas thumped the table, 'Enough! Let's go sing-song!' Everyone was so surprised that they all stopped arguing. He started off in a booming voice; *'What shall we do wi' ze drunken sailor? What shall we do wi' ze drunken sailor?'*

Juliet joined in and soon most of the table were singing along. After that, Devon got them onto Beatles songs and Chuck was finally persuaded to sing 'Nothing like a Dame' from South Pacific. He couldn't sing for toffee, but Peach and Ruth clapped like he was the Great Caruso. Ruth was an even bigger surprise than the silent Tomas; she sang a haunting folk song about a dark island, sitting on the edge of her seat looking like Marianne Faithful, long blonde hair falling across her face as her voice rose high and strong and tuneful around the smoky room.

Afterwards, there was this moment of silence, when the clatter of plates in the kitchen sounded magnified and they all sat absorbing the shockwave of her soulful voice and wondered if it really belonged to this slip of a lass who couldn't hold her drink and looked about fifteen. For once, Cassidy thought, she seemed calm and in control and as if she understood more about the universe than the rest of them put together. But then maybe he'd just had too much raki.

Suddenly Ekrem was showering her with attention. 'Now I will have to marry you,' he declared. 'Stay in Istanbul with me forever, please.'

Ruth laughed and shook her head and looked gauche again. But later she let Ekrem sit holding her hand while the rest of them smoked hookahs and downed shots of raki late into the evening, toasting Atatürk and John Lennon and Rumi and Super Mac and half the football team at Galatasaray. Cassidy wished he had the guts to reach out for Juliet's hand – clasp her long fingers with turquoise rings and healthy pearly nails like shells. Then he felt guilty for even thinking it.

Perhaps it was Peach who decided that they'd been there far too long, Cassidy wasn't sure. He had a memory of being lead through a warren of back streets and then magically they were back on the bus.

'I'm not driving the bugger back,' Cassidy said, though it came out more like, 'bagger buck.' 'Marcus,' he slurred, 'where's Marcus? Said he'd do it.'

But Marcus didn't seem to be there.

Catriona pulled a face. 'You'll have a long wait – he's gone back to Ekrem's with Ruth.'

'What! Ruth's on her own with Ekrem and Marcus?'

'No, Juliet went too.' Catriona didn't look happy.

Cassidy felt suddenly deflated. Juliet and Marcus.

'Have to sleep on the bus,' he said, past caring. Peach began protesting. Cassidy thought Chuck said something about contacting the MD or UFO first thing in the morning. But Cassidy was already lying down on the two front seats. Seconds later he was asleep.

***

When he awoke, Ginger Baker was playing drums in his temples and the night sky was lightening in the east like torchlight behind canvas. For a moment he didn't have a clue where he was, who he was. Then he saw last night's revellers sprawled about the bus like dead bodies, limbs contorted, necks cricked. Chuck was snoring softly like water being sucked down a plughole. Only Peach was awake.

She was sitting upright, looking right at him. He winced at her expression. It wasn't cross or tearful, but pitying, as if to say that her son Gerald would never have let them down like that or got too drunk to drive them home.

'Sorry Peach,' Cassidy mumbled.

He got up, steadying himself on the rail. There was no sign of the missing three. He climbed into the driver's seat, turned on the engine, revved and let it warm for a minute or two. They wouldn't be coming now; they must have crashed at Ekrem's. Well, Marcus and Juliet were old enough to look after themselves – and Juliet would keep an eye on Ruth.

Pulling the bus into the deserted street, he headed out of the city.

CHAPTER 20

Newcastle
Amber
Cassidy put on heavy-framed spectacles and studied the photos spread out on the shed table, whistling through nicotine-stained teeth.

'Aye, that's your aunt,' he pointed. 'And those were the German lads – and that was one of the Aussies, but I can't remember his name. There's Peach in the background chopping up cabbage – she was American, drove everyone potty, but I liked her. And that one's Maggie – Irish, pretty, but hard as bell metal. Don't remember the names of those two lasses – couple of the Poshettes, as I called them.' Cassidy grinned in remembrance.

'Where was it taken?' Amber asked.

'Probably Anatalya or Side – somewhere on the Turkish Med – judging by the campsite and the fact it's stopped raining. I might even have taken this one myself. Ruth was always asking others to snap her with friends.'

Amber could feel Cassidy relaxing, his interest quickening. 'Can you remember anything about the time in Istanbul? Most of Ruth's diary is missing from that bit – just a couple of short entries. Then there's a gap of nearly two weeks. When it starts up again, it's just full of how wonderful Marcus is – and a woman called Juliet.'

Cassidy grunted. 'The unholy Trinity.'

Amber looked quizzical.

'That's what Maggie called them – Ruth, Juliet and Marcus. After Istanbul they were joined at the hip – for a while anyway. We'd all had a hum-dinger of a night out with this Turkish student, someone Marcus had picked up – he was good at that. But instead of coming back to the bus, the three of them went off with the Turk. We were supposed to be leaving for Gallipoli the next day, but they didn't turn up till the evening so we had to put the tents up again and stay another night.'

'Bet they were popular,' Amber said.

'Aye but it was me got it in the neck. The Yanks and Maggie – even this canny New Zealand couple that never said boo to a goose – were all giving me grief. But the Three Musketeers came flying back high as kites – not on booze or dope just happiness – and said they were really sorry.'

'Where had they been?'

Cassidy snorted, 'God knows. Had some garbled story about how they'd just missed the bus and went for breakfast instead and ended up on a fishing boat and made friends with this guy whose cousin ran a hotel in Pumakale. Marcus won most people round cos when we got to Pumakale, this cousin let us camp in the grounds and swim in the hot lime pools for free. Posh Boy had this knack of chatting up the right people and getting them to do things.' He picked up one of the photos and

65

studied it. 'For a while I thought Marcus and Forbsy were going to get it together – long term, I mean – she seemed that keen.'

'Forbsy?'

'My nickname for Juliet – Juliet Forbes.'

'Which one's Juliet?'

'That's her,' Cassidy said gently, his finger lingering over a tall handsome woman in a peasant headscarf, with almond-shaped eyes and a large grinning mouth. Older looking than a lot of them but quite sexy, in Amber's opinion.

'Did you keep in touch with her?'

'No.' Abruptly, Cassidy dropped the photo back on the table.

'Or any of the others from that trip?'

'Once a trip's over, the group breaks up and you never see them again – or hardly ever.'

'But weren't they interviewed over the disappearances?'

Cassidy poured another shot of whisky into his cold tea. 'Maybe,' he shrugged. 'But how should I know? They'd all long gone.'

'Bit strange, isn't it, that no one kept in touch?'

'They might have with each other,' Cassidy said in irritation, 'but not with me. I heard things on the grapevine about one or two of them, that's all. It was no big deal back then to lose touch - we didn't have mobiles and all that crap – we just lived for the moment and moved on.'

Amber was bursting with more questions but saw the man's agitation. She was stirring up memories and feelings that must be difficult and painful for Ruth's driver. But she didn't have long; she was due to get an early evening train.

'Tell me about this guy Marcus,' Amber urged. 'You didn't like him?'

'Posh prat,' Cassidy grunted. 'But to give him his due, he was a useful driver – good at sweet talking officials at border posts and giving just the right amount of *baksheesh*. Not much good with a wrench. And he was always trying to change the route to suit himself – drove me bloody nuts.'

'Why did he do that?'

Cassidy slugged at his tea. 'Oh, there was all sorts going on – I never knew the half of it.' He stood up. 'Listen lass, I've got some planting to do.'

'Cool, I can help,' Amber offered at once.

Cassidy gave her a sceptical look.

'Hey, I work in a garden centre,' Amber smiled, 'and I used to love helping out on Gran's smallholding.'

The older man nodded and led her outside. While Amber pegged and marked out the beds with twine, Cassidy fetched trays of seedlings. Together they plugged the plants into neat rows. As they worked together under a heavy grey sky, Amber talked about her degree in archaeology and her mother's catering business and how she had inherited Sarah's cottage in Weardale.

'Be cool to spend more time up there,' Amber said, 'have a go at living off the land and maybe let backpackers crash at the house.'

'Couch surfing?' Cassidy asked.

66

Amber grinned at him in surprise.

Cassidy laughed. 'I'm not a complete fossil. My upstairs neighbour does that, puts people up. But you should be more careful – being a lass.'

'Jez, you mean?'

'Aye, you met him?'

'He's looking after my bag. Seems nice. Is he a student?'

Cassidy nodded. 'Post-grad. Doing something clever with genetics, but don't ask me what.'

He bent down again to press the dark damp soil around a plant. Amber went off to fill the watering can, wondering why she'd told this stranger about plans that she'd never spoken of to anyone else, had hardly even formed in her own mind.

When she returned, Cassidy said, 'passengers might have come and gone, but there was a real brotherhood among us drivers. Some of the closest mates I ever had. Lads you could trust and have a laugh with – the ones that didn't mind getting their hands dirty.' He smiled, 'the kind who could fix a broken shaft in the middle of nowhere with a bit of scrap and a blowtorch.'

Amber looked up from her watering. 'Wicked. Was Marcus like that?'

Cassidy snorted. 'Hardly.'

'But he knew the hippy trail well, yeah?'

'That's what I thought.'

'Meaning he didn't?' Amber puzzled.

Cassidy said, 'Souter not tell you?'

'Tell me what? We didn't have much time.'

Cassidy gave her a long considering look. 'It turned out Marcus wasn't who we thought he was at all.'

CHAPTER 21

Ruth's diary
Sat 30th October - Day 35
Konya

Last night we danced round the campfire – me and Marcus and Juliet. Cassidy said we looked like whirling dervishes and Juliet said that's just what we are. It's all about expressing our love and getting to the highest level of ecstasy or something. It all makes sense when Marcus and Juliet are talking about it. I'm so happy now. J's more like a mother to me than my real one. She looks after me and I feel safe with her. And Marcus is the greatest. They're my best friends ever! ♥

Cassidy's in a moody-blues today, driving a bit fast over potholes so it's quite hard to write this. Says we've lost another day because of detour to Konya but Marcus said we really had to see it. And it was Republic Day and the place was full of red flags and musicians playing in the streets.

Saw my first camel train today! Donkeys with them and herds of black goats. Next stop Goreme and the cave houses and the Zelve Valley. Photos in Peach's brochure make the rocks look like giant toadstools, weird! Lucy (Kiwi) says it scares her (she's been a bit tearful lately so I think she's homesick or maybe she's had a row with Shane). But I don't find any of it scary – I love the big distances, the long roads going on and on forever and ever, and the way the sun shines off the rocks so brightly it hurts your eyes. And the sky so high and with no clouds, like a big blue tent over the world.

The colour of my true love's eyes is blue. The colour of Turkey is turquoise.

CHAPTER 22

'To know Turkey I must go right into the homes of the people of Anatolia, and the thought of spending my days on horseback and my nights sometimes in the homes of the primitive Turks, sometimes under the starlit sky, with the glorious Eastern moon to kiss me to sleep, gave me courage to break away for a while from my matter-of-fact grinding existence of the West ... When I think of London at this moment, shrouded in fog, whilst we are surrounded by a blue sky, trees in all their autumn glory, and the air which caresses my face like iced velvet, I am thankful ...'

An Englishwoman in a Turkish Harem, by Grace Ellison, 1915

Eastern Turkey
Juliet

The hired truck bumped its way down the mountainside, the headlamps lurching like searchlights in the dark, trying to pick out the dirt track. They sat squashed together wrapped in blankets, cold air biting their cheeks after the heat of the day. Overhead, stars littered the sky.

The Londoners were singing *'Show me the way to go home'* and Devon was beating out a rhythm on the side of the truck. Under the blanket, Juliet groped for the warmth of Marcus's hand and squeezed it in time to the song. Her skin still tingled from the dust and sun at the top of the mountain, and the strange sight of the giant carved stone heads of Nemrut Dagi marooned in the rubble like the remains from some mass beheading of the gods. The distant Euphrates had twisted like a thin snake and disappeared east between endless mountain ranges. Kurt had told her they stood on the burial ground of Antioch I, chosen so that he could reach up to heaven. The silence in the thin air was so intense that it felt like a human presence.

She still felt spellbound by the strangeness of Eastern Turkey, with its outposts of biblical villages – mud houses clinging to the hillsides with goats grazing on their grass roofs and children breaking off from tending cattle to run after the truck shouting, 'bye-bye tourists!'

The truck slowed and rolled like a ship as it juddered down to a stone bridge. Moonlight bathed the cliffs of the gorge and caressed the black water of the river, turning it to rippling silk. Softly, Devon began to sing a Bob Dylan song. People dozed, their heads lolling on neighbouring shoulders. The journey back to camp was taking hours, but Juliet didn't want the day to end. She glanced at Ruth on her other side. She was curled up tight in a sleeping bag with only her crown of blonde hair showing, a hibernating mouse.

What an odd threesome they made: Marcus, herself and the young Ruth who craved their companionship, and wouldn't let them out of her sight. It was trying at times – times when all she wanted to do was be alone with Marcus. Her physical need for him was like being constantly hungry, and yet they had still not made love. Juliet knew it was only a matter of time. She was very fond of Ruth and ever since that bewildering night back in Istanbul when things had changed so abruptly, had felt her need to be protected.

Juliet turned to face Marcus. His eyes glittered and a warm cloud of breath escaped from his slightly parted lips – plump sensual lips. He gave his playful quizzical smile. The truck reached the far side and revved at the slope ahead. Closing her eyes, she marvelled again at that night in Istanbul. On the way back to the bus Marcus had taken her by the arm and she had flinched as if from static. 'Better follow Ruth – looks like she's going off with Ekrem.'

She had slipped her hand into his as they walked, and they had ended up in a chilly high-ceilinged room in a tall shabby house that Ekrem appeared to share with his sister Fatima, a radical journalist. They had smoked a scented hookah and drank *ararak* and talked late into the night. At some stage, her throat raw from too much smoking, talking and fiery alcohol, she had fallen asleep on a pile of cushions. The next time she had woken, dawn was imminent, and Ruth was there snuggled between her and Marcus. Marcus had said something about promising to drive the bus back for Cassidy, so they had crept out without disturbing their hosts.

Juliet would never forget that hushed moment, Ruth holding hands between them. The sea of Marmara, glimpsed through the dark cypress trees and minarets, was a rucked carpet of purple, red and gold. The clear call of the muezzin heralded the dawn. They passed under a balcony of cascading wisteria; a fountain trickled in a courtyard beyond rusty gates. The sky had lightened and the city stirred; water splashed from standpipes, birds trilled, shutters banged.

Azure had seeped into the sky as they approached the Hippodrome. Amazingly their Rainbow bus was still parked there. They must have been a hundred yards from it when, with a cough of black exhaust, it swung out and pulled away.

'Oh hell,' Ruth had said. 'What do we do now?'

'Don't worry,' Marcus had said, looking scruffy and piratical with unshaven chin and tousled hair. Somewhere along the way he had lost his fez. His face had creased into a grin. 'Breakfast!' he had ordered and taken them both by the hand.

His hands, Juliet thought, were the most sensual she had ever known in a man. They were medium sized with dexterous fingers: sportsman's hands. Juliet glanced around, convinced that someone must be aware of her longing for Marcus – surely it came off her like a hot blast? – but her fellow passengers were lulled into their own thoughts by the lumbering truck.

Juliet knew how some of the others talked about them – thought they were into some kinky *ménage a trois* sharing a tent together. But it wasn't like that. Ruth saw them as her guardians; they were so much older and more worldly-wise than she. Marcus said that the love they shared between the three was akin to the state of pure joy that Sufis

70

thirsted after. Mystics all over the east, he said, spent their lives trying to attain the spiritual ecstasy that they already had.

Juliet had not expected to find such a strange heady relationship on the trip, but it coloured her experience of Turkey. Every sight, sound and smell was even more vibrant and fascinating than she had dared hope. The ruins at Pergamon, swimming at night in warm lime pools strewn with ancient columns, grinning school children offering posies of flowers, Rumi's green-domed shrine at Konya, the surreal volcanic landscape of Goreme and the hospitality of the people: all were overwhelming. Marcus charmed the locals wherever they went and so they got invited into homes for tea and sticky cakes. In Side they found themselves guests at a circumcision party sharing sweet wine and cigarettes, and in Troy and Konya they got the best guides around the ancient sites. With Marcus it was like experiencing a monochrome world in vivid Technicolor. And to cap it all, he read and loved the same travel books.

There was a sudden commotion at the other end of the truck. Someone struggled to stand, gripping the side of the truck.

'Watch it!'

'I feel sick. ' It was New Zealand Lucy.

The sound of her retching galvanised others to move away.

'Oh my giddy aunt! Watch my jacket!'

'Someone help her,' Peach called out.

Lucy gave a wail of distress as husband Shane and Devon held her up.

'Okay girl,' Shane soothed, holding her dark hair away from her face. 'Nearly back now - just hang on.'

'I can't,' Lucy cried and vomited over the side.

Torches went on. People shuffled out of the way.

'Here's a hanky,' Catriona offered.

Ten minutes later they chugged into Kahta where they were camped in the lee of a hotel wall. It was bitingly cold as they disembarked. Lucy was in tears and trying to apologise. Cassidy got water boiling for hot drinks. Half the group had dispersed by the time tea was brewed. Shane coaxed his wife to drink but she grimaced and pushed the mug away.

'You look like death warmed up,' Maggie told a grey-faced Lucy. 'You okay?'

'Chilled to the bone I'd say,' Juliet said. 'Why don't you book into the hotel for tonight?'

'That's a good idea,' Cassidy agreed. 'Get a good night's kip. We've got a long drive tomorrow up to Lake Van.'

Shane went off to negotiate a room.

Juliet touched Marcus on the shoulder. 'Why don't we do the same?'

He smiled, 'Yes, let's.'

The hotel turned out to be little warmer than the tent and to Juliet's frustration Ruth came too. Their basic room held two single iron-framed beds that squeaked at the slightest movement. Ruth took the one by the door and Juliet the other next to a draughty window. Marcus laid out his sleeping bag on the floor. Ruth appeared subdued or maybe just tired, and Juliet felt a gloom descend on the spartan room and began to regret

71

their move out of the tent. Marcus fell asleep at once but she couldn't get warm.

She finally dozed off only to be woken in the dead of night by raised voices in the next room. A door banged open and feet thumped up the corridor. All went quiet and she was huddling under the covers again when a shriek brought her bolt upright. A woman was crying out in distress. Ruth! Juliet struggled out of bed, climbing over Marcus and stumbling in the pitch black towards the other bed. Ruth was still fast asleep. Yet in her befuddled state it had sounded just like the girl. Had she been dreaming? She listened out but all was quiet.

Juliet stood shivering, undecided. A moment later, she padded into the corridor just to make sure. A light was showing under the bathroom door at the far end. As she drew nearer, she could hear a woman sobbing and a man's voice low and insistent. Juliet banged on the door.

'Are you all right?'

There was sudden silence. Juliet tried the handle. It opened. The stark electric light showed a smear of blood on the floor. Lucy was curled up on the cold tiles in bloodstained pants. Shane was crouched beside her.

'What on earth's happened?'

'My baby!' Lucy whimpered. 'Please don't take my baby.'

Shane gave Juliet a bewildered pleading look. 'Help us. I think she's miscarrying.'

CHAPTER 23

Ruth's diary
Wed 3rd November – Day 39
Turkey-Iran border

Had a really scary moment today. We stopped in village after dark to spend last Turkish lire. All piled in this tearoom. But word went round quickly and all the men and boys followed us in and sat staring and laughing and poking us while we tried to drink tea. Cassidy came in and told us all to get out quick and just leave the money. By then there were even more men outside all trying to cram in and see what was going on. There was a lot of shouting and pushing and pulling as we tried to leave. Catriona's shoe came off in the crush and she held onto me and asked me to help look for it. I had a panic and started screaming. Juliet wasn't there. Marcus forced his way back inside and pulled me out and onto the bus. Cassidy had the engine running. Catriona never got her shoe. Cassidy drove till we got to the border. He doesn't want us to camp in the wild tonight as he says it's too dangerous with bandits and wild animals. It's like something out of the Good Samaritan story. Marcus is my Good Samaritan.

Tonight we're dossing down in the customs hall on the Iranian side of the border. It's clean, with proper toilets and the policemen are very handsome and well dressed but they don't stare at us. There's a vicious looking sheepdog, but it lets me pet it.

It's calm now but there's been a bad atmosphere ever since Lucy nearly miscarried. She lies on the back seat and cries all the time and says she wants to go back to New Zealand as soon as possible. Peach is really upset for her too. They both cry together, even though Shane keeps saying it's all going to be hunky-dory. The local doctor said there was still a chance the baby would be all right as long as she rested and tried not to move. Cassidy says we're going to drive straight to Tehran and get her checked out at the hospital. Some people are kicking up a fuss cos they don't want to go to Tehran cos it's supposed to be boring and polluted and with nothing nice to look at. Juliet wants to go there to visit some handwriting expert that she's been in touch with.

Thurs 4th November – Day 40
I don't want to go to sleep in case I dream. Should I tell someone about what I saw at the top of Nemrut Dagi? That dead baby with blue lips lying in a woman's lap and the woman's long hair falling down over her face hiding her tears. Does it mean Lucy's baby is going to die? She blames the bumpy truck ride for her problems, but I think it was always going to happen. You can't change things that are predestined, can you? I saw it and it makes me very sad. I want to talk to Juliet about it but all she wants to do is read her book about Persia and talk to Marcus.

Sun 7th November – Day 43

They were right, Tehran is a hole. Traffic's mad too. Lucy's in hospital having tests. She says that whatever the doctors tell her she just wants to go home now. That's what Shane told Cassidy. They're going to look into flights. There were no letters for me at *post restante*.

Mon 8th November – Day 44

Doesn't look like Shane can persuade Lucy to carry on with the trip, even though the doctors say she can as long as she rests up for a week. Marcus is offering to take some of us down to Esfahan with him and wait there. Says it's much nicer. Everyone's voted to do that, except Peach and Chuck who want to stay with Lucy until she decides what to do, and Juliet who hasn't managed to meet up with her handwriting friend yet. He's out of the city until the weekend. Cassidy says he'll stay and help Shane sort things out. He's got a soft spot for Lucy. He's given Marcus all the details about the route and campsite in Esfahan but Marcus says he knows it well and not to worry.

I don't like to leave Juliet but I can't not be with Marcus. She's annoyed with him for splitting up the group but it's not his fault. He was just stopping all the arguments.

CHAPTER 24

'We proceeded to the garden and found a most agreeable retreat; long alleys of large orange trees, whose spreading branches completely over-canopied the walks; and the date and the cypress, both in full perfection, flourishing close by each other ... The storm that had burst on us but the preceding evening, had purified the atmosphere; and every tree, and bush, and blade of verdure, breathed forth a perfume, which at once delighted the senses and invigorated and expanded the mind.'
Travels in Assyria, Media and Persia, by J. S. Buckingham, 1829

Iran, November
Juliet

Five days: that's how long they had been apart. Separation from Marcus felt like toothache, a constant and nagging pain. She longed to be with him again, yet the unwelcome words from Rehman the graphologist plagued her thoughts. *'This man is in the peak of health. He is very driven and single-minded – but secretive – look how those letters curl back on themselves. And do you see that dagger stroke on the cross of the "t"? A sign of ruthlessness. Beware of this man.'*

She regretted now that she had wasted these precious days in Tehran, tracking down a so-called expert whose diagnoses were so wide of the mark. Where he saw Marcus as self-obsessed, she saw a healthy sense of self. Where he detected suppressed anger, she saw calm self-control. The only thing they agreed on was that Marcus was an optimist with a strong imagination.

There had been no time to dwell on the disappointing encounter. Shane and Lucy had said tearful goodbyes at the airport.

'You take real good care of her,' Peach had said. 'You're gonna have that baby.'

'And you have a great reunion with Gerald in Kathmandu,' Lucy had cried.

'You betch ya.' Peach had hugged her and wept loudly. All the way back to the hotel in the taxi Chuck had patted her while Peach had sniffed, 'she's gonna have that child, I just know it.'

That night Juliet and Cassidy had got mildly drunk with the Americans as they toasted the New Zealanders good luck and turned their thoughts to the trip ahead. Juliet floated the idea of reaching Pakistan via the southern desert; Rehman had eulogised about the ruined city of Bam and she was keen to see what she could of Baluchistan.

'He says the route is safe, Cass,' she had assured, 'and I really want to get to see Quetta and try and find my father's old friend. It would mean so much.'

Cassidy had been in mellow mood, relieved that Lucy was safely on her way home and that he had done what he could.

'We'll see Forbsy.'

Now they were stopped at a wayside tea-stall under trees, half way to Esfahan, waiting for the driver of the local bus to finish his meal of mast and flat crispy bread. Under a lopsided picture of the Shah and Empress, Cassidy sat cross-legged with him drinking *cay* and talking about carburettors. Peach and Chuck were still pouring over a newspaper bought in Tehran early that morning that told them they had a new President, Jimmy Carter, and wondering if this was good or bad. He was a southerner like them, but a Democrat. 'Gerald would be pleased,' Peach conceded with a sigh.

Juliet was too tense to eat anything. Rehman had said disturbing things about Ruth too, things that Juliet had puzzled over but been unsure about.

'This girl is not in a healthy state. Look at the upper sphere of her writing – the disjointed strokes and dashes - and the gaps between letters. There is no joined up thinking. I would worry about her. She is under mental stress. These visions she claims to have could be signs of a possible breakdown. Either that or she is a fantasist.'

As the rooftops of Esfahan finally appeared on the beige horizon like winking jewels, Juliet felt sick with anticipation at the thought of imminent reunion with Marcus. She suspected Rehman had over-exaggerated Ruth's weaknesses too, but she needed to talk to someone about her. Marcus was the only one who knew the girl as well as she did, and the only person she wanted to confide in about it all.

At Chuck's insistence, they were dropped in the city centre close to Maiden Shah. Despite her eagerness to find the others, Juliet was captivated by the broad sweep of green lawns that had once been a royal polo ground, surrounded on all sides by elegant mosques and pavilioned buildings. They explored the bazaar with its busy workshops of metalworkers and printers. She imagined Catriona rushing from stall to stall buying presents for her large family, and wished she'd been there too. Strolling outside in mild sunshine, the air was so clear that the distant mountains looked close enough to touch.

They bought kebabs in flat bread with hunks of tomatoes and raw onion and sat on the grass watching the passers-by; tradesmen pushing barrows, elegant young women in jeans and high heels under long flimsy veils, the occasional turbaned holy man. Juliet scanned them for signs of their fellow passengers without success.

While Chuck and Peach went off to explore, Cassidy took Juliet to the blue-domed Shah's mosque and through huge silver-plated wooden doors. Immediately she was struck by a deep sense of tranquillity. They walked in silence through its courtyards, under elegant arches of blue and turquoise mosaics and listened to the plash of doves drinking at the water tanks, their whiteness shimmering against sky blue water. Cassidy led her into a smaller courtyard lined with trees, purple flowers and a pool of goldfish.

They sat in the shade of blue and yellow arches, and dozed. For a few minutes she managed to let go of her turbulent thoughts. She understood completely how Grace Ellison had felt so at home with Islam. When Juliet opened her eyes again, Cassidy was looking at her. They smiled.

'It's so beautiful here,' she murmured.

'I knew you'd like it,' he said, offering her a hand and pulling her to | feet.

As they emerged into the square she said, 'You're a nice man, Cass. What you did for Lucy – I'm sure it was over and above your duty as driver. Shane could have arranged it all.'

'Aye, but I was sorry for the lass. Didn't want any harm to come to her and her bairn – maybes I'd driven too hard through Eastern Turkey.'

'Don't you go blaming yourself,' Juliet insisted. 'Life's full of risks. They chose to come on this trip.'

When his eyes met hers they were full of sadness.

'Cassidy, has something like this happened before? Happened to you, I mean?'

He glanced away and pulled out a squashed cigarette from behind his ear.

'Look, there's Pearl & Dean,' he pointed at the Americans and quickened his pace.

They got to the campsite shortly before dusk. Juliet's heart quickened at the sight of the Rainbow bus. But before they got near it, Cassidy said, 'That's not mine.'

They found the lugubrious Don who had helped them load up the bus in London, sitting behind the wheel reading a battered copy of *Time Magazine*.

'They're not here,' he seemed to take delight in telling them. 'Haven't been for a few days. Had problems with grit in the fuel – wouldn't let me help – took it to a local guy who bled the pipes.'

Cassidy cursed. 'Bloody told him not to let the fuel run low or the pipes would clog. I should never have let him go off with me bus.'

'Where have they gone?' Juliet asked in dismay. 'They were supposed to wait here until we came, then we were all going on to Persepolis.'

Don shrugged. He turned and shouted to someone down the bus if they knew.

'Shiraz, I think!'

'What about Persepolis?' Chuck demanded. 'We can't miss out on that.'

Don said, 'my trip isn't full. You can come along with us tomorrow. Day after that I can drop you off in Shiraz.'

Juliet could have kissed him for being unexpectedly co-operative, but Cassidy looked furious. 'This isn't good,' he muttered, 'I knew I shouldn't have let him nick off with my bus.'

'He hasn't nicked it,' Juliet said. 'He was doing you a favour remember? The others must have got bored and hassled him to move on.'

Cassidy turned to Don. 'Which mechanic did he use?'

Don shrugged. 'Nobody I'd ever heard of.'

Cassidy swore in annoyance. Juliet tried to shake Rehman's words from her mind but couldn't. *'Beware of this man. I wouldn't trust him.'*

As soon as Juliet set eyes on Marcus in Shiraz, relaxing in a restaurant garden, she knew that something had changed. He and Ruth were sitting close together, Marcus's hand resting on the girl's thigh. The look that passed between the pair before he waved – a chummy sort of wave – made her stomach knot. Juliet hesitated, checking her impulse to rush forward. It was Ruth, face radiant, who sprang towards her, knocking over a chair in her hurry. She hugged her like a long lost friend; she smelt of intimacy with Marcus.

'We've missed you so much!' she cried. 'Haven't we Marcus?'

'Of course,' he said.

Juliet bent towards him and he planted a kiss on her cheek. A Judas kiss. Now she was sure of it; Marcus and Ruth were lovers.

CHAPTER 25

Ruth's diary
Not sure of day or date
Shiraz

They make the best banana milkshakes in the world here. Two whole bananas – really creamy. You just buy them in the street at these little stalls. Marcus had an amazing chilled pomegranate juice too. We drank half each and then swapped! The nougat is fab – they call it "gaz". 'Life's a gaz,' says Marcus! I've never been so happy!! ♥♥♥

Juliet and Cassidy and Peach and Chuck came in on the other Rainbow bus today! It was brilliant to see them again – I've missed them all so much.

There's a row going on about what route to take next. Cassidy wants to head north for Yezd and Mashhad. The Germans want to go south through the desert and see canals or something. Juliet and Marcus are really keen too. Juliet's been funny with me since she got back. There was a nasty slanging match her first night in Shiraz. It's not the same between the three of us. I think she's jealous that I've had all this time with Marcus. But she's the one chose to stay in Tehran. Marcus said she wasn't the jealous type and I believed him. I hope it gets better again, cos I still love her. ♥

Juliet gave me two letters from the *post restante* in Tehran. I haven't opened them yet.
Home is so far away now, like another world.

CHAPTER 26

Southern Iran
Cassidy

He focused all his concentration on steering the bus up the hairpin pass; rock face to one side, sheer drop to the other. The road – no more than a track – was riddled with channels that kept catching at the wheels like some malign sprite trying to trip them up. Last night they had camped on rocky scrubland using stones to peg down the tents, and woken to a biting wind and a gaggle of curious nomads who had gathered to watch the morning ritual.

For better or worse he had given into the majority demand to travel through the southern desert and cross the border at Zahedan. Juliet was determined to go via Baluchistan and Marcus was backing her up. Cassidy thought his co-driver was just trying to get back into her good books; it was obvious they'd had a bust up. Kurt had lobbied hard to see his beloved *kanats*. Cassidy wondered what all the fuss was about – they were just mounds in the desert with deep holes that he had to warn people not to get too close to.

But it was Peach's opinion that had swung it for him; he was growing fond of the mother hen.

'I think it's real important that Juliet goes to Quetta,' she had said firmly. 'It's where her father lived before he died. It's like a pilgrimage.'

Surprised, Cassidy had pointed out, 'if we do that, Peach, you'll miss out on Mashhad and Herat. And you've been looking forward to seeing them.'

'This trip ain't just about me and Chucky and what we want.'

Juliet had hugged her. The Aussies and Poshettes had grown excited at the thought of heading off along the arduous, little travelled southern route, and the others hadn't been fussed. Cassidy had a bad feeling but ignored it; this is what his group wanted.

It was three or four years since he had driven this way, but part of him relished the challenge. Like the captain of a small ship buffeted by the elements, he rode the high mountain passes and used his skill and nerve to negotiate the treacherous roads. Not trusting Marcus's unknown motor mechanic in Esfahan, Cassidy had given the bus a thorough checking over before leaving Shiraz, and refuelled.

Now that they were on the move again he was happier. The arguing had done his head in. He was back in control of his beloved bus.

CHAPTER 27

Ruth's diary
Desert, Iran – Day 48 – or is it 49?
The Maiden's Castle. Where was it? Cassidy told us that story.
Somewhere in Turkey – before we left the sea. On a rock in the sea. The
father locks her up because of a prophecy that she would die from a
snakebite. But one day a fruit basket is brought in with a serpent in it and
it stings the maiden and she dies. So you can't avoid it. If the evil is
there you can't stop it harming you. He tried to protect her, but he
couldn't. He let the serpent come in so it was his fault his daughter died.

CHAPTER 28

'A stony, unbroken desert, intersected here and there by low ranges of barren, bleak and rocky hills, stretches on every side, as far as the eye can reach; and neither beast, bird, shrub, tree, twig, nor human being, breaks the impressive monotony.'
Eastern Persia: an Account of the Journeys of the Persian Boundary Commission, by Major Euan Smith, 1876

South East Iran
Juliet

Each day the landscape grew more stark. They rode through jagged mountains and across empty rock-strewn desert – vast salt encrusted plains that shimmered from afar but crumbled on approach – resembling cracked leather. Cassidy battled with the terrain: freak rainfall had made the road across the usually dry salt lake unusable and so he had to take the disused track around it. The only other traffic was an occasional donkey. Several times a day, Cassidy had to order his passengers off the bus while he negotiated gullies and channels, and twice they had to pile out and help shore up the road with stones where it had been washed away by flash floods and wind.

At times, the grey rock would give way to sudden lushness and thriving towns – Sirjan, Kerman, Mahan – where they bought fresh bread from communal ovens, huge cabbages, tomatoes and grapes from the markets, and bargained for woolly hats and blankets for the freezing nights.

Cassidy pressed on, driving long hours, stopping only for provisions or to let passengers squat behind the bus to urinate. When the sunset stretched behind them like a crimson banner, he would pull over and they would pitch camp, the futile sound of hammering metal into stone ringing through the darkness.

Juliet welcomed the ceaseless movement, the monotony, and the barren landscape forever repeating itself beyond the bus windows. It lulled her fractious thoughts, her fear that the best of the trip was already over. She had rowed with Marcus that night in Shiraz, when she had met up with them again after separation in Tehran. When Ruth had gone to the washroom, Juliet's hurt had spilled out.

'You're sleeping with her, aren't you?'

Marcus had said calmly, 'So are you.'

'I don't mean just sleeping, I mean having sex.'

He said nothing.

'You can see it all over your faces. I feel such a fool.'

'You shouldn't. It's not what you think. She really needs me just now.'

He had reached over to touch her, but she had pushed him away.

'I thought us two would – I hoped we had something special.'

'We do, girl.'

'She's much too young for you.'

'Age doesn't come into it.'

'Why did you encourage me,' Juliet accused, 'when it's Ruth you want?'

'You're making too big a deal of this,' Marcus sighed.

'She's unstable you know – I've seen it in her handwriting – you mustn't take advantage.'

Suddenly he had gripped her arm. 'I'd never take advantage of her, don't ever say that.'

Their argument was cut short by Ruth's return. Juliet had started to pack up her things.

'What are you doing?' the girl had asked.

'Leaving you two to get on with it.'

'Why? Stop her Marcus.'

'I can't force her.'

'Don't go,' Ruth had said in agitation, pulling clothes back out of Juliet's bag, 'please don't.'

'I can't stay – not if you two are lovers.'

Ruth had looked astonished. 'You think this is about sex?'

'Isn't it?'

'We're above all that,' Ruth cried. 'What we've got is more important. Tell her Marcus.'

Juliet had looked at him in bewilderment.

'Ruth wants you to stay,' he said. 'I want you to stay. I don't know what lies this graphologist has been peddling about us, but he's wrong.'

'Yes,' Ruth had said, 'we three are meant to be together. Don't spoil it Juliet, please!' She had burst into tears.

Alarmed at Ruth's distress, Juliet had comforted her. She had stayed. Juliet was still sharing a tent with them. But it wasn't the same. She had misjudged the whole situation. Marcus didn't desire her and Ruth just saw her as some kind of comfort blanket. Yet Marcus didn't appear interested in having sex with either of them. They lay on the hard ground mummified in layers of clothing, huddled against each other for warmth. Juliet blamed herself for spoiling their previous innocent intimacy like a grown-up ruining a child's game of make-believe. Ruth had begun to moan and babble in her sleep once more.

During the day, Marcus and Ruth sat together. Juliet changed seats around the bus, sometimes sitting half way down with Kurt and Tomas, or Peach and Chuck, and sometimes at the front with Devon changing the tapes and helping Cassidy navigate gullies and boulders.

As they travelled on, the emotional distance between Juliet and her two tent-mates grew. Ruth was subdued. Late one night she had gone back out to the dying fire, torn up the letters Juliet had picked up for her in Tehran and thrown them on the flames. The charred remains had still been there the following morning; frosted fragments that read, "good idea, don't you th-" "springtime once y-" "God's protec-" "love from -".

Outwardly Marcus was cheerful, but now she wondered how much of it was a front. On the day they stopped at Mahan, she caught him weeping at the shrine of a Sufi poet, Shah Nematollah Vali. He was kneeling on a prayer mat in front of a table laden with roses and books, soft lamplight glancing off the white archways. His eyes were closed but his face was wet with tears. She drew back, not wanting to intrude. But he saw her and followed her out.

'I think it's best if you move out of our tent,' he said. 'I'm sorry.'

Juliet searched his face for clues, but it was impassive. He gave no explanation and she did not ask for one.

That night, once more in the desert, they ate risotto huddled around the stove, Maggie complaining her fingers were so cold they were sticking to the metal containers. Juliet moved in with Catriona, and Australians Fran and Gwennie. Marcus got drunk on cherry brandy with the Londoners and snored loudly until dawn. Juliet was exhausted but could not sleep.

She rose early to catch the sunrise. Cassidy had advised the women, 'if you walk into the rising sun and squat down, no one can see you having a piss. Got to time it right, mind.'

There was ice on the flysheet and an eerie red light behind the distant hills as if a hidden city were on fire. Perhaps it was the lack of sleep, but Juliet felt on edge. Some unnamed fear clawed at her insides. As light rapidly flooded the grey plain, turning it beige, she looked back at their huddle of tents and thought how insignificant they were in the vast landscape. In an hour or so they would be gone and within a day or two nothing would remain to indicate they had ever been. Was this how it would be when she looked for traces of her father: a futile search in endless tracts of desert that yielded up nothing?

In the distance, Ruth emerged from Marcus's tent, arms hugging herself for warmth. She walked a few paces away from the camp, bent over double and seemed to stare at the ground. Juliet watched, wondering what she was doing. A minute later, Ruth looked around, and stared straight at her. Juliet waved. The girl continued to gaze at her but did not wave back. Something was going on that Juliet couldn't comprehend but was too worn down by the emotions of the past week – by Ruth's neediness and Marcus's rejection - to work it out.

Juliet felt out of sorts all morning as they plunged south and deeper into the wilderness. They stopped at the ruined Persian city of Bam, and paid 10 rials each to explore the vast, empty citadel of mud houses enclosed by crumbling ramparts. Juliet wandered around the maze of abandoned streets with Kurt and some of the Australians but got separated trying to find the mosque. She stopped and listened out for voices or footsteps, but heard nothing. The silence was oppressive like the sudden hot sun.

Juliet pressed on, climbing through the ruins, nearly treading on a scorpion. There had been a dozen or more of the group clambering about the site, so it was a matter of time before she bumped into someone. Twenty minutes later, she was still alone and quite lost. Two ugly black birds wheeled overhead, their cawing making their throats rattle. Her chest tightened in fear. She imagined Kurt walking back to the new town in its oasis of palm trees, thinking that she had joined up with others. A memory from early in the trip returned unbidden: *'you'll get lost in the desert'* Ruth had predicted.

Suddenly, she was paralysed by terrifying thoughts: she was alone, abandoned, the bus had left and no one had noticed her missing, she might round a corner and step on a snake at any moment, she would be bitten and die. Just like her father, the desert would claim her, but it would be her fault because she had chosen to come here. She was tempting fate.

Juliet took deep breaths to smother her panic. She fixed on a section of the city wall and headed towards it. If she could gain height she would see where she was. Scrambling onto a narrow ledge, she saw that she was at the furthest point from the entrance. In the far distance lay the emerald green smudge of the modern city. There was no one else about. A sudden movement to her left made her cry out in fright. A large lizard scuttled into a crack. As quickly as she could, Juliet groped her way along the ramparts, clinging on where the ledge fell away to a few footholds.

Negative thoughts pursued her and slowed her progress. *I'm a small speck of dust, a mote in the sun. Others have tried to tame this place and failed. I am quite alone in the world. There is no one to claim me. Who will repatriate my body when I die? Like the Zoroastrians I will be left to the elements. Those birds will shred my flesh and the sun will bleach my bones. This is my tower of silence. I am bone meal.*

'Juliet? Juliet!'

Squinting into the fierce light, Juliet saw a slim figure waving to her near the entrance. Ruth's pink t-shirt. She swallowed a sob of relief and waved back.

'Here, over here!'

Five minutes later, Juliet was back on the ground, outside the fortress and hugging Ruth.

'Thank you,' she gasped, half laughing in relief.

But Ruth was upset. 'I knew you were still in there. They thought you'd gone back to town. Don't ever go off like that again!'

'I'm sorry.'

They hurried back to town, passed veiled women washing in the open drains. Kurt apologised for losing her and Marcus fussed over Ruth. Juliet was grateful to the girl. She felt guilty for the bad thoughts she had harboured against her recently over Marcus. In the safety of the sunny bustling town, her fear of Ruth's premonition now seemed ridiculous. She had allowed superstition to overcome common sense. Yet Rehman's diagnosis that Ruth could be heading for a breakdown, still nagged. She must keep an eye on the girl.

Later that day, Cassidy stopped at a lone desert lighthouse, an edifice of mud bricks that towered over the empty road.

'I see no ships!' joked a Londoner.

'It's so camel trains can see where they're going,' Gwennie read from the tour brochure.

'See how lost they are, you mean.'

People piled out and larked around in the sun, chucking stones and racing up the tower. A hot breeze was blowing. From the top, one of the Liverpudlians shouted down, 'Hey, there's a super tanker on the horizon.'

'Let's hope it's full of beer,' a Poshette shouted back.

Cassidy touched Juliet on the elbow. 'Want to help me make a cuppa?'

She nodded. 'I've had enough of climbing for one day.'

In the shelter of two abandoned truck tyres, they set up the stove and made tea and coffee. Juliet noticed how Marcus had taken himself off to lie on a blanket and doze, not joining in.

'You all right Forbsy?' Cassidy eyed her.

Juliet nodded. 'I don't know why I panicked. It was such an eerie place.'

'Aye, gives me the creeps an' all. Dead places always do.'

'Dead?'

Suddenly there was a high-pitched scream from the lighthouse. They looked up to see a figure leaning over the parapet.

'No don't! Christ, someone grab her!'

'Get away, don't touch me!'

The screaming filled the air, bouncing off the bald rock all about. Juliet's heart lurched. 'It's Ruth,' she gasped, leaping up. Appalled she watched as the girl clawed at the stone, trying to haul herself over. Kurt had a hold of her legs.

'It's too late,' she babbled, 'too late. Why me? I hate her, hate her!'

Juliet rushed to the bottom and shouted up. 'Ruth, it's okay. Calm down. I'll come up.'

'I'll go,' Marcus dashed past her and disappeared into the tower.

Others were hanging onto her now, trying to avoid her flailing arms. Below, the rest of the group looked on in horror as she yelled and fought with them. A minute later Marcus was at the top, pushing his way towards Ruth and enveloping her in a bear hug.

She screamed his name. She disappeared from view, but they could still hear her wails of distress. Juliet and Cassidy waited at the bottom of the steps. It seemed an age before the others descended, one by one, eager to be back on ground. Out of view they could hear Marcus gently coaxing, his voice echoing around the inside. Finally he emerged with Ruth. Her face was ashen, her hair lank with sweat. She looked dazed, and when Juliet stepped forward, flinched away, burying her face in Marcus's chest. For a moment everyone stood around wondering what to say; some gave Juliet curious looks.

'Hot sweet tea,' Peach declared, 'that's what you need, Miss Ruth.'

She guided her over to the tyres but Ruth wouldn't let go of Marcus. Together they shared a mug. They packed up quickly and moved on. Ruth lay curled up on the back seat and slept, Marcus keeping guard over her. Around the bus, people had hushed conversations.

'What was all that about?'

'Search me.'

'Too much sun.'

'She's a head case.'

86

'Can't see her coping with working in an orphanage, can you?'

'Pity the orphans.'

'Surprised if she lasts the trip, mate.'

'If you ask me, it's all a lot of screaming over nothing.'

'Or screaming over Marcus. That's love triangles for you – they never work.'

'How does that guy do it?'

'Makes them think they're special.'

'Yea, like sneaking a look at Juliet's books so he can spout off about them.'

'He doesn't do that does he?'

'Too right he does!'

Juliet went red with humiliation to hear them gossip. They were wrong about Marcus, surely? He was cultured and well read in his own right. She did not recognise this cynic they described. But worse was her guilt over Ruth. Had she triggered the girl's hysteria by accusing her of sleeping with Marcus, or even for getting lost that morning? Was she the one Ruth now hated? The girl seemed so emotionally fragile since the row in Shiraz that the slightest thing upset her. Juliet gulped back tears. Whatever had possessed her to get into such an emotional mess?

Devon leaned over and murmured. 'Don't listen to them, man.' He offered her a half-smoked cigarette.

Gratefully Juliet took it. 'Thanks.'

Cassidy glanced round; his expression told her he understood. 'Hey, Forbsy, we could do with some music.'

CHAPTER 29

South East Iran
Cassidy

What a crazy day: Juliet getting lost in Bam and Ruth screaming like a banshee and trying to hurl herself off the lighthouse. That had really shaken him up. Maggie was right, the lass was a head-case, but then so were plenty of overlanders. You had to be a little bit daft to share a bus for months with complete strangers, camp in sub-zero temperatures, stink for days on end and piss in groups.

Even so, as Cassidy erected his one-man tent that evening, he wondered what to do about Ruth. Should he flag up to head office that he had a problem? Trouble was they were still a day's ride from the Pakistan border, in the middle of nowhere and it would be almost impossible to send any messages to anyone until they reached Quetta in three or four days time. By then the friction between Ruth, Juliet and Marcus might have calmed down anyway.

Cassidy noticed how Juliet had moved back in with Catriona. From what he could see, Marcus had not tried to stop her. As for Ruth, she looked completely out of it, her eyes all unfocused. He wondered if Marcus had sedated her with something; he seemed to have a ready supply of hash. Cassidy crawled thankfully into his sleeping bag and fell into exhausted sleep.

A blare of music erupted in the camp and brought Cassidy wide-awake. Someone had got onto the bus and was blasting out *Supertramp*. Cassidy recognised the disturbing song about someone in crisis – cold, demons, screaming, hiding in their shell – the words rang around the empty night. Who the hell was messing on at this hour?

He raced to the bus, the cold throttling his breath. He clattered on board. Ruth lay on the floor, cradled in Marcus's arms, her eyes wild. She was half singing, half sobbing, her long hair stuck to her face with tears. Cassidy lurched for the tape deck and silenced the music.

'What the fuck, Marcus man!'

'I thought the music would calm her down. She needs to let it all out.'

'Not on my bus at three in the morning, you tosser.'

Juliet appeared in the door, her face registering shock. 'What's happened?'

Ruth grew more agitated. 'There was blood everywhere,' she moaned. 'And faces staring – dead faces staring. I couldn't stop them.'

'It was a bad dream, girl,' Marcus crooned, 'just a bad dream. Let's get you back to bed.'

Cassidy helped him lift her to her feet. Marcus gave an apologetic smile. 'Thought the joint would calm her.'

Outside the bus, Ruth stopped and touched Juliet with a clammy hand. 'You were there. I saw you there.'

Juliet flinched. Marcus steered her away.

Cassidy put an arm round her shoulder. She looked really shaken up. 'She's high as a kite, talking gibberish.'

Juliet nodded. Yet he could tell from her face that she half-believed the girl's ranting. Ruth had got under her skin like a poison. It made Cassidy furious to see her so upset. If the Weardale lass and Marcus were going to carry on disrupting his trip, he was going to have to do something about them.

CHAPTER 30

Newcastle
Amber
They sat around a low table on cushions, eating couscous and vegetable stew in Cassidy's flat. Jez had joined them. Maybe that was why Amber had missed her train south. She would call home later, and text work to say she wouldn't be in. She wanted to hear more of Cassidy's tales, of bizarre goings-on in the desert that might explain why her aunt had disappeared just two weeks later.

'Was it drugs?' Amber asked. 'You thought Marcus was getting her stoned a lot.'

'Yeah,' Jez agreed, 'that could explain her weird outbursts.'

Cassidy shrugged. 'Possibly. But -' He shrugged again.

'Possibly what? Say what you think, I won't stress,' Amber said.

'Well, sometimes I used to wonder if she was just putting it on – all that screaming and prophesying business – like she was playing a part.'

'You make her sound like a telly evangelist,' Jez snorted.

'When we started out she was just this young lass from the Durham Dales,' Cassidy said, 'quite ordinary. But the more she got involved with that Marcus, the odder she got. He was this larger than life big-mouth, always grabbing the limelight. It was like she was trying to impress him – be the mad bohemian girlfriend she thought he wanted.'

Jez leaned across and nudged Cassidy's arm. 'Wow, Cass, when did you turn all Freudian?'

He batted him off. 'Cheeky sod.'

'You don't believe she was seeing visions then?' Amber asked.

'No, it's bollocks.'

Amber said, 'My gran believed in all that heavy stuff and she wasn't nuts. She said some people had a sort of gift and they should use it to stop bad things happening.'

'Well Ruth didn't,' Cassidy replied. 'She just went into herself – cut herself off from everyone except Marcus.'

Jez passed round a plate of halva and refilled their tumblers of wine. When his hand brushed Amber's she felt a ridiculous thrill; he was so good-looking she found it hard not to gaze.

'My grandfather was a shaman,' Jez said. 'My mum says he would go into a trance – singing and dancing - then make predictions. Said his soul could travel and leave the body when he did this, and that it was the ancestors speaking through him. But it was also to ward off evil. He would call up the spirits of our ancestors to protect the family from harm. Perhaps she was trying to protect herself – or someone else?'

'It's beyond me,' Cassidy said, lighting up a b*eedie.* He blew out scented blue smoke and nodded at Amber. 'Mind you, Souter – your journalist friend – had a theory about all that. He was well into this prophesying business once he'd made friends with your grandmother.'

90

'Oh yeah, what did he think?'

'Well, about a week or so after Ruth was screaming her head off about seeing dead bodies and faces of blood, there was a massive earthquake around Lake Van in Eastern Turkey – just where we'd been camping. Being on the road we didn't hear about it for weeks afterwards, of course. Souter thought Ruth must have predicted it.'

'You're kidding? But why that disaster?' Amber asked. 'There've been loads of violent stuff in that part of the world since.'

'True, but according to Souter, the people who have second-sight type experiences usually see things that are just about to happen – an accident or someone's funeral.'

Amber said, 'but you don't agree?'

Cassidy shook his head. 'If you ask me, I think the trip was too tough for her and she wanted out.'

'Enough to take her own life?' Jez asked quietly.

Cassidy shrugged. They fell into silence. Amber gnawed at her thoughts. What had her grandparents made of their daughter's relationship with Marcus? Or with the eccentric sounding Juliet who danced like a dervish and thought she was the reincarnation of an Edwardian traveller? They must have been shocked to discover how different the trip was from the one they thought she was taking. Yet none of that must have mattered in the face of her disappearance; her gran had never stopped yearning for Ruth's return till the day she died.

Another thought resurfaced. At the allotment Cassidy had been on the point of telling her more about Marcus when a neighbouring gardener had appeared and distracted his attention over onions.

'You said something earlier about Marcus not being what he seemed. What did you mean by that?'

Cassidy gave a grunt. 'Thought Souter would have filled you in on all that.'

'He's going to send me his old articles.'

Cassidy ground out his *beedie* and gathered his thoughts.

'He wasn't who he said he was, that's all I know. His passport said Marcus Barclay – I remember checking it when he joined as relief driver – but the police kept asking me about that over and over. Was I sure? Apparently there was nothing in his rucksack that gave any clues; no letters, no diary, no address book.'

'And no passport?' Amber queried.

'And no passport.'

'Why take your passport if you're thinking of topping yourself?' Jez murmured.

'What about Ruth's?' asked Amber.

Cassidy tugged on his moustache. 'She hadn't taken hers. That's one of the reasons your father thought Marcus had planned her murder – left notes that made them sound suicidal – then taken his passport for a quick escape.'

'But why?'

'Maybe he was in trouble. How should I know?'

'So who was he?'

'All they had to go on was what me and some of the others must have told them; that he was Marcus Barclay and he'd been at Oxford and he'd spent most of the time since travelling round Asia.'

'Whoa, so what are you saying?' asked Jez. 'That Marcus Barclay didn't exist?'

'Oh he existed. He went to Oxford University in the '60s – that part was true.'

'But he lied about India and the travelling?' Amber guessed.

Cassidy finished off his wine in one long glug. 'Marcus Barclay never left Oxford. He died of meningitis just before his finals.'

CHAPTER 31

London
Amber

While coffee brewed, Amber spread out Ruth's photos on the parquet floor. Her mum had never understood why she preferred to sit and work on the floor rather than at a table. She liked to spread into space and see it all in front of her like a map.

The glass patio doors were wide-open letting in the noise of traffic. Black and yellow tulips that she had planted for her mum in old Wellington boots, basked in the late spring sunshine on the tiny fourth floor balcony. Opposite loomed an identical brick factory building converted into high-ceilinged flats, as severe and utilitarian as her mother's. Music played from her ipod: an Afro-Celtic CD she had bought from a shop near Newcastle station before leaving.

She paced between the kitchen area and the dining-cum-sitting-room, rearranging the photos like pieces of a jigsaw. She had listed their names on the back from what Cassidy could remember of the group.

Ruth and Marcus on the Galata Bridge, grinning.

Ruth, Juliet and Catriona, arms around each other, posing by a soggy looking tent, towels draped over the flysheet.

Ruth and Gino? (Cassidy wasn't sure of the name but he knew he was Australian) sitting close together on the bus.

A group of young women drinking beer in a beach bar – two blonde, one dark, one with tiny braids – the "Poshettes".

Lots of scenic shots with tiny figures in the distance that could be anybody – long hair and jeans - waving.

Marcus, Kurt and Juliet wearing towels round their heads like turbans and holding kitchen knives in their teeth. (Cassidy recalled them giving a tipsy performance of being bandits. They'd been drinking with some Turkish guys on Republic Day).

Peach and Chuck smiling outside Topkapi Palace.

A group in a dimly lit restaurant, the table cluttered with bottles and Tomas, the bearded German, giving the thumbs up.

A picture of school children posing under a Turkish flag.

A small boy standing in a huge pair of scuffed men's shoes, laughing at the photographer. (Cassidy thought the mosque in the background was Iranian, possibly in Shiraz).

Juliet squinting into fierce sunlight; the dusty bus and pale mountains in the background.

Cassidy looking up from cleaning some engine piece, smiling quizzically.

Devon playing guitar on a beach; Marcus with an arm round a Poshette (possibly called Mixie?)

Two blurred figures dancing, arms outstretched as if twirling in circles (Almost definitely Marcus and Juliet)

So what did these cheap amateur snaps tell her? That the overlanders were mostly young – twenties and early thirties – and having a good time (or at least putting on a smile for the camera). That they seemed a typical holiday group enjoying the moment and forming friendships, however transient or superficial. So what were they doing now? Were they all still alive? She doubted that the middle-aged Americans were, over thirty years on.

Souter's articles, which had come in the post a couple of weeks ago, told her little of the other members. The journalist had been focused on trying to flesh out Ruth and Marcus for his readers, their backgrounds and life stories, so he had gone after family members and old friends. The owners of Rainbow Tours had refused to give out names and addresses of any of the passengers to the press.

But Souter had tracked down a reluctant Cassidy and Maggie from Dublin (who had said the missing couple were mad as March hares and well capable of suicide) and a New Zealand couple over the telephone – but they had left the trip in Tehran.

The rest appeared to have scattered to the ends of the earth.

Amber had a sudden thought. What if, after all these years, some of the group were as curious as she was to find out what had become of the others? Perhaps they had reunited across the Web?

Her mum came in two hours later to find her still at her laptop, leg jiggling with suppressed energy.

'I'm onto something,' she told her excitedly. Before Helen had time to dump down her box of groceries, Amber was pulling her over to the screen.

'Hang on a minute - '

'Look Mum, there's a website for overland trips – it's amazing! One of the drivers from Asian Greyhound has set it up. See here, there are links to other companies and people are sending in photos and trying to contact others on their trip. It goes right back to the sixties.'

Amber clicked and scrolled. 'There're a few for Rainbow Tours. Listen to this one: Pat from Brisbane has emailed with stuff about her trip – Eastbound, 1976, left in autumn from London – that fits, doesn't it? She wants people to get in touch.'

Helen plonked the veg box on the floor. 'Does she mention any names?'

'Umm … yea: Lucy, Fran, Paul and two Americans she can't remember the names of. I'll ring Cassidy and see if he remembers Pat.'

Helen frowned at the screen. 'And if it is Ruth's trip, what will you do?'

'Get in touch with this Pat of course, find out more.'

Helen gave a worried smile. 'Sweetheart, why is this so important all of a sudden?'

Amber scooped back her hair. 'Dunno. Something to do with Gran maybe. Like I'm taking up where she left off – doing it for her I guess.'

Helen touched Amber's head in affection. 'Don't feel bad about not seeing her before she died. She knew how much you cared.'

Amber's eyes smarted. 'Yeah, I know.'

Out on the balcony she phoned Jez on his mobile. Her heart rate doubled at the sound of his voice.

'Sounds promising,' he said. 'Give me a minute and I'll nip downstairs. I'll get Cass to ring you back, okay?'

'If you're sure – or I could ring again in five?'

'No problem, he can use my mobile.'

She rang off wishing she could have thought of more to say to keep him talking longer. It was twenty minutes before her phone rang, showing Jez's number.

'Not my trip lass,' said Cassidy on hearing the details. 'It was Kiwi Don's – took the trip out after mine, two weeks later.'

Amber sighed in disappointment.

'Sounds an interesting site, mind,' Cassidy added. 'Got much about the buses?'

Amber smiled. 'Loads – photos too. You guys can get really excited over knackered old motors, can't you?'

Cassidy chuckled. 'I'll have to get Jez to show me on his computer thingy.'

Amber asked, 'don't you think it's strange that not one person off your trip has posted a comment on the site?'

'Not really, not when you think what happened.'

'I know, but people still had a cool time for most of it, didn't they? If I was one of them I'd want to know how all the others ended up.'

'Maybe they will.'

'Cassidy,' Amber hesitated. 'Would you let me put your name on? I could be your email contact, then if someone answers, you can decide if you want to get back in touch or not. There might be guys from your other trips too. All your fans out there.'

Cassidy snorted. 'If I didn't know you were such a sweet lass I might think you were taking the piss.'

'Me? Never,' Amber grinned.

'All right then. Wouldn't mind hearing from a few of the drivers.'

Amber registered with the site and posted a comment from Cassidy. Over the next two weeks, several replies came in reminiscing about long ago trips and asking for news. But not one of them was from the Rainbow Tours bus that her aunt had taken eastbound in the autumn of '76.

CHAPTER 32

'At Gúrg there is a stream so salt and bitter that none of our animals even would touch it ... The old road to Sistán used to follow the Gúrg valley, but robbers caused its desertion. Remains of kanats and mud-houses and a caravanserai afford proof that at one time a vain attempt was made to inhabit these inhospitable latitudes, which though so bitterly cold at the time we traversed them, are so hot in summer that the infrequent traveller has to wrap bandages round his stirrups to prevent his horse or camel being wounded from contact therewith.'

Major Euan Smith, Eastern Persia: an Account of the Journeys of the Persian Boundary Commission, 1876

Iran-Pakistan Border (Baluchistan province), mid November
Juliet

'But I thought you wanted to see Baluchistan?' Juliet cried in dismay. Abruptly, Kurt and Tomas had elected to leave the trip at Zahedan before crossing the border into Pakistan. Cassidy was extracting their backpacks from the roof-rack.

'We're already in it according to the Baluch,' Kurt said with his wry smile. 'All this area once belonged to them.'

'You know what I mean – the Baluchistan that my father knew.' Juliet felt ridiculously disappointed that they were going. Kurt had been a steady friend throughout the journey. She would miss his kindness and wry comments.

He touched her arm. 'I'm sorry but Tomas wants to visit Seistan and see what's left of the *Hamun* and the watercourses. And I'm keen to visit the Parthian remains at Kuh-e Khajeh.'

'But what about Quetta?'

'We think we might go there after the trip is over.'

'So you're meeting up with us again?'

Kurt smiled. 'Of course. We shall join you in Afghanistan.'

'Oh Good,' Juliet brightened. 'I'm relying on you to be my guide.'

There were hugs goodbye and instructions from Cassidy about where to meet up in Kandahar or Kabul. The Germans waved them away, disappearing in a cloud of dust as the bus gained speed.

'I told you they were spies,' Catriona joked.

That night the group crossed the border and slept in the custom's yard. Juliet felt her appetite for adventure return. She was ashamed at feeling so sorry for herself over the previous few days. Finally she was in Baluchistan! Would this most remote province of Pakistan be as vast, arid and empty as the desert they had just passed through? Sleepless at the thought, she rose at dawn to help her tent-mates make breakfast. Already the officials were setting up tables and chairs to conduct their business in the open air.

Suddenly, out of the morning mist came a wail of music as a brightly painted local bus hove into the compound. Spilling from it were blanketed figures, muffled against the cold with woollen scarves wrapped around large turbans, rugs slung over their shoulders like plaids and thick baggy trousers gathered at the ankles. The air crackled with the sound of throat-wracking spits and the bleat of a goat being carried off the bus.

'There are your Baluch,' Cassidy said, nodding at the moustachioed men.

Juliet gazed in fascination.

'Let's have a nose at that bus,' said Fran.

Every inch – even the ladder at the rear - was covered in multi-coloured designs: flowers, hearts, curling script and pictures of snow-capped mountains. Tinsel and mirrors adorned the windscreen and a small Christmas tree dangled inside the cab.

While they peered at the Pakistani bus, the Baluch came to gaze at theirs. Soon more buses and trucks were arriving, each more fantastical in its decoration. Passengers piled out and greeted each other. The customs yard filled up with moneychangers, cigarette sellers and blind beggars led around on sticks by small boys.

Juliet and Fran chatted with two Englishmen off one local bus while waiting to buy rupees.

'Hen laid an egg in the seat behind me,' one of them laughed. 'Wished we'd taken the train, but it only runs once a week if you're lucky.'

Cassidy questioned them about the route ahead. 'Had any trouble coming through?'

'No hassle, mate. Slept most of the way.'

The other one was less sure. 'Soldiers are a bit jumpy. There's a curfew in Nushki and Quetta.'

Juliet spent the day sitting upfront, gazing out of the window at the changing scene. She was glad that Marcus and Ruth had taken up residence on the back seat, sprawled out dozing, keeping to themselves. They'd hardly exchanged two words with her since Ruth's late night outburst.

The desert appeared sandier than before, the scrub more bushy and the villages neater with people sitting outside their mud huts on rush mats watching them pass by. At times the road petered out and Cassidy followed the tracks of camel traffic until they overtook their makers: long trains of heavily laden camels and their herders. It delighted Juliet to suddenly spot a cyclist riding through the desert.

'Where on earth has he come from?' she cried, waving at the man as they trundled past.

'Took a wrong turn at Dorking,' said Cassidy.

Further on, the landscape grew rockier and more stark; the plain littered with hills of shale like blackened sugar mounds.

'They look like slag heaps,' said Maggie.

'That should make Cassidy feel at home then,' quipped a Londoner. 'Isn't that right, mate?' he called out. 'It's all coal mines up your way.'

'Not enough pubs round here to keep me happy, bonny lad.'

97

Juliet was spellbound by the mysterious landscape. Other camels roamed without packs or attendants. Were they wild? Tomas had been knowledgeable about them. Kurt had interpreted a conversation around the campfire near Sirjan the week before.

'The single-humped were used on the Western Silk Route, the double-humped on the Eastern stretch. The two-humped camel is larger and slower but better suited to the desert – they can survive without water for two weeks after a long drink and grow thick winter coats for the freezing nights. Some say they can predict the desert winds and that they have a homing instinct – they have a habit of running off but always return when they are hungry.'

'Just like humans,' Juliet had joked.

It puzzled her that Kurt and Tomas should leave the trip at this point. Whenever they had talked about this part of the trip they had been enthusiastic, and they had helped persuade Cassidy to take the southern route. But perhaps Kurt thought he would find some of his beloved Buddhist petroglyphs around Seistan and by missing out the long drive to Quetta he would have more time to explore this shadowy borderland.

The hills grew into jagged ranges once more. They rolled away into the distance as petrified waves. Juliet caught glimpses of dark shadowy ravines, scarred with dried up watercourses, and an encampment of black nomadic tents with a woman in a red skirt bending over a fire. A line of goats made their way up a sheer cliff-face with a faint tinkle of bells, a thin black stream pouring itself into the mountainside and disappearing as if by magic.

When the fierce light mellowed behind the grey-purple mountains, Cassidy pulled into the walled compound of an army resthouse and got permission to pitch camp for the night. They cooked up rice and vegetable stew as the sky turned magenta. An army patrol returned and locked the gates behind them.

Cassidy took Juliet to drink tea, share cigarettes and talk cricket with the officer in charge. They sat in faded canvas camp chairs in a bare room made cosy by lamplight.

'We chain off the roads at night,' the Pakistani commander explained, 'to discourage our Baluch friends from making trouble after dark. That is when they are most lively.'

He seemed baffled as to why she would chose to come here. Juliet told him about her father. He nodded.

'Quetta can be charming in the spring,' he conceded, 'but this place -' He spread his hands in despair. 'It is nothing but sand and rock. Why the Baluch should want to fight over it is quite beyond comprehension. They should be glad that Pakistan is willing to share the benefits of a modern state.' He gave her a charming smile. 'Madam, you must visit Lahore – there you will see the heart of our great country – culture, good food and cricket.'

They struck camp early. A patrol went out ahead and heaved in the chains.

Shortly before reaching Nushki, Juliet rummaged in her bag for the threadbare old reconnaissance map that had belonged to her father. Long ago, her grandfather had marked on it where they thought his plane had come down. She couldn't find it. She searched again more frantically. When was the last time she had looked at it? She had a vague memory of spreading it out on a table in Tehran to show some of the others: the Londoners and Gwennie, and Kurt and Tomas. Surely no one would have taken it? She must have packed it away in her suitcase. She would check when they got to Quetta.

***

The bus rattled and jarred over the un-metalled road; for most of the day they sat in dust clouds with towels over their heads like faux nomads. Juliet's throat was parched and her eyes gritty. She couldn't even read, and she had long grown tired of staring at the desert. By afternoon they were climbing steeply through a ring of purple mountains.

The colours of the city came as a shock to the senses after long days in a world of tan and beige. Wide streets of neat white bungalows were shaded by green and gold trees, an open stall was stacked with bolts of turquoise and crimson cloth, while scooter-rickshaws painted in crazy hallucinogenic purples and reds raced them down the road.

They checked into the Ferdausi Hotel, and then strolled into town in the dying light to eat. There were signs in English as well as Urdu. After the silence of the desert, Quetta burst about them with the blare of hooters, bicycle bells, pop music and cries of street vendors.

'Baksheesh!' cried the crippled beggars.

'Hashish?' offered a youth.

'You are my like!' grinned a slim boy in a white baggy shirt with a gaggle of giggling friends who trailed the blonde Poshettes.

Cassidy recommended The Farah on Jinnah Road. 'Does toast and scrambled egg, and tea with milk.'

Juliet and Catriona joined him.

'Bread's like pan loaf,' Catriona said in delight.

'My Nan's favourite,' Juliet smiled.

After weeks of flat unleavened bread and Persian script, Juliet found it dislocating yet strangely comforting to find the familiar among the eastern. She knew much about Quetta from books; that it had once been no more than a sleepy *caravanserai* of mud huts until the British chose it as an army outpost for sorties into Afghanistan and the surrounding tribal areas; that alongside the civilian town was built a cantonment of barracks, hospital, church and club which became the largest garrison in British India; that an earthquake in 1935 had caused devastation, and when her father visited ten years later it was still being rebuilt. But she had not expected to find road signs in English or instant coffee or omelettes or *Chirpy-Chirpy-Cheap-Cheap* playing from a tinny loudspeaker.

She talked to Cassidy about tracking down Aziz Baloch.

'You'd be better searching tomorrow,' he said. 'There's a nine o'clock curfew.'

The bazaars were closing up as they emerged from the restaurant; a tension crept in with the falling night. Gas heaters in the bedrooms meant the first comfortable night's sleep for weeks and Juliet slept in. Peach and Chuck had waited for her.

'Mr Cassidy's taken the Australians to get visas for Afghanistan,' Chuck explained.

'Do you want some help finding your father's friend?' Peach asked.

Juliet wanted to go alone, but saw the eagerness in Peach's lined face. 'Thanks, that would be kind.'

Chuck insisted they had breakfast first; he chose the Metropole and ordered up steak and chips, coffee and pastries. Juliet forced down some tea and cake. She asked the waiter for directions to the address she had.

'In bazaar,' he told her, 'you ask in bazaar.'

Juliet's insides knotted in excitement as she led the way. Her father must have walked this maze of lanes. Here was the pulse of the place, the overgrown *caravanserai* of travellers and merchants and unveiled tribal women with kohl-eyed children on their hips. It turned out there were several bazaars, each merging into the next. Weaving their way through, they sidestepped camels pulling carts and boys carrying trays of tea on their heads. The air was pungent with the smell of fried samosas. Food kiosks sold sugar beet sticks, nuts and lurid sweets. Colourful scarves and hats hung like exotic birds in open-fronted stalls and clothes-sellers beckoned them in.

'Come! Come and drink *cay*!'

Peach was easily side-tracked.

'Just look at those dresses, ain't they just so pretty? Do you think Sherrie would like one, Chuck honey?'

The owner swept them in, sat them on a gaudily painted trunk and plied them with sweet milky tea, while a sea of beautiful clothes were spread before them: embroidered dresses of rippling golden velvet and caps stitched with winking mirrors. Peach fingered and sighed and dithered.

'There's just too much choice.'

Impatiently, Juliet showed the owner the address she had.

'Do you know Mr Baloch?'

The man's smile faltered. 'There are many called Baloch – it is common name.'

'But Aziz Baloch of Pishin Street?' she persisted. 'He had a clothes shop. Look.' She unwrapped the tiny waistcoat that her father had commissioned.

The shopkeeper inspected it. 'This is local made,' he admitted, 'is Baluch made.'

'But you don't know him?'

He waggled his head.

Juliet explained about her father. 'They made friends when he was stationed here at the end of the War.'

'I'm sorry. My family not here then. We in Delhi. I do not know this Mr Baloch.'

He turned smartly back to Peach. Juliet wondered if she had offended him. Then it struck her: he was a *mohajir*, one of the refugees who had fled India at Partition. Perhaps local traders like Aziz resented this outsider from Delhi. The man was just keeping his head down.

They made slow progress, Peach wanting to stop at every stall. Chuck gently reminded her of Juliet's search.

'Honey, I'm so sorry! We must find your man at once.'

She instantly became a woman with a mission, waving Juliet's piece of paper and loudly accosting each stallholder with requests for Aziz Baloch. A group of laughing boys gathered about and followed in their wake. 'You English? You take picture! Say cheese, English!'

But to Juliet's frustration, no one appeared to have any knowledge of the man who had sent postcards from Quetta. For someone who had traded in this town for decades, it was baffling how no one knew him. They gave up and returned to Jinnah Road to eat.

That night, standing under the stars sharing cigarettes with Cassidy, she puzzled over it all.

'There's something not right.'

'Must be a long shot trying to find him,' Cassidy pointed out. 'Most likely the bloke's dead.'

Juliet nodded. 'That's exactly it. It wouldn't have surprised me at all. But no one said that. It's like the guy never lived round here.'

'He could've moved or retired. Maybes it was just a trading address and he lived somewhere else.'

'Yes, but if so, why did no one tell me that?' She ground the cigarette butt under her boot. 'You know what's really strange? All along the trip people have bent over backwards to help, to offer themselves as guides and show us around. The people here are just as friendly, but when me and Peach asked for Aziz they just clammed up. You could see the shutters coming down.'

Cassidy gave his wry smile. 'Forbsy, I think you're being a bit over-sensitive.'

'I'm not! Come with me tomorrow if you don't believe me.'

'All right.'

***

They began at Manna Chowk and Suraj Ganj Bazaar. Cassidy did the asking. He did not mention Aziz by name and was soon directed to Pishin Street in the Mizan Chowk area. But all they could find were grocers selling piles of nuts, apricots and melons, and none of them knew Aziz. They searched the Liaquat Bazaar and the Rug market off Masjid Road; they peered into dark noisy workshops but were directed back the way they had come. On the point of giving up, a young bearded man in a wool tunic and baggy trousers appeared at their side.

'Please, I am Gulam. I can help. Follow me.'

101

Juliet glanced in surprise. 'You know Aziz Baloch?'

'Just come.'

As they walked, he told them he was a teacher from Kalat and that he went around the tribal areas trying to encourage the villagers to send their children to school. He knew Aziz because the merchant had given money to help teach illiterate villagers. Five minutes later they stopped outside a boarded up stall in a narrow side street. The windows above were shuttered and barred.

'He has gone away,' he said.

Disappointment engulfed Juliet. 'Where to?'

'Perhaps his village. Aziz is an old man, a sick man.'

'Where is that?'

Gulam hesitated. 'Dalbandin, long way west.'

'Oh!' Juliet cried. 'We drove past it two days ago.' How frustrating to think they might have driven right by Aziz's home.

'But the shop,' she persisted, 'does he still own it? He has family. Perhaps someone will come and open up soon. Is it worth giving a knock?'

Alarm flickered across the man's face and he glanced around. 'No, there is no one.'

'But I know he has sons – he mentioned them in letters to - '

Galum held up his hands. 'That is all I can say.'

'But I don't understand - '

Cassidy intervened. 'It's very good of you to help us. Perhaps we could buy you a *cay*?'

The man looked about to refuse, and then nodded in assent. At a tea stall two streets away, they perched on stools. The teacher talked earnestly about his job.

Finally Juliet asked, 'Is the Baloch family in some sort of trouble?'

He hesitated.

'There is trouble among some Baluch,' he said, dropping his voice so low she had to lean closer. 'Hot heads. Aziz has son like this. He is also called Aziz. He makes it dangerous for his family. That is why they leave.'

'So this son, he's a separatist?' When Galum looked quizzical, Juliet said, 'he wants an independent Baluchistan.'

He darted a look up the street, then nodded.

'So where is young Aziz? In prison?'

Galum shrugged and quickly finished his tea. 'I will guide you back to Mizan Chowk.' He walked quickly as if eager to be rid of them. As the streets broadened out, he stopped and pointed the way. Juliet knew this was her last chance.

'Please tell me how I can find Aziz now?'

His face grew stern. 'It is best not to ask these questions. Aziz is a good man. I am sorry he is gone, but you will not find him here.'

Cassidy gave Juliet a warning look. 'Thanks for your help mate.'

As the teacher turned to go, Juliet said, 'If you see him, will you tell him I came to find him? Thank him for his postcards.'

Galum gave the ghost of a smile and nodded. She watched him melt into the crowd.

CHAPTER 33

London
Amber

Kurt. Amber was in the middle of planting up a flowerbed at the entrance of the garden centre when the thought occurred. She had seen Kurt's face somewhere before, she was sure of it. She stood up and gazed along the half-planted row of impatiens. A month ago, she had packed away the photos and articles, deciding it a waste of time. What could she unearth that was new? It was over thirty years ago and she was no detective.

But Kurt's face was definitely familiar: perhaps from a textbook? Amber's interest at university had been Iron Age Britain, whereas Cassidy remembered the German archaeologist being obsessed with some kind of 'swirly rock symbols and anything ruined in the desert'. But Amber could still have come across Kurt's work in the course of her degree.

'They won't plant themselves!' her supervisor shouted. 'Get on with it, my lovely.'

Impatient for the end of her shift, Amber went on the Internet as soon as she got home. She trawled through sites matching Kurt and Archaeology. On the fourth attempt she found an article in an academic magazine, but it was all in German. The photo of the deceased man looked similar to the one in Ruth's instamatics. Kurt Kiefer. Amber googled the full name.

It threw up two references: one was as a speaker at a symposium in honour of a celebrated Cambridge academic and linguist, Professor Harold Bailey. Kurt Kiefer's work had led to a major find of Bactrian treasure in Afghanistan in 1978. Through these priceless artefacts of jewellery, coins and writing tablets, Professor Bailey had pieced together much of their long forgotten language and thrown valuable light on the mysterious civilization of Bactria.

The second was a short obituary in The Guardian newspaper of Kurt Kiefer, one-time curator of Middle Asian artefacts at the British Museum in the 1960s. It mentioned the Bactrian find and then listed some academic work on Buddhist petroglyphs in the late 1990s. Kiefer had set up a retreat called Bulbulak in former East Germany based on Buddhist principles, where he had died peacefully in July of last year. He leaves behind a wife, Roxane and a son, Al.

That's where Amber had seen this article before, on a long bus journey up to Weardale to visit her gran. She had read this edition of the newspaper from front to back. The mention of the archaeologist had lodged in her mind.

Amber re-read the article several times, trying to glean clues from the spare text. Kurt must have gone back out to Afghanistan after the trip, or had stayed out there until at least 1978. Where had all the treasure been stored after his breakthrough find? Kabul museum perhaps? Amber remembered hearing that some of the museum's artefacts had been smashed and defaced by the Taliban regime after the American bombings in 2001. The Taliban had blown up the giant Buddhas at Bamiyan too. Was that the museum that had been badly looted after the fall of the Taliban, or was she confusing it with the one in Baghdad and the Iraq war?

What had Kurt done between 1978 and his article writing of the 1990s? Afghanistan would have been off-limits to the archaeologist after the Russian invasion in 1980. And she guessed he couldn't have set up his retreat until after the Berlin Wall came down at the end of 1989. Had he stayed out east during the eighties or returned to Europe?

According to Cassidy, Kurt had been one of the passengers closest to Juliet. Had he been close to Ruth or Marcus too? Amber thought of the photo with Kurt, Juliet and Marcus drunkenly clowning about in Turkey. How frustrating that the one man who might be able to tell her something important was now dead.

Amber wondered what had become of Kurt's travelling companion, Tomas. And the retreat in East Germany: was it still running or had it collapsed with its founder? Bulbulak. It sounded Middle Eastern. What on earth did it mean?

CHAPTER 34

Amber's mobile woke her.

'I've been thinking 'bout what you said lass – bout Kurt and that.'

'Cassidy?' Amber asked, her head groggy.

'Aye. It was in Istanbul. The Scotch lass Catriona told me how Kurt was ganin' on about ancient symbols in the desert and Juliet was all excited cos she thought he could tell her more about Baluchistan where her father died. Well Marcus being Marcus had to go one better – he said he was related to some fella who'd mapped the whole of the area for the Brits in India – drawn up the boundaries or something. You know, Marcus made out he was well connected. Course we know now that was all bollocks. But it impressed Kurt and Juliet no end.'

Amber tried to focus. 'Can you remember who she said it was – the man who did the maps?'

She could hear Cassidy sucking in his cheeks as he thought back. 'Na. Name's long gone. Marcus was probably making it up any road.'

'Did Marcus have any old maps of Baluchistan?'

'I never saw him with one. But by the time we got to Pakistan, he and Ruth were keeping their heads down. We were in Quetta three days and I never saw them once. They booked into a different hotel from the rest of us – that's what they did until they disappeared – kept themselves apart. Juliet thought it was her fault – that it was her they were trying to avoid.'

Amber yawned and squinted at the digital clock by the bed. 'So why are you ringing me at half past two in the morning to tell me you can't remember the name of some map maker who probably didn't exist?'

Cassidy laughed. 'Is it that late? Sorry lass. It's just that it's spinning round in me head a lot of the time. Maybe there were things I should have noticed and didn't.'

'No, it's my fault for digging it all up again,' Amber said. 'Never meant to give you sleepless nights.'

Amber could hear Cassidy take a slug of something. Perhaps he was drinking and just felt lonely.

'How's Jez?' she asked.

'Canny. Working hard on some paper that needs to be finished soon. I remind him to eat.'

'Tell him good luck from me.'

'Will do. You coming up this way again?'

'I'd like to, but it's busy at work just now.' Amber yawned again.

'There was a map,' Cassidy said abruptly.

'Of Baluchistan?'

'Aye, Juliet had one – an old reconnaissance map from the Second World War - falling to bits but much more detailed that the tourist ones. She'd marked on where her father was supposed to have crashed in the Chagai mountains.'

Amber let him talk. She'd noticed how Cassidy liked to speak about Juliet, how his voice softened when he did.

'Map went missing. She thought the Germans had nicked it at first. But they swore blind they hadn't. She was upset like – wanted to show it to this Aziz Baloch in Quetta who knew her father. But it wasn't on the bus. Much later on – I think it was Benares - we had a big clear out before heading for Kathmandu – there was a rat on board nesting under the pedals. Found the rat but never found the map.'

'What about Marcus?' Amber asked. 'Could he have taken it?'

'That's what I thought. Juliet blamed herself, said she must have left it on a café table in Tehran. But I sort of convinced her it might be Marcus. Well he could've flogged it to buy dope, couldn't he?'

'So did she have it out with him?'

Cassidy let out a juddering sigh. 'Aye. There was this big nasty ding-dong. We were all a bit drunk – well I was – and I was getting a lot off me chest about Marcus screwing up the trip and being worse than useless as a co-driver. Apparently Juliet accused him of half-inching the map an' all. Marcus denied it and Juliet stormed off.'

'Did you sort things out with him later?'

'No, never had the chance.' Amber could hear Cassidy swallowing hard. 'It was the night they disappeared.'

* * *

Unable to get back to sleep, Amber made a black coffee with three sugars and padded into the living room. The blinds were open and some insomniac bird was trilling into the May night sky. She tore off bits of telephone pad, labelled them and placed them in a circle on the floor.

Juliet. Marcus and Ruth. Kurt. Cassidy. Map of Baluchistan. Brit-Indian boundary/map maker – 19th century? Juliet's father in plane crash. Buddhist Petroglyphs. Baluchistan – dangerous place to travel in 70s? Bactrian horde – relevant? Afghanistan. Buddhas of Bamiyan.

Amber swapped the pieces of paper around. How did they all fit together? Were they connected or was she just trying to force a fit? The mapmaker intrigued her. Perhaps Marcus had known something about him even if he wasn't an ancestor. This mapmaker – if he existed - must have been quite a guy to have travelled the wild tribal areas marking out borders, just to suit a bunch of Brits sitting in far off offices drawing random lines across vast tracts of desert. Lines that would mean nothing to the Baluch and Afghans whose land it was.

What a huge undertaking it must have been: surveyors and engineers, soldiers to guard them, local scouts to show the way, servants and cooks, pack horses and camels laden with supplies and cooking equipment. Amber thought of all the logistics needed on a modern archaeology field trip, let alone a survey expedition into remote Baluchistan in Victorian times. Surely there must be a record of it? The British were second to none at bureaucracy.

Amber tore off a blank sheet and placed it in the middle of the circle. Something would tie this all together. It was only a hunch, but she would go after it.

She dozed off on the sofa in her oversize Simpsons t-shirt. The sky was leaching pink when she came fully awake with a sudden thought. What if the real Marcus *had* been related to the mapmaker and the man posing as Marcus knew about the connection?

Amber scribbled 'the real Marcus' on another piece of paper. She placed it in the centre of her paper circle. If the mapmaker was a flesh and bone historical person, and the real Marcus had been related to him, then for Ruth's 'Marcus' to have known about this, he must have known the real Marcus pretty well indeed.

Cassidy, Souter and the police had all assumed that the impostor Marcus had picked an identity at random, chosen a man of similar age from a headstone or a death register. No one at Oxford had recognised the photo of impostor Marcus that Maggie had provided the investigation. Neither had the Barclay family. Souter had reported how Marcus's mother had become tearful at the suggestion that the man who had stolen her son's identity could be mistaken for her beloved child: her Marcus was taller and more athletic and he would never have grown a scruffy beard, or if he had it wouldn't have been ginger.

Amber stared at the two paper Marcuses. Could there be a link between the two that had been missed simply because no one had gone looking for it?

CHAPTER 35

Quetta, West Pakistan, mid November 1976
Cassidy

That night a group of them ate curry and rice pudding at the Liberty Cafe. The Aussies were having a noisy get-together with some fellow countrymen off an Encounter Overland truck. Cassidy tried to cheer-up a subdued Juliet.

'At least you tried. And you found where he lived – that was something.'

Juliet ground out a cigarette on her half-touched meal. She sighed, 'I know I was expecting too much, but he's always been this living link to my dad. I so wanted to meet him Cass.'

'I know,' he said gently, touching her hand. He hated to see her this down in the dumps. She drew back and lit up another cigarette. Perhaps he should get her some hash; help her chill out?

'Fancy a nightcap?' he asked. 'I've got a bottle of Johnny Walker back at the hotel.'

She smiled at last. 'I thought you were keeping that for bribing our way into India?'

'I've got more than one,' Cassidy grinned.

On the point of getting up, two posh blokes with neat moustaches who had walked in a couple of minutes before (he had noticed their thick well-cut overcoats) strolled up to their table. They introduced themselves as a doctor and lawyer, and welcomed them to their town. Cassidy was used to the casual friendliness of strangers on the road, but right now he was keen to get back to the hotel and whisky with Juliet. But they won him over when they started asking him about the bus and wanted to know how it had performed along the desert roads.

'Would you like to go for a drink?' the lawyer said with a conspiratorial wink. 'I mean a proper drink.'

'We were just heading back to the hotel,' Cassidy said, aware of Juliet's eyes glazing over at talk of motors.

'Please,' the lawyer exclaimed, 'you must let us take you to the club.'

'The old army club?' Juliet burst into life. 'In the cantonment?'

'Yes,' he beamed. 'You know it?'

'My father wrote about it – he was here many years ago.'

'Then you must come and see.'

The other added, 'perhaps some of your friends would like to join us? We will make a party.'

Before Cassidy could lob in an objection, the men were rounding up two Poshettes, Catriona and Fran, and ushering them all into the back of a large black 1940s Bentley. Cassidy found Aussie Fran on his knee.

'Geez this looks like fun!'

The doctor pulled Juliet into the front seat with him. As they raced through dark streets, Cassidy was aware of something hard digging into his buttocks. When they piled out he saw that a rifle lay across the back seat.

The lawyer unlocked large doors and in they went. Cassidy thought it was like a Hammer Horror film set: long corridors of dark panelled wood and red carpet, and not a dickie-bird around. The Poshettes whispered nervously, overawed. Finally they reached a huge room with two wood fires burning at either end, and a long polished bar down its length. Their footsteps echoed across the floor; the only furniture a few chairs.

Suddenly, half a dozen waiters popped up like Jack-in-the-boxes from behind the bar, dressed in green livery.

'Gin, whisky, beer?' the lawyer cried. 'Order what you like!'

As the drinks flowed, the girls grew noisy and the laughter of their hosts – who seemed to be drinking just as much whisky as Cassidy - echoed around the room. At one point, the doctor called for music and a waiter switched on a tape machine. The soundtrack to West Side Story boomed out.

'Dance Fran,' the doctor insisted, pulling the Australian to her feet and causing her to slosh beer on the polished floor.

'Doctor's orders!' the other one joked, as Fran tried to resist.

Cassidy noticed how the lawyer put his head close to Juliet and smiled at everything she said. He began to feel drunk; it was weeks since he had drunk this much, probably Turkey. He went off to find the toilet. One of the waiters came after him and steered him down a corridor to an enormous washroom with marble-topped basins and wooden seats on china bowls. Cassidy splashed icy water from a rattling tap on to his unshaven face. How on earth had they ended up here? He felt a flicker of alarm that he should be trying to get them back to the hotel. It must be well past curfew. These men, however rich, presumably couldn't give two fingers to the military.

Back in the bar, he saw Juliet standing alone at the furthest fireplace. She was smoking fiercely.

'What's up?' he asked.

'I want to go.'

'Aye, me too. Have you asked them?'

She nodded. 'They're not listening.'

It took another half hour to persuade the men to break up the party and drive them back to town. This time Juliet climbed in the back, Fran sat in the front. The lawyer drove too fast. Cassidy glanced nervously out of the window. Armed guards were patrolling the street.

They had to knock for the *chowkidar* to let them in. Outside her bedroom door, Juliet lingered as if she had something to say.

'Was that lawyer bothering you?' Cassidy asked.

'I'm not sure he was a lawyer.'

'Why not?'

'He knew I'd been asking for Aziz. How would a lawyer know that?'

Cassidy thought of the gun in the back of the car, but didn't want to make a big deal of it. 'Small towns talk, you know.'

She shook her head. 'There was something about him – about them both. Too watchful – like police.'

'What else did he say?'

'Said I shouldn't waste any more time trying to find him.' Her eyes welled up with tears. 'Said he was sorry to have to tell me, but Aziz was dead.'

CHAPTER 36

London
Amber

Helen worried about how much of her free time Amber spent closeted away in the British Library pouring over old books in the India room.

'What's so interesting?'

'The past, I guess,' she smiled.

Her mum did not believe in looking back or dwelling on things that couldn't be changed. She and her business partner Morella were busy putting together a new range of salads and deserts for their summer catering brochure. They were due to go to Le Marché in Italy shortly to source some organic olive oil.

'Why don't you contact some of your friends?' she suggested. 'Go out and enjoy yourself. I don't like to think of you rattling around the flat with no company while I'm away. Someone of your age shouldn't be …'

Amber eyed her. 'Don't stress; I'm not turning into a strange old grump like Dad if that's what's worrying you.'

Helen laughed self-consciously. 'I wasn't thinking that. I just want you to have some fun.' Her mum looked at the mosaic of paper scraps on the floor, anchored against the breeze by half-drunk mugs of coffee and jars of pasta. 'My sitting-room is turning into an archaeological site. How long is this going to go on do you think?'

'I'll clear it up soon,' Amber grinned, 'Brownie's promise.'

Her mother sighed and went to take a shower.

***

Amber sat at a wide desk making notes with the pencil she was allowed to take into the glinting modern library on Euston Road. Her ipod, mobile and biros were stored in a locker downstairs. A see-through plastic bag contained her purse and notebook. She re-read her latest notes.

Baluchistan – now called Balochistan – low level civil war since 1940s and Partition of India/Pakistan. British treaty of 1876 promised to respect sovereignty and independence.

Baluch chiefs wanted autonomy from Pakistan. Uprisings in 50s, 60s and again in 1973.

War between West and East Pakistan – East breaks away – becomes Bangladesh. Army then sent into Balochistan. Fighting until 1977. President Z.A. Bhutto – repression of Baloch. Martial law never lifted. Still occupied?

What was Britain's role at time of Independence? Did they promise Baloch autonomy?

Sandeman in charge of drawing up borders with Afghanistan and Persia (Iran). Pacified Baluch tribes by giving them positions and some power within British Indian administration – allowed own courts and customs, paid them for services such as guiding and intelligence. Sandeman learnt their language, treated with respect.
Check maps.

Amber logged her request for two tomes of reports of the Boundary Commission, and Stanford's Compendium of Geography: Asia Vol. II, by A H Keane, 1896. She went for coffee. Outside she could see office workers sunning themselves and chatting over sandwiches. *This is mad.* She suddenly yearned to be outside mixing with the living rather than ghosts from the past. Her limbs twitched with unspent energy. Why bother going back upstairs? It was all mildly interesting, but her research told her nothing about her aunt or travellers from the 1970s. None of this stuff was relevant.

Still, the librarians had bothered to summon up the material from some deep archive, so the least she could do was give it a quick flick through. Then she would stop. And take a weekend off. And maybe visit her dad. And stop off in Newcastle to see Cassidy. And Jez. Thinking about him gave her a buzzy feel in her stomach.

Back at her desk, the pile of books awaited. Amber leafed through the top one: a report from Sandeman about the Commission. She set it aside. Stanford's Compendium looked interesting but dense. Perhaps another time. The third one was a slim volume of maps drawn by surveyors of the new Afghan border with extracts from a journal dated 1884. Amber caught her breath at the author's name: Algernon Barclay.

Baluchistan, British India, 1884

'After days of dreary desert, of grey rock and violent sandstorms, the surprise of finding this mountain oasis could not have been greater. The sound of running water and the billing of doves appeared to come from inside the cliff wall itself, but the Baluchi goatherd showed us how to climb into the cave (the last resting place of some revered Mohammedan saint) and to the enclosed vale beyond.

We came out by a thundering waterfall that emptied into a deep green pool surrounded by tamarisks, junipers and date palms. Water was skilfully channelled along steep terraces that dropped away to the valley floor, where fat-tailed sheep grazed and unveiled women were threshing corn. The emerald and golden view, the puzzling scent of roses and the splash of fresh water, dazzled our desert-numbed senses.

What appeared from above to be crudely made huts of brushwood were, on closer inspection, solid mud-brick houses thatched with tamarisk boughs and overhung with wild vines. Men dozed with prayer beads or smoked their hubble-bubble pipes under a grove of mulberries. They claimed to be Sabaris, a fiercesome nomadic tribe of freebooters who inhabit the Afghan-Baluchi border. But they welcomed us with offers of green tea, curds and tobacco, and refilled our goatskins with water that was not in the least brackish. We were loathe to leave this Shangri-La, but had to make haste for the next staging post before nightfall, promising to visit on our return.

The nomads call this place Bulbulak which, I am told, is Persian for Hissing Water.

Capt. Algernon Barclay, Afghan Boundary Commission.

Amber sat back. Bulbulak. Was this the place after which Kurt had named his retreat? Had the German been there or just read about it as Amber had? It sounded mythical, too good to be true. Amber leafed through the rest of the report but there was no further mention of it. The soldier did not appear to have returned. Perhaps he'd been unable to find it again? Amber turned back to the original entry to study the accompanying map. She couldn't find it, yet it was listed in the index. She ran her finger down the crease where it should have been. Someone – maybe years ago - had carefully cut out the map with a sharp blade.

CHAPTER 37

Ruth's diary
Mon 22nd Nov – Day 58
Kabul, Afghanistan
Can't eat. Marcus brought me apple pie but couldn't face it. Electricity went off so room was dark and freezing. Smoked dope. Marcus has promised we won't be here much longer. All the others are staying at the Mustafa.

Had hot shower this morning and felt better. Marcus took me to Sigis' Restaurant and had an omelette. Cat Stevens was playing. There's a giant chess set in the courtyard that's lit up at night. No one's playing. Went to Istanbul Restaurant for something sweet. Marcus ate a huge bit of sponge cake with chocolate and raisins and grapefruit segments.

Juliet's knocking around with Kurt and Tomas; seems really pleased they've met up again. She's wearing a new Afghan coat. It's freezing all the time. Marcus haggled for some woollen boots for me, but the soles stink of animals. I don't see the point of buying anything. Not now. Marcus puts on a brave face, keeps saying it's not long to go. Soon it'll all be over. I wish it could've been different, but I don't see any other way out. He's brave for the two of us. I wish the end would hurry up and come.

CHAPTER 38

London
Amber

A well-spoken elderly voice belonging to a Hugh Coatsworth answered her query at the alumni office at Oxford University. Yes, Marcus Barclay had been at Lincoln College from 1964 to 1967.

'He studied Classics, rowed for the college. Died before completing his degree. Absolutely tragic.'

'What about guys who were there at the same time?' Amber asked. 'Are there any I could speak to - anyone who might remember him?'

'I could cross-check names against any who are still active in supporting our college events and appeals,' he said. 'Though I'd need their prior permission before you approached anybody.'

'Sure, and thanks.'

'Did you say you were a relation of the deceased?'

'Er, not exactly, but I'm doing research into the Barclay family. Did you know that one of Marcus's ancestors was a soldier on the Afghan frontier in the 1880s?'

'Really? How fascinating!'

Amber left her mobile number and email address and rang off before the archivist questioned her too closely.

She checked the Overlanders website for the first time in a week. There was a posting for Cassidy.

'Hi! You don't know me, but my parents were on your trip in '76 – Lucy and Shane Lavery. My mum says I've you to thank for being alive! I'm the baby she nearly miscarried. So just to say thanks. We still live in Napier – me and mum. Dad died of a heart attack five years ago. She'd love to hear from you – think she had a soft spot! Any news would be great. All the best, Jilly.'

With Cassidy's permission, Amber emailed a reply giving out his address in Newcastle to Lucy. He sounded pleased to hear from Lucy's daughter.

'I'm chuffed about that,' he said over the phone. 'Always worried that she might have lost the kiddy. That's made my day. Sorry about poor Shane like.'

A few days later, there was another new posting from Sid and Mixie in Australia. They had split up after the trip but got together five years later when Mixie had gone out to Australia to work. They'd been married now for twenty years and lived in Brisbane. Mixie had kept in touch with Suzy and Fay for a while but had lost contact ages ago. She had no news of any of the others.

'One of the Poshettes,' Cassidy said about Mixie. 'Never would have put money on those two staying together. Chalk and cheese. She was la-di-da and he was an Aussie miner. Good on 'em.'

'I'm due a couple of days off,' Amber told him. 'Do you need any help on the allotment?'

'Aye. Can always use a spare pair of hands.'

Amber booked a train ticket for the middle of the following week. She checked Jez's status on Facebook: it was still single. The day before she travelled a call came through from Hugh Coatsworth at Oxford.

'I've got a possible contact for you: Alex Wheeler. He was a contemporary of Marcus Barclay and rowed with him. Wheeler worked for Oxfam, and then did something in government. He's a consultant now, semi-retired. Lives in Yorkshire. Says he doesn't mind speaking to you, though he doesn't think he'll be much help.'

Amber scribbled down the details. 'Thanks anyway.'

That night, as she packed a bag, she almost rang her dad. It upset her that he was so alone in the world. She still felt bad about her pathetic reaction to Daniel's fessing up to his German-Scottish birth parents. Perhaps she should be trying to track down her father's real family – *her* real grandparents - instead of spending so much time and energy on Ruth's tragic story?

Amber brought up Daniel's number on her mobile, and then lost courage. Her dad was hopeless on the phone and she always ended up talking for her country to fill up the awkward silences. Daniel didn't have Internet access at home either, despite Amber's nagging. Instead, she scribbled him a chatty postcard that told nothing about her researches into Ruth's trip, and posted it on the way to the station.

CHAPTER 39

'Thence we were conducted to Bamian by the precipitous defile of Pimuri and the volcanic valley of Zohawk. The Pimuri defile is of a peculiarly wild character. The mountains that wall this narrow ravine have evidently been rent asunder by some tremendous subterranean convulsion. Their bases nearly join, and their sides rise almost perpendicularly. Beetling crags threaten the traveller from above, whilst immediately below his insecure pathway, a brawling stream cascades through the length of the chasm. At one place the stream is bridged over for a distance of two hundred paces by a portion of the mountain that has fallen across the ravine.'

Journey to the Source of the River Oxus, by Capt John Wood, Indian Navy, 1872.

Bamiyan, Afghanistan, late November 1976
Juliet

She had felt on edge all day. Perhaps it was the sight of the local bus jack-knifing on the bridge in front of them and blocking the mountain road. Cassidy had sent them to a local tea shop while they waited for the way to clear. Juliet knew she should be relishing the moment, but couldn't. The views of snowy mountains and rushing rivers were stunning. The autumnal trees glowed golden in the sunlight and the air was so clear and pure it was like drinking iced water. Foothills of spices, dried fruits and watermelons lined the roadside. The Afghan passengers sat around patiently chatting and drinking tea. It was a peaceful mellow scene in a beautiful country and yet Juliet couldn't fully enjoy it.

She still smarted from her disappointment in Quetta. Finding Aziz Baloch would have been the highlight of the trip, cancelling out her bruising humiliation over Marcus and Ruth's rejection. From the teahouse she watched the pair walking up a nearby slope, hand in hand, ignoring Cassidy's instructions not to wander off, then turn to gaze at the distant peaks of the Hindu Kush. Juliet's resentment had grown as the day went on. When Marcus had high-handedly ordered them all off the bus on an icy hairpin bend, she had snapped, 'you're not the driver, it's up to Cassidy.'

In defiance, she had remained on the bus, but her nerves had been frayed by the bus slipping backwards and Cassidy asking her to get off just in case.

Now the group was packed into a snug teahouse as the temperature plunged and night fell. There was a general feeling of euphoria at having safely reached the high valley of the Buddha statues. The friendly waiter brought out endless trays of food and tea, kept the central stove stoked up and grinned at his customers as they sang songs, played cards and lay back on their sleeping bags.

'Have a swig of this Forbsy,' Cassidy said, shuffling over to her side in the dim lamplight.

Juliet drank from the bottle of brandy he proffered. The spirit ripped down her throat like fire.

'Thanks,' she gasped and took another gulp. It warmed and numbed her at the same time.

Cassidy reached for an empty tea glass and filled it for her.
'What's eating you?'

Juliet sighed. 'The whole Quetta thing. And bloody Marcus. Rehman was right; he's a manipulative, cold-hearted bastard.'

'I'll drink to that.' Cassidy took a long slug from the bottle. 'So you're better off without him.'

'Yes, but I worry about Ruth. He completely dominates her.'

'That's her choice.'

'It's like she's under his spell. I know how he can turn on the charm. I think he's deliberately keeping her away from the group – they're not even in the same *chaikhana* as the rest of us. What's the point of being on the trip?'

They talked and drank. Cassidy tried to divert her with talk of seeing the giant Buddhas the next day. But her mind kept coming back to what rankled.

'Do you think it was Marcus who stole my father's map?'

Cassidy nodded. 'Who else?'

'I could've left it somewhere.'

'You're not that careless, not with something so precious.'

'But why? It's really getting to me.'

Cassidy put an arm about her.

'Hey Forbsy, I'll not have him upsetting you any more. Come on, we'll gan and have it out with him.'

He struggled to his feet and pulled her up. Outside in the frozen air they staggered unevenly in the darkness. The brandy had taken effect quicker than she'd realised.

The sight of Marcus and Ruth holding hands across the rough wooden table ignited Juliet's anger.

'Where is it?' she demanded. Ruth looked startled. She'd been crying. 'My father's bloody map! You took it and I want it back.'

Marcus gave her a pitying look. 'Not guilty. Ask Kurt and Tomas about it.' He turned back to Ruth. It was obvious they had interrupted an emotional moment.

Juliet jabbed him in the back. 'Don't turn your back on me! Prove to me you don't have it.'

Marcus shifted round. 'You two have been drinking, haven't you?' He teasingly wagged a finger. 'Let me order up some tea to clear the head. Let's all try and be civilized.'

Suddenly Cassidy sprang forward. 'Don't patronise us, you stuck-up prick! I've had it up to here with you. You've been bad news right from the start. All you've done is use my trip as your own play thing. Couldn't care less about anybody else. You're not even a half-decent

119

driver. You wouldn't know a carburettor if it jumped up and bit you on the arse.'

To Juliet's fury, Marcus barked with laughter. 'You're absolutely right there old chap. Got me in one.'

She wanted to slap his face, but Ruth's anxious look held her in check. Well the wretched girl was welcome to him.

'I'm not staying to listen to anymore,' Juliet cried. 'You're an arrogant pig! I feel ashamed I was taken in by you for so long. I don't know why the pair of you bother to stick around – except it's a free ride for you all the way to Kathmandu, isn't it, Marcus?'

She spun round and stormed out of the *chaikhana*.

Lying on the floor of the other teahouse, head spinning, she felt bad for deserting Cassidy but couldn't have borne another minute under Marcus's gaze. His blue eyes had been almost feverish with suppressed excitement, the way they always were when he succeeded in provoking an argument. Cassidy returned but said nothing. He sat polishing off the brandy, slurring the words to American Pie.

Juliet woke, stiff and disorientated. Someone stepped over her. She saw Cassidy heading out of the door. Was he going to check on Marcus and Ruth? Suddenly she was engulfed with guilt about the tongue-lashing she and Cassidy had given them. She had no proof about the map. Sober, her outburst seemed petty and immature – it must have sounded like sour grapes at being spurned as Marcus's lover. And she should never have said such hurtful things in front of Ruth.

Quickly, Juliet got up, pulled on her boots and followed Cassidy outside. Glancing up the road in the mauve dawn light, she was surprised to see him making off towards the cliffs and the Buddhas. Something wasn't right.

She barged into the *chaikhana* opposite. Two figures stirred under blankets close to the stove.

'Ruth – Marcus – I'm really sorry about last night -'

A round-faced youth squinted up at her and an older man scrambled to his feet.

'*Cay* lady?'

Juliet peered around the room. Two grubby foam mattresses – the kind used by Rainbow Tours – lay against the far wall, empty.

'Where are they?' Juliet asked, pointing.

The men looked as baffled as she was.

Moments later, she was running up the road, guilt trapped in her chest, to tell Cassidy that Marcus and Ruth were gone.

CHAPTER 40

Kabul, Afghanistan
Cassidy

The day after Bamiyan, Cassidy got them cleaning out the bus. It was choked with dust. He did a day's maintenance: checking spark plugs, replacing hose, greasing pipes, buying petrol before leaving Kabul. If he kept busy he didn't have to think about Posh Boy and Ruth. The next day he sensed a restlessness in the group; they had bought what they wanted and eaten in most of the cafes on Chicken Street. Two Poshettes and Devon had the shits.

'Everything's going straight through me, man. It's like Niagara Falls.'

Cassidy told them to drink sweet tea and eat dried toast. 'Apple that's gone brown helps an' all.' He gave them drops of tincture of iodine for their water bottles. 'Sterilising tablets are bugger all use against amoebic bacteria. This'll sort you out.'

'Hey, Papa Cass to the rescue,' Devon grinned before diving off to the toilet once more.

Juliet had the opposite problem, her stomach so bloated she couldn't do up the zip on her skirt. Cassidy gave her Senacot and bought her a huge bunch of grapes and dried figs.

'Keep the fluids up Forbsy.'

He was glad to help. Practical stuff he could cope with; mind games stressed him out. By this stage in any trip, conversation always boiled down to what went in the top end and out the bottom. Forget the forts and palaces; overlanders could talk all day about the state of their stools – or lack of them.

Early next morning he packed up the bus in the dark to the blare of music, traffic and the early calls from vendors. With no sign of his wayward co-driver and girlfriend after four days – he hadn't expected them to turn up – Cassidy extracted their rucksacks and Marcus's tent and left them at the Mustafa with a note to say they had gone ahead.

Soon they were leaving the broad plain and twisting down the Kabul Gorge. Dizzying drops and hairpin bends plunged them deeper down the dark canyon. Cassidy held his nerve at the wheel as they passed wrecked vans left at cliff edges as cautionary tales. By the end of the day, they were driving through a fertile valley to Jalalabad, surrounded by trees and irrigated fields. Sundown beat them to the border, so they camped on the Afghan side, lying out in the mild open air without bothering to pitch tents.

Cassidy lay listening to the night sounds: a donkey braying, a wailing singer, a night watchman shouting into the night, and Catriona snoring. He felt a protective swell of affection for the group. He might have been landed with all the driving to do from now on, but he would make sure they all arrived safely in Kathmandu before Christmas.

'Stop worrying about them,' Juliet whispered.

Cassidy had not realised she was lying so close in the dark.

'It's not your fault.' She rolled a little closer. 'I talked to Kurt about it yesterday. He thinks they've been planning to jump ship since Iran. He made me feel a whole lot better.' She stretched out a hand and laid it on his shoulder. 'You okay?'

'Aye, I'm all right.'

He watched her roll onto her back, her nose and cheekbones outlined like marble, and felt a sweet yearning.

'God, aren't those stars beautiful?'

His chest tightened at the wonder in her voice; it was just how he felt about her.

'I read somewhere,' she went on, 'that the Milky Way is the path of Prophet Mohammed racing through the night sky on his winged horse? Isn't that the most romantic thought?' she murmured. 'Galloping stars.'

Cassidy wished in that moment he could tell her he loved her. But guilt held him back and he never said the words that heaved in his throat.

They woke to find themselves sleeping on a thoroughfare, Afghan travellers stepping over them to get to the border crossing. After a lengthy wait and search of the bus by border officials – inside, on top, in the boot – they passed on to Pakistan and a scruffy border post of money-changers and simple *cay* shops with big wicker benches like hammocks swinging in the dust.

'You can't be seen taking photos down the Khyber Pass,' Cassidy instructed, 'and we can't stop on the road. So you'll have to take them while we're moving – but don't let the truck behind see any cameras. All right?'

They drove on down the barren mountain pass, speeding past pack ponies with small boys in attendance and stopping briefly at Landi Kotal, a village of tall fortified houses and a dark bazaar with open drains selling hunks of dripping meat, knives and hashish. The locals strolled around with guns slung over their shoulders like workers with haversacks. Cassidy was always wary of stopping in the middle of Pathan country and soon had them rounded up and away.

At Peshawar they were stopped at a checkpoint searching for fruit and veg. A guard slit their Afghan fruit, chucked some out and waved them on. When they crossed the Indus at Attock Fort, the countryside began to roll out into a magic carpet of green fields and the clashing colours of noisy market towns. Cassidy felt happier the further on they drove. The Punjab: one of his favourites. Everything was warmer and livelier, more energetic and pulsating, ridiculously cinematic – like seeing England on acid. He whistled as he drove. The following day they reached Lahore.

CHAPTER 41

Newcastle
Amber

As the train slowed over the Tyne and Amber saw the series of bridges leaping away downriver, her excitement quickened. She imagined finding Jez at his flat, and having tea with him before going to look for Cassidy who would be pottering about at the allotment.

'Jez is out,' Cassidy said, appearing at his door in baggy pantaloons, bare-chested and bleary eyed like a pantomime pirate. 'Haven't heard him since yesterday. Celebrating with a friend whose exams have just ended.'

'God you look rough,' Amber grinned, hiding her disappointment and following him inside.

'Feel like death warmed up,' Cassidy grunted, 'or not very warmed up. I meant to get the place tidy, get the bed settee made up before you came.'

'No worries, I'll do it later.' Amber dumped down her bag. The sitting-room was even more cluttered than she'd remembered with mismatched furniture in mustard yellow and browns, two ancient TVs and a bicycle in bits. Faded hangings of printed horsemen and exotic birds hung loosely on red and yellow walls. Dusty spider plants and ferns sprouted from glazed pots and fought for light on the windowsill.

Amber pushed Cassidy into a chair and went to make a pot of tea.

When she returned he said, 'Found the old tour brochure.' Cassidy waved nicotined fingers at a tattered booklet with the picture of a bus by a turquoise lake. 'Thought you might be interested.'

'You bet!'

Amber leafed through it, marvelling at the string of famous names: Tehran, Kabul, the Khyber Pass, Amritsar, Kashmir, Delhi, the Taj Mahal, Kathmandu. When she looked up, Cassidy was hunched on the floor with eyes closed.

'You okay?' she asked.

'Aye, lass.'

'Can I get you anything?'

'Just pour the tea, pet.'

Amber told him about her researching at the British Library, the missing map and her hunch that impostor Marcus knew the real one well. Cassidy said little. Amber worried that she shouldn't have come.

'I could find somewhere else to stay, no sweat,' she offered.

'Not a bit of it,' Cassidy rallied. 'I'm sorry lass. It's just I'm not sleeping well.'

Amber said no more about Marcus and Ruth. She encouraged Cassidy out into the June sunshine and sat him in a deck chair while she weeded the allotment and lifted some new potatoes. She insisted on cooking for him that evening and sent a text to Jez inviting him down to eat.

He found them sharing Cassidy's hookah and listening to Peter Frampton on an old portable record player. The vegetable chilli had dried out but they ate it washed down with a bottle of red wine Amber had brought as a present.

'Shiraz,' Cassidy said, 'Forbsy's favourite.'

Clearing up in the kitchen, Jez whispered to Amber, 'he's been talking a lot about her lately – Juliet – and that trip. Think he's remembering stuff he's not thought about for years – perhaps not wanted to.'

He was wearing a green t-shirt, his feet were bare, and he smelt of musky aftershave. Amber felt small shocks like electric prods each time she met his look.

'Perhaps I shouldn't go on about it anymore. I think it's making him ill.'

He touched her arm. 'No, I think he wants to talk. As long as we're here to support him if he finds it tough.'

Amber nodded. She liked the way he included her. He wanted her to stick around, or she hoped that's what he meant. Later, after they'd gone to the corner shop for another bottle of wine, Amber spread out her paper circle.

'Why would Kurt name his retreat in Germany after a place in the Baluchistan desert that might never have existed? I can't find any other reference to this Bulbulak anywhere.'

'He must have read the same book you did,' Jez suggested. 'You said he used to work in London in the 60s. He might be the one who cut out the map.'

'But what was so important about it?'

Cassidy said, 'he was dead set on finding some rock carvings in that area. He and Tomas jumped ship in Zahedan on the Iranian border to gan off and look at some ruins. Didn't see them again until Kabul a week later. Maybe he found this Bulbulak place.'

Amber sat cross-legged moving the pieces of paper around, her large silver thumb ring glinting in the candlelight. Jez sat opposite, his chin resting on a fist, frowning in concentration.

'Okay,' Jez said, 'so even if Kurt and Tomas were up to something – on the look out for archaeological treasure say – what has that got to do with Marcus and Ruth's disappearance?'

Amber sighed. 'Maybe nothing.'

'Maybe something,' Cassidy said quietly. They both looked at him and waited. 'Kurt didn't seem that surprised that the pair of them had up and left and gone north. Juliet told me later on that Marcus had shown a lot of interest in Kurt's theory about Bactrian treasure. Kurt said it was a matter of time before something was found – a rich civilization couldn't just vanish into thin air. Kurt thought Marcus might have headed off to try his luck.'

'Sounds a bit far-fetched,' Jez said. 'Marcus wouldn't know where to start, would he?'

'And winter was coming on,' Amber added, 'it would have been a crazy thing to do.'

124

'Well he was always one to take the daft option if he could,' Cassidy grunted. 'He might have holed up somewhere for the winter and started searching in the spring.'

'Okay,' Amber said, pushing hair behind her ears, 'but wouldn't the police have found them when they started searching?'

'Have you any idea how remote those mountains are? Even the Afghans don't know all the pathways through the Hindu Kush. Would be a needle in a haystack job.'

'What about Ruth?' Jez asked. 'Would she have survived hiding out in the mountains?'

'She was hardy enough,' Cassidy conceded. 'Ruth was never one to get sick or have the squits like half the others. Don't remember her going missing at mealtimes either – not until she went all unsociable.'

Amber said, 'Did you tell the police about your hunch?'

'Not my hunch; Juliet and Kurt's.' Cassidy looked uncomfortable. 'Told them what I knew, that they'd headed north to Lake Band e-Amir. I thought all Kurt's talk of treasure hunts was a bit too James Bond at the time. How was I to know he'd discover a horde of gold a couple of years later? Anyways, I knew nothing about any of it till you told me the other day.'

'That's right, you weren't to know,' Amber said quickly, 'none of you did.'

Jez continued to puzzle over the paper jigsaw. 'But it doesn't tie in with Bulbulak, does it? Marcus and Ruth went north; Bulbulak's to the south in Pakistan. Where's the connection?'

'Maybe there's more than one Bulbulak,' Amber suggested. 'It means Hissing Water – like a waterfall or a spring I suppose – so it might have been a common name but just never written down.'

Cassidy struggled to his feet. 'I need me pit. I'll leave you two Indiana Joneses to work it all out.'

Amber made tea. She didn't want Jez to disappear upstairs. She settled down close to him on the sofa, their shoulders touching. They spoke softly so as not to disturb Cassidy.

'I think he had a thing going with this Juliet,' Jez confided.

'Can't have been for very long,' Amber mused. 'Once the trip was over he never saw her again did he?'

'I'm not sure – he's never actually said.'

'Has he got a partner now?' Amber asked. 'One of Souter's articles mentioned him with a Paula.'

'No one since I've known him. I've got a feeling he was married once though – long time ago. There's a photo at the allotment of him in a smart suit and shorter hair with this pretty girl in a huge floppy hat – real retro looking. I asked him who it was and he just said someone from his past and not to be so nosy.'

'It's a nice nose,' Amber said, touching the tip of it playfully. When he smiled, she leaned towards him and brushed his lips with a questioning kiss. They looked at each other for a long moment.

'You've got fantastic eyes,' Jez said.

'I've been thinking the same about you. Can't get them out of my head.'

'That's nice.' He leaned against her and pressed his lips to hers. They kissed long and slow, touching each other, exploring.

After a while, Jez murmured, 'you don't have to sleep on Cassidy's lumpy sofa, you know.'

Amber's insides lurched. 'Oh, yeah?'

'Yeah.' He kissed her again. 'I really like you Amber. I'd really like ...'

Her heart pumped harder. 'Cool,' she smiled, 'me too.'

She held his hand as he led her upstairs.

His bed was unmade. 'God, sorry about the mess.' He turfed a pile of clothes onto the floor.

'I like your mess,' she said.

He laughed and stripped off. The sky beyond the un-curtained window was still violet with dying light as he helped Amber shed her clothes too. The bed smelt of his spicy body spray and a musky male smell. She was almost sick with wanting him.

After they made love, Jez pulled a sheet over them and Amber lay with her head on his chest. His heart hammered below her ear. She shook with small tremors from released energy like aftershocks.

'Wow, Amber, that was lively,' he said, his breath slowing.

'This was such a good idea,' Amber grinned.

They lay like dozing cats, Jez playing with her hair, she stroking his arm.

'What about Ruth's friends?' he asked.

For a moment she wondered what he was talking about. She was still in a dreamlike, semi-euphoric state.

'Friends?'

'From catering college. Perhaps she wrote things to them that she never told her parents. Isn't that what girls do all the time, message each other?'

'Umm, that's a thought. Souter might have spoken to them. Not that he quotes any friends in his articles.' Amber drew circles on his arm with a finger. 'But you're right – Ruth was in Edinburgh for two years before the trip – she must have made some friends. Dad said she had a good time there.'

Jez fell asleep with an arm curved around her waist. Amber lay awake not quite believing her luck. Some time in the night she heard Cassidy moving around downstairs, flushing the toilet, running a tap, maybe putting on a kettle. The soft beat of music – possibly Dylan – murmured below. She felt a pang for the solitary man and wondered if she should slip downstairs to see if he was okay. What did he think of her not being there? Or was his mind too distracted by ghosts from the past to care?

Something was keeping him awake at night. What was it that Cassidy couldn't tell her?

CHAPTER 42

'Life in a Kashmir house-boat is very like a summer holiday spent in one on the Thames. But how infinitely more enchanting are our surroundings! The Dal Lake is one of the great attractions to Kashmir's visitors. The water is so clear that the reflections of the surrounding mountains are perfect. Chenars and willows, picturesque chalets, dark cypresses, blue distance, and snow mountains, make a picture hard to equal anywhere. Graceful little fishing-boats, called "Shikharas," skim about with sails like white wings.'
Kashmir, by Hon. Mrs C.G. Bruce (Finetta Campbell), 1911

Srinagar, Kashmir, India, early December 1976
Juliet
On the houseboat, standing in the antiquated tin bath under a hot shower, Juliet felt the tensions of the past weeks wash away. She had misjudged Marcus, and over-mothered Ruth. Neither needed her. Their threesome had been a bit of naïve fun, their friendship shallow and transient. The more she thought about it, the more she realised that Marcus and Ruth only wanted each other – probably had done for weeks. Nothing to do but write it down to experience. She hoped this stop in Kashmir would give others a fillip too.

Since Kabul, the group had been jaded; beset with petty bickering, stomach upsets, homesickness and lethargy. Maggie had left Australian Gino's tent and was back with Devon. Chuck was being snappy with Peach, while the Liverpudlians had stopped speaking to each other altogether except to hurl insults the length of the bus.

Only Cassidy seemed in buoyant mood, trying to rally people's spirits. 'Everyone gets sick of the bus at some point – then they get their second wind.' To which Fran had said, 'Struth, I've got enough wind to power a hot air balloon.'

Beyond the spray of warm water, the air was icy cold, but Juliet could smell rich cooking coming from the kitchen in the boat behind. Vegetable soup, duck and roast potatoes, stewed pear: that's what their houseboy Noor had announced when he'd rowed them back across Dal Lake in the slim shikara, after a day's sight-seeing around Srinagar town.

Houseboy! What a ridiculous title: he was her age or older. For several generations, his family had run The Golden Bell houseboat and lived on a draughty vessel at the back. She imagined nothing much had changed on the Bell since Edwardian days: the dark panelling, the heavy furnishings and pictures, the old wood burning stove and oil lamps when the electricity faltered.

For the first time in weeks, they sat down at a dining table again – Fran and Gwennie, Kurt and Tomas, Catriona and herself – and ate to stupefaction. The following day was just as indulgent. A breakfast of porridge, omelette, tea and toast was followed by another shikara trip across the lake to brown wintry Mughal gardens, their bare trees stark against the ice-capped mountains, and then back - a flash of blue kingfisher leading the way - for a lunch of lamb and vegetables. That afternoon, sellers of shawls, jewels, carpets and knives called and spread out their wares for the tourists. Juliet bought a garnet to set in a ring and lazed about reading until supper was served. Noor dressed up in a crisp white jacket to serve them curried mutton, cauliflower and rice, followed by bananas and custard.

Later that evening, raised voices echoing across the calm water announced the arrival of visitors who broke their soporific state. Chuck and Peach, Cassidy, Devon, Maggie and Gino clattered into their sitting-room with a blast of cold air.

'We've come to play charades!' Maggie announced. 'We've been on the gin and limes so our acting will be better than yours.'

Cassidy plonked a bottle of brandy on the table. Chuck, who didn't normally drink, sloshed large measures into their empty teacups. Juliet sensed a belligerence about them, something simmering in the air, as if they had come here only to divert an argument. Too long cooped up together no doubt. Kurt must have felt it too, for he hurried to fetch chocolates bought from a passing shikara and handed them round.

'Film titles,' Maggie ordered. 'Two teams. We give you one to do then we swap.'

Tomas was first up and mimed Gone with the Wind, which Juliet guessed in seconds. They gave Cassidy the Erotic Adventures of Zorro; his team failed to get one word in the time allowed. This provoked a loud argument and accusations of foul play. They gave Kurt, All Quiet on the Western Front. This was followed by two more British war films for the Golden Bell team. The atmosphere grew heated.

'That's not fair and you know it,' Juliet protested.

'It's okay,' Kurt tried to calm things, 'we'll give them Nietzsche's existential holiday.'

'Foreign movies shouldn't be allowed,' Chuck growled, 'especially not Nazi ones.'

'Nietzsche,' Juliet stifled a giggle, 'not Nazi.'

'There's no such film,' retorted Maggie.

'*Ja*, it was a joke.'

'Come off it you guys,' shouted Fran, 'we Aussies don't know any of these Pommy films either.'

'Everyone knows the Dambusters,' said Chuck, glaring at Kurt. 'Plucky Brits against your Hitler.'

As the game disintegrated ill-temperedly, Devon aimed a jibe at Chuck. 'Had enough flag waving for one day, dude? Bet even your underwear's made outta them.'

'I wouldn't expect a draft-dodger like you to stick up for your own kind.'

'He's not -' Cassidy began.

Devon laughed back manically. 'Man, I wish I'd had the balls to dodge 'Nam. I wouldn't be so fuckin' crazy.'

'People like you make me sick.'

'What, crazy people or nigger people?'

Instantly the atmosphere tensed.

'People who run down my country,' Chuck spat out his words. 'My brother died in France so that you low-lifes could be free.'

'Free?' Devon sneered. 'Yea, free to napalm Charlies, while you old men hide at home behind your flags.'

They squared up to each other across the table.

'I was the wrong age - I'm not afraid to fight!'

'Steady lads.' Cassidy stood up to intervene.

Devon taunted. 'Must kill ya to have a son in the Peace Corp, eh dude? And workin' for all them darky Nepalese too.'

'Don't you dare bring Gerald into this!'

'Oh no,' Maggie joined in, 'we mustn't say anything about Saint Gerald. Was the feckin' Immaculate Conception when he was born.'

Juliet saw the shock on Peach's face and said, 'Maggie, lay off.'

Maggie snorted, 'don't pretend you're all holier than thou – you're just as sick of all the Gerald this, Gerald that crap we have to listen to. We've all laughed behind their backs.'

'No we haven't.'

All at once Peach sprang up, knocking over her chair. 'Stop it all of you! Just stop it!' She burst into tears.

Catriona rushed over. 'Now look what you've all done.' Hugging Peach, she said, 'don't listen; they're all smashed. I canna wait to meet Gerry, he sounds brilliant.'

Peach continued to sob. Juliet shot a look at Cassidy.

'Let's call it a day, eh?' he said.

'Tell them,' Chuck said harshly.

Peach looked up with puffy red eyes.

'Tell them the truth, Peach.'

'Not now, Chucky.' She looked scared.

'If you won't, then I will,' he snapped.

'Please, Chuck -' She gripped onto Catriona.

'It's okay,' Catriona soothed.

'It's not okay,' Chuck bawled, 'it'll never be okay! This whole darn idea was a stupid mistake – coming with you people – pretending to be young and hip like we could recapture what Gerry felt, what Gerry did - '

'Don't,' Peach wailed.

'As if it could turn back the clock,' Chuck ranted. 'We shouldn't be here. We shoulda gone straight to Nepal and got it over with, instead of weeks with you guys – watching you drink and drug your way to the goddam east – wasting your lives. It makes me so damn mad!'

'Get what over with?' Juliet asked. 'Why are you so angry with us?'

He swung round and glared, 'because you're alive and Gerald's dead!'

Silence fell. The room felt stiflingly hot. Peach buried her face in Catriona's shoulder. Chuck bowed his head, his body still trembling with rage.

'Shit,' said Fran. 'What happened?'

Chuck stared hard at the table, gripping on as if he was in danger of losing balance. When he spoke his voice was monotone. 'He was working in some village near Pokhara, building a bridge. Truck got caught in a mudslide, went off the road. Gerry and two Nepalese …' He clamped his mouth shut, swallowing tears.

'Oh you poor things,' Juliet said, reaching out to touch Chuck's arm. He stiffened.

Peach looked across. 'We're on a pilgrimage. We're gonna see Gerald. We thought he'd want to stay there – where he's been happy.'

Chuck met her look. 'We're gonna see where he's buried. *Buried* Peach.'

His wife's face crumpled again.

Devon stepped round the table and gripped Chuck's shoulder. 'Sorry, man. Real sorry.'

Chuck sagged, his anger deflating. Nobody moved. Nobody knew what to say. It was Peach who broke the anguished silence.

'Gerald's houseboat was the Maid of the Mountain,' she said. 'But he stayed in the summer when it was beautiful and green and all the flowers were out.' Her voice was tender. 'Happy Valley they call it. Ain't that pretty?'

CHAPTER 43

London
Amber
Back in London Amber spent her spare time on the Internet pursuing leads and sending out messages to network groups. Bulbulak, the Buddhist retreat, did not have a website but she found a postal address and wrote asking for details and if it was possible to visit. She regularly skyped Jez. It was tantalising to see and hear him on the computer and not be able to touch. The way she missed him was like being hungry all the time. Her mother was pleased she had interest in a flesh and blood human and not just the dead.

'He's lovely. Don't spoil it by harping on about your aunt all the time. He might think it's weird.'

'He doesn't. He's as keen as I am to find out more.'

'Still.'

Helen left the word hanging like a warning as she kicked off her sandals and went to change. Her mum would never stop fretting about her, no matter how old she got; that's what mothers did. They had always been close and Amber loved her to bits even when she fussed too much. It started her wondering about her grandmother's relationship with Ruth.

Amber knew Gran had loved her daughter and missed her really badly, but what about Ruth? The entries in her diary did not make them sound particularly close. If anything there was a hint of jealousy that Daniel was the favoured one and Ruth never seemed interested in reading her mail from home. In fact she'd burned her letters in the desert. That seemed a bit extreme.

The irony was that Daniel had never had a good word to say about his mother. There was no love lost there. Or had there been love before he discovered he was adopted? Poor Gran. And what of her grandfather John whom Amber hardly remembered? The more she heard about him the less she liked; he'd been cruel to her dad and a racist. She didn't blame Daniel for not having a good word to say about his father; she was on her dad's side on that one. Yet Amber's gran had never openly criticised her husband; she had talked of him with sadness and resignation. 'Your grandfather died of a broken heart. Ruth going missing – he couldn't live with the not knowing.'

Amber had always been struck by those words; they did not sound like those of a man without feeling. Dorothy at the care home had been dismissive. She had nursed old John as a trainee. 'He died of cancer, Amber. No one really dies of a broken heart.'

Alex Wheeler, the Oxford friend of Marcus, was frustratingly elusive. He had been away from home when Amber had travelled back south. Now he was holidaying in Madeira. Amber left a message on his answer phone asking to meet up in July when he returned.

There were no new entries on the overland website for Cassidy, despite Amber putting out pleas for more of the group, and Juliet in particular, to get in touch. She turned her attention to tracing people from Ruth's catering course. Souter remembered interviewing a girl called Moira, but she'd been too upset to tell him very much. 'The whole thing really put the wind up her,' Souter said over the phone. 'As if she thought bad luck was contagious. I've got an old number for her, but she's probably long gone.'

The number was no longer in use. Neither was the college. It had been amalgamated with a larger institution and the records from the seventies appeared to have been shredded. Amber put out feelers on Facebook and other social networks. She wasn't too hopeful. Ruth's generation didn't do Internet friendships as much as hers.

Then one evening, a message popped up from Elise in Canada.

'I roomed with your Auntie Ruth and another friend Moira MacLean. We had lots of laughs together. Ruth was very kind to my wee sister when she came to visit. She was great with kids – much better than cooking! That's what she really wanted to do – work with disadvantaged children. I think she only did catering to get away from home. Not that I'm saying there was anything wrong with your family. We were all like that, enjoying our first taste of freedom. We had a lot of fun those two years. Too much probably. That's why Ruth failed her course. I really liked her. She was a much nicer person than me or Moira! Nothing was ever too much effort. And loyal too. Ruth would stick up for us – cover for us if our parents rang and we were out with boys or at the pub. Anyway that's enough of me prattling on about things. We were really upset when Ruth killed herself. It was such a shock. A real tragedy. I live in Vancouver now. Hope this helps.'

Amber rang Jez and told him straight away. 'I never knew Ruth failed her course. Not sure my gran ever did either. She certainly never said so.'

'Could be another reason why she took off for India,' Jez suggested, 'then she'd never have to tell her parents.'

'Yeah,' Amber agreed. 'And if she was kicked off her course, maybe she couldn't face going home again.'

'So this Elise liked her?' Jez asked.

'Umm. She made Ruth sound cool – really normal – not some freaked-out hippy who couldn't hold it together.'

'What about boyfriends?' Jez said. 'Sounds like this Elise is up front about stuff.'

'Yeah, I'll ask her.'

'I miss you, sexy eyes. When you coming back up?'

Amber's stomach fluttered with yearning. 'I get two days off next week.'

'Come then.'

Amber promised she would even though she couldn't afford it.

Two days later, Elise wrote again.

'She was quite a one for the boys I have to say. We all went a bit mad our first year – like kids let loose in the sweety shop. But Ruth's parents were over-protective – she'd hardly ever spoken to boys before let alone gone out with them – so she made up for lost time.'

Amber messaged back. 'Was there anyone special?'

'Moira and I used to wonder. Sometimes she would disappear off and not say where. And there was one guy who stayed a couple of times. She was a bit mysterious about him. I think he worked on the rigs or something. It was boom time then of course and there were lots of boys about with money to spend. Moira was a bit jealous. Why did they always fancy Ruth? She was always complaining!'

'Can you remember his name – the guy off the rigs?'

'No sorry. It's too long ago. I can't even think what he looked like now, just that he seemed very keen on her.'

CHAPTER 44

Northern India, early December 1976
Cassidy
A pink sun rose over the line of tents and the misty trees behind. Cassidy smoked his first b*eedie* of the day. This was when he loved India best: in the cool purposeful morning when the world was starting afresh. Across the road, four men were arriving with six white oxen to irrigate the fields.

He watched them work, admiring the simple age-old mechanics of drawing water. Two men threw large leather bags into the well; the other two set off down a small slope riding on ropes pulled by two pairs of oxen. Cassidy liked the symmetry, the binary numbers. As the four oxen pulled out the roped bags from the well like a line of magician's hankies, the two men at the top emptied each bag in turn into a channel that fed water away into the green fields. The young lad sang cheerfully as he worked the bags, like labourers the world over. On the verge, a peacock opened its feathers like a fan of cards and called for its mate.

Cassidy heard someone emerge from a tent with a jangle of bracelets. He glanced round hoping to see Juliet – to share this special moment – but saw Mixie wave and disappear behind a tree. Juliet was not a morning person; he knew that by now. She yawned and fired on half-cylinders till after mid-morning and several cups of tea or coffee. Evenings were when she came most alive and had stamina for late nights and long conversations. Their energy levels surged and dipped in direct opposition, like independently wired circuits.

Cassidy sighed. They'd been on the road for 75 days. In a week's time they would be in Kathmandu and the trip would be over. His passengers would scatter. Some might hang around together for a day or two – like prisoners on release scared of their sudden freedom – but most wouldn't. Already they were talking of the next stage, of travelling on and flights to catch, of getting home for Christmas or New Year. He didn't want to think of going home.

Still, there was a lot to see and do before the end. The group had all loved Delhi with its Red Fort, its imperial boulevards and seething old city. He had hung out with other bus drivers in Connaught Place, having done the tourist bit enough times. Jez, Jaipur, Fatehpur Sikri, and tonight Agra. Time was ticking. In a week or so he would have a big decision to make.

Cassidy ground out his cigarette and went to wake the cooks.

CHAPTER 45

'The peerless Taj-Mahal. This mausoleum, raised by Shah Jehan at a cost of three millions sterling over the grave of his beloved empress Mumtaz-i-Mahal, combines within itself more varied elements of beauty than almost any other building in the world.'

Stanford's Compendium of Geography: Asia Vol II, A.H. Keane, 1896

Agra, India, early December 1976
Juliet

She imagined this was what it felt like to walk onto a film set. The image was so familiar, so glamorous that it could not be real. The long water tank and fountains spread like a glass VIP carpet up to the marble mausoleum, while vivid green trees and pink bougainvillea gave way to red gateways and pagoda-roofed towers blushing in the evening sun.

The Taj Mahal. Her father had written about visiting here on a few days snatched leave. Juliet had expected to be disappointed, had braced herself for it, but was immediately won over. From afar it was dazzlingly white and simple, from up close intricately complex and subtly hued.

'And the setting is pure romantic Hollywood,' she enthused later to Kurt and Fran as they sat in the café of the International Youth Hostel drinking coffee. Stevie Wonder was playing on an old turntable at half speed. The tables were lit with candles. Outside on the lawn, Devon's cooking group were preparing salad to go with tinned corned beef. A strong smell of cannabis wafted in the night air.

'Wait till you see it tonight,' Cassidy walked in on the conversation.

'Will it be open?' Juliet asked in excitement.

'Aye, I've just checked. Fourth night after the full moon so it's the last night open this month.'

Ten of them walked down after supper towards the river. From the outer archway of the complex all was in darkness and half of them decided it wasn't worth paying to get in again.

'We'll see something,' Cassidy promised.

Juliet and Kurt stayed, as did Australians Fran and Gwennie.

From the inner archway it was possible to see that the eastern face of the mausoleum was bathed in moonlight. The rest of its bulk was cloaked in shadow. As they walked towards it, hushed by its beauty, a pale reflection dipped into the still water of the tank. They circled the building, moonlight flooding onto its right flank of arches and minarets.

'Bright as car headlights, isn't it?' Cassidy whispered.

Juliet nodded, spellbound.

Sitting on the steps in front, she murmured, 'it's like another moon reflecting the real moon, isn't it?'

'*Ja,*' Kurt agreed. 'It's tomorrow's sun shining on us tonight.'

'Or is it yesterday's?' asked Gwennie.

'Are you guys drunk or something?' Fran snorted.

'My thoughts exactly,' said Cassidy.

'No,' grinned Juliet, 'we're just romantics.'

'I could sit here all night,' said Gwennie, 'and just breathe it in.'

'Wow, Gwen, you've not even opened your guide book,' teased Fran. 'It must be love.'

'Well if you can't feel love here, there's no hope for you,' Juliet said. 'Isn't that right, Gwennie?'

'Not really,' said Gwennie, 'it's just too dark to read.'

Cassidy started to chuckle, then it spread and they were all laughing. They were happy to be there, happy in each other's company, happy in the moment. Juliet wanted to capture the feeling, imprint on her memory forever: the group of friends, the peaceful garden with the ethereal tomb, and the warmth of laughter.

A pack of tourists spilled into the moonlight, raucous and excited. Their voices exploded in the dark like firecrackers, and the moment vanished.

CHAPTER 46

Newcastle
Amber

Jez and Amber walked with their arms linked around each other along the promenade at Whitley Bay. It was breezy and grey, with moisture spattering their faces that could have been sea spray or the beginnings of rain. Neither minded.

'I keep thinking about this mystery guy from the rigs,' Amber said. 'And maybe I'm making too big a deal of it, but what if he had more to do with Ruth taking off for India than some missionary woman that my dad blamed?'

'Yeah go on.'

'Okay, from what Elise in Canada says, Ruth wasn't exactly the religious type, right? She chucked all that as soon as she got away from home – right party animal. So maybe she just made up all that stuff about being 'called' to work with orphans. Maybe it was just an excuse to get right beyond her parents' reach and meet up with this guy.'

'But why all the way to India?' Jez questioned. 'They could have run off to Bournemouth.'

'Maybe he was already out there.'

Jez stopped and frowned. 'But she never made it to India. If she was really keen on this guy and was prepared to make up a pack of lies to be with him out there, why did she let herself be sidetracked by Marcus? It doesn't make sense.'

'No it doesn't,' Amber sighed. 'Unless Marcus wanted her so badly he wasn't prepared to let her go? Did away with her, like my dad thought.'

They stared out at the choppy sea. Amber snuggled into him.

'Shit,' Jez gasped.

'What's wrong?'

'There's another possibility.' He looked at her. 'What if it was *Marcus* who was the man off the rigs?'

Amber stared. 'You mean Ruth might have known him from before the trip?'

Jez nodded. 'What if they planned the whole thing right from the start?'

CHAPTER 47

Nepal, mid December 1976
Cassidy
The bus laboured up the tree-covered slopes of the foothills. Terraces of lime green rice fields were stacked like cards into the sides of hairpin bends. Cassidy had to stop at frequent road tolls as they trundled further into Nepal. His passengers were seized with a sudden desire to photograph everything as if making up for weeks of not snapping enough: thatched houses on stilts, hens on verandas, a village granny in a purple padded wrap-over jacket pouring *cay*, children carrying baskets strapped on with headbands, and cattle feeding on steaming hay.

They reached Pokhara in the late afternoon, the high white peaks of the Annapurna range thrusting out of fluffy clouds and turning pink. The valley was in shadow. The place was full of soldiers. Decorative archways across the road with pictures of the royal family announced that the king was in residence at the nearby palace.

'They're a menace,' Cassidy muttered, trying to negotiate the bus under a festive arch without taking it with him. 'Everyone up to the front!'

The bus dipped with the weight of passengers. He edged it forward.

'Right – run to the back!' he ordered.

Their laughter had a note of hysteria; they knew this was the last time they would camp together. Tomorrow was Kathmandu.

'Nearly took off the king's head there, mate,' shouted one of the London brothers. After three months Cassidy still had trouble telling which was which.

'Aye, well I'm a Republican.'

'So were we,' Peach exclaimed. 'But Nixon was such a disappointment.'

'No Peach,' snorted Maggie, 'he doesn't mean that kind - '

'Leave it, she's cool,' Devon said and drew Maggie into a kiss.

The village, with its string of little restaurants, was perched on the edge of a glassy lake. They camped in the grounds of a cheap hotel, putting up the tents for the final time.

'We've baked beans to use up,' Cassidy told the cooks, extracting the final tins from the roof-rack.

'That'll go nicely with the cabbage stew,' grunted Gino.

'Yeah, we'll all explode with gas,' said Fran.

'You're sleeping outside the tent tonight, Frances,' ordered Gwennie.

'Can't - there's a curfew.'

'Should be a curfew on your farts.'

'Oh my God, you guys,' laughed Mixie, 'don't you ever stop talking about your bodily functions?'

'No,' said Fran, 'unless it's to talk about someone else's.'

Cassidy went with Chuck and Peach to find them a guide for their following day's trek. He treated them to tea and a cheesy paratha while he negotiated with the hotel owner. Chuck showed him the map and pointed to the village where Gerald had been living.

'It's not far,' the Nepali told them. 'Two hours walk. You want to stay there for night?'

'Oh yes,' said Peach, 'we do. It's our son you see.'

As they walked back in the dark, the lights of the village glinting on the still water, Chuck said, 'we plan to stay around here for awhile, Mr Cassidy. We may not see you again.'

'Oh, Chucky, I'm sure we'll bump into Cassidy in Kathmandu later.'

'But maybe we won't.' He stopped and turned to his driver. 'Just in case, we'd like to say thank you for bringing us safely to Nepal. I know I was sometimes a bit critical of you, but I meant no offence.'

'None taken,' Cassidy said. 'I've had a lot worse, believe me. You've been a teddy bear compared to some of the buggers I've had on board.'

Chuck gave him a quizzical look, and then smiled.

That night, some went off exploring, following a rumour there was Tibetan dancing to see. Others sat around a dying fire, chatting quietly while Devon strummed guitar. By ten there was a curfew, and at the sight of soldiers patrolling with guns, people turned in for the night.

At dawn, Cassidy woke them all with a loud banging of pan lids.

'Haway, you lazy lot, you've got to see this!'

Campers emerged bleary-eyed, fumbling into warm clothes, cursing him. But the view silenced their protests. Behind the thatched huts, behind the dark wooded foothills, the crystal clear Himalayas sprang out of pink light. The only sound Cassidy could hear was the frantic clicking of cameras. He looked round and caught sight of Juliet standing with her arm around Peach, their faces turned up to the sunrise. They looked awe-struck. He felt his chest constrict. He would never need a photograph to remind him of how beautiful Juliet looked in that moment.

She must have sensed him staring, because she glanced over. They smiled, and then he had to look away, his eyes filling up.

As the peak of Machhupuchre whitened and disappeared in morning cloud, they set about eating breakfast – the end of the previous night's stew and beans – and then a brisk cleaning of the bus and its equipment before it got stowed away for the last time.

Cassidy hauled down Peach and Chuck's matching tartan cases. Devon and Gino helped Chuck carry the luggage across to the hotel. On their return, Chuck began a round of awkward goodbyes.

'Can't go yet mate,' said Cassidy, 'the girls have gone off with your missus.'

'Where?'

Cassidy nodded towards the lake. 'Said you were to come when you were ready.'

They walked through the wet grass. Mist was rolling back to reveal still water. A group muffled in coats and hats stood along the shore, arms linked, singing disjointedly. Snatches of song rose into the sharp air one after the other: The Skye Boat Song, Kumbyya, Show Me the Way to Go Home, Waltzing Matilda. As each song tailed off in forgotten words, someone else would start off another. In the middle of the line was Peach, a garland of flowers, pinched from a festive arch, strung around her neck.

Aware of the men appearing, Juliet beckoned them to join in. The women broke ranks to pull Chuck into their middle and stand beside his wife. Devon began a soulful rendition of Blowing in the Wind. Other voices died away as they listened to his song filling the silence. He finished. No one spoke. The lake threw back a perfect inversion of the mountains behind.

Cassidy became aware of Juliet fumbling with gloved hands for something in her pocket. She stepped forward.

'For Gerry,' she said, and threw a handful of petals onto the water.

Others followed – Catriona, Fran, Gwennie, Maggie, Mixie – scattering flower heads, leaves and twigs that they had picked up that morning. Juliet grabbed Peach's hands and heaped them with leftover petals. The bereft woman stood paralysed, tears streaming down her face. Chuck put an arm around his wife and encouraged her forward. Together they hurled the broken flowers and cried out their son's name. The water rippled and shook the image of the mountains under the flotsam.

The couple stood, gripping each other, wrapped in grief. Cassidy caught Juliet's eye and nodded. It was time to go.

One by one, they hugged or shook hands with the Americans.

'See you soon.'

'Take care, won't you?'

'Chin up mate.'

'We're all brothers, dude.'

'Sorry I was such a feckin' pain, Peach.'

'We must keep in touch, yeah?'

'I'll write, I promise.'

'If you ever make it across the pond, be sure to come and stay.'

Cassidy listened to their farewells, the promises touching and sincere, yet most would never be kept. The same ritual would be repeated over the next few days as the group dispersed. He had heard it all before. Ships passing in the night, that's what they really were.

The bus pulled away, everyone pressed up against the windows, waving and mouthing goodbyes. Peach and Chuck stood in their blue jackets watching them leave, Peach shaking a hankie. Devon gave a salute. Cassidy wasn't sure if it was made in jest. But glancing in his mirror he saw Chuck raise his hand and return a peace sign.

It was twenty minutes before conversations broke out around the bus. The talk was of food and hot showers.

CHAPTER 48

York
Amber

She got to the meeting place in York early. She'd put on a print dress, borrowed one of her mum's smart jackets and tied back her hair; this guy was ex-Oxford and ex-government, so she wanted to appear the earnest researcher. The coffee shop was in a converted convent a few minutes walk from the station. It appeared to be a hostel and conference centre too.

'Hi, I'm here to meet Alex Wheeler.'

'Mr Wheeler's not in yet,' the receptionist smiled. 'You could wait in the café if you like.'

Amber found it hard to sit still. She kept glancing at the door. Twenty minutes late a tanned balding man in cargo shorts and lime green polo shirt strode in, scanned the room and raised a hand in greeting.

'Amber?' he held out a hand and gave a crushing handshake. 'Sorry. Bike got a puncture. Traffic a nightmare. Coffee or tea? Cake here is superb.' He ushered Amber to the counter to choose and chatted to the staff by name. 'Let's take it out into the courtyard. Far too nice to be sitting inside.'

Amber followed. There were a handful of others reading books or snacking at tables. The yard was hemmed in by high walls and softened with healthy shrubs in terracotta pots. Classical music played through an open window. It was sheltered and cool. Her mum would like this place.

Alex Wheeler needed little prompting to talk about his Oxford days. He hopped from subject to subject, scattering opinions like crumbs. Amber found him lively and engaging, with a self-confidence that teetered on arrogance. He must be mid-sixties but looked a weathered forty-five. After going off on a tangent about water privatisation in Dar-es-Salam, Amber steered him back to Marcus Barclay.

'Jolly good rower of course. And first rate mind. Marcus was much more thorough than Sabby or me. He would have made an excellent diplomat – wonderful way with people – all walks of life. Or an academic. Always had his head buried in some vast tome in the Bodleian. Room looked like a lending library. But he could be tremendous fun too. Life and soul. Girls went silly around him. Not that he noticed.'

'Was there any girl in particular?' Amber asked through a mouthful of cake.

'Umm, don't think so. To be frank,' Alex lowered his voice a little, 'I'm not sure girls really interested him. It didn't occur to me at the time, but thinking about it now, it wouldn't surprise me if he'd been gay.'

'Really?'

'Yah. But who knows. It wasn't something we ever talked about.'

'So was there a special guy in his life do you think?'

Alex gave her an uncomfortable look. 'Goodness, I just wouldn't know. I shouldn't really have mentioned it. Just thinking aloud. He died so young you see, and his life was so full, no time for a big romance ...'

For the first time in half an hour he seemed stuck for words. Amber hid a smile as she rummaged in her handbag and produced Ruth's photographs. Alex pulled out a pair of spectacles from his top pocket and viewed them one by one.

'That's the man who pretended to be Marcus,' Amber prompted.

'Yes,' Alex nodded. 'I was shown his picture by police at the time. Never seen him before. Extraordinary thing, wasn't it? Very upsetting for the parents. Went to see them, but got the feeling they didn't want his friends around – too painful – reminded them of what they'd lost. Bloody awful.'

He slurped his cold coffee, leaving the photos out of their packet.

'So he didn't look like the real Marcus at all?' Amber asked.

'Difficult to tell from these. Not great quality. We all grew beards and long hair in those days.' He tapped one photograph with the arm of his spectacles. 'But that one – that could be Marcus – at a push. The way he's standing with his hands clasped behind his head – the smile – yes that could be him.'

Amber leaned forward to look. It was the one of Marcus standing on the Galata Bridge in Istanbul. Ruth was gazing up at him. There was a look passing between them - Amber had not noticed it before – as if they were sharing an in-joke. Juliet must have taken it.

'I have this hunch,' Amber said, 'that that man – whoever he was – must've known Marcus pretty well. He knew so much about him – his family history.'

'Well it wasn't one of the college men – I knew everyone at Lincoln by sight at least.'

'Did he have any relatives who came to stay? Friends from home?'

'Possibly. But it was so long ago. I really can't remember.'

Alex looked at his watch. Amber swallowed her frustration; she had really hoped this student friend would uncover some piece of the jigsaw. If he couldn't no one else would after all this time.

'Can I buy you a coffee in return?' she asked.

'Kind, but no thanks. I have a lunch appointment. I'm sorry if I haven't been much help.'

'No, you've been great. Thanks.'

Alex picked up the photos, tapped them into an orderly pile and handed them back.

'It must be ghastly not knowing about your aunt. But I'm afraid it's not so uncommon. People go missing every day of the year. Just walk out. Never seen again. One of life's mysteries.'

He carried the tray of empty cups and plates back to the café. For something to say, Amber asked, 'Who was the man you called Sabby? It's a strange name.'

'Sabby? Oh, he was a character. Sabari was his real name. We used to tease him he was an eastern prince. Made him furious. He got a bad dose of Communism at Oxford – did PPE. Old Taj. First rate polo player and horseman. Gave it all up – said it was far too bourgeois. Father was some sort of clan chief – sold horses and camels to the British army – rich as stink. Sent Taj to Oxford to give him the trappings of an English gentleman and got a raving commie in his place. Impossibly idealistic. Great man, Taj Sabari.'

Amber felt the hairs prickle on the back of her neck. Impulsively she grabbed his arm. 'This Taj – where did he come from? It wasn't Balochistan was it?'

Alex gave her an astonished look. 'Yes it was. Good heavens, do you know him?'

CHAPTER 49

'Kathmandu, the present capital of Nepal, including the old capital of Patan close by, lies in a productive and well-watered valley in the heart of the country. The two capitals together make a very interesting locality, with good streets, pleasant houses, many temples of unique style and beauty, in its appearance betraying a certain mixture of Indian and Chinese elements.'

Stanford's Compendium of Geography: Asia Vol II, A.H. Keane, 1896

Kathmandu, Nepal, late December 1976
Juliet

By Christmas Eve there were a dozen of the group still in the capital, most staying in the Thali district at the Asia Hotel and Hotel Star. Sometimes Juliet would come across two or three when cycling into Durbar Square and they would greet each other like long lost friends and go for coffee and cake. But mostly she avoided the crowded downtown streets and the travellers' hangouts around Freak Street – Aunt Jane's and the Ra Ra Restaurant - preferring to eat spring rolls and read in the garden of the Shangri-La or write letters in KC's Restaurant and eat huge chunks of apple pie.

Devon and Maggie had discovered KC's on the first night. 'The young guy who runs it looks like Frank Zappa,' said Devon, 'a real cool dude.'

KC laid on breakfasts of porridge, fried eggs and toast, packed lunches of bread, cheese and tomatoes and evening meals of steaks, soups, hamburgers, salads, rotis and apple crumble. Across the street, his sister ran a cake shop and there were few days when Juliet did not stop by with Fran and Gwennie or Catriona and Mixie to eat fruit salad pie or chocolate sponge cake. At night they would sit on drinking 'Night Lifes' (rum and lemons) and swap stories about where they had been – the medieval town of Bhaktapur with its Buddhist temple and Tibetan craftsmen or breathless climbs up to the flag-strewn stupas of Swayambhu and Boudhanath.

Cassidy ran a trip to the Tibetan border and Gwennie discovered an evening performance of the Messiah at an ex-pat school across town. But Juliet liked best the aimless wandering along narrow back streets and small squares of tall brick houses and carved wooden doors, sidestepping fruit sellers, roaming buffalo, dogs and rickshaws. Finally there was no need to rush onto the next place. At first she had missed the safe predictability of the bus, the rhythm of travel, the packing up and moving on. Now she welcomed putting down roots, however temporary.

'We should have a Christmas party for Cassidy,' Maggie suggested over coffee, 'as a thank you.'

'Aye,' agreed Catriona, 'I've hardly seen him. Just a couple of times at Yeti Travels picking up post.'

'I saw him at the Post Office trying to put a call in,' Mixie said. 'Looked a bit upset.'

'Probably trying to get the cricket scores,' Sid joked.

'I may be wrong but I think he's having trouble getting paid,' said Juliet.

'Is that why he's not eating out with us much?' Catriona guessed.

Mixie frowned. 'I got the feeling the call was more personal – like he was trying to calm someone down. Has anyone any idea of his home life?'

There were shrugs and head shaking. Then Devon said, 'He mentioned a girl once when he was high – some name like Pauline or Paula – but he wasn't making a whole lotta sense. Mister Mysterious, that's our Pappa Cass.'

'Well if he's having hassle,' said Mixie, 'all the more reason to give him a party.'

They all agreed. Juliet, who was sharing a room with Fran and Gwennie, offered to host it. They got in spicy nuts and made up a hot punch of local 'country liquor', rum and orange. Kurt and Tomas came from across town where they were staying at the upmarket Crystal and brought puffed up cheese breads called jaffles and a bottle of Johnny Walker Red Label. Mixie and Sid came with sweets and biscuits and a couple of Canadians from a Swagman bus who were staying at the Asia. Devon and Maggie made hash brownies and stuck in candles begged from KC. Catriona and Suzy made paper streamers and brought vodka.

Cassidy was told by Gwennie that he was invited for a quiet lunchtime drink on Christmas Day to look through some of her guide books and advise her onward travel. He stepped through the door to a raucous shouting of 'Merry Christmas!' and a tin mug of potent punch thrust into his hand.

They partied all afternoon. The noise attracted in a Norwegian called Anders and an Irishman who could recite poetry. At some point fire-crackers were let off on the open-air corridor and Juliet decided they should go and eat. Half of them disappeared into town. Sid, Mixie, Devon, Maggie, Catriona, Cassidy, Juliet, and the Irish Poet ended up eating a huge Chinese meal at the Utze.

Emerging into the half dark, Maggie cried, 'let's go and eat cake!' and led them in the direction of KC's. Juliet stopped to breathe in the scented air of wood-smoke. Around her, stalls were lit and busy. The moon and evening star glowed like lamps as the mist settled on the surrounding hills.

'Couldn't eat or drink another thing,' she sighed in contentment.

'Me neither,' said Cassidy. 'Fancy a stroll?'

They set off down the street in the opposite direction to the others. No one seemed to notice. Juliet felt light-headed and full of bonhomie.

'I love how this place is already so familiar,' she said. 'In fact I love everything about it.'

'Will you stick around here for a while then?' Cassidy asked.

'Why not? I've got nothing to rush home for. Maybe I'll start writing poetry or get a job in a cake shop.'

'You'd eat all the profits.'

'Cheeky,' Juliet laughed and gave him a playful push. She hung onto his arm as they walked on. 'What about you?'

'I'll hang around till my pay comes through. Maybe run a few local trips. I don't have to take a group back to London till May.'

'Is there a problem?'

Cassidy gave her a wary look. 'What do you mean?'

'Well if you're short of money I could lend you some.'

Cassidy's face relaxed. 'It's nowt to worry about, just a mix up with the bank. I can always threaten to sell the bus if they don't pay up.'

'Well, just let me know if I can help, won't you?'

They walked on, arm in arm, Juliet enjoying the feeling of their closeness. She wondered whether to ask him about the upsetting phone call or if there was someone waiting for him at home. It seemed unlikely, given that he wasn't rushing back to Newcastle as soon as the trip was over. Suddenly she didn't want there to be anyone in Cassidy's life. She felt a surge of tenderness for him.

'I'm glad you're not leaving,' she said with a sideways glance. 'Maybe we could do a bit of trekking together – if you like?'

He stopped and looked at her, grinning. 'Are you propositioning me or just drunk?'

'Probably both.'

Just then, the sound of drums beating rhythmically grew out of the evening crowd. Juliet turned around. Through the dusk came a band of musicians playing shepherds' pipes and small drums, and ringing bells. They were swathed in homespun tunics and cloaks, with colourful Nepalese hats. She gazed at them in wonder as they passed. They appeared to be playing for no other reason than the simple joy of it. The music filled her with a deep sense of well-being; a Christmas gift. She couldn't remember such a happy Christmas Day since she was a child.

Cassidy placed his hands around her face and wiped the tears from her cheeks with his thumbs. Until that moment, she had not known she was crying.

'I'm not sad,' she began.

He pulled her face to his and pressed a kiss to her lips. He tasted of salty soy sauce and country liquor. When he stopped, she slipped her arms around his neck and kissed him back, opening her mouth to suck at his lips, his moustache, and flick his salty tongue with hers. They stood in the street embracing as the sound of the young musicians faded into the night. A cyclist swerved around them, ringing his bell.

'Can we do this?' Juliet murmured.

'I want to,' Cassidy said.

'So do I.'

She could feel him trembling as he took her hand. They hurried back to the hotel without a word. Her heart thumped and made her breathless.

146

Inside his room, under the stark electric light, Cassidy seemed less eager. His single bed was neatly made, and his few belongings stowed under it or hung on hooks.

'Are you sure?' he looked anxious.

Juliet was already unbuttoning her jacket. 'Yes. It's too cold to hang about Cass. Let's get under those blankets.'

He switched off the light. He sat down and undid his boots. Half undressed Juliet paused. She sensed his awkwardness. Perhaps she had misread the situation? 'Is something wrong?' she asked. 'We don't have to if you don't want – I just thought - '

She peered at him in the dark. Outside she could hear people laughing in the courtyard, shouting in another language.

'By heck I want to,' Cassidy groaned and reached out for her.

The next moment she was straddling him on the bed and they were fumbling with frantic fingers to take each other's clothes off. They kissed with a hunger and urgency that surprised them both. They climaxed in a flurry of discarded clothes and blankets.

Juliet lay with her hand on his chest, feeling it rise and fall with the racing of his heart.

'Where did that come from?' Juliet asked. 'I didn't realise how much I fancied you.'

'God, woman, I've been wanting to do that for bloody weeks.'

Juliet smiled. 'Really?'

'Aye, really.'

'Since when?'

'Probably the moment I saw you strutting up the bus in your undies when someone was sick on your skirt. I liked the way you didn't give a toss.'

Juliet laughed. 'I don't believe you.'

Cassidy kissed her hair. 'Don't then, but it's true.'

'When were you ever going to tell me? If it hadn't been for those musicians we might never have got it together. I could have gone off trekking and you could have driven off to India - '

He silenced her with another kiss. Much later, Juliet drifted off to the sound of someone singing in French in the room above, her arms and legs entwined around Cassidy's. She felt deeply content. For the first time in over a month she went to sleep without a thought for either Marcus or Ruth.

CHAPTER 50

Nepal, New Year 1977
Cassidy

Nobody, apart from himself, seemed surprised when Juliet moved in with him.

'That's cool, man,' Devon grinned.

'About time,' said Maggie. 'She wasted too many feckin' weeks going after that mad Marcus.' Cassidy took this as a thumb's up to the new relationship.

Fran and Gwennie cheered; Catriona claimed she'd predicted it from the word go. Even Kurt seemed pleased, though Cassidy thought he saw a wistful look in the man's eye as he wished them goodbye and good luck. The Germans were heading off on a jungle trek in the south of Nepal. Juliet and Kurt swapped addresses and promised to keep in touch.

Two days later, Cassidy drove Fran and Gwennie to the airport and they said a tearful farewell. They were heading home to Australia via Bangkok and Bali. A day later they put Catriona on a flight to Delhi; she was going to spend a fortnight at an ashram before returning to Glasgow.

'You'll never be able to keep quiet that long,' Juliet teased.

'I just hope I lose a bit of the flab,' Catriona grimaced. 'I used to be like Twiggy.'

'You're a much better cuddle than Twiggy,' Cassidy said, pulling her into a hug. 'Take care lass.'

Juliet and Catriona cried as they hugged goodbye. 'The last of our tent,' Catriona sighed.

'Maggie's still around,' Juliet reminded.

'She was never there long enough to count.'

Cassidy watched them. Neither mentioned Ruth, but he knew they both thought of her. She was a loose thread in the story of their adventure that they would tell in years to come: *do you remember that girl from Weardale who went off with the relief driver – I wonder whatever happened to her?*

'We'll all meet up next Christmas,' said Catriona, 'and have a reunion – a few bevvies – Newcastle or Glasgow, eh?'

Both Juliet and Cassidy agreed that they would. Soon afterwards, Mixie, Sid and Suzy joined a busload going south to Goa for New Year. Devon and Maggie moved to a cheaper room in the heart of the city. Cassidy saw them once, doped up to the eyeballs in a café on Freak Street. They made arrangements to meet on New Year's Eve but never showed up.

'Didn't think they'd remember,' Cassidy said, half way through the evening. By then, he and Juliet had made new friends – an Australian couple working for the World Health Organisation, a Spanish motor mechanic and a former nun from Manchester – and ended the evening at a party in the Blue Star drinking vodka and singing Auld Lang Syne.

148

'Let's head for the hills,' Juliet said the next day, nursing a hangover.

A couple of days later, they packed up a bag of clothes and a bag of books and took the trolley bus to Bhaktapur. In Durbar Square they piled into a minibus alongside milk churns and sacks of grain, stopping frequently to pick up more and more passengers who squeezed in around them. At Karapati they got out and started to walk. The path was immediately steep and rocky; the sun was growing hot and the air thin. Small boys appeared at their sides to chat and guide them.

'Goodness, I'm unfit!' Juliet gasped, as they reached a small hamlet of thatched cottages painted yellow and orange. Kids and hens rushed around. Women pounded and sieved grain outside a small store heaped with nuts and flour. A cow blocked their way. 'It's a sign that we should stop and drink tea,' she panted.

Cassidy ordered *cay*. He peeled an orange and fed it in bits to Juliet. Two black goats came close and stared. The children laughed. When they moved on, their small friends ran along beside for a few yards shouting, 'Hello, bye-bye!'

All day, they wound their way higher, the valley and distant jungle spreading below them like a rich green carpet. The rock rang with their footsteps. Juliet breathed as if she had just run a marathon.

'How come you're so fit?' she complained at one tea stop. 'And you smoke loads.'

'Less sticky cakes for the last four months,' he grinned.

'You should have stopped me,' Juliet laughed.

By four o'clock they reached Nagarkot. From here the Himalayas swept around in a huge arc from Annapurna to beyond Everest. They were drinking coffee at a nearby stall when the sun set in a blaze of orange behind the mountains, filling the far off valley with soft light and plunging the wooded foothills into darkness.

Juliet spent so long gawping at the sight, that they found themselves rushing around in the near dark trying to find somewhere to stay. Eventually, they dropped steeply down the hill again and banged on the door of the Everest Cottage. The owners opened up for them – there was no one else staying – and lit a huge fire in the large central room.

By candlelight, they wolfed down a meal of vegetable curry, dhal, rice, omelette and a round of stodgy Tibetan bread. The young owner put on a tape of The Eagles and Cassidy shared his bottle of Country Liquor by the fire. They went to bed early, lying in a vast bed partitioned off from the main room, the light from the candle dancing across the high matted ceiling.

'I can hear a mouse running around up there,' Juliet whispered.

'Aye, cosy, isn't it?' Cassidy smiled, pulling her into his arms and kissing her.

They stayed there for two weeks like hideaways, avoiding company except their own, absorbed in their newfound passion. They would stay in bed late, eat a large breakfast then go for short walks or sit on the terraced steps, drink tea and read. Cassidy found himself enjoying Juliet's books on eccentric travellers, and discussing them with her.

'Me favourite's that one who lived for ages among a bunch of Turks.'

'Grace Ellison?' Juliet asked. She was stretched out on a blanket in the sun like a contented cat.

'Aye, that's the one. That's proper travelling in my eyes. Most overlanders - me included - don't have the bottle for that.'

'She had plenty of time and no problem with money,' Juliet pointed out. 'I'm sure that helps.'

Cassidy lay propped on an elbow beside her, tracing his finger down her arm. He never tired of touching her, breathing in the scented warmth of her, of watching a smile pull at the corners of her full mouth.

'I'm the reincarnation of Grace Ellison,' she said in a dreamy voice. 'She's the one who gave me the courage to set out on this trip.'

'Amazin' Grace,' he grunted, leaning forward to kiss the hollow of her neck. 'No wonder I fell for you.'

She stroked his head, and rubbed his scalp with long fingers.

'I wish,' she began, and then let the words hang.

'Your wish is my command,' he smiled.

'I wish I had the guts to find where my father died. If only Aziz had been there, maybe he could have shown me.'

Cassidy was dismayed; he thought she had put the Aziz thing behind her. He said, 'even if you'd found him, it's hardly likely he would have known anything. He was just your old man's tailor.'

She sighed. 'You're right. It's just something I have to accept.'

'It's not good to hark on the past,' Cassidy said. 'Enjoy what we have now, that's what's important – at least to me it is.'

She swivelled to look him in the eye. 'And me,' she said quickly, kissing him. 'Cass, this isn't just a holiday fling is it? It feels like more than that to me. You're not going to suddenly tell me you've got a wife and five kids back in Newcastle are you?'

His stomach knotted. 'Course not. I want this time to go on for ever.' He kissed her to stem any further awkward questions.

One morning he left her to sleep, creeping out into the raw dawn to watch the sunrise over the distant peak of Everest. He took a blanket and strode up the slope as the mist rose out of the valley. Sitting huddled in the blanket staring at the dark blue mountains, Cassidy wrestled with his thoughts.

He should tell Juliet about Paula. It was only fair. In a day or two they would have to go back to Kathmandu and check on the bus, only then could he sort out the mess he had left at home. He wished he hadn't tried to ring Paula – it had only been a nagging guilt over Christmas – but she had started having a go at him, wanting him back. That was the last thing he had expected. Then this fantastic thing had happened with Juliet. Now all he wanted was to be with her. He would leave Newcastle behind forever if it meant living a life with Juliet – anywhere in the world she wanted to go. But for that to happen, Juliet needed to know the full picture: all the cards on the table.

Deep pink light began to seep into the valley and catch at the peaks. As a brilliant orange sun rose, the snow appeared to burn in the dawn.

Everest, remote and ice blue, was crowned by a copper cloud. From far below, the chanting of a group of girls walking to school tinkled like bells. Cassidy's heart swelled. He felt alive. He was in love. Anything was possible.

As he scrambled down towards the guesthouse, he saw Juliet peering out, Afghan coat thrown over her pyjamas. Her breath exhaled in a cloud.

'Where've you been?'

'Watching the sun come up.'

She smiled in relief. 'I thought you'd done a runner.'

'Course not. Why would I do that?'

'Mister Mysterious, that's what Devon calls you.'

Cassidy went to her and held her close. 'I love you lass. There are things I need to tell you though.'

'Not now,' Juliet said quickly, 'not here. Don't spoil things in our place.'

'It's not so bad,' he began to laugh.

'Then it can wait,' she smiled. 'Can't it?'

'Aye, of course it can.'

She shivered. 'Come back to bed then and warm me up.'

CHAPTER 51

London
Amber

When she got in from work, Amber found a large brown envelope on the doormat. Inside was a colour brochure on recycled matt paper from the Bulbulak Centre for Holistic Study. It was in German, English and French. Amber kicked off her dusty boots and padded across the wooden floor, throwing open the balcony windows to let in some air. Pouring a glass of milk, she sat on the floor and flicked through it. There were photos of painted wooden houses surrounded by trees, long stretches of flat coastline and sand dunes, and a colourful stupa with fluttering prayer flags. Inside shots showed smiling people in saffron-coloured clothes, a library, a communal dining-hall and children doing yoga.

The last page gave a contact telephone number and an email address, but no names. There was a piece of rough yellow paper – the kind scrapbooks were made of – enclosed with the brochure. In large looping writing, a message had been written: *You are welcome to visit. We don't charge a daily rate, but ask for contributions towards bed and food. If you wish to stay, please ring. In peace. Al Kiefer.*

Amber checked the name with Kurt's obituary; Al Kiefer was his son. So the retreat was still in existence. Amber gulped down the icy milk and went to take a shower. She finished off with cold water until her whole body tingled, then wrapped her hair in a towel and lay down on the sofa, promptly falling asleep.

She was awoken by her mobile buzzing. There was a text from Jez saying *ring me, <3 u* and a message on call register: *Alex Wheeler here, had a thought about those photos, maybe barking up the wrong tree but there again it could be something. Call me back when you have a moment. I'll be out after seven.*

Amber was keen to hear Jez's voice, but it was ten to seven. She rang Alex back first.

'There's been something niggling at the back of my mind,' Alex got straight to the point. 'Do you have the photos to hand?'

Letting her damp towel drop, Amber scrambled through the desk drawer. 'Yeah got them in front of me.' She scattered them across the floor.

'One of the beach ones,' said Alex. 'There's a black man playing the guitar and I think Marcus is sitting beside him?'

'Yeah, that's right; it's a close-up.'

'Marcus has a tattoo on his upper arm. What is it?'

Amber flicked back dishevelled hair and studied the photo. 'Looks like an eagle.'

'Yah! That's what I thought. An eagle with talons.'

'Did Marcus have a tattoo like that?' Amber asked.

'Good lord no! One didn't in those days. But I do remember someone who did. One of the college scouts.'

'Scouts?'

'They were the men who cleaned our rooms, ran errands, generally looked after us. The chap on Marcus's corridor was younger than most – very obliging and cheerful – quick on the uptake Marcus used to say. Sabby had the same scout but hated all that servant stuff so wouldn't let him clean up. Gave him presents for his family – silver ornaments and an emerald-studded hunting knife – anything of value Taj simply gave away.'

Amber's heart thumped as she asked, 'Do you think this could be the pretend Marcus? Did they look anything alike – the scout and your friend?'

'Well, not dissimilar. The scout had short back and sides, but he was fairish like Marcus. Not as tall. But both had boyish good looks, smiled and laughed readily. Marcus was far more well-spoken, of course, but people can change their accents, can't they?'

'Do you remember his name?' Amber held her breath.

'Yes, it was Robin. We joked about it, rather unkindly, because of the eagle tattoo. He couldn't wait to show us when he had it done. A common and garden Robin who saw himself as a noble eagle. Taj ticked us off for being snobs, and he was right. But it was just the callousness of youth, we meant no harm by it, and certainly never teased him to his face.'

Amber felt a pang of pity for the young cleaner showing off to the privileged students, perhaps aping their ways, while they laughed about him behind his back.

'Robin who?'

'Umm, Robin Baker or Barker, some name like that. I could probably find out for you if you really want to know.'

'Yeah, please.' Then Amber asked, 'if it was this Robin who got it together with my aunt on the trip, why would he go to all the trouble of pretending to be Marcus Barclay?'

'That's what I've been wondering,' Alex grunted. 'I can only think that the boy must've admired Marcus greatly – saw him as some sort of role model. Maybe he was living out some fantasy. Or maybe it was much more mundane and he just needed to skip the country with an ID he knew he could get away with.'

Amber gazed at the grinning image of the handsome imposter. She could see why Ruth had been attracted to him. 'How long did he work at the college?'

'I can't really recall,' Alex said. 'I think he was still there when I left, but I can't be sure.'

He rang off. Amber wrapped herself in a cotton throw and sat deep in thought as the evening light streamed into the room, dust motes dancing in its beam. She imagined Robin, quick to learn and eager to please, running around after Marcus and Alex and their fellow students, studying their mannerisms and ways of speech, sneaking a look at their books

153

between chores and amassing knowledge like an eager jackdaw. No doubt he was aware of the fun they had at his expense, but he tolerated it because they opened a door on a world of learning, athleticism and privilege: a university education by proxy. She felt a swell of admiration for this Robin who, judging by Ruth's diary had made her aunt so happy. Ruth had been nuts about him.

It made Amber think warmly of Jez and his message. Eagerly she dialled him up. He answered after a couple of rings. She launched straight into the retelling of her conversation with Alex.

'Isn't that amazing? It's the first time we've even come close to finding out something about Ruth's Marcus. It's beginning to make some sense. And the other thing is, I've got the brochure from Bulbulak and its still running. Looks a cool place. I was wondering whether me and you – could – well – perhaps - '

'Amber.'

The way he said her name made her insides plunge.

'What? Is something wrong?'

There was silence at the other end.

'Tell me, Jez.'

'It's Cass.' She could hear him swallowing.

'What's happened?'

'I made him go to the doctor's a couple of weeks ago. They did tests. He's been losing weight …not eating …'

Amber's stomach clenched. 'And?'

'He's got cancer.'

CHAPTER 52

Nepal, mid January 1977
Cassidy

Back in Kathmandu, a message awaited Cassidy at the Hotel Star. There was a telex for him at Yeti Travels: sounded urgent.

'I'll come with you,' said Juliet.

'No need,' Cassidy said hastily, 'I'll deal with it. Meet you at KC's later for a coffee?'

Borrowing a bicycle from the hotel, he rode with mounting dread. It was bound to be from Paula – a threat or ultimatum or a tearful pleading to start again. He was going to have to be firm, remind her that it was she who had walked away.

It was with partial relief that he found the telex – only three days old - was from head office. Ring at once. More hassle with wages probably. He hadn't had time to check with the bank and see if he'd been paid. He booked a call for the afternoon and went to meet Juliet.

She was reassuring. 'Maybe they've got some extra work for you. Whatever it is, stop worrying – we'll deal with it together.'

But as the time came to make the call, Cassidy felt increasingly on edge. Perhaps Rainbow Tours were about to go bust? Juliet stood crammed next to him in the small wooden booth. 'Don't let them walk all over you, Cass.'

Janine, the office gofer, answered on a crackling line. 'Hi! Dave wants a word but he's not here. Bout that girl. Mother's been on every day.'

'What girl?' He had to shout for her to hear.

'Ruth English. Dave says you should've told him she'd gone missing.'

Cassidy saw Juliet's eyes widen in shock.

'She hasn't. She just jumped ship with her boyfriend – in Afghanistan.'

'That's not what Dave says. Her mother's been in touch with some place near Delhi – orphanage I think – anyway, Ruth never turned up. Should've been there for Christmas. Dave wants to know when you last heard from her and why you didn't report that she'd gone off.'

'You can't force people to stay on the bus.' Cassidy felt sweat break out on the back of his neck. Juliet was pressing a hand to her mouth. 'It wasn't like she was on her own – she had this guy Marcus with her. Obviously didn't fancy doing the orphanage thing once she hitched up with him.'

'Well you'll have to explain it all to Dave,' Janine said. He could hear her tapping a pen against her teeth. 'Give him the jen on this guy Mark.'

'Marcus. He was my co-driver.'

'Umm, Marcus? Don't recognise the name. Is he on our books?'

'Not really – I co-opted him in Venice.'

'Blimey, it doesn't get any better. So what was he thinking, quitting the bus?'

Cassidy tugged on his moustache. 'He got friendly with Ruth – kept an eye on her like. Then I suppose they got it together.' Juliet was colouring; he couldn't meet her look.

Janine whistled. 'Don't think Ruth's old doll is going to like the sound of that. Do you know,' she smirked, 'she thinks we're some sort of religious travel agent?'

Cassidy sighed. 'What does Dave expect me to do?'

'Dunno. You'll have to ring back. Expect he just wants some info to tell Mrs English – where Ruth might have gone, that sort of thing.'

'I know they headed off to the lakes at Band e-Amir,' Cassidy said. Then he thought to add, 'and I left their rucksacks at the Mustafa Hotel in Kabul. He could check if they ever turned up to collect them.'

The line went dead and he wasn't sure if Janine had heard him.

Juliet pushed at the door and fell out into the winter sunshine. She stood breathing hard. Cassidy lit a cigarette and handed it over. She drew on it deeply and handed it back.

'God, Cass, what's happened to them?'

'Probably nothing. Just her mother over-reacting.'

Juliet shook her head. 'I have a really bad feeling about this – I did at the time – the way we argued with them – them going off without a word.'

'They're grown ups, Juliet,' he said in irritation, 'it was their decision to hop it. Anyway, you said that you and Kurt weren't surprised they'd gone north. Do you know more than you're letting on?'

'No! How can you think that?' She turned her back on him.

'Sorry,' Cassidy said at once, 'I didn't mean to snap at you.'

Juliet sighed. 'I'm sorry too. It was just a hunch Kurt had. Marcus had pumped him for information on archaeological digs – the Bactrian stuff Kurt's into – seemed to get all excited at the thought of ancient treasure. You know what Marcus is like – he gets sudden enthusiasms. Kurt thought he might have gone off to try his luck – some dig near the Minaret of Jam or further north, I can't remember.'

Cassidy ground out the cigarette and took hold of her hands. 'A few phone calls and it'll all get sorted out - once word goes out on the grapevine. They're probably living it up in Lahore or somewhere, watching cricket.'

'If anything's happened to them, I'll never forgive myself,' Juliet said. The look she gave him seemed to say, and I'll never forgive you either. But maybe that was his guilty conscience.

That night they dined quietly at the Utze, but Cassidy could tell Juliet was dwelling on Ruth and Marcus for she said very little. It pained him to remember how happy and lively their previous meals had been there over Christmas and New Year. Now no one was left from the group except the two of them. He was almost relieved when the friendly Irish poet they had befriended on Christmas Day, came over to chat.

Over the next couple of days, Cassidy tried and failed to get through to Dave. At the end of the week another telex arrived at Yeti Travels: *Rucksacks still in Kabul. Police now involved. Send details on Marcus.*

156

Trying to reply, he realised with a shock how little he knew about his co-driver. His name was Marcus Barclay and he was a competent driver. He was occasionally helpful and frequently full of bullshit. Cassidy found it awkward asking Juliet for more details. She grew defensive.

'How should I know?'

'You shared a -' Cassidy stopped himself.

She reddened. 'He's thirty-something, went to Oxford. He's well-read. A gentleman traveller.'

Cassidy snorted at this and she clammed up.

Worry over the whereabouts of the missing pair began to blight their happy state. It hung over them like a rain cloud. Another week passed and no further word came from head office. While he wanted to let sleeping dogs lie, Juliet badgered him to ring and find out the latest. Finally Cassidy spoke to Dave.

After a couple of minutes ranting, Dave told him, 'Mrs English is insisting on going out east to search for Ruth. Her son's coming with her; the old man's not fit enough to travel. It's a bloody needle in a haystack job but if it'll keep the old bird off my back then good luck to her. You can make yourself useful by helping.'

'Me? How can I - '

'You've got our bus,' Dave snapped. 'You can ferry them around if needs be. Just keep her happy. You've got nothing else to do till May.'

'Well you can pay me wages first,' Cassidy said angrily.

'Keep your hair on – I'll sort it out,' Dave said and put down the phone.

Cassidy and Juliet existed in limbo waiting for instructions. A few days later they were sitting smoking in the Shangri-La Restaurant garden, discussing what to do when a cry went up across the courtyard.

'My friends! You're still here! Haven't you moved from that dining table since we left?'

Juliet sprang up and rushed across to greet Kurt. He kissed her cheeks.

'Oh, it's wonderful to see you!' Juliet cried. 'Come and sit down. How was your jungle trip? Where's Tomas?'

'At the hotel having a long hot soak.'

They chatted for a minute or two, but soon Juliet was telling him about the disappearance of Ruth and Marcus.

'It's all taking a more sinister turn,' she said, her face anguished.

'We don't know that,' Cassidy tried to sound up beat. 'If something terrible had happened, wouldn't they have found – you know – bodies?'

Juliet flinched.

Kurt said, '*Ja*, that's true. Don't think the worst. Marcus and Ruth may not think they are lost at all!'

They ordered pancakes and Kurt talked of his latest trip. Cassidy was grateful to the German for lifting Juliet's mood. That evening they joined Kurt and Tomas for a meal at their hotel, for which Kurt insisted on paying. Before the evening was over, Kurt was suggesting they all go trekking from Pokhara into the Annapurna range.

'That sounds great,' Juliet said, 'but we're waiting to hear what Cass has to do about Ruth's mother.'

157

'Whatever happens,' Cassidy said, 'you must go. No point having your holiday in Nepal spoilt.'

Juliet put a hand over his. 'No, if you have to go, I'm going with you.'

They carried on making plans to go to Pokhara, Cassidy hopeful that the Englishes would hear news of Ruth before embarking on such a daunting search. He wanted to rekindle the closeness between him and Juliet and knew that Pokhara by its fairytale lake would be just the place.

Just before setting off, a telex arrived telling Cassidy to go to Delhi and meet Sarah and Daniel English. Mother and son were flying in the following Thursday.

'Why Delhi?' asked Kurt.

'Perhaps they want to start at the orphanage, see if they can pick up any leads?' guessed Juliet.

'Probably just the quickest flight they could get out east,' Cassidy answered.

'We could all come,' Kurt offered, 'if you think it would help.'

Cassidy gave a wistful smile. 'I appreciate it. But I think it's all a waste of time. There's no point ruining everyone's trip. It's my responsibility.' He turned to Juliet. 'And you must go with the lads. I'll probably just be gone a week or two – long enough to talk some sense into Ruth's mam.'

She protested that she wanted to go with him, but later when they were alone he persuaded her it was for the best.

'I want to think of you here, enjoying yourself – not too much mind! – and waiting for me. When I get back we can do a trip just the two of us, eh? Or I can send word from Delhi and we can do a bit travelling down south – Goa and Kerela.'

He sensed her relief that he was letting her off the hook.

'Well, if you really don't mind. I'd really like to see more of Nepal. It's such a beautiful country and I might never afford to come back.'

On the day before he left, they walked out to Swayambunath crossing a muddy river and through brown fields where boys busied themselves making mud bricks and farmers carried baskets of earth balanced on long poles across their shoulders. Hand in hand Cassidy and Juliet climbed up to the stupa, their silence masked by the screech of monkeys and the chanting of worshippers around the shrine. Cropped-haired monks in maroon robes circled the brightly painted edifice, spinning prayer wheels. A horn blew from deep inside the temple.

Cassidy found a pie shop and bought Juliet a slice of apple pie. They sat on the terrace while she ate it.

'Tell me what you were going to tell me at Nagarkot,' she said, picking at the pie half-heartedly.

Cassidy let out a long breath. 'I don't want this to come out the wrong way.'

'Is it something to do with Pauline – or Paula?'

He started. 'How do you know about – who told you?'

She shrugged. 'Someone mentioned a phone call.'

'It's not what it seems,' he said. 'She's this lass back home. It's over now – at least it is for me. But a bad thing happened – I blamed myself.'

Juliet scrutinised his face. 'Remember when I asked you about Lucy nearly miscarrying – whether something like that had happened for you? Is that what you're trying to tell me?'

Cassidy nodded. It was more complicated than that, but it made no difference.

'Does this woman expect you to go back to her?' Juliet touched his arm. 'Be truthful.'

'It doesn't matter what she expects,' Cassidy said, swallowing down panic. 'It's you I want to be with – only you!' He gripped her hand, willing her to believe him. 'I've never felt like this about anyone before. I love you – and I've never said that to any lass before either. Do you believe me?'

She gazed at him with large troubled eyes, and then suddenly, miraculously, her face broke into a broad smile.

'I do believe you.' She leaned forward and kissed him on the lips. Her tenderness made his eyes sting.

They went to bed early and made love with the bittersweet urgency of those about to be parted.

'It won't be for long,' he whispered.

'I'll wait for you here after the trek,' she promised.

The streets were quiet and the sky dark with clouds in the early morning. The only sound was the twitter of birds in nearby trees and the dogs in the courtyard beginning to snuffle and stir.

'Stay in bed,' Cassidy urged, kissing a sleepy Juliet. 'I know how much you hate mornings.' Her cheek was flushed and warm. He breathed in her scent. 'Look after yourself Forbsy.'

She smiled and murmured. 'Love you.'

His last sight of her was the grey light playing across her wavy brown hair and pale forehead, the curve of her mouth. Then he shut the door and walked out into the cold dawn.

CHAPTER 53

'My dearest,
Last week I was part of a reconnaissance survey over the Arabian Sea.
We spotted an island that wasn't on our maps. It just seems to have risen
out of the sea! I'm back up north again in Quetta. The desert here is
terrific in the spring, flowers everywhere. I'm having a waistcoat made
for our unborn. He will look like a little prince in it, I can tell you! I
hope you and the parents are keeping well; you especially my love.
With <u>lashings</u> of love
Harry xx'
(Letter from Harold Forbes, March 1945)

Kathmandu, Nepal, late February 1977
Juliet

It was the end of February before Juliet returned to Kathmandu. Bad
weather had held up her trek with Kurt and Tomas for two weeks, so they
had idled away time in Pokhara, eating well and reading through the dog-
eared novels left by other travellers at the hotel.

Juliet fully expected to find Cassidy waiting for her at the Star, but there
was no sign of him.

'Are you sure there are no messages for me?'

The clerk gave an apologetic shrug. Her disappointment deepened
when she could not book the room she had shared with Cassidy; someone
else was in it now. She took a room on the floor below. There was
nothing at *post restante* either.

'Why don't you try Yeti Travels?' Kurt suggested. 'They might have
news from Rainbow Tours.'

To Juliet's delight there was a quickly scrawled postcard from Cassidy,
posted in Delhi nearly a month previously. *No luck so far. Sarah English*
very canny. Daniel's got a temper but can't blame him. Trying to
arrange visas for Afghanistan. Sarah determined to go to Kabul. This
may take longer than I thought. Will keep in touch. Miss you. Cassidy.

Her initial relief turned swiftly to doubt. The postcard was nearly a
month old. There had been no further word. Why had he not written to
her since? Was he in Afghanistan or India? Was he still at the beck and
call of Ruth's mother? And what on earth had happened to poor Ruth – to
Marcus? Lying sleepless at night, Juliet allowed negative voices to
whisper the unthinkable: Ruth and Marcus had been kidnapped or
murdered. Cassidy had changed his mind about her and headed home.

In the brightness of day, such thoughts were banished. She went to the
Nepal Bank on New Road and arranged to have the rest of her savings
transferred out; there was enough to last until May, maybe June if she was
careful. She would wait for Cassidy. Every other day she checked for
mail at the post office and Yeti Travels. Nothing came. Then one day, at

the *post restante*, she saw an airmail letter for Cassidy. The postmark was from Newcastle. She took it for him. It lay unopened on her bedside table.

March wore on. Tomas left to meet up in Pakistan with Rudi – the friend he had talked of in Istanbul - before returning to Germany. Kurt kept her company, but eventually said, 'I have to move on. I promised Tomas I'd join him before he goes back home.'

'Of course you must,' Juliet said, hiding her dismay. 'I'll be fine.'

A couple of days before Kurt was due to go, he came rushing to find Juliet. She was attempting to write poetry in the hotel courtyard. She looked up to see his face ashen.

'Take a look,' he said, spreading out a newspaper on the table. It was a month old copy of *The Times*. 'Someone left it at my hotel.'

Ruth's face – a younger version with a short fringe and a hint of school tie below her elfin chin – grinned out above the headline: *Missing British Girl in Suspected Suicide Pact*. Juliet's heart thumped in shock.

'Please God no!' She looked at Kurt in horror. 'This can't be true.'

He sat beside her. 'You should read it,' he said gently.

With shaking hands, Juliet read the article. The Afghan police believed that Ruth English and Marcus Barclay had taken their own lives somewhere in the remote central mountains. The police have now revealed that suicide notes were discovered in the rucksacks of the missing British pair. The short notes were identically worded and stated they were sick of modern living and wished to pass over to the other side. So far no trace of the couple had been found. Ruth's mother, Sarah English, was hopeful her daughter was still alive. Brother, Daniel English, speaking on behalf of the family, said they were very keen to find out more about Mr Barclay and he was not ruling out foul play. They appealed for any information or sightings that other travellers might have had.

At the end of the article it mentioned a Steven Cassidy. The driver of the fated bus tour had been interviewed by police. He was still helping the English family with their search. Juliet's insides twisted at the quote in the final paragraph. It was from his 'common law' wife, Paula Jenkins in Newcastle. *It's a terrible tragedy but from what I hear, that couple weren't very stable. I'm sure Steve has done all he can to help but I just want him back home now. I never wanted him to take the job in the first place. In future he'll be driving local buses.*

Juliet felt bile fill her throat. She couldn't take it in at first. Common law wife: what did that mean? Women were only called that if they had lived together with their partners for years, weren't they? She read it again.

'He's been in touch with her,' she said in a flat voice, 'he must've been.' She looked at Kurt with hurt-filled eyes. 'He's been in touch with her but not with me.'

Kurt said, 'You don't know that. She might be making it up. Some nosy journalist looking for a quote. Maybe she likes the – what you call it – limelight, *ja*?'

161

'Maybe,' Juliet said, grateful for any reassurance. Yet doubt immediately took over. 'But they must have got her details from Cassidy, surely? Why didn't he tell them to come to me or you for an opinion? We were on the bloody trip after all!'

Kurt put a hand on her shoulder. 'Don't judge him until you've heard his side of the story.'

Juliet's lips trembled. 'Oh Kurt, when is that going to be? I miss him so much.'

He pulled her into a hug. 'Cassidy is mad for you,' he encouraged. 'He is still in Kabul helping. That is the only reason he is not here with you. Okay?'

'Okay,' she tried to smile as tears leaked down her cheeks.

'That's good,' Kurt said, giving her his handkerchief.

'I can't take it in about Ruth and Marcus. It's so horrible. She was so young-'

'*Ja*,' Kurt sighed, 'I find it hard to believe.'

Juliet blew her nose hard and handed back his handkerchief. 'Did you know Cass was called Steven?'

'No,' admitted Kurt.

'Neither did I.'

That night, they bumped into a forlorn Devon. Maggie had up and left two weeks ago, or maybe three, he couldn't remember.

'Went off with some French dude with gold teeth,' he said morosely. 'Gonna chill out in Sri Lanka – or maybe it was Thailand. Bad karma, man.'

The three of them got drunk on Cleopatra whisky, but it only made Devon more maudlin. He couldn't stop crying about Ruth and Marcus. In the end, Juliet was so worried that she bedded him down in her room and slept on the floor. Except she could not sleep. Her mind whirred with anxiety and dark thoughts: how had Ruth and Marcus killed themselves? If she had stayed friends with them would they still be alive? What must her poor family be going through? It didn't bear thinking about.

Tossing and turning in her sleeping bag, Juliet seesawed between longing for Cassidy and fury at him for leaving her in limbo. The newspaper article had been written weeks ago; surely he had done all he could by now? Why hadn't he come back or at least sent her word?

He had told her it was over with Paula; but the woman spoke as if she expected him back any day. The postcard from India told her Cassidy missed her, so why had he not written to her from Kabul? It rankled that Paula knew him as Steve as if she had access to a whole different part of his personality – a private part he shared only with her. Juliet could never imagine calling him Steve or Steven.

In the early hours of the morning, she went out onto the balcony and smoked one of the cigarettes Cassidy had left her: Rhinos. When she had finished, she eased open the airmail letter that had come for him, swallowing down guilt. As she had feared, it was a long out-pouring from this Paula, begging him to come home. One sentence in particular seared her.

I miss our bairn so much, the one we should have had and I want us to try for another more than anything.

Juliet quickly folded up the letter; its neediness and misery were overwhelming. This woman was still very much in love with Cassidy. If she were in Paula's shoes, she would be devastated to know that he was carrying on with someone else. She leant her brow against the cold concrete pillar. God! Was that all she was to Cassidy: a bit of carry on? She could hear him saying it to Paula, dismissing their affair as 'a bit of daft carry on', just as he had played down the Paula relationship to her.

Suddenly she was crying: tears of regret and fury and loss and bewilderment. She tore up the letter and threw the shreds over the parapet. They danced away into the dark. Juliet refused to feel guilty. She hated Paula for dashing her hopes and hated Cassidy for his betrayal. Most of all she rebuked herself for falling in love with him. She didn't even know who this Steven Cassidy was.

'God, I'm crap at choosing men,' she hissed into the shadows. At that moment she wished she really was Grace Ellison and could retire to some cloistered comfortable harem to enjoy the segregated companionship of cultured women. Unexpectedly, an image came to her of Ruth's mother, plucky Sarah English, travelling from remote Weardale to the forbidding mountains of Afghanistan to look for her daughter. Wild horses couldn't keep her away. Juliet felt a gut-wrenching loss that she had never had a mother to care for her like that. She felt dizzyingly alone.

Worn out with it all, Juliet crawled into her sleeping bag and slept. When she awoke it was early afternoon and Devon was nowhere to be seen. He had left a note thanking her for looking after him. She found him in KC's eating dhal and rice.

'I'm going to travel on,' Juliet told him. 'Do you want to come?'

'Where to, man?'

'Back to Quetta. I want to find my dad – where he ended up.'

He looked at her from under his unkempt hair. 'What about waiting for Cassidy?'

She steeled herself. 'I want to do this before my money runs out.'

He put down his spoon. 'This is real important for you, right?'

'Right.'

'Uh-hu,' Devon nodded. 'Sure I'll come along with you.'

Juliet smiled at him. 'Great. Thanks.'

CHAPTER 54

Newcastle
Amber

Amber and Cassidy sat in the allotment shed with the rain drumming on the tin roof like clashing pans. The stove was lit. The room smelt earthy, of onions and wilting lettuce. Three empty bottles of beer stood on the table between them. Amber had drunk two of them. She had tried to get Cassidy to talk of his illness and was being upbeat about homeopathic remedies and Jez's insistence on juicing vegetables and drinking food supplements. Cassidy laughed it off as if it was a joke. Amber was trying really hard not to be tearful. She had become really fond of this man in the short time of knowing him. She was still grieving for her lovely gran; it was too cruel to think she might lose this gruff loveable Geordie too.

'Jez says they're offering you radiotherapy, but that you won't take it.'

Cassidy pulled out another cigarette, and then pushed it behind his ear.

'Why won't you?' Amber pleaded.

'Hospitals,' he snorted, 'they're for sick people.'

'You're sick,' Amber gulped down tears. 'They can help you, Cass.'

Cassidy coughed and leaned forward. 'I'm not sick, I'm dying. It's terminal, finito. All the vitamins in the world won't repair me oesophagus. Too many bastard cheap cigarettes.' He began to light up another.

Amber buried her face in her hands and stifled a sob.

'Hey,' Cassidy said gently and leaned over, pushing a crumpled checked handkerchief at her.

Amber grabbed it and burst into tears. The squeeze he gave her shoulder only made her want to cry more.

'Sorry, Cass.' She made a big effort to stop. 'I just want to help you.' She wiped her eyes and blew her nose hard.

'Tell me about this Robin Baker,' Cassidy changed the subject. 'Have you found out any more about him?'

Amber swallowed. 'No,' she admitted, 'I've hit a brick wall. The college had an address for him - digs in the town – but now it's a boutique hotel. No one has a clue where he came from. I've put a letter in the local paper asking for info – but it's a long shot. He may not have been from Oxford at all.'

Cassidy gave a rueful laugh. 'You gotta hand it to Posh Boy - had me fooled – Juliet too - she was always ganin on about how well read he was.'

'I wonder if Ruth ever found out who he really was,' Amber sighed.

'I think she would have stuck with him whatever,' Cassidy said. 'She depended on him – he was the only one she wanted when things got tough – the only one who could handle her outbursts. Juliet knew that too. When she'd calmed down about Marcus ganin off with Ruth behind her back, she admitted how much they suited each other – needed each other.'

'So Juliet talked to you quite a lot, yeah?'

Cassidy slid Amber a look. 'Aye, later on.'

'Did you two …? Jez thought you might have got friendly.'

'None of your business,' Cassidy snorted.

'Sorry.' She gave him a watery smile and squeezed his hand.

They sat in silence. The rain eased off. The smell of tobacco hung in the air.

'I was in love with her,' Cassidy said softly, 'Juliet. But it was complicated. The year before, I'd been living with this lass Paula. She got pregnant. I wanted us to have the bairn but she wanted an abortion – said she wasn't ready to settle down.' He paused. 'I handled it badly – angry like – said I'd gan off on another trip if that's what she wanted. Then before anything was settled, she miscarried.' His eyes glittered with unshed tears. 'We split up. I signed up for the eastbound trip your aunt was on. But I felt that guilty – all the arguing – maybe I'd caused the bairn to - ?' He broke off and let out a long sigh.

'I knew I should've stayed and tried to mend things between me and Paula. But then I met Juliet. She was different from the other lasses – a born traveller like me – everything excited her. I began to see the world through her eyes – fresh eyes. And I fancied her rotten. Never thought I had a chance mind. Was clear as a bell she had the hots for Marcus. But when he disappeared off the scene, we got a lot closer. For a while at least.'

Cassidy lapsed back into silence.

Eventually Amber asked, 'so what happened?'

Cassidy let go a long breath. 'We were still in Nepal when word came through there was a hunt on for Ruth and Marcus – when your aunt didn't turn up at the orphanage. Head Office told me to get my arse back to Delhi and meet your grandmother – she was flying out to look for her – and your dad too. Juliet said she would wait for me in Kathmandu. It took a lot longer than I thought - what with winter and not being able to search properly till the spring. Your grandma wouldn't take no for an answer. Had me driving all over searching, back into India an' all.' He paused to light up a cigarette.

'I got back to Kathmandu in May expecting to take a busload west again. But there was a telex telling me I was sacked. Apparently there was a bit of a hoo-ha ganin on at home in the papers and Rainbow Tours was getting the wrong kind of publicity. I was their scapegoat. And to cap it all, Juliet wasn't there either. I'd written a couple of postcards from Afghanistan, but I don't know if she ever got them. I didn't really expect her to have waited all that time. I hoped she might have left word where she'd gone but she didn't.'

'So what did you do?'

'I thought bugger it! They hadn't paid me for months so I held onto the bus and did a trip down to Goa – it was easy in them days to pick up passengers in any of the big cities. I half hoped I'd come across Juliet again, but I didn't. In the end I headed home with the bus half full. Stayed in Newcastle for a few months doing coach tours to Blackpool.

Got back with Paula but it didn't last. She married this lad from Vickers. I went out east again. Ran trips for different companies till the Iranian Revolution. Soon as the Ayatollah took over, they closed the borders. Killed the overland business stone dead. Once the eighties came, drivers like me looked to Africa and South America for long haul trips, or tootled around Europe with old aged pensioners.'

Cassidy smoked and stared beyond the rain-spattered window. The dark clouds were breaking up and moving on. Amber felt the sadness in the room like a separate presence. Cassidy's relationship with Juliet had been another casualty of Ruth's disappearance. Or perhaps Juliet had never felt as strongly as her driver had? Maybe he had only ever been a temporary consolation after breaking up with Marcus. After all, Juliet had neither waited for him nor tried to stay in touch. She felt a wave of resentment towards Cassidy's lover for dumping him.

Gently Amber asked, 'Did you ever see or hear from Juliet again?'

Cassidy appeared to ignore the question. He carried on smoking and gazing into the distance. After a minute or two he said, 'not exactly.'

Amber waited.

'I tried to track her down the following year after I came home – thought she'd be back in Durham by then and I had her address from the passenger list. But it was a rented house and someone else was living there. They'd heard the previous tenant had gone to live abroad. I contacted the motor tax department where she'd worked and one of the lasses said she'd signed over her car to her cos she wasn't coming back. Said she'd met a man. I gave up after that.'

Cassidy ground out his cigarette and pulled on his moustache. Amber kept quiet, sensing there was more to come.

'A few years later, when I was back out east, I bumped into this guy – real dope head – think it was in Amritsar – and he was reading one of Juliet's travel books. Had her name in it. Well, I had him up against the wall. Where did he get it? Had he nicked it? Swore blind he'd bought it in a bazaar in Quetta. Well that got me thinking. Maybe she'd gone back there to try and find this guy Aziz who used to know her dad and had a shop. So later that summer I took the train up there and tried to find the shop but it all looked different – place was full of Afghan refugees. I asked around the hotels: same thing. No one knew of Juliet - or Aziz for that matter.'

Cassidy stopped and rubbed his temples.

Amber said, 'the guy was probably lying about the book just to get you off his back. He could've picked it up from anywhere.'

'Aye, I know, but I just had this feeling. When I was in Quetta it *felt* like she was there.' Cassidy gave an embarrassed grunt. 'In fact I made a right fool of myself. I caught sight of this woman on a tonga – she was dressed like a local with a veil and that, but I could tell she was European – big feet in hippy sandals. Something about her reminded me of Juliet – the way she sat, her hands. She had her arm around this little lad. I remember it clear as day. He looked local: dark hair but fair skin and green eyes like a lot of Pathans. I ran after them shouting. This guy who was with them – big strapping bearded lad with a rifle – warned me off.'

Cassidy slumped back in his seat. 'Daft of me, but I was clutching at straws. Of course it couldn't have been her.' He gave the ghost of a laugh. 'Mind you, it wouldn't have surprised me if she'd gone native. That's what I imagine she did - settled out there and married – but not some head-case with a rifle. Juliet will have ended up with a maharajah or as companion to a mad old dowager.'

Amber saw how tired he looked. She stood up and cleared the bottles into a box. She would make soup tonight from the asparagus and radishes: soft food to coax his appetite.

'I hope you're right,' said Amber, 'and she didn't go back to Balochistan. Sounds like it was a dangerous place to be – civil war, then Afghan refugee camps – and it's probably worse now with the Taliban hanging out in the region.'

Cassidy snorted. 'You've been doing your homework.'

Amber smiled. 'Yeah, I did get a bit obsessed with Afghan boundary commissions.' She loaded a bag with mud-encrusted vegetables. As Cassidy hauled himself to his feet, Amber had to restrain herself from going to help. Treating him like an invalid would just get on his nerves.

'Do you believe in this place Bulbulak?' Amber asked.

'What, your Buddhist Kraut retreat?'

Amber rolled his eyes. 'No, the one in Balochistan that Marcus's ancestor discovered. The Shangri-la type place.'

Cassidy was dismissive. 'There were rumours on the trail about somewhere in the desert, but I never believed it. There's nowt out there but dust and rocks. Think the old soldier was on the whacky-baccy.'

Later, after Amber and Jez had encouraged their friend to swallow some soup and cheesy mashed potato, Cassidy returned to the subject that occupied his thoughts.

'There was one lad off the trip I did see again: Devon. What a state he was in,' Cassidy sucked in his breath. 'Hepatitis, dysentery, drugged up to the eyeballs. It was a crying shame cos he was a canny fella. Think he'd had a spell in the nick for possession, but it was hard to make out what he was on about.'

'Where did you meet him?' Jez asked, pouring him more green tea.

'He was begging on the streets of Delhi. Didn't recognise me at first, but when he did he started babbling on about blood and fire and how I had to do something to stop it. I think he was having flashbacks to Vietnam – it was really freaking him out poor bugger. I got him into a hostel and said I'd contact his embassy, but when I came back he'd gone. Never saw him again. Probably died years since, the way he was going.'

'When was that?' Amber asked, as she leaned in under Jez's arm.

'Early nineties?' Cassidy guessed. 'I took a tour round Mughal palaces in '94, must've been then.'

They sipped at their tea. Amber asked, 'so you had no idea where Devon had been all that time between the trip and finding him down-and-out in Delhi?'

Cassidy hesitated then shook his head. 'He talked a load of rubbish.'

'Such as?'

'I told him if he didn't get his act together he'd be in heaven or hell before Christmas. He said a weird thing: "I've been to heaven man, it's got ice 'n' roses", then he laughed like a hyena. Started a long ramble about mountains. But it's the ice and roses that stuck in my mind.'

'Poor guy,' said Amber.

'Aye,' Cassidy sighed, 'but at least he was happier thinking of roses than all the bad stuff he must have seen in Vietnam.'

After a moment, Amber said, 'what if it wasn't Vietnam he was talking about?'

'What do you mean?' Cassidy asked.

'Don't you think it's strange that he should talk to you about blood and death, Cass, the moment he knew it was you? Perhaps he was trying to tell you something.'

'He was off his head.'

'Yeah, I suppose so.'

Jez laced his fingers between Amber's. 'I think it's strange too,' he said. 'You know what it reminds me of Cass?'

'What?'

'That stuff you told us about Ruth screaming her head off in the desert. Wasn't she going on about seeing dead bodies too?'

CHAPTER 55

'LAHORE: a large city in the Panjab... Its population in 1881 numbered 149,369, chiefly Muhammadans and Hindus, with a small number of Sikhs. Situated on the high road from Afghanistan, Lahore has been visited by every invader of India, from Alexander downwards... The artisans now, instead of [manufacturing] Sikh armour, inlay caskets and studs, vases, paper-cutters, letter weights, and other fancy articles.'
The Cyclopaedia of India, Vol II, by Surgeon General Edward Balfour, 1885

Lahore, Pakistan, April 1977
Juliet

In the end, Juliet and Devon left Kathmandu with Kurt. Their friend was due to meet Tomas in Lahore. A week later, they were in the old Pakistani city. Juliet tried not to dwell on the last time they had been there, wandering around the lush gardens of the Fort and the vast beautiful red sandstone Badshahi Mosque, and watching cricket nearby. Cassidy's favourite game.

Tomas was not at the address in Golberg that he had telegrammed to Kurt. Juliet wasn't surprised; this prosperous-looking suburb looked too expensive for budget travellers like them.

'He's gone onto Quetta with Rudi,' Kurt reported.

'Quetta?' Juliet cried. 'That's great. We can all go together.'

Kurt looked pensive.

'Is everything okay?' Juliet asked.

'It's just Rudi. I'm not sure about him. Tomas said he would wait here.'

'Perhaps they're running out of time and want to press on,' Juliet suggested.

'*Ja*,' Kurt smiled, 'probably you are right.'

Before they left the city, Juliet visited the consulate and gave a statement about knowing Marcus and Ruth, and her belief that Ruth's mental state had been deteriorating en route. The more she thought about it, the more she came to believe that the girl was capable of taking her own life. Marcus she was not so sure about.

They went west by train, chugging through spectacular mountains, back into Baluchistan. With a pang, Juliet thought how familiar Quetta looked, yet subtly altered, blooming with early spring flowers. It seemed an age since she and Cassidy had roamed its crowded streets looking for Aziz's house. At the time she had been too wounded by exclusion from Marcus and Ruth to realise how much she had really cared for their driver. He had been so kind to her then. Why had she spoilt their friendship by encouraging him to become her lover? And yet she could not regret those few sweet weeks with Cassidy. As Kathmandu receded in vividness, she began to think of her time there as some strange intense dream. Not real at all.

After two days of asking around, it became apparent that Tomas and Rudi had moved on again. Juliet found a cursory note pinned up on a hotel notice board in German from Tomas. They had gone on to Nushki.

'They must be heading home then?' Juliet guessed. 'That's on the road back to Iran.'

Kurt shook his head, perplexed. 'I have a bad feeling about this.'

'Why man?' Devon asked.

But Kurt just shrugged.

Devon seemed content to laze around in the spring sunshine or smoke dope in his room, but Juliet determined she would travel out to Dalbandin to try and find Aziz's family. She made enquiries about hiring a taxi but it turned out there was an Exodus truck going west in two days time, so she begged a lift.

Devon was reluctant. 'I hate all that desert stuff. I'm just gonna stay here – mellow-yellow – till you come back.'

Kurt insisted on going with her. 'It's not safe on your own.'

He had been subdued and preoccupied since leaving Lahore, so Juliet was glad to see him take an interest. Perhaps it was just travel fatigue but she sensed it was more. His face was grey with tension; he looked his age now.

'Are you worried about Tomas?' she asked, the night before they left.

Kurt nodded.

'Is Rudi not reliable?'

'He is quite strong-minded,' Kurt said cautiously. 'Like Tomas he is an idealist.'

'That's good isn't it?' Juliet smiled.

'Of course. But I think it might get them into trouble. And I blame myself.'

She searched his troubled face. 'I don't understand. Tell me.' She put a hand over his.

'Rudi is looking for somewhere,' he said so quietly she had to lean close. 'For some people. I think it is – what you call – wild goose chase? But I have a map and I showed Tomas where it might be.'

'What sort of place?' Juliet asked.

Kurt shrugged. 'It doesn't have a name.'

She didn't believe him; he was keeping something back.

'Is this something to do with your Buddhist petroglyphs?'

Kurt glanced around. 'That was my interest but Tomas thought there was a secret commune. Rudi talked of it.'

Juliet puzzled. 'Is that why you left the bus in Zahedan? Were you looking for this place?'

Kurt looked about them, as if worried there were eavesdroppers.

'Yes, we looked but found nothing. I thought Tomas had given up. I was pleased. Tomas is a good doctor. He must go back to Germany and work. But Rudi ...' he broke off with a sigh.

Juliet squeezed his hand. 'After we have been to Dalbandin, I'll help you find them.'

The next day, they left Devon with enough money for rent and food for a week, and urged him to eat properly. The overland truck dropped them off in the desert town. Juliet was pleasantly surprised by the splashes of spring green, the tamarisk trees and grasses waving in the warm evening breeze. They found an old *caravanserai* with rooms to rent around a dusty courtyard busy with pack animals tethered to iron stakes. Juliet lost no time in asking around for the home of Aziz Baloch, the tailor. A young man who worked at the *caravanserai* looking after the livestock and spoke some English offered to be their guide. He could take them to someone who knew someone who knew Aziz.

'Is he still alive?' Juliet asked in excitement.

'Alive, yes,' the youth nodded.

He arranged to take them the following evening. Kurt was wary.

'Why do we go after it is dark? There is a curfew. I'm not happy.'

'Please come with me,' Juliet pleaded. 'This guy seems harmless. It might be my only chance. I knew those men in Quetta were lying about Aziz being dead.'

'Maybe they had their reasons. You could be getting mixed up in Baluch trouble,' Kurt cautioned.

'He was a friend to my father and my family, that's all. Anyone in authority will see that's my only interest. I'm just a tourist.'

'You're no longer in a tourist place.'

'Look Kurt, I'm going along anyway. Stay here if you want to.'

Kurt scratched his shaggy greying hair. 'No, I will come with you.'

***

Devon didn't worry for a week. He read one of the books Juliet had left behind about some crazy woman who rode about on camels and got on down with the natives. Obviously stoned half the time. He hung out with some overlanders at the Liberty Café and found a plentiful supply of cheap hashish in the bazaars.

It was nearly the end of the second week before he began to worry about his friends. Money was running out again. He moved out of the hotel and kipped on the floor of some dude who was waiting for a visa. He scrounged the odd meal. He read another of Juliet's books about another crazy babe who knew all about the opium trade in China.

By the end of three weeks, Juliet and Kurt had still not returned. Devon tried to recall what arrangements they had made. He was pretty sure they had said they would return to Quetta. Had he missed them or had they decided to head back west without him?

Devon made friends with an overland driver and offered to stay guard on the bus at night for a meal and a chance to kip in the gangway. He hung around and spoke to any trips arriving from the desert. Had they seen a tall hippy Brit girl with a middle aged German dude? The answer

171

was always no. Devon tried to remember the name of the place Juliet had gone to, but his mind was a blank. He sold his guitar.

At the beginning of May, when the temperature suddenly leapt and a hot dry wind began to blow, Devon sold Juliet's books to an Armenian dealer. Feeling guilty, he gave away half the money to the legless beggar who sat on a makeshift trolley outside the Farah Hotel. The rest he used to buy a one-way bus ticket to Nushki. The name rang a bell. He was pretty sure that was the place Juliet and Kurt had mentioned.

Early one morning, he boarded a noisy local bus that was already hot and airless, and set off for the desert.

CHAPTER 56

London
Amber

Back in London, Amber found a letter awaiting her from her dad. In it was a cheque for three months' rent for her grandmother's cottage in Weardale. Probate was now sorted out and in future she would get the money from the Cleggs paid directly into her bank account.

'The bills and house maintenance will be all yours from now on too,' Daniel wrote. 'The Cleggs want to stay until the end of the year, then buy their own place. Unless you want to sell them your house? Worth thinking about, then you'd not be stuck with having to look after the smallholding from hundreds of miles away.'

Amber shrieked and kissed the cheque. What a windfall! She rang Jez straight away.

'How about a week in Germany all expenses paid?'

Jez laughed. 'Are we talking luxury cruise down the Rhine or a week of cold sea bathing with a bunch of East German Buddhists?'

'Not too cold at this time of year,' Amber grinned. She told him about the cheque.

'I'd love to but …' Jez hesitated.

'Go on.'

'I'm worried about Cass. You know he won't eat a thing if one of us isn't there to bully him. Perhaps we should just wait a bit and see – go in the autumn – what do you think?'

Amber felt a flood of warmth for Jez. 'You're such a good mate to him,' she said, 'and you're right; we can't leave him on his own.'

It was Helen, coming in much later, who found the other letter tucked under the mat where it had lodged perhaps for days.

Dear Ms English

I got quite a shock to read your letter in the paper. I had a brother Robin who worked at one of the colleges. He was there four or five years. We grew up on a farm ten miles away but he always wanted to see the world and do better than our father who was a dairyman. We were quite close as children but I never saw much of him after he left school. After Oxford he worked on lorries. Long distance driving. If you think it's the Robin Baker you want to know about then you can give me a ring, but I can't tell you much more.

Yours truly,

Susan Webster (neé Baker)

It took several attempts over two days before Susan answered the phone to Amber. She spoke with a marked Oxfordshire accent, cautious at first then warming to Amber's friendly voice and her assurance that she was just filling in gaps in her family history, such as her aunt's friends.

173

'Wasted life really,' Susan confided. 'Robin was bright as a button but didn't get on at school. I think he's what you'd call today dyslexic or something. Anyway he was always getting into scrapes – too much energy and head full of fancy ideas. I wish I'd known him better as an adult.'

'So he didn't keep in touch?' Amber asked.

'No. Had itchy feet. Took jobs all over. Loved it out east, but that was his undoing. He was killed in a road accident in Pakistan. At least that's where the letter came from. His friend wrote to me, you see. It was ever so kind really. Robin had known him for years apparently. Anyway he sent me Robin's money and passport and a little silver box that he'd bought to send to me. I've still got it.'

'Can you remember the name of Robin's friend?' Amber asked.

'Yes, posh name: Marcus something.'

Amber tensed. 'When did you get the news of Robin's death?'

Susan sighed. 'It was shortly before Christmas, 1976. He'd died in the November.'

'Did he ever mention my auntie, Ruth English?'

'No dear. He had quite a few girlfriends by all accounts, but I don't remember that name.'

Amber said, 'Thanks for taking the trouble to contact me, I really appreciate it.' She paused. 'Just out of interest, do you happen to remember where the letter was posted from – the one that Marcus sent?'

'Oh, yes, I do. It was such a pretty name. Quetta: that's where he was. Nice isn't it?'

***

That night, Amber lay awake thinking of Ruth in Quetta. This Robin Baker stuff was mind-blowing. Had Auntie Ruth known that Marcus was cutting his final ties with home, discarding his true identity as Robin Baker for the last time, killing him off? Had she helped him compose the letter of condolence to his unsuspecting sister Susan? Or had Marcus done it without her knowing, sneaking away to post it while she dozed or wandered the bazaars? Surely Ruth would not have gone along with such a hurtful act? It was far more likely that Marcus had planned it all himself. He had shed his old life completely and taken on the identity of his fantasy hero, so that no one would think of coming looking for him. He was untraceable. But for what reason? Was he already planning a suicide pact with Ruth, but leaving himself an escape route if it all went wrong? Or was Marcus the calculating murderer that her dad had always maintained he was?

Unable to sleep, Amber got up and padded out to the balcony. She found the restless sounds of the city soothing; she wasn't alone in her wakefulness. She smoked one of Cassidy's *beedies,* for which, to her mum's dismay, she was acquiring a taste.

174

All her leads were hitting dead ends: Marcus's friends, Robin's family, Ruth's flatmates, Juliet, Devon. Was there anything left to explore before she called it a day?

There was Kurt. She hadn't fully delved into the life of the gifted archaeologist, or the traces he left behind at Bulbulak. Amber suddenly yearned to get away and follow her curiosity to eastern Germany. If nothing else it would be a different sort of holiday; a change from digging in peat bogs in Ireland for Iron Age pots. But there was only one problem. She so wanted Jez with her and hated the thought of going away without him.

As she stubbed out the *beedie*, the answer came to her.

'Jez? Sorry to wake you but I've had a cool idea.'

'Umm?'

She could visualise him, warm and sleepy, hair tousled, phone to his ear.

'Let's take Cassidy with us to Bulbulak. He'll love it – probably bunch of old hippies smoking weed and levitating. And it might just do him some good – the holistic thing. They're big on health and all round well-being. What do you think?'

'Cool,' Jez murmured, 'I'll ask him in the morning.'

'Great!' Amber felt light-headed with excitement. 'Maybe stress the happy hippy side more than the healthy stuff, yeah?'

'Yeah,' agreed Jez. Amber was about to ring off when he added, 'I love you, Missy Zen Buddhist sexy eyes.'

Amber's heart squeezed. 'You too,' she grinned.

CHAPTER 57

'Hi, it's Amber English. Sorry to bother you again Susan. There's just one thing I wanted to ask.'

It was the week before she was due to travel to Germany with Jez and Cassidy.

'That's okay dear,' Susan replied.

'You said that your brother Robin drove long distance lorries?'

'Yes, that's right.'

'But did he ever work on the rigs up north?' Amber held her breath.

Susan paused. 'No, never on the rigs. Not that I knew of.'

She hid her disappointment. 'No worries. I just thought he might have known my Auntie Ruth from when she lived in Edinburgh.'

They made small talk about work and the weather. Amber was about to ring off when Susan said, 'did you say Edinburgh?'

'Yes. My aunt lived there for a couple of years.'

'Robin did go there. He drove refrigerated lorries down to London full of fish. Brought me Edinburgh rock. Stayed there for the Festival – he liked music and acting and things like that. I think he had a friend he could stay with. Yes I'd forgotten that.'

Amber's heartbeat quickened. 'Cool. Can you remember exactly when that was?'

'Let me think. Umm, must've been mid-seventies – '74, '75? – cos after that I never heard anything until the accident. So could he have known your Auntie Ruth?'

Amber's pulse beat in her throat. 'Yes, he could.'

CHAPTER 58

Kühlungsborn, Germany
Amber

Cassidy wouldn't fly, so they took the overnight ferry from Newcastle to Amsterdam and a series of trains through Holland and Germany: Amersfoort, Enschede, Münster, Bremen, Hamburg. The vast station was teeming with travellers, commuters and backpackers. They ate soft Frankfurters in pea soup from a stall outside the Hauptbahnhof listening to classical music over the tannoy among t-shirted crowds enjoying the evening sun.

Pressing on eastwards, Amber gazed at the sun setting over woodland and canals, and wondered where her German grandfather had come from?

'Germany?' Daniel had asked suspiciously, when Amber had rung to tell her dad. 'What d'you want to go there for?'

'For a holiday with Jez.'

'You hardly know him.'

'I know him enough to want to go on holiday.' She knew that disapproving tone; that's why she hadn't yet taken Jez to meet him, even though her dad only lived an hour north of Newcastle.

'When do I get to meet him then?'

'Soon.' Amber had hesitated then added, 'we're taking Cassidy with us to Germany.'

'You're joking? Don't be such an idiot. Two men that you've only just met -'

'It'll be fine. We're really close friends.'

'That man,' Daniel had hissed, 'is no friend of our family's.'

'Oh Dad, don't be like that. Cass is a friend of mine, and he's got cancer. I want to be there for him.'

'For God's sake be careful.'

'Don't fuss. I'll send you a postcard. Love you Dad.'

Schwerin's station was a fancy brick building like a mini St Pancras; a train carrying logs sat in a siding. The town was surrounded by lush gardens and orchards. After that, the countryside grew more undulating and peppered with small lakes. A deer stood poised on the fringe of grassland between water and woods. By Rostock night had fallen and they changed trains for the last time for Bad Doberan.

Cassidy looked grey-faced and exhausted, so Amber was glad she had arranged the first night in a comfortable hotel. Twenty minutes after reaching their final stop, a taxi was driving them to the coast and up the strand at Kühlungsborn. A row of ornate hotels with wooden turrets and balconies overlooked a windbreak of swaying pine trees and the Baltic Sea. Deposited at the Polar-Stern, a large wooden-clad hotel painted in white and blue, they were given a cheerful reception by the owners Albrecht and Dagmar who spoke immaculate English.

The jocular Albrecht, who knew Scotland well, gave Cassidy a complementary whisky before the old driver turned in for bed. From their bedroom balcony Amber and Jez could smell the spicy resinous smell of the trees in the warm night air and hear the sighing of the sea.

'This is great,' Jez said, slipping his arms around her waist. 'Wouldn't mind staying here all week.'

'Yeah,' Amber smiled, 'let's pack Cassidy off to the retreat to eat lentils and we'll do luxury.'

She gazed into his dark eyes and felt the familiar kick of yearning inside. A whole week together. Even if she discovered nothing further about her aunt, she was going to enjoy this holiday to the full.

When they emerged late the next morning, Cassidy was drinking tea and chatting with Albrecht and Dagmar about the resort.

'Been for a swim an' all,' Cassidy said proudly, 'never swum in the Baltic before.'

'Another one to add to your list then,' Amber smiled, kissing him on the head as she sat down.

They discussed what to do that day. The picturesque-ness of the old resort had taken them by surprise and no one was in a hurry to leave for Bulbulak. Albrecht offered them bicycles on which to explore and Dagmar recommended a trip on the Molli, a vintage steam train that ran to the seaside spa, Heiligendamm. While Amber and Jez took the bicycles, Cassidy elected to relax and read on the beach. They found him later, snoozing in a strand-korb, a double-seated wicker contraption that was part deck chair, part windbreak.

'We've found just the place for you to eat tonight,' Amber said. 'It's a restaurant inside the local brewery. We've booked a table. You can have a tour round it first.'

Cassidy grinned, 'this is my kind of town. You can leave me here when you go.'

They stayed another two nights and then, despite loving every minute of their stay, Amber became restless; Bulbulak still beckoned. Their friends at the hotel were vague about the place. They knew that it was located in the forest to the east, in huts that had once housed factory workers from Leipzig on their annual holidays in the days of Communism. There had been mild publicity when Kurt Kiefer had died, but the commune kept largely to itself. They grew their own food, ran occasional yoga classes on the beach and sold honey and jam made from local sanndorn berries. Sometimes locals came across them chanting in the woods or dancing among the sand dunes. They were seen as eccentric but harmless.

Amber rang ahead to double check they could be accommodated for four or five nights. A woman answered in German but changed into English at Amber's faltering attempts to reply. Her accent sounded French.

'Staying is no problem. It's bunk beds. You said you are three people? That's okay if you don't mind sharing.'

She gave directions from the nearest bus stop. It was a mile through the woods from the Bad Doberan road.

The day was hot and the sun fierce on the open highway, but walking down the track through the trees was cool and pine scented. Amber walked between the two men.

'There's still wild boar in the forests inland,' Cassidy told them cheerfully, keeping up a good pace. 'It's grand to be somewhere where it's not completely tame and safe – adds a bit o' spice to life, eh?'

'As long as they stay wild and boaring in their own forest and not this one,' Amber replied, giving his hand a squeeze.

The first sign of the retreat was the sound of children's voices at play. Their laughter and high-pitched chatter rang through the trees. They came up to a high fence made of wooden stakes threaded with reeds that offered privacy rather than defence, and pulled at a bell rope in front of a large wooden gate.

CHAPTER 59

Bulbulak, Germany
Amber

A young woman in long shorts and baggy t-shirt, her hair tied up in a bright pink headscarf, answered their ringing.

'Namaste!' she greeted them breezily. 'You're Amber right? Come right in.' She sounded American. After Amber introduced the others, the woman said, 'You're welcome. You can drop off your packs first, then I'll show you round. I'm Sunshine by the way.'

'You can tell,' said Cassidy, following in her wake.

They were shown into an ochre coloured cabin with orange blinds at the windows. The room held two sets of bunk beds, a couple of wooden chairs, a chest of drawers and a green and orange hand-woven rug on the bare wooden floor. Sunshine pointed out the washrooms in a long building opposite and gave them each a pillowcase, inner sheet and a small threadbare towel. She left them to unpack.

Cassidy sat down on a bottom bunk. 'I warn you now I snore.'

'We know,' Amber and Jez chorused.

Cassidy chuckled. He leaned over and fingered the heavy, rough woollen blanket, then plunged his face into its dark brown mass.

'Goat's hair,' he said. 'Reminds me of Kandahar.' He laughed at their puzzled faces. 'We used to stop over at this cheap hotel – same rates for a floor as camping. Good kebabs – played Bob Dylan – and heavy blankets that kept you warm as toast no matter if it was sub-zero outside. Was a beautiful place Kandahar.' He sniffed at his bedding again. 'Aye, takes me right back.'

Amber rolled her eyes at Jez. 'Well, he's easily pleased. All we have to do is sing him to sleep with Mr Tambourine Man.'

'Yeah,' Jez laughed and sang the first line of the song.

Cassidy snorted, 'glad you young'uns know your Dylan.'

'You play him every day below me, remember?' Jez teased.

Sunshine returned and gave them a guided tour around the camp. A central communal building stood like a high-bowed ship with huge glass windows giving views onto the sea. Peering in, they could see rows of cheap Formica-topped tables and plastic chairs, while in the upper room they glimpsed bookcases.

'Up top is the library and yoga space,' explained the young American.

Radiating out from this central hub were rows of huts along sandy footpaths and an outer ring of workshops and poly-tunnels. Beyond were clearings cultivated with vegetable beds and fruit bushes.

'We forage in the woods,' their guide said with a wave of her arm at the forest beyond, 'nuts and berries and beehives. We have tree houses too, so that guys can go off and be solitary - like if they need space, you know? Kurt did a lot of that.'

'What was he like?' Amber asked.

'Oh, he was a great guy,' she enthused, 'so into nature and peace. A real quiet guy.'

'That's not how I remember him,' Cassidy grunted. 'He could talk all night and drink you under the table thirty odd years ago.'

'You knew Kurt Kiefer?' she gasped in admiration.

'Aye, took him all the way to Kathmandu on a bus in '76. Did he never mention it?'

She shrugged. 'Well, I can't say I got to know him well. By the time I came he was like this hermit sorta guy, real old, you know? Lived out in the woods. Al and Roxane would take him his food. Sometimes he'd come out for dawn meditation or to swim in the sea by moonlight.'

'I like the sound of that,' said Cassidy.

'Al's Kurt's son, right?' Amber asked, as they made their way towards the beach.

Sunshine nodded. 'He's awesome.'

'Can we meet him?'

'Sure. He's away today taking produce to market. But maybe tomorrow.'

'What about Kurt's wife Roxane?' Amber persisted. 'Is she still here? Can I talk to her?'

Sunshine gave her a surprised look. 'I dunno. She's at the retreat house. You're not a journalist are you?'

'No she's not,' Jez said quickly, 'she's an archaeologist. Amber's just keen to learn about Kurt and his work that's all.'

'Awesome,' Sunshine smiled.

As they emerged onto the beach, a westerly breeze was whipping up the sand. Amber shaded her eyes and squinted. A group of children were running in and out of the sea, splashing and shrieking. At the mouth of a voluminous Bedouin-style tent, some adults were picnicking. Behind them, a disused concrete watchtower had been painted a riot of gaudy colours, around a large unblinking eye that gazed out to sea. Sunshine left the three visitors there to share the bread and tomatoes and boiled eggs.

'I'll catch you later. Enjoy!'

The conversation was carried on in a mix of German, English and Italian. Once Cassidy had been offered a beer, he relaxed and tried out his rusty German, boasting that it was Kurt who had taught him a few phrases.

'Is there a lad called Tomas Schwartz here? He was a good friend of Kurt's. Tall, dark bushy beard.'

They shook their heads. There was no one here of that name. Cassidy exchanged looks with Amber. Amber was discouraged. It didn't look like they were going to uncover anything earth shattering here.

The afternoon was spent relaxing on the beach. A meal was served in the dining hall in the early evening. Amber counted thirty adults (including kitchen staff), nine children and four more that looked teenaged. Sunshine sat with her visitors, along with a young Italian called Giorgio who had been on the beach.

'Everyone who comes to live,' he told them, 'must stay for one year here. Maybe more. But see the year go round – each season – understand the earth better, *si*?'

'How long have you been here?' Jez asked.

'Four years,' he smiled.

'How did you find this place?' Amber asked.

'I hear from friend at university. We come together but he not stay. It is not good life for everybody, I think. In winter is hard.'

'It's nearly all word of mouth,' Sunshine added. 'Isn't that how you guys got here?'

'No,' Amber said, 'I read about it in Kurt's obituary then sent for information.'

'Oh, well,' Sunshine grinned, 'either way you were meant to come.'

'So where does the Buddhist stuff come in?' Jez asked. 'I don't see lots of blokes in orange robes and prayer wheels.'

Sunshine shook her head. 'It's not really that religious – more spiritual. You can meditate or pray in groups or on your own, or you can just chill out. As long as you stick to the ideas of love and peace and helping those around you, then it's cool.'

'We don't eat meat, we don't carry guns,' said Giorgio.

'Well as long as you haven't signed the pledge,' grunted Cassidy, 'then this place suits me down to the ground.'

'The pledge?' queried Giorgio.

'Booze lad. As long as you can still have a drink.'

'I think what Cassidy is trying to say,' explained Amber, 'is can he have another beer?'

That night, returning up the pathway lit by solar lamps to their guest hut, Amber said, 'I'd like to help Sunshine pick berries tomorrow. How about you Cass?'

'Aye, maybe. Swim first mind.'

They settled onto their bunks. In the dark Cassidy said, 'funny name Sunshine. Do you think she just made it up?'

Amber said, 'I bet her parents were a couple of hippies.'

'Is Roxane a German name?' Jez asked.

Amber yawned, 'No. Roxane was the Afghan wife of Alexander the Great – they married after he'd occupied and ripped off her country.'

'Nice way to meet,' Jez said dryly.

'Didn't think Afghanistan existed in the time of Alexander,' murmured Cassidy.

'No, you're right,' Amber said. 'It was probably still called Bactria in those days.'

***

The next morning Cassidy was lacking in energy and refusing breakfast.

'Think I'll lie here a bit longer,' he told his friends and turned over to sleep.

They left him alone but Amber was concerned. 'He doesn't even want to swim.'

Jez took her hand. 'It's probably all the travelling catching up. He's going to have good days and bad.'

'Maybe we should cut our losses and go back to the Polar Stern – pamper him for a few nights? It's a bit basic here.'

'But you want to find out more about Kurt, don't you?'

Amber sighed. 'Yeah, but Cassidy comes first. And my gut feeling is there's nothing more to find out.'

'Give it another day,' Jez suggested. 'We'll get Cass out in the sunshine later.'

They spent the day helping out: Jez in the poly-tunnels picking salad and Amber in the woods harvesting wild berries. In the late afternoon they joined Cassidy on the beach where he was refereeing a game of children's football from an old camp chair, shouting and gesticulating. Pleased to see him reviving, Amber and Jez joined in. It ended in chaos with half the players losing interest and running off with the ball into the sea.

Afterwards, they sat on the shore as the light softened, Giorgio bringing out some cold beers to share with them. The beach went into shadow; the children disappeared. Eventually a gong boomed, announcing the evening meal.

'*Andiamo*!' said Giorgio, taking their empty beer bottles. 'Or we are last in queue for food. Not good.'

Reluctantly, the three stood up.

'Not last,' said Jez, nodding down the beach.

A woman was standing at the water's edge, blue skirt hitched up as the sea sucked around her ankles. Her hair was bound up in a green scarf like a turban. She stood very still and straight-backed, her face tilted to the last of the sun's rays.

'Who is she?' Amber asked.

Giorgio said, 'Ah, that is Roxane. She likes the *spaggia* when it is empty.'

'We better leave her to it then,' said Jez. Both Amber and Cassidy were staring at the poised figure. 'Amber?'

She turned and nodded, taking his hand. All at once, Cassidy took off, running down the beach.

'Cassidy!' Amber shouted after him.

'What the hell's he doing?' Jez exclaimed.

Giorgio cursed and started after him, Jez and Amber following. Turning back from the sea, Roxane caught sight of the commotion. Alarmed, she retreated quickly towards the trees.

'Wait!' Cassidy called out, panting as he ran. 'Let me talk to you!'

Giorgio caught him up and grabbed his arm. 'Hey, stop. She don't want to talk.'

Cassidy bent double, heaving for breath. As Amber and Jez reached him, he stood up wheezing. 'Go – after - her – please.'

Amber put an arm round his shoulder. 'Hey Cass, you look terrible.'

At that moment, a lean man with close-cropped brown hair and a hooped earring glinting in the sunset, strode out of the woods.

'What's all this?'

Giorgio said, 'Sorry Al, this guy go crazy when he see Roxane.'

'You must leave my mother in peace,' he chided. 'She's in mourning.'

'I'm sorry,' Cassidy, his face putty-grey and glistening, said. 'I thought I -' he faltered. His shoulders caved in defeat.

Al looked at them properly, his annoyance subsiding. 'Are you the English visitors?'

'Yes,' said Amber, 'I was the one who wrote to you.'

Al shook her hand. 'So you are the archaeologist who knew of my father? I'm sorry I wasn't here to greet you.'

Amber introduced her friends. 'Cassidy knew your dad in person – they travelled to India together in '76.'

Al gaped at the older man, quite taken aback. He held onto Cassidy's hand. 'You knew him?'

Cassidy nodded. 'I was his bus driver – took him overland. We shared many a late night drink and putting the world to rights.'

Al's eyes shone with emotion. They waited for him to find his words. 'Forgive me; it's just the shock of meeting someone from my father's past.' He let go of Cassidy's hand. 'Last month was the first anniversary of his death. That is why Mutti is on retreat and not seeing people.'

'I'm sorry lad,' Cassidy said. 'I liked your dad. It must be hard on you both.'

Al nodded.

Just then, Amber caught sight of Roxane emerging from the tree line, barefoot and cautious. Close up, she was middle-aged, her handsome face scored by lines. She stared open-mouthed, as if distrusting what she saw.

'Cassidy?' She said his name softly, quizzically.

Cassidy jerked around. He cried out, half pained, half triumphant. 'I knew it! I knew it was you.'

Then his knees buckled.

CHAPTER 60

Al helped Amber get Cassidy into the Bedouin tent. Weak legged, Cassidy sank down onto cushions. His eyes brimmed with tears.

'I'm sorry,' Roxane said, 'I didn't mean to upset you. It's a shock for me too, to find you here.'

Cassidy just stared at her, beyond speech. Amber and Jez exchanged anxious glances. Amber had no idea what was going on. Al fetched a bottle of water from a cool box. Cassidy drank it with difficulty, spluttering as if his throat were plugged.

Roxane squatted beside him, resting a hand on his shoulder. Blue veins like cords knotted the backs of her hands, betraying her age more than her face.

Cassidy wiped his clammy face with his sleeve. With an effort he found his voice.

'All this time? You and Kurt together?'

'Yes.'

'And the lad?' Cassidy nodded towards Al. 'He's yours too?'

Roxane nodded.

Cassidy bowed his head. A moment later, a deep sob broke out of him. Roxane leaned forward to comfort him, but Cassidy pulled away. 'I'm all right.'

She asked, 'How did you find us?'

'I didn't,' Cassidy said, 'Amber did.'

She fixed Amber with vital eyes – young eyes in an old face. 'You're an archaeologist?'

Amber nodded. 'I read about Kurt in the newspaper – wanted to find out about Bulbulak – I wish I'd met him – I've so many questions.'

Roxane looked mystified. 'I can try and answer them if you like, but I'm no expert in Kurt's work.'

'The lass isn't after that,' Cassidy broke in. 'She wants to find out what happened on our trip. That's why we've come all this way.'

Roxane tensed.

'Amber is Ruth's niece.'

Roxane stared at Amber.

'Aye, Daniel's lass,' said Cassidy. 'So if you know anything I don't know, you have to tell her.'

Roxane pressed a trembling hand to her mouth.

'Cassidy,' Amber said, 'tell me what's going on.'

'This is the woman I used to -' he broke off with a sigh of regret. 'This is Juliet.'

CHAPTER 61

'There were white, green and blue hangings, fastened with cords of fine linen and purple to silver rings and pillars of marble; the beds were of gold and silver, upon a pavement of red and blue and white and black marble.'
The Book of Esther, chapter 1, verse 6.

Baluchistan, West Pakistan, April 1977
Juliet
Her mind resurfaced from some deep place to the sound of a woodpigeon. For a moment Juliet thought she was back in her grandparent's house in Durham. But it did not feel like her bed and there was an animal smell like untreated hide. She tried to open her eyes, but her head thumped in pain and she closed them again. Where was she? She fumbled to remember her last conscious thoughts: Kurt and she had gone with the stable boy to a house in the town. Two men. A woman had served them tea. Had they gone somewhere else with the men? Got into a taxi? Or was that somewhere else? Perhaps she was back at the *caravanserai*. God, how her head hurt!

Kurt. She tried to say his name, to call out for him, but found she couldn't. His name rang around in her head. Juliet lost consciousness again.

***

The door creaking open woke her up. Juliet squinted. A stocky, broad-shouldered man in baggy white Baluch clothes stepped into the room. He had a rifle slung over his shoulder. He looked severe under his large turban and thick dark beard. Juliet's heart lurched. He stared at her. She lay completely still. He turned away. She appeared to be in a crude hut, lying on a mattress covered in an animal skin. A shuttered window let in arrows of light between what looked like slats of leaves. Had she been kidnapped? Fear throttled her.

The guard aimed a spit at the doorway. It stained the ground red with betel nut juice. She moved a fraction and he noticed at once. He shouted out in a language she didn't know. Juliet shrank back.

A few moments later an unveiled woman with short black hair and male *shalwar kameez* padded into the hut bearing a pottery bowl.

She crouched down beside Juliet and spoke in accented English. 'Drink. It's sherbet.' A cool hand touched her brow.

Juliet tensed. Her lips felt thick and parched.

'It's okay, I don't hurt you. Now drink.' The young woman helped prop Juliet up. The cool sweet sherbet dribbled down her chin as Juliet tried to gulp. 'Slowly, slowly, that's good.'

It tasted like nectar, like her Nan's homemade lemonade. 'Thanks,' Juliet whispered.

The stranger's expression was guarded.

Juliet croaked, 'What's your name?'

The woman did not answer.

'What's happened to me? Why am I here?' The woman stood up. 'Don't go yet. Please speak to me. Where is Kurt? Is he all right?'

She hesitated then said, 'Your friend is okay. He too is sleeping off hangover.'

'Hangover?' Juliet had no recollection of drinking any alcohol. She felt light-headed with confusion.

'We had to drug you. You were asking too many questions.'

The guard returned and grunted something. Juliet gave him a frightened look.

The woman said something back in his language. He replied, sounding severe.

'What's going on?' Juliet asked, scared and disorientated.

'Your friend is also awake,' she said.

'Can I see him?'

The woman ignored her plea and made for the door.

Briefly, Juliet glimpsed another hut of baked mud with a roof of untidy tamarisk branches.

'But where on earth am I?' she asked. 'Is this Dalbandin?'

'Don't ask us questions,' the woman said, 'we can't tell you. You will speak to our commanders. Then they will decide what to do with you.'

CHAPTER 62

Juliet was brought a basin of water for washing and a bucket to use as a toilet. Twenty minutes later, Kurt was led in blindfold by the same guard. As soon as he removed the blindfold Juliet threw her arms around Kurt and burst into tears.

He hugged her back. 'You're safe, thank God.' They pulled apart and surveyed each other. Kurt smiled, but she could see the strain on his unshaven face. The guard propped himself in the doorway.

'Where are we?' Juliet whispered. 'And who are these people?'

Kurt dropped his voice too. 'They didn't like you asking about Aziz. Perhaps they are Baluch separatists. I've tried to explain we don't want to cause them any trouble.'

'Oh, Kurt, I'm so sorry for dragging you into this.'

'Don't be. I would have come looking for Tomas anyway.'

The woman returned with a tray of food: bowls of pulao, hard-boiled eggs and flat bread, which she placed on the bare floor. She poured them water from an earthenware jug. Juliet smelt it suspiciously.

'The water is good,' the woman said, pouring some into the palm of her hand and scooping it into her mouth. 'See?'

She left them alone, but Juliet was too anxious to eat. She watched Kurt squeeze handfuls of rice into balls and pop them in his mouth while she chewed on a piece of bread.

The woman returned. 'They will see you now. You must hide your eyes.' She held up two scarves.

Outside, Juliet could feel the heat of the sun bearing down on the top of her head as she groped forward. A hot wind blew. The path under their feet was uneven and stony. From a distance she could hear a muffled sound of bells - sheep or goats perhaps? - and a strange whirring noise that she could not place at all.

'Hold onto me,' the woman instructed, 'it is narrow and steep.'

Juliet had the impression they were scaling the side of a cliff or mountain. The air was dry and thin, and the crunch of their footsteps seemed to echo off rock. After ten minutes it felt cooler; they had gone into shade. The sounds changed. There was birdsong and the crackle of crickets. She could smell perfume: a heady scent of lilies. Surely she was mistaken?

They halted. Their blindfolds were removed. They were standing in front of an open-sided pavilion, its mud-baked walls painted ochre and its archways hung with muslin. Raised voices came from inside: an angry woman's and a placating man's. Juliet looked quickly about her, but thick bushes alive with the cooing and chirruping of birds obscured any view. Baffled, she followed Kurt behind the gauzy curtain.

Juliet caught her breath; the walls were adorned with a mosaic of blue and orange tiles, their reflection shimmering in a central water tank with a fountain. On a raised platform, a tall woman with Slavic features and pale hair, dressed in dusty overalls and hands on hips, stood among scattered cushions.

A scholarly looking man with wild black hair and glasses, dressed in a crumpled blue shirt and baggy pantaloons, sprang to his feet. His lean face looked tense. 'Please, come and sit down. Would you like tea?'

'Tea?' the blonde woman derided. 'I don't believe this!'

'I'll make some,' the dark-haired woman said and quickly disappeared.

They perched awkwardly on cushions while the man folded himself neatly into a squatting position. Juliet noticed his long-fingered hands that he used expressively as he spoke in a cultured voice.

'I apologise for the manner in which you have been brought here. It was not ideal. But we have to be cautious. We need to know your business.'

Before they could answer, the tall woman rounded on them. 'You've been asking for Aziz Baloch. Why? Who sent you?'

'No one sent us,' Juliet answered.

'I don't believe you,' she snapped. 'We know you met with police agents in Quetta last year.'

'Agents? Never -'

'At the Club. You were recognised by one of our comrades.'

Juliet felt panic. 'I didn't know -'

'See!' the woman turned in accusation to the man. 'They can't be trusted. I say get rid of them now.'

'Calm down Lena.'

'Don't tell them my name!'

'Sorry.' He held up his hands to ward off further verbal attack. 'Please comrade, sit down and let them speak for themselves.'

Juliet's throat was tight with fear. Kurt spoke.

'We don't wish to make trouble. Please believe us. Juliet's father died in a plane crash in this area – many years ago before she was born. Aziz Baloch was one of the last people to know him. Juliet simply wants to meet him and thank him for being her father's friend. It is personal, nothing to do with police.'

'You mean you are looking for the old tailor?' Lena demanded.

Kurt and Juliet nodded. Their interrogators exchanged looks.

'We thought you were after his son Aziz,' the man said quietly.

'Don't explain,' Lena warned then turned on Juliet. 'The old man is dead. Three months ago. You have wasted your trip.'

Juliet felt winded. 'Are you sure?'

'I'm sorry,' the man nodded. 'And I'm sorry about your father.'

'Always sorry, sorry,' Lena muttered.

He ignored her. 'And you?' he asked Kurt. 'You are just helping?'

Kurt hesitated. 'I'm looking for a friend – Dr Tomas Schwartz. We came out east together on the same bus as Juliet. He's travelling with a man called Rudi.'

'But you haven't found them?'

'No.'

'Were they going back West?'

189

Kurt eyed him. 'They were looking for a secret commune in the desert.'

Looks shot between Lena and their questioner.

Juliet blurted out, 'is this where we are? Is Tomas here?'

Lena jabbed a finger at her. 'Shut up and stop asking questions! There is no one called Tomas here.' She turned to the bespectacled man. 'I've got work to do. Don't waste any more time on these two.'

She barged out of the pavilion. They stared after her.

'You won't harm us will you?' Juliet asked anxiously.

The man looked offended. 'While you are here you have our protection. I apologise for my comrade. She is worried you are spies.' His mouth twitched. 'But I don't think you are.'

'Obviously not very good ones,' Kurt said dryly.

Abruptly the man smiled. 'Tell me something of yourselves.'

'Kurt is the interesting one,' Juliet said, 'he's an archaeologist and an expert on Bactria. All he really wanted to do was search for Buddhist holy sites and I got him into all this.'

'Kurt?' the man leaned forward, his dark eyes behind the owlish glasses sparking with interest. 'Not Professor Kurt Kiefer from the British Museum?'

'Yes.' Kurt's eyes widened in surprise.

The man explained. 'I studied at Oxford in the 60s. As a Baluch I was interested in your work. There are traces of Buddhism in this valley.'

'There are?' Kurt asked in sudden excitement. 'Would it be possible - ?'

'That depends.'

'On what?'

'Whether you stay or go.'

Juliet's insides clenched. Her instinct was to get away as quickly as possible and yet part of her thirsted to know more. This strange intense man intrigued her, and even though Aziz was dead, he might be able to tell her something about her father's friend.

'Who are you?' she asked.

He hesitated then said, 'I am Comrade Taj.'

'Can't you tell us anything about this place?'

He pressed his palms together and considered her. 'It is no bourgeois hippy commune. Here we nurture food and socialism in equal measure.' He checked himself. 'But to tell you more might endanger my comrades. Tell me, are you acting alone?'

'Yes,' Juliet said, and then wished she hadn't.

'I need to know if anyone else is likely to come looking for you. Does anyone else know of your trip to Dalbandin? You must be truthful.'

Kurt and Juliet exchanged wary glances. Juliet thought of Cassidy. She had left him no clue as to her onward travel plans, too hurt by his dishonesty over Paula to care. Now with a pang, she wished she had left him word of where she had gone.

'There's Devon, a friend in Quetta,' said Kurt.

'Yes,' Juliet agreed. 'He'll expect us back.'

'When he runs out of hash,' Kurt added.

Taj raised an eyebrow. 'He has a drug problem?'

'Just cannabis,' Juliet said.

Kurt added, 'He picked up the habit in Vietnam.'

Taj nodded. 'That terrible imperialist war. We grow a little hashish here for medicinal purposes. But nothing stronger. Marx said that religion is the opium of the people. But from what I've seen, it is opium itself we should fear – it rots the soul quicker than anything. My grandfather's health was ruined by it. There will *never* be poppy-growing in this valley.'

He fixed them with his searching look, his body taut with suppressed energy. 'I should probably arrange for you to go back to Quetta at once. That's what Lena wants.'

'Do we have a choice?' Kurt asked.

Taj spread his hands. 'If you have courage and a taste for hard work, you can stay and help us here in our commune.'

'Help with what?' Juliet asked. 'How can we decide when we don't know where we are or what you're really doing? Is it something to do with making Baluchistan independent? Because you don't look very warlike.'

Taj gave a sudden laugh. 'No, we believe in peaceful revolution. If we can create utopia here in this rocky wilderness then we can do it anywhere. My family has been trying to get justice and autonomy for us Baluch for a hundred years – ever since the British promised to protect our independence and then didn't - but I am sick of waiting.' Taj leapt up and paced the pavilion.

'You've travelled through here, you've seen how the people live. In hovels or in tents – struggling to live in a barren land – rounded up and persecuted by the Pakistani army – ill educated and ground down. So what do they do? Fight among themselves for a little bit of power. Instead of working together to overthrow the system they play into the hands of their oppressors – they carry on blood feuds and revenge for things done two generations ago. Divide and rule. That's the classic strategy of those who wield power and have no intention of giving it up.'

He threw his arms wide, his look passionate. 'But not here. We are showing how the land can be made rich – how it can support our people. We recruit comrades with knowledge – in agriculture, medicine, engineering, teaching – and they commit to our revolution. This place was once an oasis where my ancestors farmed. Then a plague wiped half of them out. After that it was said that the valley was cursed and no one wanted to come here. But we don't let such superstitions get in our way.'

'So why do you keep it secret?' Juliet asked. 'Surely you should be telling everyone about it if you want to spread good farming methods.'

'It is not that simple. We live in dangerous times. There are those who would see us fail – think us godless communists. And there are others who think we are hiding Baluch separatists. So for the time being we must guard our commune from the unwanted attention of the army and others. That is why we feared you might lead our enemies to us.'

'We're sorry,' said Juliet, 'we had no idea.'

'And are you hiding separatists?' Kurt asked.

Taj eyed him. 'I can tell you no more unless you make a commitment to stay. But if you go, that is it. You will never find us again and you must never try to return.'

Juliet knew that staying was her only chance of learning anything about the life of Aziz. But if they did, what would happen to Devon?

She asked, 'If we stay, then decide the life is not for us, is it possible to leave?'

'You must commit for a year. The commune has been running for eight. No one has ever wanted to leave,' he smiled, 'so you would be the first.'

'Can't we just see round the commune before we make up our minds?'

'I'm sorry I cannot allow that.'

'But what is there for us to do here?' Kurt demanded. 'I am an academic. I have my work back in Germany.'

Taj gestured beyond. 'You are in the middle of rich archaeological land. You would be free to survey and dig in the valley. We encourage the pursuit of culture – it is not enough just to own the means of production. Here you will find traces of your Buddhist monks.'

'Petroglyphs?' Kurt asked, his eyes alighting.

Taj nodded. 'You would have to help out with some of the chores, but there would be plenty of chance to pursue your studies. And I have contacts across the border in Afghanistan. It would not be impossible for you to spend some time out of the commune if it was important research.'

Juliet could see Kurt's interest quicken. Taj was either an idealist or a clever manipulator.

Kurt said, 'How long will you give us to decide?'

'Till nightfall.'

Impulsively, Kurt said, 'I want to stay.' He gave Juliet a pleading look. 'What's a year out of a whole lifetime? We could do something really worthwhile here. Stay Juliet, please.'

She agonised, casting around the beautiful pavilion for an answer. Grace Ellison would have jumped at the opportunity.

'I'll stay on one condition.'

'You're hardly in a position to demand conditions,' Taj said dryly, 'but what is it?'

'That our friend Devon is allowed to join us.'

Taj shook his head. 'No. No more. This is no place for drugged up hippies.'

'He's a casualty of imperialism, you said as much yourself,' Juliet challenged. 'And he's penniless – he'll not survive alone.'

Taj threw up his hands. 'Lena will kill me,' he muttered. 'Okay, your friend can come.'

'Thank you!'

'But he works hard and stays off the weed.'

'We'll be responsible for him,' Juliet promised, feeling a surge of nervous excitement.

Just then, the dark-haired woman reappeared with a teapot and small glasses and a plate of figs on a tray. '*Voila*! You are staying?'

'Yes,' Juliet grinned.

The woman smiled for the first time. 'I'm Eloïse.' She poured out cardamom tea and handed it round. 'Welcome to Bulbulak.'

CHAPTER 63

Bulbulak, Baluchistan, West Pakistan, April 1977

Juliet was not prepared for the view that greeted her as they emerged from the bushes around Taj's pavilion. Colour assaulted her senses. Trailing vines crisscrossed overhead to create a shady walkway between a dozen huts. At the end of this leafy tunnel, terracing dropped away to fields of swaying green wheat and barley. A web of channels gurgling with water zigzagged between them. Goats and fat-tailed sheep grazed in the shade of willows, mulberries and pistachio trees.

They were in a steep-sided gorge, with the settlement facing north and in partial shade. Strong sun glinted off the rock, and a hot wind turned a series of windmills that clattered below. That had been the whirring noise that had so perplexed her when blindfolded. Above were the mouths of caves and a scattering of other mud buildings half hidden behind banks off spiky bushes.

On every available ledge, flowers burst out of crevices and brightly painted pots.

'The eating house is on the next level,' the young woman explained, leading them up the path. Juliet caught sight of a dove flitting into a slit in the rock.

'That's what I heard when I first woke up,' she panted, trying to keep up. 'It was a dove.'

'Some say they carry the souls of the departed,' Eloïse replied.

At an open-sided chamber furnished with brightly woven rugs and long low tables, they were introduced to Marco the cook, a thin balding Italian, who offered them sweet cool water.

'It tastes wonderful,' Juliet said. 'Where does it come from?'

'Mansur will show you.'

Mansur turned out to be a handsome Kashmiri who had trained with the Indian Forestry Commission. He was very enthusiastic about the hydrology of the valley.

'We have revived the ancient system of underground tunnels and water pumps. It's amazing what we can grow here – everything from plums and chickpeas to beetroot and melons. And always a clean water supply.'

As they climbed along the terraced cliff, Juliet could hear the low murmur of water falling but saw no trace of it. Mansur ducked under a thick overhanging bush and seemed to disappear into the rock.

'Come, come, follow me!' his voice echoed from beyond.

They found themselves in a dark crevice wide enough to take a pack pony with a shaft of cool light beyond. Mansur beckoned them on. As they emerged onto a narrow ledge, a deafening thunder of water met them. Juliet gasped.

In front of her a waterfall spilled out of the cliff face about thirty feet above and plunged into a large green pool at her feet. From there it disappeared into the rock again and rumbled underground like a distant

194

train. Date palms and creepers had sprouted around the water source and small birds flitted overhead.

'The Rud i- Perian,' Mansur said with a sweep of his hand, 'the Fairy Pool. We come here to bathe in the evening. And that is the source of our life – Bulbulak – the Hissing Water. Without this we could not be here. It is also our way in and our way out.'

Juliet gawped at him. 'I don't see how …?'

He pointed at the waterfall. 'Behind there is a cave. It leads into the Chagai Hills.'

'Is that how we got here?' Kurt asked in disbelief.

Mansur grinned. 'Yes, on the back of a donkey like a sack of rice.'

'So does all this land belong to Taj?' Juliet asked.

'It belongs to us all,' Mansur said proudly.

'So the other Baluch around here don't mind?'

He gave an evasive shrug. 'Taj's father is well-respected – his word is rule around Kacha Kuh – the Black Hills. We have the Khan's protection.'

He led them back. As they passed a cave mouth with roughly-hewn pillars supporting a lintel, Kurt gave a gasp.

'Wait, stop! What are those?' He stretched up and ran his hand across some markings on the lintel: round circles, wheels and dots. 'Petroglyphs,' he cried in delight. 'This must be the cell of a Buddhist pilgrim.' He spun round, his face lit up. 'Juliet this is it, it really exists, just as Taj said! Do you know what this means? It shows some Chinese pilgrims used a westerly route through the Hindu Kush to India.'

Mansur gave him a baffled look. 'Buddhists? There are no Buddhists here.'

Kurt laughed. 'No, not for a couple of thousand years. But they were here. Can I look inside?'

'I'm sorry, no,' said Mansur. 'This cave is for isolation.'

'For people who are ill?' Juliet asked.

Mansur shook his head. 'For meditation, for thinking. There may be someone in there. Do not disturb,' he smiled.

They descended by a different path. Juliet noticed a track that ended at a large low lying hut almost hidden in flowering creepers. Mansur followed her look.

'That is the house for women,' he said with a bashful smile. 'They can go there to be without men or to have babies.'

'How very civilised,' she laughed.

'Sometimes there is need. If a woman is having bad pregnancy, she is allowed rest and no work. Other women look after her.'

Eloïse met them as they came down the path. 'I'll show you to your room.'

They followed her down the vine-covered walkway. She stopped outside a small hut that clung to the cliff edge. Inside, it was dingy and smelt of drains but the mud floor was covered in a bright red and black carpet. Bedrolls, blankets and a pile of cushions were stored in one alcove and a washstand with bowl and pitcher stood in another. There

195

were niches in the walls for candles and lamps. An unshuttered window gave a spectacular view of the sheer drop down the valley and the serrated mountaintops beyond.

'You can divide the room in half,' Eloïse said, tugging at a curtain that was tied back at one end of the small room. 'It's up to you.'

It was then that Juliet realised she was expected to share with Kurt. Perhaps they had assumed they were a couple? 'Evening meal is at sundown,' Eloïse told them and left.

Kurt and Juliet looked at each other warily. 'Which side do you want?' Juliet asked.

'You choose.' Kurt said, turning to gaze out of the window. With his back to her he said, 'don't worry, I don't snore.'

'Good. But I'm afraid I'm told I do.'

He turned round and smiled. 'Well if it gets too bad, I'll banish you to the Women's House.'

'I knew that would make you jealous,' she grinned.

***

That evening, a sea of faces greeted them around a long candlelit communal table: Charlotte (a bubbly potter from Cumbria), Ziggi (an Israeli plumber with a line in bad Jewish jokes), Masjid (an Iranian science teacher), Kasim (their guard who was a cousin of Taj's) and a dozen others whose names Juliet couldn't remember. The conversation was lively and carried out in several languages. Only Lena refused to acknowledge them and sat at the far end throwing contemptuous looks. At a smaller table in an adjoining room half a dozen young children squatted around a smaller table eating falafels and dhal, chattering like starlings.

Charlotte told them that there were others who were absent: a medical team giving inoculations to the children of nomads passing through to the summer pastures, and a further dozen at the Helmand River, fishing and gathering reeds while the spring watercourses were still plentiful and the weather bearable.

'Once the Bad-i-Sad-u-Bist-Ruz begins to blow,' explained Masjid, 'the wind of a hundred and twenty days, then it is too hot on the plain for anyone who isn't a camel.'

They dined on lamb biryani and vegetable paratha, followed by a bread pudding enriched with pistachios, almonds, raisins and cream. Afterwards, people relaxed back on their cushions to smoke and drink tea. The wind had dropped and brilliant stars pulsed in the night sky. Mansur and another man fetched instruments – a sitar and drums – and began to play a rhythmic and haunting melody while an older woman sang.

'Abida is a Sufi poet from South Pakistan,' murmured Eloïse, 'very well respected. Related to Taj on his mother's side.'

Juliet let the music wash over her. She and Kurt appeared to have stumbled into paradise. Already she felt completely at home. The guiding hand of Grace Ellison had led her here, she was sure of it. How

Cassidy would love this place! Juliet felt a sharp pang of regret and then chided herself: this was a new start among new friends.

Someone jabbed her in the back. She turned to see Lena leaning close as she passed by.

'Taj is soft person,' she hissed, 'but I am not. You work hard and keep out of my way. Understand, Bourgeoise?'

She walked off.

Juliet felt indignant. 'What's her problem?'

Charlotte whispered, 'She hates anyone that Taj takes a shine to. Lena is Taj's partner.'

'Prima donna,' Juliet muttered.

'Don't underestimate her,' Charlotte warned.   'She's the brains behind the commune – the practical stuff – best engineer we've got. But then they train them well in the Soviet Union don't they?'

'Is that where Lena's from?'

'Yeah.'

'How did she meet Taj?'

'A summer work camp in the Ukraine or somewhere.'

'How romantic,' Juliet said with a wry laugh.

But Charlotte looked uncomfortable. 'Take my advice; don't cross her or she'll make your life hell.'

CHAPTER 64

Juliet was given the most menial jobs and knew Lena had had a hand in it. Day after day, she did the back-breaking task of filling water skins for the kitchens and communal washhouse, and cleaning out the primitive latrines. Even after a fortnight, she still retched every time she did that chore.

Kurt was despatched to help in the metal workshop, bashing old tins into hooks, candleholders and plates. Late at night, they would lie out on the flat roof of their hut smoking cigarettes, almost too exhausted to speak.

'She's a bitch,' Juliet complained.

'It doesn't help that you call her the Tsarina behind her back,' Kurt said in amusement. 'Someone's bound to have told her.'

'Well she's a despot. And she won't let me anywhere near Taj to ask about Aziz or even about Devon. They promised he could join us.'

'Perhaps they can't find him. He could have travelled on.'

'I think the Tsarina's put her foot down. Taj is scared of her.'

'We're all scared of her.'

Juliet sighed. 'I'm not sure I can stand a month of this, let alone a year.'

They fell silent, listening to the hum of crickets and watching the trace of shooting stars over the black mountains.

***

The days grew rapidly hotter. One night a thunderstorm rolled down the valley like a volley of canon-fire, pursued by a northerly wind. Ten days of calm hot weather followed.

'There'll be another storm shortly,' Mansur told her as he helped her fill up the water-skins and strap them to a contrary donkey nicknamed the Shah. 'Then the summer winds will come.'

That night, a dozen of them went up to the Fairy Pool, stripped off and swam in the cool water under a moon with a bright halo. It glittered on the dark water like molten silver. Lena kept a watchful eye on the other women, and made a show of kissing Taj as they tread water. Juliet kept her distance.

There was no warning at what happened next. One minute they were splashing around, chatting over the noise of the waterfall, the next there were screams and the crack of gunfire. Dark figures spilled out from behind the waterfall brandishing rifles. A volley of gunfire went off. Juliet's shriek was a noiseless gasp of terror. The swimmers scrambled for the ledge. She felt Kurt grab her arms and haul her out.

Taj bawled out commands as he reached for his gun.

'Stop, stop!' Kasim shouted down from a lookout above. 'No shoot! No shoot!'

Taj wheeled around. 'What - ?'

'It's fishing men!'

The attackers emerged from the shadows into the moonlight and round the side of the pool. All were heavily laden but only two with firearms. Their faces grinned in the ghostly light.

'Comrades!' one of them cried, gleeful at the mayhem caused. 'Always swim with your pants on!'

'You bastards!' Lena shouted, grabbing at her clothes. There was a hasty wrapping in blankets and loud cursing from the swimmers. Juliet struggled into her loose kaftan, heart still pounding with shock.

Only Taj laughed. 'Rustum, our joker in the pack. I shall have to double the guard.'

'Your guard was easily bribed with an ounce of best Afghan,' the man chuckled, throwing down a pack and unwinding his turban.

Suddenly Kurt clenched Juliet's arm. 'My God ...'

'Good fishing, my friend?' Taj asked.

'Excellent,' the man replied, pulling off his boots and plunging feet in the cool water. 'Caught the biggest sturgeon I've ever seen. So Lena you can have caviar for breakfast just like Comrade Brezhnev.'

'Along with your balls,' Lena retorted.

The man threw back his head and laughed. Juliet stared. A shiver went down her spine: that laugh. She started to shake. Holding onto Kurt she stepped forward.

'It can't be - ? Marcus, is it really you?'

CHAPTER 65

At first Marcus seemed as stunned at the sight of Juliet and Kurt as they were of him. He stared back, lost for words. It was Taj who took command.

'You must be mistaken. This is our Comrade Rustum.' He took Juliet by the elbow. 'You've had a bit of a shock. And these chaps need something to eat. Come, we shall talk over a plate of food.'

On the way downhill, Taj murmured to Juliet. 'You know this man?'

'He was on our bus trip,' Juliet gulped. 'Went missing with a young girl.' 'They're looking for them - '

'Please say nothing about this just now,' Taj interrupted. 'I know this man from Oxford.'

'But – '

'I have my reasons for asking,' said Taj. 'The safety of the commune is paramount. You can ask your questions later.'

The fishing troupe was given big bowls of spicy soup and hunks of bread. Juliet and Kurt hovered in the shadows watching Marcus eating and boasting about their expedition as if he had been living among them for years. Juliet could hardly contain herself, seized by a mixture of disbelief and impotent rage. The worry he had put everyone through! And where in God's name was Ruth? Eloïse appeared at her side.

'Taj wants you to wait at the peace house. He'll bring Rustum there to speak with you. *D'accord?*'

At the secluded pavilion, Eloïse lit lamps and closed the rattan shutters, then left. Kurt sat with his head in his hands. Juliet smoked furiously. They didn't have long to wait. Taj entered with Lena and Marcus. Marcus attempted to embrace Juliet, but she pushed him off.

'What have you done with Ruth?' she demanded.

Marcus exchanged quick looks with Taj. Taj nodded.

'I haven't done anything with her. She's okay.'

'Then where is she?'

'She's being cared for – here in the commune.'

'We haven't seen her. Why should we believe you?'

Lena cut in. 'Who cares what you believe, Bourgeoise? You have only just come here, yet you think you can boss around - '

'Lena, please,' Taj warned.

'Do you realise,' Juliet continued uncowed, 'there's a major hunt on for this man and his girlfriend in Afghanistan – and all over the place? It's in the British newspapers.'

Taj said calmly, 'they needed a place of sanctuary.'

'Sanctuary?' Kurt said in exasperation. 'Sanctuary from what?'

'Our old lives,' Marcus said.

'How bloody selfish!' Juliet cried. 'Have you any idea what havoc you're caused to other people's lives? Cassidy's been searching all over with Ruth's family.'

'Must be his guilty conscience,' Marcus retaliated.

200

'Meaning what exactly?'

He gave her a pitying look. 'Meaning he encouraged us to go. Your salt-of-the-earth honest Geordie gave me a wad of cash to get rid of us. He didn't care a stuff about Ruth's welfare.'

'That's rubbish,' she cried.

'It's true. All he wanted was us two out of the way so he could have you all to himself. Bet he cosied up to you after we went,' Marcus challenged, 'didn't he?'

Juliet flushed crimson. Kurt came to her rescue.

'It makes no difference if Cassidy tried to pay you off – you were disrupting his trip. The fact still remains; you planned the whole disappearance with suicide notes. You faked your deaths,' Kurt said with contempt.

'Not faked,' Marcus replied, 'Marcus and the old Ruth are dead.'

'But you're not,' Juliet retorted. 'And what about Ruth's family? Can you imagine what you're putting them through? You have to let them know you're alive, you have to!'

Lena snapped, 'they'll do nothing. If they make contact, it could lead our enemies to the commune. We could be wiped out.'

'Don't be so dramatic,' Juliet exclaimed. 'All it would take would be a phone call.'

'No,' Marcus said, 'we don't want to make contact with the old world. That's behind us now.'

'Maybe for you, but what about Ruth?' Juliet challenged.

'She doesn't want it either.'

'Why ever not?'

'Because,' Taj intervened, 'she has chosen to reject the corrupt bourgeois world that she came from – a world that betrayed her.'

'What do you mean?' Kurt asked tersely.

'Tell them,' Taj ordered quietly.

Marcus took a deep breath. 'When Ruth was younger, she was abused by someone she trusted. Not a relation, but a close friend of the family.'

'Oh, God,' Juliet groaned.

'She blames her family for not protecting her – especially her mother,' Marcus added. 'She wants nothing more to do with them.'

There was silence but for the tinkle of the fountain. Shadows contorted on the walls in the flickering lamplight. Kurt bowed his head and let out a soft moan. Juliet's fury drained out of her.

'Oh poor, poor girl,' she murmured. She looked around the tense faces. 'I'm sorry.'

Taj nodded. 'How could you know?'

'It explains so much I suppose,' Juliet said quietly. 'So where is she now?'

'In the Women's House,' Taj answered.

Juliet said, 'helping out?'

Marcus lifted his chin. 'No,' he said, 'she's resting.'

Juliet caught a look on his face. 'Oh?'

'Yes. Ruth is expecting my baby.'

CHAPTER 66

The next day, she was allowed a few minutes with Ruth. Juliet found her in the shady inner courtyard of the Women's House lying on a charpoy. The heady scent of roses filled the warm air. As soon as Ruth spotted her she burst into tears.

'I never thought I'd see you - '

They hugged. Juliet felt the hard warmth of Ruth's distended belly.

'I'm so sorry the way we left,' Ruth sobbed.

'It's okay,' Juliet reassured, 'I'm just thankful you're safe and well.'

'I wanted to tell you but Marcus said - '

'Don't you mean Rustum?' Juliet mocked.

Ruth pulled away. 'You're angry with him? Don't be. He's been fantastic. He sorted everything out. I think I really would have killed myself if it hadn't been for him, I really do!'

Juliet saw her agitation and swallowed down her string of questions. She took Ruth's hands in hers. They had plumped out, as had her face.

'You look well. They must be looking after you.'

Ruth nodded.

Juliet smiled. 'This will be a special place to bring up a child. Are you excited? Marcus seems very proud.'

Ruth looked down, her long hair falling across her face. 'I'm frightened.'

'Well that's only natural, but there are experienced people to help deliver the baby.'

Ruth shook her head. 'It's not the birth,' she said. 'I can put up with pain.'

'What then?'

For a long time Ruth said nothing. Juliet realised there were tears running down the girl's face. 'Tell me,' Juliet urged.

'It's going to die,' Ruth whispered. 'I keep seeing it – blue and dead. The baby.'

'Oh Ruth, you're just being over-anxious. It's not exactly been a normal pregnancy for you, has it? You've just got to relax about things. You're safe now. Nothings going to happen to you here – or to your baby. So don't go worrying over silly dreams.'

'Not dreams,' Ruth hissed. 'I *see* it. It's been happening from before I even knew I was pregnant. At Nemrut Dagi – I thought it was Lucy's baby that was going to die – but now I realise it's mine!'

Ruth's nails dug into Juliet's palms as she clung on. Juliet winced.

'You mustn't get upset like this; it's not doing you any good.'

'Do you think it's my punishment,' Ruth fretted, 'for all the bad things I've done?'

'No, of course not. Come on, relax.' Juliet pushed her gently into a lying position and stroked back her damp hair. 'Let me get you a drink. Some of Eloïse's lovely sherbet.'

But when she tried to stand up, Ruth clung onto her.

'Will you stay with me here Juliet? Until the baby comes?'

Juliet hesitated. Marcus might see it as interfering, Lena as shirking. But Ruth looked so lost and terrified.

'If that's what you want, then of course I'll stay.'

CHAPTER 67

Juliet remained a month in the Women's House, keeping Ruth company and helping with the daily chores. She had imagined it would be like a religious retreat, full of quiet and contemplation, but it was run by a bubbly nurse called Heidi; the handful of women who came and went filled the house with laughter and singing and sometimes shouts and tears. They cooked for each other, gave massages and read out loud. At night they gathered in the courtyard to chat and as the summer heat intensified, slept out on the roof to catch any breeze.

Juliet found nothing onerous in caring for Ruth; the girl seemed to relax in the company of the women and regain some of the light-hearted playfulness of old. Juliet quickly became Ruth's confidante. She learnt how Ruth had first met Marcus in Edinburgh a year before the trip, how Marcus had planned Ruth's escape to India when she had failed her course, how he had tailed the bus and taken advantage of Cassidy's need for a driver (spiking the relief driver's food with laxatives) and how they had concocted their final disappearance once they knew of her pregnancy. As Juliet suspected, Marcus had never been romantically interested in her, she had just been co-opted into the threesome as a bizarre cover, feeding his need for excitement and intrigue, and Ruth's need for a female figure she could trust. All Marcus had ever really wanted from her was her father's detailed reconnaissance map; Ruth admitted that they had stolen it.

'Marcus had picked up rumours about the commune on his travels, but didn't take them seriously until Tomas and Kurt started asking questions about Baluchistan. He remembered that Taj was from here – they'd been at Oxford together – so in Esfahan he made contact with Taj through a Baluchi mechanic. By the time we reached Quetta, Marcus had set up a meeting. By then we'd decided to disappear forever. Taj's people helped plan our escape route down the Helmand River. You see,' Ruth said with an anxious smile, 'we were meant to find this place, it was our destiny.'

One evening as they sat under a mulberry tree, propped up on cushions, Ruth returned to the subject that most troubled her: the elaborate hoax of her disappearance with Marcus.

'We didn't set out to lie to you – to any of you. It all just got out of hand. My visions,' Ruth said, 'really began to scare me and Marcus.'

Juliet was brushing out Ruth's fine blonde hair, an act that relaxed and calmed her. She was prone to panic attacks and Heidi came frequently to monitor her blood pressure. Juliet was tiring of Ruth's obsessive raking over of the trip, of how it had gone sour, but she sensed a deep-seated unhappiness. Despite all that had happened, she still felt a strong protectiveness towards the girl.

'Perhaps the bad things you see will stop after the baby is born,' Juliet encouraged. 'Maybe it's hormonal imbalance or something.'

'Yes,' Ruth seized on the idea. 'Once it comes everything will be different, won't it?'

'Yeah, you'll have your son or daughter to look after – you won't have time to worry about anything else.'

'Just me and Marcus,' Ruth said, as if Juliet had not spoken, 'just as we always planned it would be.'

Ruth went into labour on a scorching June day. The hot desert wind carried the taste of salt to the lips. Ruth, pacing in agony, chose to stay in the Women's House.

'I don't want Marcus to see me like this,' she wailed.

They stripped off her clothes and let her wallow in the courtyard pool while the birthing room was prepared. Juliet watered the leaves in the slatted shutters to create a cooling breeze. Someone arrived with ice from the store they kept deep in a cave and broke it into slivers for Ruth to suck. The labour was long and arduous; by evening Ruth was worn out.

'Perhaps Dr Abrahams should come in,' Heidi said in concern.

'No,' Ruth hissed, 'no men.'

At two in the morning, exhausted and sweat-soaked, Ruth gave birth to a tiny boy. 'Let me see!' she panted.

Juliet helped her sit up while Heidi placed the slippery baby on Ruth's chest. He gave a small whimper, his rosebud mouth opening. Juliet felt her eyes sting with tears.

'He's gorgeous,' she smiled.

Ruth recoiled. 'Give him to Rustum.'

'Just hold him a moment,' Juliet encouraged. 'You've done all the hard work.'

Ruth closed her eyes and sank back. 'Not now.'

Heidi and Juliet exchanged worried glances. Then the nurse snipped and tied off the umbilical cord, wiped and wrapped the baby in a clean piece of cotton and handed him to Juliet. 'I'll see to Ruth.'

Marcus was roused from his vigil on the eating terrace. He burst into tears at the sight of his son. 'I'm a father!' he cried. 'Rustum and his son Sohrab! How is Ruth? Can I go and see her? My God, I feel like I've drunk a flagon of wine!'

Taj broke open two bottles of Shiraz from a store kept for special occasions, and others emerged from their huts at the noise. Mansur played a celebratory roll on his tabla. Kurt appeared with a lean figure wrapped in a dirty blanket.

'Good karma, dude,' a deep voice chuckled.

'*Devon*?' Juliet exclaimed.

The American opened wide his blanket and enveloped her in a musty hug.

'Why did no one tell me you were here?' she chided.

'You had your hands full, man,' said Devon.

'They picked him up in Nushki two weeks ago,' Kurt explained.

'Thought I was a holy man,' Devon laughed. 'This place is wild.'

The party and drumming went on until sunrise, but long before that Heidi had rescued Sohrab for a first feed and Juliet had followed them back to the Women's House to sleep.

CHAPTER 68

Bulbulak, Baluchistan, summer 1977

Ruth moved into a hut with Marcus and baby Sohrab. Marcus doted on his son but Ruth would not allow anyone else near him. She turned Heidi away when she came to check on mother and baby; even Juliet was not allowed over their threshold. Ruth stayed indoors, while Marcus fetched everything they needed.

'She's fine,' Marcus said briskly when anyone asked, 'finding her feet. Doesn't want to bring Sohrab out in this wind – too much dust, too many flies.'

'Is the feeding going well?' Heidi asked.

'Oh, yes, she's a natural mother.'

Taj and Lena were more sanguine. 'Leave them alone,' Lena said, 'they don't want people fussing around them every five minutes.'

'If they need help,' Taj said, 'they'll ask.'

At night the baby's plaintive crying carried down to Juliet's hut. 'I think she's terrified of letting Sohrab out of her sight in case he stops breathing or something.'

'His lungs sound healthy to me,' Kurt grunted.

'But it's not healthy for her,' Juliet fretted.

Once, Juliet thought Marcus was going to confide in her. He waylaid her carrying fruit up to the kitchen. His eyes were dark-ringed. He made a joke about sleepless nights, and then said, 'I've told her she should see her friends. It's not me that's keeping her away, you know.'

'Shall I call round?' Juliet suggested.

He looked relieved, and then shrugged. 'If you want. It's not that we can't manage, you understand.'

But calling round proved fruitless. Knocks went unanswered; all Juliet and her friends could do was to leave gifts of food and clothing on their doorstep. After a month, Juliet and Heidi decided to act. They went to see Ruth when they knew Marcus was down in the orchard smoking with Devon. The door was bolted. No one answered their calling. Going round to the side, Juliet wrenched open the reed shutter and peered in the narrow window. Fetid air hit her.

'Ruth? Ruth, are you awake?'

A whimpering sound came from the corner opposite. Juliet saw a figure huddled in a blanket. 'Go away,' Ruth wailed. 'You can't have him.'

'It's me, Juliet.'

'I won't let you have him! Just fuck off!'

Suddenly it struck Juliet how there was no sound of the baby. She turned to Heidi. 'Go and get Mansur – and Kasim – we need to break in now.'

Heidi tore off. Juliet hauled herself up at the window.

'I'm Juliet, your friend. I'm here to help you.'

Ruth sprang up and tried to push her out again, scratching at Juliet's arms and face. 'You're the Devil! You just look like Juliet. You can't kid me.'

Juliet slipped back. 'Ruth, don't be afraid. Just show me Sohrab. Is he sleeping?'

'He's not here,' Ruth shrieked, 'I've put him somewhere safe. You'll never find him. He's safe in the arms of Jesus. Our Father Who art in Heaven,' she began a frantic recital of the Lord's Prayer.

'Oh Ruth,' Juliet called in distress, 'just let me in.'

Five minutes later Kasim and Mansur were battering down the door. Ruth hurled herself at Juliet like a wild animal. The men pulled her off. Heidi rushed around looking for Sohrab. She found him behind a curtain in a basket covered in dried up rose petals.

'Is he alive?' gasped Juliet.

'Yes, alive!' cried Heidi. 'He's very dehydrated. She can't have been feeding him.'

Heidi whisked the baby away, to howls of rage from Ruth. Juliet and Mansur stayed with Ruth while Kasim went to fetch Marcus. He threw himself at Ruth's feet and sobbed, 'I'm sorry girl, it's my fault. I should have done something sooner.'

Ruth wept and clung onto him. 'They've taken him away. I tried to stop them but you weren't here. Now he'll die.'

'No, no he won't! No one's going to die. I'm going to take care of you both, I promise.'

Ruth's face was tight with fear. 'You can't. The Devil's got him now.'

Marcus looked round helplessly at Juliet and the men. 'What should I do? Help me please.'

***

Ruth was taken back to the Women's House at Marcus's request. Sohrab was wet-nursed by Kasim's wife, Safina, who was still breast-feeding their third child. Once a day, the baby was brought to Ruth.

'She's not interested,' Juliet discussed her with Heidi and Eloïse. 'Stares at him like she's not quite sure what she's supposed to do. Hardly ever picks him up. She's gone from one extreme to the other.'

'Is it post-natal depression?' Eloïse asked.

'I think it's a severe case,' Heidi said. 'I wouldn't trust her with the baby on her own. We must be watchful.'

'Can't we get her any help?' Juliet suggested. 'We're out of our depth on this.'

'We don't have a psychiatrist in the commune,' Heidi answered, 'but we can treat her with herbal drugs, and lots of rest. In time her body will adjust to giving birth.'

'But what about her mind?' asked Eloïse.

Heidi sighed. 'That is difficult to say.' She eyed Juliet. 'You are the closest to her. Get Ruth to talk about her past. She must let go of her demons.'

***

For a long time, Juliet thought Ruth had quite lost her mind. Her actions were unpredictable and her words bizarre. She would tear out of the Women's House screaming for Marcus at all times of the day and night. He never knew if she would punch and kick him or smother him in kisses. Marcus grew wary and left her largely to the care of the women. But he delighted in his son, strapping him in a sling across his chest and taking him about the place.

One time, in the late summer, Juliet found Ruth snipping roses in the courtyard, swaddling them in a blanket and laying them in a basket. When Juliet asked her what she was doing, Ruth gave her a look of surprise.

'You told me to. I have to save their souls, remember?'

Later, talking it over with Kurt and Devon, Juliet sighed, 'in Turkey there were dying roses in a courtyard – Konya or somewhere. Marcus was going to snap off two and give them to me and Ruth, and I said not to do it because some people believed that at night the souls of the unborn inhabit roses so it's bad luck to cut them in the evening.'

Devon shook his head. 'She's in a bad place, going through some bad shit.'

Kurt said, 'I think she should be kept away from Sohrab while she's in this state.'

'That's what Heidi thinks,' said Juliet, 'but won't it make her even worse?'

Devon said quietly, 'she needs to be loved, man. Loved back to life.'

CHAPTER 69

Kurt spent the autumn excavating the caves and underground tunnels of the valley. Juliet and some of the others joined in, and under his expert guidance, made discoveries of pottery, coins, a bronze armlet and some amber beads. Kurt was more excited about the crude geometric carvings in the Cave of Silence, but it was the small haul of treasure that impressed Marcus.

'Just think, the historical Rustum might have worn this very armlet when he fought around Seistan! Perhaps he gave it as a gift to some warrior who had pleased him.'

He badgered Taj to let him have it for Sohrab. 'A gift for a young prince, what do you say?'

Taj let him keep it, but it lead to an argument with Lena and some of the others.

'It should be the common property of the commune,' she rebuked, 'we could sell it to buy kerosene and material. You shouldn't be indulging that man in his stupid fantasies!'

To keep the peace, Kurt stopped excavating, but Juliet could tell he found it frustrating. So she was glad when they both volunteered to go on the half-yearly trip with Kasim and Masjid to the oasis at Duzdap to barter with nomadic traders and re-stock supplies of fuel, thread, needles, tools, blocks of rock salt and raw sugar. As the oasis was on the border with Iran, Kurt's knowledge of Farsi was useful.

Despite having to put on an all-enveloping chador, Juliet enjoyed once more the bustle of a busy bazaar and glimpsing the world outside. With a twinge of envy, she watched some Europeans clamber out of a VW campervan to explore. A year ago she had been doing just that; her friendship with Cassidy blossoming. Pushing him painfully from her mind, she loaded up with imported cigarettes before the two day trip back to Bulbulak.

Winter returned with snow on the mountaintops and bitter winds. They all moved into cave houses for extra warmth and lived off their stores of dried fruit and grains. They wove rugs, played backgammon and told stories to wile away the dead time. Ruth's health improved, but arguments flared easily and Lena was quick to blame the newcomers for any upsets. Juliet knew that, in the Russian's eyes, all five of the overlanders were decadent bourgeoisie and not to be trusted.

When the snows melted and the first snake of spring was seen basking in the lower valley, word came through that the Khan, Taj's father was gravely ill. Taj set off for the Kacha Kuh and was gone for over a month. Lena took charge. She ordered everyone back to their huts and to work in the fields. After the confines of the caves and the bitter weather, Juliet was glad to be busy again.

'And it's time Ruth earned her keep around here,' Lena told Marcus bluntly. 'Sohrab can go to the crèche.'

Marcus protested that the boy needed his mother, but Ruth said that she would do her bit and volunteered to help Devon with the hens. 'I grew up among chickens and I can fix a stone wall too.'

Juliet saw how Ruth's spirits revived with the outdoor life and Devon's cheerful kindness. In turn, Devon seemed as content and happy as Juliet had ever seen him. Sohrab was a sunny natured baby who thrived among the other children and basked in the attention of the adults who cared for him. He took his first steps at ten months and Marcus boasted as if he had completed a Herculean feat.

Taj returned. His father was dead and his older brother Reza had taken on the chiefship of the clan. He was quick to reassure his comrades that the change of leadership would not affect Bulbulak.

'Reza has no interest in our commune,' Taj said. 'And he is bound to protect us by *mayar*, our code of loyalty.'

Taj was full of another piece of news. In Afghanistan, the Communists had taken over power, ousting the King's nephew.

'This is a good sign,' he enthused. 'The people are throwing off the despots; they are ready to come out of the dark ages. Education will be a priority.'

'Yes,' agreed Lena, 'especially for girls.'

Using his contacts in Afghanistan, Taj arranged for Kurt to undertake an expedition to northern Afghanistan to meet up with some Russian archaeologists and help on their dig. A Sabari from Taj's clan would guide him and Masjid across the Border at the Helmand River. Marcus, sensing a new adventure, persuaded Taj to let him go too. But as the time grew near, it sparked off a row between Marcus and Ruth.

'Why do you have to go?' Ruth demanded. 'I need you here to help with Sohrab.'

'It won't be for long,' Marcus blustered.

'It could be for months. You'll be gone for Sohrab's first birthday. How could you?'

'We'll celebrate it before I go. He'll not know the difference.'

'I'll know!' Ruth shouted. 'What kind of father are you?'

'Don't say that.' Marcus was stung.

'Well stay then,' she pleaded.

'I can't be cooped up in one place all the time, you know that. I brought you here for your own safety. I did it for you, remember? Now you throw it back in my face as if it's my fault.'

Ruth seized on this. 'Well it might not be safe for you to travel across Afghanistan. What if you are recognised? They'll still be looking for us. You'll get arrested.'

The wrangling spilled out into the wider commune. Juliet overheard Lena complaining to Marco and a couple of longer serving members.

'I knew they'd be trouble. That's what comes of allowing in people we haven't hand picked.'

There were grunts of agreement. Marco said, 'and how many more are going to turn up from that bloody bus trip?'

'It's not our fault,' Lena said. 'Taj is too easy going. He feels responsible for Rustum just because they were at Oxford together.'

'Why? Rustum is such a typical privileged bourgeois.'

Lena snorted. 'Rustum wasn't one of the students. All that college stuff is bullshit. He was Taj's servant. Taj puts up with him and his girlfriend out of pity.'

Juliet was dumbfounded. She thought Lena must be mistaken – or just being spiteful – for Marcus's learning was self-evident. But she was left feeling uneasy: Lena despised the recent arrivals. She only tolerated them for Taj's sake, but for how long?

In the end, Marcus was prevented from going. Both Taj and Lena thought the likelihood of Marcus being picked up by police and questioned was too much of a risk. He took his frustration out on Ruth, accusing her of preferring her hens to Sohrab and of spending too much time with Devon. Over the summer Marcus moved out of their hut and had a brief affair with Charlotte the potter. Taj, pained by all the disruption, sent Marcus off with Mansur to fish in the Helmand River. When they returned, Marcus appeared contrite and eager to make amends with Ruth.

'He's asked me to marry him,' Ruth told Juliet tearfully, 'and we're going to try for another baby. Marcus wants lots of babies!'

They wrote their own vows and had a simple ceremony in the Peace House, standing hand in hand with seventeen month-old Sohrab between them and surrounded by their comrades. The youngest children threw rose petals like confetti.

It wasn't till the spring of 1979 that Kurt and Masjid returned from Afghanistan, ecstatic about their dig. They had helped unearth a horde of Bactrian treasure on such an immense scale that no one quite knew what to do with it all.

But they came bearing other momentous news: revolution had broken out in Iran and the Shah had fled. Ayatollah Khomeini had returned from exile to head the Revolution.

'But it is communist led,' Masjid said excitedly, 'the people don't want to swap a secular despot for a religious one.'

They threw a party in celebration. Juliet teased Kurt that he was like Alexander the Great, returning triumphant from a long campaign with so many spoils of war. That night, heady on homemade wine and realising how much they had missed each other, Juliet and Kurt took down the dividing curtain, pushed their mattresses together and made love for the first time. Kurt's lovemaking was gentle and diffident. Juliet was glad he did not remind her of Cassidy for it helped her bury her lingering feelings for her former lover.

'If I am Alexander,' Kurt said tenderly, 'then you are my Roxane – his beautiful Afghan spouse.'

But Masjid was no longer content. He yearned to return to Iran to help in the Revolution.

'It's important that the Communists and Socialists are not squeezed out by the Fundamentalists. I'm needed more at home than here!'

Everyone talked and argued about it for days. Lena was against his going.

'It will send out the wrong signal, once one goes then others will follow. Masjid's duty lies with the commune. He's been gone long enough on this treasure hunt.'

Juliet privately agreed - Bulbulak needed single-minded commitment to survive – but stayed out of the argument. Taj finally ruled that Masjid should be allowed to go.

'We mustn't lose sight of the greater goal of Revolution for all oppressed peoples throughout the region. We cannot be selfish and keep Masjid here against his will. He's given us nearly ten years of loyal service.'

'And I'll return to give more once the Revolution is complete,' Masjid promised.

Lena needled Marcus. 'Perhaps our other Persian hero Rustum would like to test his warrior skills and go with Masjid?'

Marcus laughed and declined. 'My wife wouldn't let me.'

***

In June, Sohrab celebrated his second birthday. He was an active small boy, forever clambering onto roofs or trying to climb after the older children, his stocky determined figure and close cropped hair a familiar sight at Juliet's door.

'Dates Yuliet!' he would cry, stomping into her house and raiding her fruit bowl.

'Say please,' she would demand.

'Pease!' he would grin, his blue eyes creasing in merriment.

They would munch dates, figs and apricots while he sat in her lap and she told him stories: Three Little Pigs, Bonnie Prince Charlie or the Genie and the Lamp. His favourite was the heroic tale of Sohrab and Rustum, even though it ended with the father killing the son by mistake.

'Tell the one about me and dad,' he would demand again and again.

That autumn, both Ruth and Lena fell pregnant. Lena carried on with manual work until the day before she gave birth, while Ruth had a terrible time of sickness, swollen ankles and anxiety attacks. Often Juliet and Kurt took Sohrab for the night to give Ruth some peace; his restless activity irritated her more than usual.

Lena and Taj's son, Lenin, was born two days before Sohrab's third birthday. Lena was back milling flour a week later, with Lenin carried about in a small basket alongside her tool bag. Ruth endured another long and painful birth. Marcus named their daughter Rose. Juliet watched out for signs of depression in Ruth, but apart from constant tiredness, she showed only happiness at her newborn. Ruth's bonding with Rose was instant and all consuming. Increasingly, Sohrab would turn up at Juliet's door for attention and stories.

'All these babies are making me broody,' Juliet confessed to Kurt. 'I'm 35 you know.'

'And I'm 54,' he laughed, 'so we better get to it.'

That summer as they tried for a baby, they were cocooned from the outside world and preoccupied with small routines. It was Kasim who came back from a hunting trip with the news. The Afghan Communists were running into difficulties. They had called on Russia for help.

'Russian troops are everywhere – even in Helmand. The borders are closed.'

Soon after, Taj was called away to a *jirga*, a meeting of the local Baluch family leaders. By the time he returned, the area was being overrun with Afghan refugees fleeing the Russians.

'Even in Duzdap and the Chagai Hills,' Taj told them sombrely.

'What does it all mean?' Juliet asked.

'My brother Reza has told us to keep our heads down,' Taj said.

'But the Russians won't harm us,' Lena cried, 'we're working for revolution too.'

'Still,' Taj warned, 'no one goes anywhere until it all becomes clearer.'

A month later, when uncertainty hung over them all like a storm cloud, tragedy struck. Marcus accidentally rolled onto baby Rose in the night and smothered her to death.

CHAPTER 70

Germany
Amber

Amber watched Juliet twist a large ruby ring around her index finger. Her deep voice was hoarse from talking. She had broken off to drink more water. Inside the tent was so still Amber could hear the glug of liquid moving down her throat. Her initial flurry of questions had petered out as Cassidy told her just to listen and let Juliet have her say.

Through the dark could be heard the murmur of the sea and the hoot of an owl. The whole tale sounded so fantastical Amber wondered if she were dreaming – or whether Juliet was making it up like some story teller from the Arabian Nights. But Cassidy looked ashen.

'The poor buggers. How did they recover from that?'

'They didn't – not really.' Juliet's voice sounded old and very tired. 'Ruth was inconsolable and Marcus ridden with guilt. He began smoking dope heavily. Neither could comfort the other. Ruth's grief turned inwards and soon she was blaming herself for the baby's death. She believed she'd somehow brought it all on with her visions, as if it was some sort of self fulfilling prophecy.'

Amber felt sick with a clash of emotions: fury that for years Ruth had lived her hippy life and not attempted to get word back to her family that she was alive, and yet deep pity for her aunt. How deeply unhappy and troubled she must have been to have suffered early abuse, and how horrific to have lost her baby daughter in such a way. Amber could only imagine how traumatised Ruth would have been. Did she at that stage long for her mother back in Weardale or wish that she could leave?

Anxiety clawed her stomach; she dreaded asking what no one else dared.

'How did it all end? You said that Ruth isn't alive ...'

Juliet's eyes shimmered with sorrow. 'Your aunt is dead, yes. I'm so sorry.'

Amber's throat choked with tears; she couldn't speak. Jez took her hand and held on.

'And Marcus?' he asked somberly.

'I don't know about Marcus,' Juliet said. 'He disappeared a couple of years after Rose died – went off with the Bulbulak treasure including Sohrab's armlet. But by then the commune was falling apart. Taj's brother Reza was putting pressure on Taj to take in mujahideen fighters – resistance was building against the Russian occupation and they needed a safe haven to launch attacks from. Reza backed the insurgency – the Sabaris had kin among the Afghans – but Taj wouldn't co-operate. Partly because the resistance wanted to grow opium in the valley for cash and weapons, and Taj was really anti. But he also still believed the Baluch would be better off allying themselves to the Soviets - that they would bring equality and education - whereas the arms flooding in from the West would be used by Pakistan to suppress them.'

Cassidy sighed. 'And is that what happened?'

Juliet nodded. 'By the mid 80's things were very dangerous. Reagan's administration was bankrolling General Zia's military regime in Pakistan and the Afghan insurgency. Exiled mujahideen were beginning to rule the roost in parts of Baluchistan. More than half the commune had left by then – especially those with children – and it was no longer viable. Kurt and I were ready to leave, but our main obstacle was persuading Ruth to come with us. She didn't want to go.'

'Why not?' Amber asked, her anger igniting. 'How could she be so reckless with Sohrab's life?'

'Because she thought Marcus would come back for her like he always had done. If she went he'd never be able to find her. She still loved him you see, so very much. Anyway,' Juliet sighed, 'we all kept putting off a final decision. We'd become institutionalised I suppose - and felt such loyalty to Taj – especially after Lena left.'

'Lena left Bulbulak?' Amber said in surprise. 'But the commune was as much hers as Taj's.'

'Yes,' Juliet agreed, 'but she disappeared with Mansur and took Lenin with her. Taj went after them - got the Sabaris out looking too - but I always wonder …'

'What?' Amber questioned.

'Well, word got out about Bulbulak; that it was a Communist enclave. Someone betrayed us.'

'Lena?'

'I think so.'

'It could've been Marcus,' Amber suggested.

Juliet shook her head. 'He'd been gone a long time by then. Marcus always looked after number one, but he wouldn't have done that to Ruth and Sohrab. I still believe he loved Ruth but that he couldn't face coming back because he'd let her down so badly. Lena on the other hand would fight like a tiger for herself and her son. She probably did some deal with Reza or a mujahideen faction to get out safely.'

'So what happened?'

Juliet swallowed. 'It's bad.'

'Please, you have to tell me!'

CHAPTER 71

'Wherever there is a natural or artificial watercourse, the desert immediately blooms ... A failure in the water supply necessitates the desertion of the place and explains the barren ruins that mark once fertile spots.'
Life in the Moslem East, Pierre Ponafidine, 1911

Bulbulak, Baluchistan, 1985
Juliet

It was a hot August day; the fifth anniversary of Rose's tragic death.

'We'll take Sohrab for a picnic,' Juliet suggested to Ruth. She knew her friend wanted to be left alone in the Women's House to sit in the shade of the mulberry and do some painting. Eloïse had suggested it as therapy. Ruth's miniatures – tiny figures and colourful birds – adorned the walls of the Women's House.

Ruth blew a distracted kiss to her eight year-old son who was impatient to be off. Devon had made him a sling and they were going to hit apricots out of the trees down in the orchard. As Juliet wended her way downhill with Kurt, Devon and Sohrab, she knew this would be their final summer there. The fields were drying up and reverting to sand and the water system neglected since engineer Lena and hydrologist Mansur had left.

Juliet chose a shady spot under a trailing willow and watched Sohrab and Devon splash around in the trickle of a stream.

'How can we convince Taj to come with us?' she asked Kurt. 'Do you think if we suggested Oxford he might be tempted? He talks of it with great affection. It's where he learnt his politics.'

Kurt shook his head. 'I'm not sure even Oxford would do the trick. To leave here would be to admit failure and the end of his lifelong dream. Men are not good at that.' After a pause he added, 'do you want to return to England? I wouldn't hold you back.'

Juliet squeezed his hand. 'Dear Kurt, always so thoughtful. I'm not sure I could cope with going back. It must be so different.'

'That's not what I meant,' Kurt said gently. 'I know I wasn't your first choice as a partner – or perhaps not even second.' His smile was rueful.

Juliet leant forward and kissed him. 'Don't be silly. I'm your Roxane, remember? You're not going to get rid of me that easily.'

'Good,' he grinned.

After the picnic they dozed under the trees. Even Sohrab's energy was sapped by the heat.

Juliet came wide-awake at the sound of gunfire. Not just one shot but a rapid volley.

Sohrab jumped up laughing. 'Is it Kasim?'

Kurt sprang up and immediately Juliet grabbed the boy. 'Come here Sohrabji.'

'No I want to see Kasim! He's shooting birds.'

217

'Quiet!' Kurt barked.

From afar they could hear shouts, and then screams. Another dozen shots cracked the air.

Devon's thin face looked appalled. 'Ruth,' he whispered, 'oh man.'

He scrambled to his feet but Kurt blocked his attempts to run for the path.

'We've got to save the boy,' he hissed.

Sohrab's face crumpled. 'Mummy Ruth. I want Mummy Ruth!'

Juliet held him close. 'You have to be really quiet and brave. We're going to play hide and seek, okay?' She turned to Kurt. 'The mill?'

He hesitated. 'No, the underground tunnels. Take everything with us and follow me. Quickly!'

He led them downstream, walking in water so as not to leave tracks. They soon came up against a sheer cliff of rock. Where the channel disappeared into the ground, Kurt pulled away some loose stone and lowered himself down the hole.

'Hand me Sohrab,' he called up.

One by one they slid into the narrow tunnel. 'We need to move further in,' Kurt said, inching his way forward and feeling for the sides. It was cool and damp; water lapped over their ankles. They groped in the increasing blackness and found a ledge above the water. Crouched together, they listened out for any sounds. Juliet's heart thumped so loudly she thought she would give them away. Sohrab shook with fear, his sobbing muffled in Juliet's arms. She hummed softly to him but Kurt told her to stop.

They waited for the men with guns to come. Hours went by. Chilled to the bone, they tried to keep warm by huddling close under the picnic blanket. Juliet's mind filled with the unknown horrors of what might be happening up in the settlement. Just when she thought she could bear the not knowing any longer, there were shouts above ground. The rock seemed to vibrate with the crunch of boots. Moments later there was the sound of scrabbling at the shaft entrance and voices arguing. Someone pointed a rifle down the hole and fired off randomly into the tunnel. Bullets struck off the rock. The noise stabbed her ears and made her head ring. Juliet clung to Sohrab for dear life. He was rigid with terror.

Abruptly the firing stopped. The footsteps and shouting receded. They sat frozen in shock. Kurt spoke first, asking them if they were unharmed. No one was hurt.

'They weren't speaking Dari or Farsi,' Kurt whispered. 'Maybe Baluch or Pashtun.'

Juliet buried her head into Sohrab's soft hair and wept. Time passed. The light from the distant shaft died and left them in pitch-black darkness.

When dawn filtered in, Kurt went above ground to investigate. 'If I need to warn you, I'll hoot like an owl, okay?'

He was gone so long that Juliet was convinced he had been captured. Eventually Devon said, 'I can't stand this man, I'm going to find him.'

'No we stick together,' Juliet insisted. 'If you go, we come too.'

They waited for what felt like an eternity. Finally Kurt returned and called to them down the shaft that it was safe to come out. Up above, there was haziness and a smell of burning in the air. As soon as she saw Kurt's face, Juliet knew something horrific had happened. He told Devon to take Sohrab for a pee. Juliet thought Kurt would be sick.

'We can't let Sohrab see. It's unimaginable – terrible - '

'Oh God, tell me,' Juliet gasped.

Kurt struggled to speak. 'Taj – Kasim – Eloïse – all of them – butchered.' He swallowed hard. 'The Women's House – burnt to the ground.'

'Ruth too?'

''Yes,' he said, his voice cracking.

Juliet and Kurt groped for each other and held on. After a long moment he pulled away. 'They'll be back. We need to get out quickly.'

Devon returned and Kurt took him aside; Juliet was too numb to speak. Before they could stop him, Devon was leaping away up the path, shouting and cursing and threatening revenge. They went after him. As they got nearer the settlement, the stench of burning made Juliet retch.

'Keep the boy away!' Kurt ordered.

Juliet clung to Sohrab, paralysed with fear. Minutes later she heard Devon shriek like someone possessed, and then Kurt was dragging him away down the path.

'I think I heard voices,' Juliet hissed, pointing up towards the pool, their only route of escape.

Kurt stopped in his tracks. 'It's just the waterfall.'

'I don't think so,' Juliet trembled. 'They could be watching the entrance.'

'I'm gonna kill 'em!' Devon roared.

Kurt shook him. 'And have us all killed?'

Sohrab dissolved into tears. The sight of him crying deflated Devon's rage. Holding the boy tight Juliet mouthed to Kurt, 'How do we get out of here?'

Desperately Kurt glanced about, his face taut with indecision. Juliet was sure she heard the sound of men's voices once again, closer this time. Kurt heard it too. All of a sudden he hissed, 'we'll have to go back to the tunnel. When I was digging years ago – where Marcus found the armlet – there may be another way out.'

CHAPTER 72

Germany
Amber

Amber hid her face in her hands, unable to block out the horrific image of burning bodies. The pain and fear must have been unbearable.

Juliet said in a strained voice, 'we were underground for days trying to find a way through the mountain. We lived on water. When Devon's matches were used up, we followed the sound of the stream. Sohrab stopped speaking. I was ready to turn back and face the gunmen – a swift death seemed better than this slow suffocation underground – the claustrophobia - '

She broke off and closed her eyes. After a moment, Juliet continued. 'A camel saved us,' she gave a mirthless laugh, 'a wild camel. We heard it braying beyond the rock-face – or what we thought was solid rock – just where the water seemed to dry up. But it just dropped to another level, and then came out into a narrow ravine. There was just enough room to squeeze through. Centuries ago, a river must have run down the ravine – or perhaps flooded into it during the spring rains. The camel got the fright of its life.'

'Were you the only ones to escape alive?' Cassidy asked quietly.

'Yes, I'm sure of it.'

Cassidy looked over, but Amber was shaking and speechless. Cassidy asked the question.

'Do you have any idea who the murderers were?'

Juliet shook her head. 'I wish I could tell you for certain. A rival clan or mujahideen or roaming mercenaries – maybe even Reza - we never knew for sure. They would probably have caught up with us too if we hadn't been taken in by Baluch nomads camping nearby. They helped us without question, fed and hid us for months. When they migrated south for the winter with their herds we went with them.'

'And from there?' Jez asked, stroking Amber's back and trying to comfort.

'Eventually we made our way to India. Lived in Delhi. Kurt worked at one of the museums for a while – till we heard about the Berlin Wall coming down. After that he got this yearning to go back to Germany. Devon wouldn't come. He was in a really bad way – drugs and thieving – we tried to help but it made no difference.'

'Aye,' Cassidy said, 'I came across him in Delhi too.'

Juliet gasped, 'you did? When?'

'Mid 90s. He was off his head. Thought it was Vietnam giving him nightmares but it must've been the massacre.'

Juliet and Cassidy held each other's look.

'Poor, dear Devon,' Juliet said, and then turned to Amber. 'He loved your aunt too. If we'd all got out, I think they might have stayed together for the long term.'

Amber stared at her. From somewhere deep inside anger churned and made her nauseous. Cassidy was looking moonstruck, but it seemed to her that Juliet had failed both Ruth and Devon. She should have tried harder to get Ruth out. Why hadn't she? And how could she give up on Devon? She should have got the poor guy the help he needed.

Her heart pounded as she demanded, 'And Sohrab? What happened to Ruth's son? Did you just abandon him too?'

Juliet flinched. 'No, of course not.'

'What then?'

Jez put a hand on Amber's arm. 'Hey, steady.'

She brushed him off, her upset boiling over. 'I want to know. And that's not all.' She glared at Juliet. 'I want to know why you never bothered to get in touch with my family once you got out of Bulbulak. You knew what happened but you kept quiet all these years. Shit! Have you any idea what my family went through not knowing? My gran went to her grave five months ago still hoping Ruth was going to walk back into her life. You could have saved her all those years of grief, but you didn't! How could you be so cruel?'

Juliet said in agitation, 'I did think about it.'

'Think about it!' Amber exploded. 'For God's sake, why didn't you *do* something?'

'I know it must seem cowardly to you - '

'Damn right! Ruth disappearing split my family. My Dad's been an emotional retard ever since.'

Abruptly, Al spoke up from the shadows, his voice indignant. 'Don't take it out on my mother.' He pushed into the circle to confront Amber, his face taut as he stared down at her. 'What did you expect Mutti to say? "By the way Mrs English, your daughter Ruth lived in a commune for nine years but never once wanted to get in contact because she blamed you for being sexually abused. She never wanted to come home even when she had the chance. And then she was butchered. Have a nice day". No, Amber, I think on balance your family were better off not knowing.'

Amber flushed, stung by his attack on her grandmother. She sparked back, 'that's all right for you to say. You've had a cosy life in this place with both your parents around to love and spoil you. You don't know what it's like to come from an unhappy home.'

'Oh yes he does,' Juliet snapped. She half rose. The cat sprang away. 'He's been through far worse than you, Amber.' She thrust out an arm and pointed. 'Kurt and I adopted Al when he was ten. He's Ruth's boy Sohrab. He's your cousin.'

Amber gaped at Al. He quickly regained his composure and hunkered down opposite her.

'My middle name is Algernon, after an ancestor of Marcus's,' Al explained. 'When Juliet and Kurt adopted me, I decided to leave the name Sohrab behind. I was a different boy by then.'

Amber's heart twisted. 'But you were still Ruth's boy.'

Al nodded. 'I loved Ruth, but she wasn't a great mother to me. I let go of all that sadness a long time ago.'

Juliet said, 'After we escaped, Al didn't speak for nearly a year. We were at a Sufi shrine in the south of Pakistan when it happened. He saw a dove fly out of a tree to drink at the water tank. In his child's mind he saw Ruth in the bird and she was telling him that she was at peace and not to hold onto her anymore. After that his speech gradually returned.'

Amber was battered by conflicting emotions. Her heart ached for the young Sohrab and she struggled to grasp that this man in front of her was the same exuberant little boy; Al Kiefer seemed so sorted and self-contained. Yet here he was, Ruth's son, the cousin she never knew she had. But she was in turmoil at all the deception; these people knew about her aunt and did nothing. Sohrab should be as angry as she was that Juliet and Kurt had denied him contact with his real flesh and blood family. Anger pumped through her like hot lava.

'Dead convenient for you Juliet.'

'Convenient?'

'Yes! You ended up with everything you wanted, didn't you? You had Kurt and a comfortable life in Germany, and you got a readymade son. No wonder you didn't want to spoil things by getting in touch with my family.'

'It wasn't like that - '

'That's what it looks like to me,' Amber said, jumping to her feet. 'You denied Al the chance of knowing his grandmother. Sarah would have *loved* to know him. How could you be so selfish?'

'There were things she couldn't have coped with,' Juliet insisted.

'How dare you be the judge of that? She was a strong woman; she could have handled the truth about Ruth's death.'

Juliet shook her head. 'Ruth never wanted her to know why she'd really left home. I respected her wishes.'

'Bullshit! All that stuff about Ruth being abused by a neighbour – we only have your word for it. How do we know you didn't just make it up?'

Cassidy intervened. 'That's enough lass. I know you're upset about it all but there's no need to take it out on Juliet.'

Amber turned on him. 'I don't know why you're still defending her. She never came looking for you either. Face it Cassidy, she never gave a toss.'

'Amber, chill,' Jez pleaded. 'Why are you so mad at her?'

Amber couldn't bear the sight of Jez's pained expression or that he might be taking Juliet's side.

'Because of the damage she's done!' She gulped back furious tears. 'It's not just Gran dying without knowing, it's the person my Dad became. It poisoned him. He never really loved anyone after Ruth – certainly not my Mum – probably not me.' Amber faced Juliet, her vision blurring. 'You could have made all the difference – just one phone call – and Dad and Gran might have made up their differences and got on with their lives. Maybe my parents would still be together.' Her voice cracked. 'But no, you were too happy playing at being Roxane in your little Shangri-la with Kurt and Al to bother about anyone else.'

Suddenly Juliet seized her arm. 'You have no idea what you're talking about.'

'Guilt finally kicking in, is it?' Amber accused, trembling violently at Juliet's hold. At last there was a reaction from this devious woman. She wanted to see the real Juliet, not the controlled manipulator that fooled the others.

'I was protecting people,' she hissed, 'people I loved, including Ruth.'

'You never protected Ruth – you betrayed her and took her son.'

Juliet was furious. 'Don't you dare say that! All his life I've protected Al.'

'Mutti,' Al said, moving to intervene, 'it's okay. Amber, I think it's time you left.' He nudged Juliet aside and took Amber by the elbow. 'You've got what you came for; it's not my mother's fault if it's not what you wanted to hear.'

'*Mother*?' Amber handed him off. 'Ruth was your mother, not this woman. Don't you want to know what she needed to protect you from all these years? Cos I do.' She challenged Juliet. 'Maybe it's more lies about that bogus posh boy Marcus.'

Al clenched his jaw and shook Amber. Jez stepped in.

'Hey, take it easy.'

Al pushed him away, rounding on Amber. 'Don't speak about my father like that. He may not have been the rich student he claimed to be but I don't think any less of him. He was self-educated and that's heroic.'

Amber choked on her anger. 'Heroic? He was a conman! I know more about him than any of you. He was ordinary Robin Baker who never stuck at anything and preyed on vulnerable people like Auntie Ruth.'

Jez tried to intervene again. 'Amber babe, that's enough.'

But she couldn't stop. She never knew she had so much fury stored up inside; she was hurting so much all she could do was lash out.

'Leave me alone. I'm not the only one with a crap dad; Al needs to know about his. Robin even faked his death to his only sister – that's how caring he was. And if he was so bloody heroic, why did he leave you in the lurch in Baluchistan?'

'Shut up.' Al shoved Amber away from him. She knocked into the tent pole and set the lamp swinging.

'Don't you touch her,' Jez sprang at Al. They wrestled, taking swings at each other.

'Haway lads!' Cassidy launched between them. As Jez hesitated, Al landed a punch.

Juliet pulled at Al's shirt. 'Please stop this now!'

Amber challenged, 'Give us the truth then. What are you hiding from all of us Juliet?'

'All right,' Juliet retaliated, eyes flashing, 'I'll give you the truth! Your aunt wasn't just running away from home – she was running away from your father.'

'My Dad?' Amber retorted. 'Rubbish!'

'Not rubbish, Amber. He was adopted wasn't he?'

'Yes, so - '

'He was angry with your grandparents for lying about his adoption – so angry that he took it out on poor Ruth – the one innocent person in the whole sorry affair. It wasn't a neighbour who sexually abused Ruth, it was your father.'

Amber was stunned. 'No way! You're lying - '

'After Marcus left, Ruth told me everything. From the age of fourteen, Daniel made her have sex with him. He justified it by saying they weren't related – they were like Cathy and Heathcliffe, not brother and sister – and Ruth went along with it because she was immature and didn't know how to handle it. She still loved him and felt sorry for him, and once it started she didn't know how to make it stop.'

Her Dad? Amber felt bile rise up her throat. 'No, that's unbelievable!'

'Oh, it's true all right,' Juliet blazed. 'That's why Ruth was so screwed up. Marcus – the man you choose to despise - was her way out of the nightmare and to a new life far away where no one could touch them. Except your father wrote to her on the trip saying he was going to come out and visit her at the orphanage. She knew then she would never be rid of him unless she did something really drastic – like faking her own suicide and vanishing forever.'

Amber was nauseous. Her head reeled as an image came back to her of a pale swatch of hair tied with baby blue ribbon in a box clutched in her father's hands. She pressed her palms against her temples to stop herself fainting.

'But Dad loved Ruth. He'd never have done anything to harm her.'

'He was kidding himself.' Juliet was blunt. 'I think he punished her for being the golden child that his parents loved - would always love better than they loved him. The irony was that Ruth always believed her mother loved Daniel more than her. She thought Sarah must have known what was going on, but never tried to stop it. That's why she could never bring herself to make contact with your grandmother again.'

Amber gripped onto the tent-pole and looked around in panic. Jez was clutching his cheek and looking shocked; Cassidy was staring at her in pity.

'Tell me you don't believe all this crap?' she pleaded.

'For goodness sake, grow up Amber,' Juliet snapped.

'Why should I believe you?' she said desperately. 'Its all lies - to salve a guilty conscience.'

Juliet leapt at her, shaking her by the shoulders. 'Listen to me! Your father was still abusing his sister until she left England. Even when she went to say goodbye, he still put pressure on her. He was selfish and needy and domineering, so stop trying to make excuses for him!'

Cassidy gasped, 'Are you saying it was still going on, even after Ruth met Marcus?'

'Yes,' Juliet cried.

'You can't prove that -' Amber began.

Furious, Juliet wheeled her around. 'Yes I can, because he did the one thing she feared most. He got her pregnant. By the time she was half way to India she knew. She was so scared she tried to throw herself off a watchtower in the desert.'

Amber felt winded. 'You mean …?'

She was facing Al. The man's face was a hollow mask in the lamplight. Amber's words died.

'Mutti?' Al whispered. 'What are you saying?'

Juliet's mouth trembled. 'My darling, I'm so sorry. I never wanted you to know. You had enough to bear in your young life. And you so idolised Marcus.'

'But - but he is not my real father?'

Juliet's face was haggard. 'No. Amber's father is your father.'

For a moment, Al stood perfectly still. No one breathed a word. Suddenly he let out an anguished groan, then was pushing past Cassidy and fleeing the tent.

'Please Al, wait!' Juliet shouted and rushed after him.

On the dark sand, he whipped round. 'Don't! For God's sake, stay away from me.'

He hurtled off into the night. Juliet stood rooted. Her shoulders sagged as she began to sob.

Jez turned to Amber with a harrowed look. 'Oh God, what have you done?'

She couldn't bear the accusation in his voice. Distraught, Amber turned and clattered out of the house.

CHAPTER 73

Cassidy

He lay unable to sleep. Al had not returned. Jez had stayed with Juliet at the retreat house while Cassidy had tracked Amber down to the bunkhouse. Half a bottle of whisky later, Amber had sobbed, 'I've messed it all up, haven't I? For everyone. Ruined Al's life. Juliet hates me. Jez thinks I'm a terrible person.'

'No he doesn't.'

'He does – that look on his face. I can't possibly stay here. I'll leave in the morning.'

'Sleep on it, lass.'

As dawn broke, Cassidy forced himself up. He felt like a hundred. Amber was curled up on the floor in her sleeping bag, dark hair cascading about her face. She had cried in her sleep, and even though his heart ached for her he had felt unable to give comfort. He was still in shock at meeting Juliet again and didn't know how he felt. All these years he had borne the guilty secret that he paid off Marcus and Ruth in that teahouse in Bamiyan and had blamed himself for their disappearance, when the truth was they had planned to go missing anyway. And Amber's accusation about Juliet and him had been right too: at the end of the day, Juliet had chosen to stay with Kurt.

On the beach, Cassidy stripped off and swam naked in the calm chill sea, ducking his head and gasping for breath. For hours he had lain helpless, his mind plagued by Juliet's revelations. The seeds of the tragedy had been sown long before the trip had ever started. He wondered if Marcus had guessed the truth about Sohrab not being his son and whether that was why he'd never returned for Ruth? All that sorrow and anger and pain; all the wasted years. All because Daniel's parents had hidden the simple truth about his adoption.

'But it was common in those days to keep quiet about being adopted,' Cassidy had tried to explain to a maudlin Amber. 'It was a pride thing. Folk felt they were being judged if they couldn't have their own kiddies.'

'His own sister,' Amber had said in disgust, 'it makes me sick. How can I ever face him again?'

Cassidy didn't have the answer to that.

He came out of the sea, dried and dressed quickly as the sky lightened. Sitting on the sand he smoked a cigarette and watched the sunrise. This was the essence of life: the small pleasures that added up to something more than the individual bits. The glinting water, the smell of tobacco, the prickle of skin after a swim: these were the things he would miss. And the people he held in his heart.

Cassidy ground out his cigarette and went in search.

***

Kurt's grave was marked by a small plaque bearing his name and dates. Next to it was a statue of Buddha; a lean, aesthetic one. It reminded Cassidy of the suffering Christ that had hung on the cross of his childhood church. He wished he'd got to know Kurt better; the more he learned about the man, the more he liked and admired him.

In the tree-house overhead, he heard a movement.

'I don't blame you for being angry, Al. Do you want to share a smoke?'

A couple of minutes went by, and then Al lowered himself down the rope ladder. They sat cross-legged in the grass. It struck Cassidy for the first time how Al and Amber had the same shaped eyes, and the same quizzical frown.

'Spit it out lad,' Cassidy encouraged.

'Mutti's just as bad as Amber's grandparents – *my* grandparents,' Al said bitterly. 'She lied to me. It feels like drowning.'

Cassidy asked gently, 'What do you think it's been like for Juliet, carrying Ruth's secret all these years? I bet it was purgatory – she hates secrets and lying. She probably didn't even tell Kurt. But she was prepared to carry it to the grave. Now why would she do that?'

Al gave him a tortured look and shook his head.

Cassidy answered, 'She did it out of love for you, man. That's why.'

Al said, 'She and Kurt, they brought me up to believe that the worst thing you could be was a liar. You must be true to yourself, and be truthful to everyone else. That was their mantra.'

Cassidy put a hand on his shoulder. 'Aye, lad. And it seems to me they both did a good job.'

Later, Cassidy sought out Juliet at the retreat house. Al had refused to go with him.

'He's gone walkabout in the forest,' he told a worried Juliet. Her handsome face was grey and drawn. 'Just give him some time.'

Jez made them some coffee - his left eye was puffy and had begun to bruise where Al had hit him – and then slipped away for a swim.

'Jez won't let me fuss over him,' Juliet said.

'It's probably Amber's attention he wants,' said Cassidy.

They sat on the steps. 'Al used to take off like that as a boy,' Juliet sighed, 'whenever someone let him down.'

'Don't be so hard on yourself,' said Cassidy. 'You were just trying to do your best.'

'Thanks.' She reached out and squeezed his hand. She had tears on her face. They leaked out of her eyes without any sound from her throat.

Cassidy thought with envy of the years Kurt had spent with her and with Al. How he would have liked a life like that. And yet. Perhaps they would have tired of each other, he and Juliet, once the passion had subsided. They might have drifted apart naturally, gone their separate ways long ago. He was an itinerant by nature. What made his heart heavy was not knowing what might have been.

And he had to face the brutal truth: Amber had been right. Juliet had never attempted to get in touch with him. He had blown it right from the start by not coming clean about Paula. It was Kurt that Juliet had loved all these years, not him.

Juliet asked, 'How sick are you? Jez is obviously worried.'

Cassidy pulled away to light a cigarette. 'He should stick to worrying about Amber – it's the first time the love birds have had a falling out.'

'Cassidy, don't change the subject.' She put a hand on his arm. 'One of our benefactors here is a top oncologist. There are things that can be done. Let me help you - '

'Let's just leave that for now, Forbsy?' He stood up. 'Think I'll just go for a lie down. See you later, eh?'

***

Cassidy didn't get up again that day. The next it rained and he spent most of it sleeping in his bunk and refusing food. He found it increasingly difficult to swallow. His throat went into spasms as he fought down the reflex to vomit.

Jez told him, 'Amber wants to leave as soon as you feel up to travelling.'

'What about you?' he asked.

He shrugged. 'Maybe I'll stay on for a bit – help out. I've got nothing to rush back for. As long as you can manage at home -?'

'Don't worry about me, lad.'

Jez must have told Juliet, because she appeared soon afterwards.

'Come to the Retreat tonight. I've made some soup.'

'Hope your soup making's improved since the trip,' Cassidy grunted.

'Marginally.'

'Any sign of Al?' he asked.

Juliet shook her head.

'I'll come,' Cassidy promised.

'I'll mix us up some High Lifes.'

He felt a pang of nostalgia. 'With proper Nepalese rum?'

'As near as damn it,' she smiled.

With great effort he shaved, splashed himself with aftershave and put on his cleanest t-shirt. Juliet was waiting for him, dressed in a green cotton wrap-over top embroidered with a white dragon that he remembered her having had made in Kathmandu. She wore it with white linen trousers.

'See it still fits,' she said.

'Fits very nicely,' he agreed. 'You haven't lost your figure, lass.'

She smiled and handed him a cocktail. They stood on the porch looking out at the orange sky over the treetops. The rum burnt its way down his throat. When it didn't make him retch he took another swig. He felt a pleasant numbness seep through him. He reflected on the long ago trip.

'All that business in Greece? Did Ruth ever tell you what really happened that night outside the taverna?'

'Oh, that,' Juliet snorted. 'That was Ruth trying to make Marcus jealous – she was annoyed at the way he was chatting up the other girls. I

228

think at first, they treated the trip like a big game – until she found out she was pregnant.'

'What do you think happened to Marcus?' he asked.

Juliet sighed. 'Goodness knows. Probably made a fortune smuggling antiques out of Afghanistan knowing him. He'd already got form. Ruth said Marcus made money smuggling razor blades into India when he first went out east. I read somewhere recently that one of the main go-betweens for art theft in Afghanistan was an Englishman nicknamed the Red Pathan.'

Cassidy grunted, 'that sounds just like our Posh Boy.' They fell silent as they watched the light drain away.

'I'm sorry about the Paula thing,' Cassidy said before his courage failed, 'I was a real twat. Thought if I told you, I'd lose you. Then I lost you anyway.'

Juliet continued to stare at the sunset, her handsome face reflecting the light. Her brown hair, now threaded with silver, glowed.

'But you made a life with her anyway,' she murmured.

Cassidy stared at her. 'No, I never. We got back for a year or so, but it wasn't right. She married a mate of mine.'

Juliet considered him in surprise. 'But the newspaper said -.'

'Souter's article?' Cassidy snorted. 'He went sniffing around for a story, got Paula at a low moment and blew everything out of proportion. All that common-law wife stuff – it was rubbish. She just wanted to feel part of the tragedy. Can't blame her when she'd lost her own baby the year before.'

Juliet took a swig of her drink. 'I didn't know you'd come out to India again, in the 90s. How strange it would've been if we'd met.'

Cassidy said, 'I always hoped we would.'

'You did?'

He took a deep breath. 'It wasn't the only time I'd gone looking for you. Even went back to Quetta once – convinced I saw you on this tonga with a little lad. Maybe it was someone else from the commune – she was definitely European, about your size, big feet with an ankle chain.'

Juliet let out a long breath. 'God, it might have been Lena escaping with Lenin and Mansur. When was that? '84?'

'Could've been. I was travelling a lot then. It all merges a bit.'

'Oh Cassidy,' Juliet said, her voice hollow with regret. She led him inside and they sat among the cushions. The low table was set with bowls of gazpacho and mint flavoured mast: liquid foods that would be easy for him to eat.

'Jez advised me,' she admitted. 'He's such a kind boy. Amber doesn't deserve him.'

'Don't be too hard on the lass. She may be mixed up, but she's a million miles from being like Daniel. Amber's been really caring to me and she's usually good fun - got a thirst for life – just like Ruth was early on in the trip.'

'Caring?' Juliet pulled a face. 'She's caused mayhem. If Al's not back by tomorrow I'm calling the police.'

They ate and then afterwards Juliet lit candles that pushed back the shadows, and they shared a hookah. She continued to fret about Al.

'I don't know what all this will do to him. Is it my fault? You see, I didn't want to destroy his sense of himself as Sohrab son of Rustum. His memory of Marcus was this larger than life hero who disappeared on an adventure. It was like a lifeline to his childhood.' Her look was troubled. 'Was I wrong to keep the truth from Al? Am I just as bad as Ruth's parents? You think so, don't you? I can see it in your face.'

Swiftly Cassidy reached out across the table and gripped her hand. 'No, I don't. You've always been useless at guessing what I think.'

'Tell me.'

'I think you're an amazing woman. You've been the mother for Al that he deserved.'

Juliet squeezed his hand in return. Her chin trembled. 'Oh Cass!'

He felt a sharp pang at her use of the old endearment.

Suddenly, the wooden boards behind them creaked. They looked round. The curtain lifted. Al stood there, unshaven and dishevelled. He came towards them.

'I heard what you said.'

'Darling!' Juliet rose. 'You look exhausted.'

'Please let me speak.' He struggled to compose his features. 'I'm still really angry with you; I can't pretend I'm not. I don't want this man Daniel to be my father. But I have to live with that.' He swallowed hard. 'But if it hadn't been for you I wouldn't have survived at all. More than that. It's you who taught me to live and to love. You are my Mutti, and I love you,' he said, his voice husky, 'and no one can take that away from me, ever.'

Juliet held out her arms. Al did the same. Cassidy looked on as they hugged each other in relief.

CHAPTER 74

Amber and Cassidy

In the morning, Amber and Cassidy packed their bags. Jez looked on mutely, and then left without a word.

'I wish you'd make it up with him,' Cassidy said.

Amber didn't answer as she rammed in her wash-bag. She felt leaden inside. She'd tried to find the right words to apologise to Jez, but every time she saw his bruised cheek and black eye she winced with shame. And it was obvious by the way he was avoiding her that he thought her to blame for all the upset. Turning, she eyed Cassidy sitting listlessly on the bed. Remorse overwhelmed her.

'God, Cass, I'm sorry. This was supposed to be a holiday for you – a miracle cure.'

He grunted. 'No such thing, bonny lass. And you're apologising to the wrong person.'

Amber hesitated only a moment before springing forward, landing a big kiss on his cheek and then was out of the door. She found Juliet and Al in the kitchen garden, gathering herbs and digging. When Al looked up, Amber felt her chest clamp at the familiar look in the blue eyes – like looking in the mirror.

She went right up to them before speaking. 'I'm so sorry; to both of you. I should never have said all those things – taken it out on you – I feel really bad.' She paused to control the wobble in her voice. 'But at least I know everything. It may be bad, but now I can start to make sense of things. Somehow that feels better.'

Al nodded. 'Yes, I know what you mean.' They eyed each other awkwardly. Al said, 'Do you need a lift to the station? I could take you if you like.'

'Yeah, thanks. I'd like that.'

As she turned, Juliet said, 'Amber, don't go. At least see the week out.'

Amber's stomach twisted. Juliet had no right to be nice to her but it felt like balm on a raw wound. She stood undecided.

'If you stayed, then Cassidy would have to stay too, wouldn't he?' Juliet smiled.

Amber's heart leapt. 'Is that what you want?'

Juliet nodded. 'Of course it is. I wanted to ask him last night but he left so abruptly.'

Amber rushed forward and threw her arms around Juliet. 'Thank you so much,' she cried. She felt Juliet's answering squeeze.

They found Cassidy on the beach, sheltering from a stiff wind in a strand-korb.

'We've had a reprieve,' Amber grinned sheepishly.

Cassidy squinted up at them.

'I've decided to keep an eye on you a bit longer,' Juliet said, sitting down in the wicker seat next to him. 'The truth is Cass; I don't want to lose you a second time.'

Amber saw Cassidy's eyes glint with sudden tears. 'I'll see you later,' Amber said and left.

Juliet took his hand in hers. He stared at them: two warm gnarled hands lying together. Cassidy's heart drummed.

'I want to help you beat this cancer,' Juliet said.

With a struggle he spoke. 'You don't want to be bothered with a knackered old bus driver like me.'

'Not so knackered I bet,' she smiled.

'I don't want your pity,' he grunted.

'Oh you stubborn man, this isn't out of pity,' Juliet cried, gripping him. 'However long you've got; I just want to be with you.'

He raised her hand to his lips and pressed it with a fierce kiss.

'So you'll stay?' she asked.

Cassidy pulled her to him in answer. He was engulfed by the same strength of feeling that had gripped him over thirty years ago. To hold her in his arms and breathe in her warm sweet scent was as heady and vivid as those days in Kathmandu.

'Oh course,' he mumbled into her hair. 'I still love you, Forbsy.'

She hugged him back. 'I love it when you call me that. My only regret is that we've left it so late.'

Exultant, he cradled her face. 'No lass; no regrets. It's what we learned on the road, remember? Each day is a new day.'

'Yes,' Juliet said, eyes gleaming, 'and I want to be with you for every one of them. Oh Cass, I've missed you!'

'Good.'

As they kissed – tenderly, longingly – Cassidy thought he had never seen sea dazzle so brightly in the summer sunlight.

***

Amber thought she'd find Jez working in the poly-tunnels, but Giorgio said he hadn't turned up that morning. Making for the woods, she glanced down the path to the cabins and saw him coming out of their bunkhouse.

'Jez,' she waved.

She held her breath, wondering what he would do. He began towards her. Her heart hammered as she picked up her pace, running to meet him.

'I'm sorry Jez!'

'I thought I'd missed you,' he cried in relief.

'I love you,' Amber said fiercely, reaching out.

His arms went around her. 'Me too.'

They hugged tight. Her throat watered. 'Jez - '

'You don't have to say anything.'

'Yes I do.' She put her hands up to his face and gently touched his yellowing bruise. 'I don't know why I started all this searching for

Auntie Ruth; I think I've probably been looking for her all my life. There was just this massive empty feeling that I grew up with. But these last couple of days have been the worst ever – I thought I'd made a huge mistake unearthing all the bad stuff, me and my big mouth - and it's horrible having to think of what my dad's done.'

'I know,' Jez said.

'But the one great thing that's come out of all this is meeting Cassidy and you.'

'Cassidy and me in that order?' Jez gave a quizzical smile.

'Especially you. I think I can bear anything, except the thought of us not being together.'

Jez bent his head and kissed her lips. 'I don't want to lose you either, Sexy Eyes. I shouldn't have blamed you for things getting out of hand the other night; I bet I would have reacted just the same. Whatever you have to face from now on, I'll be there with you, okay?'

Amber felt the deep grieving ache inside her dissolve at his caring words.

'Big okay,' she smiled tearfully and kissed him back.

❁❁❁

'Who could be unhappy in a garden when the sun has drawn out all around a most perfect concert in perfumery – roses, lilies, jasmine, carnations, and violets? When I am back in my country I will see what the distiller can make of this concert; it will be to me a souvenir of this beautiful garden of the East where I have dreamt and where I was glad, and at the same time sad; where I have longed and hoped and am resigned.'

An Englishwoman in a Turkish Harem, by Grace Ellison, 1915

❁❁❁

INTERVIEW WITH THE AUTHOR

What made you chose the subject of the overland route to India?

As an 18 year old I travelled to Kathmandu on an overland bus. My grandparents had lived and worked in India in the 1920s and '30s (my granddad was a forester) and my mother had lived there as a girl, so I was brought up on stories of their trekking in the jungle. They would travel for months with my mother's pram hoist between poles and carried like the luggage. On one occasion my grandfather shot a man-eating tiger which was terrorising a village and my mother was filmed pacing out the length of its entrails. During my childhood, the snarling tiger's head hung in the porch of my grandparents' house in Edinburgh (scarily nick-named Gwendolyn), an exotic symbol of the romantic subcontinent that made me long to go east – just like the character Juliet in the novel. Going overland was also the cheapest way to travel in the 1970s!

I wanted to recreate the excitement and camaraderie of the overland route – it was always much more than a hippy trail – and of the appetite for experiencing other cultures. It was a time of simpler travel before oil crises, revolutions and wars closed the route; a freedom of the road that westerners were privileged to experience.

At the heart of the novel is a mystery: the disappearance of two overlanders. What were the dangers on the trail?

Dangers on the road can be over-stated, though there have been some very tragic cases of people going missing or being murdered over the years. The main hazard to the majority of travellers was probably to health; from routine stomach upsets to more serious dysentery or hepatitis. Travelling in a large group sometimes brought its own problems, attracting hostile attention in remote villages. On one occasion I was assaulted outside a campsite toilet at night but managed to break free and escape to the bus. But this can happen the world over. Such incidents were far outweighed by the many gestures of kindness, hospitality and friendship shown along the way. At the end of the trip I got stuck in Delhi with no ticket home; it was ordinary people who helped out, not well-paid embassy staff. But that's another story! In some cases, it was other travellers living on the cheap, smuggling or stealing who posed the greatest risk and could be a burden to their long-suffering hosts.

Most of your previous novels have been historical ones. Why did you decide to write this one as a mystery?

Why do people go missing? The theme lends itself to mystery. The overland bus was a perfect vehicle (literally) for throwing a group of characters together at close quarters for a decent length of time. They are all on a physical journey – a retirement holiday, returning home to Australia, doing a driving job – but some are on journeys of escape or reinvention or pilgrimage. These are the ones who go under the spotlight. I wanted to explore their reasons and motivations. On the one hand disappearance creates loss, bewilderment and grief; but on the other there can be personal growth on a life changing trip, a reinvented self, the shedding of old skin – even on a temporary basis like bus driver Cassidy. The overland trip is just a three month snap shot in the lives of the characters and yet it has a profound impact on them and the consequences are still reverberating a generation later. It's an intense experience yet also transient. It allows for unresolved stories, misunderstandings to arise, broken links in a chain of narrative that need to be repaired to understand the whole.

You use a split time frame for the novel, alternating between the 1970s and the present day. Why did you choose to write it like this?

I wanted the story to unfold through the young curious eyes of niece Amber – the innocent bystander whose enthusiasm and humanity drives the story forward and gradually she peels back the layers of mystery to reveal the simple tragedy at the heart of the novel. By setting it partly in the present day, it gives immediacy to the story; you can think, 'yes, I know someone like that.' Historical novels have characters that are pinned safely in the past; they're at a remove. Not here. The Vanishing of Ruth isn't just about some long ago hippies; these are people you can pass in the street. How often do we look back on our life so far and think, 'I wonder what happened to so-and-so?' This is a book about what happened to …?

Why do you use extracts from old travel books as headings for the chapters told from Juliet's point of view?

In the novel Juliet has a passion for old travel books; she lives vicariously through the experiences of intrepid Victorian and Edwardian travellers, imagining herself the reincarnation of one such woman, Grace Ellison who lived with Turkish women in purdah. These extracts are a bit of fun, contrasting Juliet's romantic expectations of travel with the often more gritty reality of her experience overland. I also wished to give a flavour of earlier times of travel and a sense of how people in the west have always been drawn east. There is nothing new about going overland to India and beyond. I do a lot of my research and writing in the Lit & Phil, a wonderful library in Newcastle upon Tyne, North East England. Sitting among the Victorian book stacks, I'm often distracted by the fantastic range of long out of print biographies and travel books; the enthusiasm of their authors for travel still leaps off the dusty pages. I had to let some of them speak for themselves!

You've written a childhood memoir, BEATLES & CHIEFS, about growing up in a boys' boarding school in the 1960s and going on family trips to the Isle of Skye. Will you write a non fiction account of your overland trip?

Anything's possible! One of the most exciting spin-offs of researching the novel is how it has conjured old travel mates out of the ether. I'm now in touch with people I haven't seen in decades – including our driver – and we've had a couple of mini reunions in London. It would be great if this could lead to more get-togethers, and discovering what happened to the others. I've been blogging my diary and photos of the trip, so maybe one day they'll become a book.

You can read about Janet's original trip at: http://janmacleodtrotter.blogspot.com

To find out more about Janet's other novels take a look at her website: www.janetmacleodtrotter.com

WHAT READING GROUPS HAVE SAID ABOUT THE NOVEL

'Loved the book – couldn't put it down!'

'I would strongly recommend this book as a good read.'

'Wonderful. Kept me guessing all the way through. A pleasure to read.'

'It would make a fabulous screenplay - the split stories, great characters, wonderful locations and a well-resolved murder mystery at its heart - and there was a lot enthusiasm in the room for the idea!'

'I thoroughly enjoyed this journey through time and distant lands without leaving the comfort of my armchair. The contrast between the Victorians, the hippies and the modern day was fascinating.'

'I really enjoyed reading this. It held my attention with a great plot. It was enthralling and I wanted to keep reading to find out what happens. Good characters which I believed in.'

'I loved it! I found the style very easy to read, I got caught up in the story very quickly, liked the characters and wanted to know where it was going. I love split-time storylines and this was perfect in that each time it jumped from one time to another there was that instant, priceless blend of "oh no, I don't want to leave" *and* "oh good we're back with the other storyline". I loved all the little descriptive details (which I assume come direct from your diaries) - they set and illustrated the scenes without straying too much into travelogue territory, and so kept the focus on the story. I loved the end too - surprisingly straightforward and very satisfactory.'

'I think everyone who read it enjoyed it. Nothing and no one is quite as it first appears. I would recommend it to another reading group.'

'I really enjoyed this book as much as I've enjoyed all your books.'

'A most enjoyable book that seemed to get better the deeper in I went. It is a book of emotions and inner struggles. I did enjoy the book and I would recommend it to others and read more of the author's work.'

'It was a very interesting read. I enjoyed the feeling of adventure and being young again.'

'A most enjoyable read, with so many interesting characters and very good descriptions of the areas visited. The end was an interesting surprise. Thank you for a captivating read.'

POINTS OF DISCUSSION FOR READING GROUPS

Who was your favourite character and why?

Was the overland trail an interesting topic? Did you learn anything new from the book?

Did you have a preference for story line – the 1970s or the present day? If you have memories of that period, do they resonate with what you read or are they very different?

Cassidy's feelings for Juliet are still as strong 30 years later. Do you think events experienced as a young person are more intense, or do we colour our memories in a nostalgic glow? How reliable are such memories?

One of the book's themes is identity. Which characters were attempting to reinvent themselves on the trip? Were any of them ultimately successful?

Discuss Marcus the anti-hero: was he selfish and coldly calculating or to be admired for his tenacity, optimism and self-education?

Compare and contrast the different forms of love portrayed in the novel: tragic, misguided, sacrificing, enriching, destructive.

At the heart of the novel lie questions about nature/nurture, birth/adoption, growing up without parents. Do the main characters have a sense of belonging? If so, with whom or what do they most strongly identify?

The novel ends with a revelation; did it surprise you?

Lightning Source UK Ltd.
Milton Keynes UK
UKOW031427010212

186452UK00001B/3/P

9 780956 642615